The
New Queen

The New Queen

THE NEW REIGN SERIES

MARTIN McALEAR

THE NEW QUEEN
THE NEW REIGN SERIES

Copyright © 2019 Martin McAlear.

All rights reserved. No part of this book may be used or reproduced by any means, graphic, electronic, or mechanical, including photocopying, recording, taping or by any information storage retrieval system without the written permission of the author except in the case of brief quotations embodied in critical articles and reviews.

Certain characters in this work are historical figures, and certain events portrayed did take place. However, this is a work of fiction. All of the other characters, names, and events as well as all places, incidents, organizations, and dialogue in this novel are either the products of the author's imagination or are used fictitiously.

iUniverse books may be ordered through booksellers or by contacting:

iUniverse
1663 Liberty Drive
Bloomington, IN 47403
www.iuniverse.com
1-800-Authors (1-800-288-4677)

Because of the dynamic nature of the Internet, any web addresses or links contained in this book may have changed since publication and may no longer be valid. The views expressed in this work are solely those of the author and do not necessarily reflect the views of the publisher, and the publisher hereby disclaims any responsibility for them.

Any people depicted in stock imagery provided by Getty Images are models, and such images are being used for illustrative purposes only.
Certain stock imagery © Getty Images.

ISBN: 978-1-5320-7484-4 (sc)
ISBN: 978-1-5320-7486-8 (hc)
ISBN: 978-1-5320-7485-1 (e)

Print information available on the last page.

iUniverse rev. date: 10/07/2019

DEDICATIONS

"We are all someone's grandchild'
This book is dedicated to all of my grand children that
are present and in the future. Let the love of reading
give you as much joy as writing does for me.

Dedications

Chapter 1
THE SHADOW ARMY

Raging fires in the kitchen ovens and stone fireplaces blaze throughout the dark, cold castle as commoners huddle around them, the warmth briefly dancing on their skin. The musty air and cloudy sky warns of an approaching storm to the east. Rabbit tracks crisscross along the dotted snow and ice on the frozen channel. Servants prepare meats in the kitchen, clergymen drink in the Great Hall, and some children run in between the commoners. It has only been a few months since the end of the war with King Richard I, and the growing kingdom starts to stabilize from the causalities and hardships brought upon them.

Samantha, a sixteen-year-old widow, ignores the cold and busies herself in the kitchen, moving spices and meat from one table to the next. Since the death of her husband, Samantha feels useful once again. Her long, straight, light brown hair outlines her pale, narrow face. Warm chocolate eyes and her slim figure attract the unwanted interests of men with knotted beards and rotting teeth. She carefully covers her bright emerald gown with a clean apron. The custom-made lace-trimmed gown was given to her as an extravagant gift from the king himself. Samantha glances to a wooden table in the far corner where a large, black-haired man holds a chalice and stares at her. He peels his lips back in a yellow and brown-toothed grin before taking a swig from his goblet. She shudders and turns back to a smoked ham hock, carving a slice for her younger sister, Elizabeth, and a slice for their young brother, Andrew.

The kingdom often gossips about Samantha's family, to her ignorance. Elizabeth is a fourteen-year-old red-haired woman who is rumored to be madly in love with the king, and Andrew is an overconfident five-year-old who killed the enemy, King Richard, with a single arrow just last year. Andrew is known as the "King Killer" for ending the war and protecting the kingdom. Like his sister, he has chocolate-coloured eyes and red frizzy hair, easily distinguishable from the other villagers in King Martin's kingdom.

Samantha glances out of a moldy green kitchen shutter at the men practicing combat on the field. She sighs, wanting to join them, but she keeps quiet, remembering what her father told her about a woman's rightful place in the kitchen. She thinks about the importance of food and when her father attempted to sell Elizabeth for money to feed himself and Andrew. She glances at the scarce crops in a small pile on the table— apples, corn, wheat, and potatoes— and starts the preparations to feed the army of people within the castle.

A ruckus of swords clashing and men yelling begins in the distance, just outside the kitchen shutter. Samantha leans in closer and listens intently as the noise grows louder. She steps back at the stench of something burning as smoke drifts through the cracks and erupts into a fire, the flames engulfing the wood.

When the king was born, his father knew he would never be royalty, so he named him Prince. The time was approaching when most men took a second name, mostly for religious reasons, or for the family. Prince took his father's name of Martin, being known as Prince or Martin. When Martin became king, his name changed to King Prince Martin, although his people only knew him as King Martin. It was a name that only lead to confusion, so Prince did not tell many his entire name. Only Simon and a few close members of his kingdom knew him as Prince.

The young fifteen-year-old Prince Martin lays in his warm bed with his eyes closed. His slim, pale body rests comfortably in his bed as he listens to the fire crackling in the fireplace at the foot of his bed. The heat from the flames warms the room and for a brief moment, he rests in peace, lulled by the faint crackling of the dying fire.

The bedchamber is partly made of rock, slate, and stone that covered the walls and the floor, with a small maroon tapestry that hangs on the wall over the fireplace. The king's bedchamber is sparse with little furnishings: a bed, a small night table, a wash table by the door, and a few chairs, all made as gifts for the king by his subjects.

A muffled clashing of metal echoes off the stone walls down the hallway leading to the center courtyard. King Martin concentrates on the sword fight, listening to sounds of struggle or sounds of laughter. He jumps out of bed at the sound of people yelling and the swift movement of more men entering the keep. The cold air briefly attacks his bare chest before he shields it with a leather top. He tiptoes across the cold slate floor to the closed shutters that face the channel to the east. He peers through the snowy slats for any sign of invasion across the channel, but the ice-cold channel remains still, as late fall holds a firm grip on the land.

King Martin closes the slats and grabs his fairly new fur-lined leather boots and the fur overcoat that hangs from the edge of the bed, given to him by Rollo, the leader of the Vikings. He straps his two thin swords diagonally across his back and swings open the heavy wooden door. Two small, frail-looking children huddle at the front of his door for warmth, but Martin steps over them and rushes down the stone staircase as his shoulder-length hair bounces from his every step. Just as he steps onto the main landing, an arrow zooms past his face and strikes the wall, skimming the top of his hair. Martin scans the room around him: sword-fighting, arrows flying, men yelling, and fist-fighting. He draws both swords and rounds the corner, ready to fight, but does not know where to start.

A guard immediately sprints to the king's side. "Sire! There is an attempt to take over the kingdom!" The guard holds his sword at the ready and faces the small main hall.

"Who are they?" Martin asks as he watches the mysterious men wearing nothing more than cotton shirts and legging with no shoes and armor.

"I think they come from Richard's kingdom, but I do not know for sure. Anyways, we must defend the kingdom!" The guard dodges an incoming arrow.

"But we beat Richard?" Martin says, confused. "And he's dead!"

"I don't know." An enemy man charges towards them with his sword out. The guard blocks the man's sword, spins around and punches him in the face. He falls unconscious.

Two more enemies charge towards the king, swinging their two-handed swords. King Martin grips his sword as his guard jumps in front of his majesty and clashes his sword with the

THE NEW QUEEN

opposing men's. One man tries to sneak around the guard, but he blocks the attack and pushes the enemy to the ground. King Martin joins the guard's fight with his two swords, standing by the closest fallen aggressor. The man jumps up towards the king, but Martin deflects the sword to the side and uses his second sword to stab at the man, missing him completely. The man swings violently at the king, knocking him in the face. Blood drips from his nose and down his chin. The king lunges forward, using his full weight behind his thrust, but the man remains standing. Suddenly, the man falls to one knee and struggles to stand back up. He grabs his chest as tears stream down his face before falling dead in front of Martin. The king glances around the room for the source of the man's death. No one was standing behind the man nor shot him with an arrow.

An arrow whizzes by, waking the King from his puzzled thoughts. Martin scans the castle hall and he sees less and less fighting as more bodies pile up on the floor. King Martin walks out of the castle and into the bright day where Simon, his Captain of the Guard, stands on top of the wall-walk. Simon remains one of the few who knew Prince Martin before he was crowned king. Simon glances above the castle wall and around the castle. As Prince Martin walks up to Simon, Samantha rushes to King Martin and grabs his arm.

"Sire! The kitchen is under attack!" Martin and Simon glance at each other.

"You!" Simon yells at a few guards. "Go and secure the kitchen!" The guards race off at their command.

"He will make sure everything is okay before you go back," Martin says to Samantha. Samantha watches the armed men run into the castle then she turns her eyes back to Martin.

"Thank you," Samantha responds, jogging back towards the castle for warmth. Prince Martin follows Simon, scanning down and around his castle.

"What happened?" King Martin asks.

"Still sorting it out, but I believe that a group from Saxton's realm infiltrated the castle grounds and tried to overtake it." Simon stands in his full leather armor with a sword in one hand and his other hand holding the wall-walk.

"I was told they could be from Richard's kingdom." Martin places his sword back in the sheath across his back.

"Saxton's, Richard's, who cares? We stopped them!" Simon adds.

"Why would they try and overtake us?"

"Power. It's all about power, isn't it? The quest, the reign, the fortune, it's what men desire."

Martin crosses his arms. "I don't understand."

"Men want power," Simon begins as they walk along the wall-walk. "Even the attempt to get power is a type of power, sire. It's like when a boy courts a girl, the chase is just as exciting as the catch. Sometimes, the catch is even better when they're married. Understand? Men chase after the power that will make him the most powerful and the strongest."

King Martin nods. "Are you sure it is not the Great Army that attacked us inside here?" Martin watches the Great Army camped just outside the other side of the hill in the far distance I mean look how many there are of them, thousands of soldiers willing to put their lives on the line for their King.

"You were once a part of the Great Army. It's not called the great army because it fails and the attempt inside certainly failed. Not only that but the great army is large, massive, enormous army of thousand and thousands of men. Do you think they fought as great as they appear, men who were trained to fight since birth?" Simon asks.

"I guess not," Martin replies. "They have been camped out there for weeks now. I am getting nervous. Do you think they are going to attack us?"

Simon points towards the channel. "Their ships still stay anchored there. Every so often, a few go to the ships, and another ship takes its place. They are camped to leave, I hope!"

"How much longer until they are all gone, do you think?"

"We know there are thousands of men in the Great Army but only three ships in total to retrieve them. How long do you think?" Simon and Prince continue their walk along the wall-walk.

"Do you think they know their king is mad?" Martin asks. "He was the one who banish us after all?"

"I am sure they have heard stories, like him killing the man who asked for food to feed his wife? The king went mad and yelled at the guy and said he cant feed the entire kingdom and he went on and on then sentenced the man to death right there and then. But they would not know anything for sure." Simon peers at the camped army again as he rests his sword against the wall.

"I don't think they will make it through the whole winter, do you? I mean, even we have been struggling for warmth inside the castle, forget camping outside." King Martin pulls the fur closer to his chest.

"Sure, why not? They have been fighting for years, and they survived all those winters." Simon replies.

"It just makes me nervous with them there, within striking distance. The Great Army might even be planning to invade us for the idea of good shelter, if nothing else!"

"True, they could be, but I doubt it. I think if that were their plan, they would have done it already."

THE SHADOW ARMY

King Martin watches as his men carry bodies from inside the castle and stack them into a pile in the center of the courtyard. The guards pat the dead and search their clothing for any valuables or weapons. "I realize that I have never been trained to fight. I mean, I know how to use a sword but not in full battle. I can defend alright, but not how to fight back." Martin rubs his leg where a scar from an arrow once landed.

"Really?" Simon asks, surprised by the honesty of his king.

"Yes. I just react at what is coming at me and defend accordingly. I don't know how to take charge and start a fight." Prince Martin looks away.

"Reacting can be a good thing, sire, but you're right, you need to know more than that. I will train you myself and make sure you are an adequate soldier in battle." Simon pats Prince on the back.

"We should start soon. With this latest attack, I have to be ready for anything. We still do not know who these invaders are for sure, do we?" King Martin notices Samantha sitting against the wall outside the castle doors. "Simon, do you think there might be a problem within the castle?"

Simon looks at her, too. "Why do you say that?"

Martin stops pacing. "Samantha is still outside the castle, and your men have not returned."

Simon grabs his sword and skips down the closest set of stairs to the group of guards at the bottom. The guards pull out their swords and together they march into the castle, leaving Martin alone along the wall-walk.

Simon and six soldiers all in leather armor move quickly through the castle, making their way towards the kitchen, only to find the room empty. Simon looks out the slatted window at a battle between his guards against the last of the foe. He watches as an enemy swiftly slices off the head of a guard and it rolls to the side in a pool of blood. Simon rushes through the closest side gate

THE NEW QUEEN

facing south to the channel entrance with his guards following closely behind.

Once Simon and his men arrive, the fallen guards lay in a pile and his men prepare the bodies for burial. Simon curses and stomps the frozen grass. He commands the small group to search the nearby trees and shrubs to ensure the absence of another surprise attack. Simon squints across the channel to the forest and all remains peaceful.

His men return shortly and dismount their horses. "Sir, we checked the surrounding areas and there are no signs of footprints or any moving army," one guard confirms with a series of coughs. Simon nods, and they march back to the castle.

King Martin peers outside the castle wall along the wall-walk at Simon's returning men. Samantha stands next to Martin, shaking from the cold. Simon pauses and looks up, nodding to King Martin, and he nods back. "I think all is well now. You can go back to the kitchen," he smiles at Samantha.

"Are you sure?" she asks, batting her eyes at Martin. Martin chuckles at her blatant attempt to make him laugh as her eyes open and close over and over.

"Go now," Martin replies as he nods towards the stairs with a broad smile. She smirks back and exists down the staircase, hiding her disappointment.

The king joins Simon in the courtyard. "Simon," Martin calls to him. Simon leaves his group of men and stands in the cold beside his king.

"You wanted me, *your majesty?*" Simon emphasizes, in case others overhear. The king smiles at Simon's attempt at being a soldier and not a comrade.

"I have been thinking...we should send a representative up to the Great Army and see if they plan to attack us." Martin crosses his arms.

THE SHADOW ARMY

"Sire," Simon pauses, watching a guard stand watch on the wall-walk ten feet from them. "Anyone we send will have to be elderly and careful because if he says or does anything, it could lead to the end of your reign." Simon steps closer to Martin and whispers, "And they might even recognize us from before."

Martin sighs. "You're right, I never thought of that. Send someone who you think you can trust, even a maiden. I don't care who you choose, but we have to know where we stand. I mean, we were just attacked, and we don't even know who they were or why they attacked us! For goodness sake, we don't even know if they were one of ours!" Prince Martin stomps away from a nearby guard to the opposite side of Simon. He looks at the ground and whispers, "I can't be king this way, with a large army from our old kingdom that we were banished from on one side and men fighting inside the walls on this side."

Simon puts his hands on Martin's shoulders. "I understand your frustration, but you know you just don't walk up to any army and say 'Oh, what are you doing here? We own this place.' As for the fighting inside the castle walls, it happened. It's going to happen again and again, and there is nothing we can do about it. Stuff like this happens all the time within kingdoms." Simon smiles. "So get used to it," he adds, poking his index finger into Prince's chest.

Prince pushes Simon's arm away and glances behind himself. "You better watch what you are doing. Someone might talk," he hisses. Prince Martin marches down the stairs of the wall-walk, trampling the snow as he walks carefully down with his teeth chattering. He nods at a guard standing at the bottom of the stairs who straightens his posture and returns the nod. The king passes the guard and continues towards the castle.

There was something curious to Martin in the way the majority of the people remain inside the keep, despite the clear skies. He pauses and watches a nearby group of children chase a fat black rat barefoot along the stone floor, laughing as it scampers into an opening in the wall. The children's feet are bright red and scaly, like the feet of the rat. Prince Martin feels a chill creep down his back as a set of dark eyes watch him. He turns to the source of his chill. In the corner of the keep, a man draped in a long black length cloak and grips his sword tightly. He steps out of the shadow and curls his lips back in a smile, showing his yellowed rotting teeth and gaping holes. His face is covered with stubble and scars from previous battles. He tosses his cloak to the ground, revealing matted brown shoulder-length hair as wild as his dark eyes. He lunges at the king with a small hand-crafted knife. Before King Martin can pull out his swords from their sheaths, the man's face impacts with the stone wall and dark blood splatters from under his head. A guard thrusts his sword into the bloodied man. He screams in surprise and lurches over. King Martin jumps to his side to avoid the dying man as he slams onto the floor with a thud. Two more guards jump in front of their king and Simon runs down the stairs with his swords pointing straight ahead.

"Are you alright?" Simon asks while looking around the keep for other assailants.

The same guard continues to drive his sword into the defenseless man over and over. The man lays in an expanding pool of his own blood, his eyes blank, staring at the clear sky.

Martin pushes past the guards to see the dead man. "Must have underestimated the stealth and skill of hiding that these men portray. Interesting plan..." He continues staring at the dead man.

"You and you," Simon points to two guards. "Stay with the king until I say differently. There is something I must do." Simon trots off in the opposite direction.

King Martin knows the two assigned guards as previous members of the Black Army from their familiar faces during the previous war with King Richard. The guards are dressed in leather armor with two thin swords strapped to their backs, same as Martin. Their boots are laced to their legs in a cross pattern over their stockings with leather straps. One guard has a scar above his right eye, and the other man has a scar across his left cheek. They stand alert, one on each side of Martin, and follow his every move.

King Martin walks into the castle followed closely by the Black Army members. On his way in, Samantha walks out with a basket of freshly baked buns. As she passes him, he grabs a bun, and although they feel soft and fresh, they burn his freezing fingers. Martin shoves the entire small bun into his mouth.

"Hey! Yours are in your room!" Samantha objects. Her king smiles with a mouthful of a fresh bun and skips away to his bedchamber in a playful manner. The two guards enter his bedchamber without invitation and close the door behind them.

"Now that we are in private, I wish to talk with you," King Martin starts. "What can you tell me about how the Black Army started and who's in it?"

"Well," a guard starts, leaning against the wall, "before our birth, our old kingdom way back when, was always under siege, so the king back then picked ten young, eager men—well, kids of eight years old— but anyways, he sent them to go as far away as possible from the kingdom and find another army and join it. Once they joined, they had to find a different method of fighting. The ones that went to the far east found out that two swords were better than one, but ones that went to the north found that a good shield can be used as a weapon as well as a shield." Martin sits on his bed and waits.

The guard continues. "Some that went further east found that the soldiers wore soft boots and dressed in black, even covering their faces, to help camouflage attacks in the night. When the six returned after years of being away, there was a new king Edward the 2nd; he was the younger heir. This new king accused the kids of

THE NEW QUEEN

being assassins and knights for hire. It was blasphemy and treason against the kingdom."

"Did you not say ten were sent out?" Martin asks.

"Yes but only six came back. It is not known what happened to the others."

"Did they look for them?" Martin asks.

"No, the king was not told of these boys' quests." The guard pauses for another question before continuing. "Each boy left with nothing and came back as men with knowledge about combat strategies. A man heard of these boys and gathered them from the king at that time before that king could make a ruling against them. This man trained them until they were to come up with a style of fighting of their own that no other army had ever seen. They could move deathly quiet when killing and were hard to be seen. Later, one more boy returned, and he was called the 'Trainer of the Stick' and trained the army to fight with only a stick or a staff. He taught them that by using basic tools around you, you can be the master of anything."

"Did the king accept him back?" Prince Martin frowns.

"No, the king did not recognize any of the boys. By the time the army was trained, yet another king had come into power, and it was this king that saw the real threat from this army."

"Was this the kingdom we were banished from?" Prince Martin hesitates and scratches his arm.

"Yes. The king wanted to have this group disbanded, but their loyalty to one another was so strong that he couldn't do it so he sent them on a quest that he thought they would all die on. The quest he assigned was to go and destroy the entire army of the northern lands Every kingdom, All of the northern lands! The northern lands kingdoms had been fighting for many years, and it cost them too many resources, too many deaths, too much food, and too many injured horses to continue. These new soldiers moved into

THE SHADOW ARMY

the castle of the northern kingdom and within a single night, the entire army vanished. When they returned, the king was told only shadows could have killed the entire army, so we became known as 'The Shadow Army'".

"And here they call you the 'Black Army,'" Martin confirms.

"Yes," the guard responds. The other guard nods his head in confirmation.

"I think that had something to do with me and the late King Richard. I could not tell him that I brought the Shadow Army with me, could I? So I told him that the army we sought after was dressed in black. That's how you got the name here, and how most people in these areas think two different armies existed."

The guard nods. "Over the years, some died of old age, and others settled down, but most of us know no other life. When the king banished us along with you, we had no kingdom until you decided to make your own."

"It was only a dream. But then you all started to kill everyone, even innocent commoners and kids." Martin clenches his teeth.

"We followed orders from Henry. He was the Captain of the Guards, after all, and he told us to follow you. Also, if we never killed anyone, you would have never gotten the land and your plan would not have worked." The guard sits on a wooden chair by the door and the other guard standing by the bed as they exchange glances.

King Martin pauses. "It is sad you found no love. No real life, only war."

"We are trained not to love, and instead, to divert our energy and thoughts on war: weapons, combat, enemies. We protect, not love. It is what we were taught to do. Some of the Great Army who sits atop of the hill were trained by us, but not as long as we were trained."

THE NEW QUEEN

"That's why the king at the time Edward, I think it was? Well he sent them to fight because he believed they were as great as you are?" Prince Martin asks.

"Not only that, but he thought he could control them better as well because they would not kill an entire village. The king knew he could not completely control us and he even tried to have us all killed at one time but the soldiers who he sent in the middle of the night all died in their attempt. The next day we knew we would have to move on, so it was a blessing of sorts to be told to leave... banished, if you will."

The bedchamber door slams open and the guard's speech is cut short. A large man dressed in commoner's clothes of a cotton shirt and stockings stumbles into the room with a short sword raised. King Martin and the guard sitting with him on the bed jumps up, and before the invader makes a second step into the room, he drops dead, killed by the guard next to the door. King Martin watches as the guard by the door drags the dead body out of the room and closes the door behind him.

The King turns to the guard beside him and comments, "I guess Simon had good reason to keep you by my side." He shuffles uncomfortably.

"I feel you are not safe here, my majesty."

"And where do you think I should go? This is my castle. As small as it is, this is my kingdom, and it is still growing...thriving, even. I will not let someone take over what we are struggling to flourish. How are these invaders getting in, is what I want to know?" Martin glares at the guard.

"They must be already within the castle walls, my king." The second guard reenters into the bedchamber. He pulls out a small leather pack covered in blood from under his arm. "Hey, bonus!" he announces as he dumps four large gold pieces onto the floor. The men look at one another with awe.

THE SHADOW ARMY

"Where would anyone get so much gold?" Prince Martin asks.

"It would seem there is a price on your head, my majesty. And a rather large one at that," the guard beside Prince Martin says.

"We better tell Simon," Martin says. "But I don't want to bring more attention to these facts more than we have to. I want you two to go ahead of me. Make sure all is fine, and I will walk on my own accord to talk with my Captain of the Guards."

"Yes, your majesty," the guards respond in unison before leaving his room.

King Martin makes his way down the stone stairs, watching and studying everyone as if they are about to kill him. Each step he takes with caution, hiding in the shadows of the rooms. Under his pale hand hides a concealed knife hastily strapped to his hip and ready to be used.

Chapter 2
WOUNDED

Simon's did not want archers on the wall walk for fear it might be taken as aggression against the Great Army, but the king orders archers to be placed on the stone wall-walk facing the Great Army against Simon's wishes not to do so. Feeling he had to be ready for a war. The King wears a long brown rabbit fur coat over his thin body and worn-down leather boots. His shoulder-length curly hair damply hangs from the continuous snowfall, and Martin squints to watch the Great Army in the distance. The hundreds of soldiers stand in a line around the castle, just far enough that Martin's archers cannot reach. The Great Army soldiers hold out small short swords and are dressed in dark furs reaching up to their mouths.

Simon stands beside his king on the wall-walk, overlooking the familiar army. His two sheathed swords crisscross on his back.

"It was only a year ago that you were working for that very army," Martin murmurs, still staring at the Great Army.

WOUNDED

"You think they are going to attack the castle?" Simon asks his king more as a surprised statement than as a question.

"It bloody well looks like it, doesn't it?" the king snaps back.

"Right then! I want you to go to the other castle. You will be safe there while we try and sort this out. They may want to come in or even raid the castle and if you're not here," Simon pauses, "at least you will still be alive."

"If something happens to you, what will I do?" Martin turns to Simon.

"There's not much you can do. With no real army left and no men to draw from Richard's kingdom, we are on our own."

"Simon, it's my kingdom now, not Richard's. We fought him and won. But if anything should happen to you, I will avenge your death. You have my word on that." King Martin looks away and Simon rests his hand on his shoulder.

"You know, it is strange that I cannot go out there and tell them we are on the same side," Simon smiles.

"Why can't you? You were second in command behind Henry, and now you are the Captain of the Guards here," Martins says as he continues watching the Great Army.

"I am also a coward for abandoning our mad king, and I am sure he would not think highly of that, would he? As for the army, they would claim this kingdom for their king, and we will lose everything all over again. We betrayed them. There is only one way to survive, and that is to kill." Simon clenches his jaw.

King Martin nods his head and walks down the broad stone steps with his head low and his hand gliding along the side of the wall. "Good luck," King Martin answers with a blank stare, looking away from Simon.

Simon orders ten guards to escort the king to our other castle. "Light the perimeter torches!" he yells to the soldiers. Martin

THE NEW QUEEN

listens to Simon bark out other orders as he leaves to prepare for the day-long trip to the other castle.

The king's escort consists of three ex-Black Army men specially trained in stealth and assassination, and the other seven are King Martin's own guards. Martin jumps onto his horse, and his guards abruptly follow.

Elizabeth rushes over to Martin, eyes narrowed, and her curly hair bouncing with each step. "Where are you going?" she asks him, grabbing his leg. King Martin looks at the guards, not sure if he should say anything.

"I'm, uh, going to the other castle to get supplies," he lies.

"We were just there. Why didn't you get supplies then? Can I come?" Elizabeth's large green eyes widen. Her thick fox fur tunic hugs her thin body and her bushy red hair sticks out from under her hood.

Martin sighs. "Do you want to join us, Elizabeth?"

Elizabeth grins. "Yes, please! I will go fetch a horse." She races back on a small auburn horse and the party of twelve rides into the forest for cover. Racing quickly among the shadows of the forest, they soon meet up with the winding path that leads to the other castle. The gentle snowfall dusts over their new tracks.

After riding in silence along the path, one guard stops. "Your majesty, we will walk our horses for a while because we have been using these same horses all day and they need some rest," a young guard declares as he examines the surrounding path. King Martin nods and slows the pace of his horse. Elizabeth follows, and they walk together while the guards shield them from the weather.

"What supplies do we need?" Elizabeth inquires.

"Did you not see the army outside the castle walls?" Martin snaps at her.

"I did," she responds, staring back at him.

"Elizabeth, sometimes I think you're so daft! If the army attacks, who will lead the people? Simon told me to leave in case such a matter happens."

Elizabeth rides in silence before she answers. "We should name the castle. Every good castle has a name, so we should have one too!"

Martin thinks for a moment. "Well, what should we name it, Elizabeth?"

"Well, it should say something about the castle. Like whose kingdom it belongs to or what it represents, like hope. That's it! We should name it Hope Castle!"

"That sounds terrible. Whoever heard of a castle named Hope?" Martin pauses. "What about Rock Castle or Castle Channel or Waterfront?"

"That's not a bad name, Waterfront Castle." Elizabeth smacks his arm and they both laugh.

"I guess you're right, though we should name the castle. We need a good name."

Elizabeth shrieks with delight. "I got it, Quarry Castle! It says a lot about the castle." Her green eyes widen at him.

The king nods his head. "I like it. We get the stones we need from the rock we built on. I think you have a good name. From now on, we will call our castle Quarry Castle."

"We need to name Richard's castle, too," she adds.

"The first time I saw that castle, it was surrounded by yellow grass about two feet high. I was told it was because the castle was full of gold, but we know that was a lie." The king pulls on the reins of the horse. "The castle did not give us gold, but it did give our kingdom a new sense of hope. Richard's castle should be called New Hope Castle, where the path of golden grass lines the way to new possibilities." Martin smiles, and Elizabeth smiles back.

THE NEW QUEEN

Elizabeth nods. "I like it, too. Now you have it, Richard's castle will now be known as New Hope Castle!"

Two guards suddenly raise their hands to stop the group from walking. The king squints through the pine trees on one side then turns to a small patch of frozen marsh on the other.

"What's wrong?" Elizabeth asks Martin.

"I don't know," Martin whispers back. "I don't see anything unusual."

A Black Army guard turns around and tilts his head to the sky. A branch snaps overhead. "Everyone, leave the horses in the trees, quickly!" the guard hisses as he hurries the group to the trees. The group scatters around, ushering their horses between the trees. Each guard quickly pulls out their weapons and stands still, joining the first guard.

King Martin pulls out his two swords across his back. Three guards accompany their king and Elizabeth as they head into the trees together. The bushes rustle and fallen twigs crunch on the frozen ground beneath them. A guard behind them screams as a group of men jump down from the trees and block the path from the group, their swords glistening in the late afternoon sun. The king's group turn back and rush down the hillside, darting between the trees as the enemies follow closely behind, lashing their swords and shooting arrows.

Martin grabs Elizabeth's arm as they run between the guards. The group rushes past another growth of bushes as more men jump from behind and join the chase, swiping the air with their swords. King Martin stops running and draws his swords, keeping them crossed, just as Simon trained him. He charges forward at the closest enemy, crossing his swords in front of him, just as a guard jumps in front of Martin and slashes the man. Another enemy yells as he charges behind the king. Martin whips around and the man forces his two-handed sword down upon him, but Martin deflects

WOUNDED

the sword with his crisscross technique. Martin violently thrusts his sword into the man's throat and blood splatters all over his hands and face. The weight of the man twists Martin's wrist, and he lets go of the sword in pain. The man falls to the ground, dead.

A short, beefy man advances towards King Martin, swinging his sword. Martin ducks and feels the wind from the slash graze his hair. He stabs the man in his leg, pulls the bloody sword out of his first foe, and slices the man's throat. Dark red blood drains from the wounds and stains the snow where he lays.

Elizabeth screams and Martin turns to her direction. She cowers against a tree with a crossbow aimed at her from some distance. The men snicker at her screams and walk towards her. One man stretches out his arms while revealing a toothless grin. Martin jumps over tree stumps and foliage, racing around one-on-one fights as he tries to reach Elizabeth. "Elizabeth, run! Move!" She gazes wildly between the approaching man and Martin, quivering and gasping. A nearby guard slices the men behind their legs and they stumble forward, collapsing on the ice as blood gushes out behind them.

"You have to move, Elizabeth! Don't just stand there!" Martin yells at Elizabeth between breaths. She screams again, and Martin spins around to see another archer aimed at his back. Martin dashes towards the archer as the archer draws his crossbow. The young king jumps off a tree stump as the archer shoots. Sword raised above his head, King Martin thrusts his sword straight into the man's chest before falling to the ground with an arrow embedded into his thigh. Martin cries out in pain and grips his leg. The tip of the arrowhead sticks out above his knee, and blood soaks his fur coat as tears quickly well up in his eyes. A scruffy man approaches from behind a tree and Martin pulls out his sword from the other attacker's chest. The man charges at Martin but he deflects the assailant's first volley through watery eyes. The man

THE NEW QUEEN

attacks again, and Martin leans back, looking for a smaller, lighter weapon for his weak body. As the attacker is about to strike the king, a knife whips through the air, hitting the man right in his chest. Martin moves his leg where the blundering man falls.

Elizabeth moves from the tree and rushes to Martin. "You're wounded," Elizabeth wheezes, kneeling beside Martin. He flinches in pain. "Give me your sword," she requests.

"No!" he yells at her. "You will not fight for me!"

"Give me the sword or you might die!" she yells back at him, grabbing the sword from his hand. "Now hold still." She saws the tip of the arrow off as Martin groans and his body shakes. Elizabeth saws faster until the tip falls off and pulls the arrow out of his leg. Warm blood soaks Martin's leg, and he gasps, his face becoming hot and sweaty. Elizabeth grabs the bottom of his fur coat, pressing it onto the open wound. "You're lucky it deflected off your thigh bone and came out above your knee. That was very brave of you to jump at that man to stop him from shooting at me. Who knew you could jump so high? You jumped higher than old Mrs. Farmer's cow when lightning hit, the poor thing," she coaxes.

Martin struggles to sit up and he stares at the sky. "Don't you know I'm good with knives?" Elizabeth continues. "You should trust me more with them." A twig snaps in the distance behind a nearby bush. Elizabeth's heart pounds in her ears as she focuses on the rustling bush. Martin motions for Elizabeth to lay on the ground, closer to a pine tree. Elizabeth crawls to the pine tree to the right and retrieves a crossbow and some fallen arrows, flinging it over her back. She crawls back to him with the loaded crossbow. Blood soaks through Martin's fur and he presses his hands on the wound, grimacing in pain. The blood soaks his hands and travels down his leg. He gasps and his eyes widen at the amount of blood around him. He drops to the side and smashes his head against

WOUNDED

a rock. Elizabeth gasps and removes the lace from the top of her smock and wraps it tightly around Martin's leg.

"Elizabeth," Martin pants. "If I pass out, you have to get away. Go to Hope Castle where and don't look back. You must do this." Elizabeth's eyes turn glossy, and she nods at him. She places her hand on his leg, and he winces again. His leg turns from warm to cold to hot, and he releases a low groan. "Maybe the cold will freeze my leg and numb the pain," Martin whispers.

Elizabeth turns to say something but another branch snaps in the nearby bush. Elizabeth bolts up and aims the crossbow towards the noise. She stares at the same spot, slowly sidestepping onto King Martin's injured leg. Martin gasps and pushes Elizabeth violently off his leg. She presses the trigger and fires an arrow into the direction of the sound. A man runs out of the bush and King Martin recognizes him as a former Black Army soldier.

"Did you shoot at me?" the Black Army soldier asks through his thick brown beard. His thick, hairy fingers pick up the arrow and he glares at Elizabeth.

"I didn't mean to." Elizabeth apologizes.

"This is no place for a girl. You should not have been here at all!" He snaps the arrow in half and tosses it aside. "We took care of the rest of them, your majesty, but we have to go now. The horses are ready." He looks at his king and pauses. "Sire, can you walk?" King Martin nods and tries to stand up but falls to the ground. Elizabeth helps him up and Martin leans on her. The soldier looks at Martin's wound, then grunts and glares at Elizabeth again. Elizabeth tears up and stares at the icy terrain. The guard waits for Elizabeth and Martin to catch up, and together they walk up the forested hill to their tied horses.

The king hobbles and pants when another man jumps out from the tree line on the opposite path. Elizabeth screams and holds onto Martin. The man draws a dagger, leaving his sword in

THE NEW QUEEN

its sheath. Elizabeth slowly takes a step back, and Martin hops, balancing with her.

"No one to save you now," the approaching man boasts, grinning as he raises his dagger. Within steps of Elizabeth and the king, the man suddenly stops. He frowns, widens his eyes and falls to his knees.

"He knows who you are," Elizabeth whispers to Martin. Elizabeth clears her throat and shouts, "You better kneel before your king!"

The man chokes and falls face first onto the snowy path with six knives protruding from his back. Elizabeth gasps and turns to Martin's chest, hiding her face from the site. His arm slips off of Elizabeth's shoulder and he tumbles backward. He thumps to the ground and wails in pain. "Elizabeth!" he snaps at her. Two guards rush over to Martin and they lift him onto his white horse. King Martin grabs his leg and feels the warm blood soaking his cold hands. He winces as he lifts his leg over the side of the horse.

"I can't move my leg to get the horse to move," he tells Elizabeth as he grasps the horse's neck. Elizabeth grabs a nearby black horse grazing off the path and mounts it. She rides over to Martin, grabs hold of Martin's reins and kicks her horse into a gallop. Martin grips the horse's neck tighter as Elizabeth's horse breaks into a sprint.

As Elizabeth urges her horse forward, a blundering guard on his black horse leaps from behind a tree and blocks their path. Elizabeth's horse neighs loudly and kicks at the ground, shaking its head. Martin's horse skids to a stop and flings Martin into the horse's mane.

"What was that for?" Elizabeth purses her lips.

"We have two guards up ahead. You have to give them time to make sure all is safe," the familiar bearded Black Army soldier replies to Elizabeth. He frowns at her.

WOUNDED

King Martin's vision blurs so he squeezes his eyes closed. The pain from his leg shoots up his body and he jerks in pain.

"We have three guards behind us, and I will stay with you two," the guard adds.

"Where are the others?" Elizabeth asks.

"They were killed," the guard replies, lighting two torches as the sun begins to set. He gives one to King Martin, then one to Elizabeth. He lights a third torch and holds it close to Martin's leg. "It looks bad." The guard turns to Elizabeth and adds, "We better move now." With a quick nod, the guard leads the way up the snowy path, holding a torch in one hand and the reins in the other.

Martin's body becomes numb, and he loosens his grip around the horse's neck. The guard glances back at Martin and Elizabeth. "Hey! Stop! Stop!" the guard yells at them. He turns around and races back to Martin. The guard reaches for Martin's limp body as it falls sideways off the horse.

A guard runs into the trees and returns with a few long reeds. He ties it tightly around Martin's leg and glances at Elizabeth. "You will have to hold on to him. We have to keep going or else he might not make it." She nods as her hands shake. The two guards secure the king onto Elizabeth's horse as she holds his weak body. The group treks on through dusk, pushing their horses faster to get to New Hope Castle.

The guards ahead of the small party arrive first at the castle and alert the other guards about a possible attack. The Black Army guard grabs Martin and places him onto his shoulder. "We need to stop his bleeding right away," he grunts.

Elizabeth nods her head, jumping off her horse. The guard follows her lead, carrying the unconscious King down the hallway, past the kitchens and into a full, dimly lit room with ten wooden framed beds on opposite sides of the walls. The floor is made up of thick, wooden beams and the walls are constructed from large on

THE NEW QUEEN

the lower half and wood on the upper half. Torches line the walls, warming the room. A few bandaged guards rest in the makeshift beds as maidens tend to their needs. One of the maidens, fair skinned, with brown and graying hair, points and gives orders to the younger maidens who do what she commands. She wears a long dress made up of rag patches sewn together with a corset in the middle. The old maiden, in her late forties, waves them over and quickly clears a bed in the far corner for her new king.

"Quickly, put him here! I must see what has happened to this poor boy." She points to a small bed and touches his neck, feeling for his pulse.

"Who are you?" Elizabeth asks, sitting by the bed and holding Martin's hand.

The maiden examines the rest of Martin's bloodied body. "I am Gwyneth, the king's personal caregiver, and Head Maiden," she responds, not looking at Elizabeth. She continues her examination. Gwyneth moves over to the bedside and Elizabeth moves to the side to allow Gwyneth to be closer to the king. Gwyneth lifts the blood-soaked lace from Martin's leg. "I will have to sew him up, that's for sure," she says, pulling out a needle from her dress pocket. She licks some thread, prepares the needle and pokes the needle into Martin's thigh.

Elizabeth screams, "Stop! What are you doing? He is not a dress to be hemmed up! He's your king! Poking more holes into him will not help him stop bleeding, you will only make him worse!" Her chest rises and falls quickly. "You have to wrap his wound!"

A guard moves over to Elizabeth and pulls her away. "She knows what she is doing, my lady. You must trust her, for the life of your king depends on it. She is the best we have." The guard reassures Elizabeth, keeping her out of Gwyneth's way. Elizabeth

WOUNDED

and the guard stand together by the bedchamber door as Elizabeth winces each time the needle goes through her king.

"It does not look too bad," Gwyneth comments, stitching his wound. "The arrow never cut any of the major veins so he should be fine, but we will know more when morning arrives. There is nothing more any of us can do now. He needs his rest." Gwyneth stands and puts the needle carefully back into her dress, just below her thigh.

Gwyneth turns to Elizabeth. "You care for your king. Are you to be the new queen?"

"I," Elizabeth hesitates. "I could only wish for such an honor, but I have no say in what the king wants." She looks back at Martin. "He is very handsome though, even covered in blood."

Gwyneth grins. "Yes, he is good looking, better than most kings I have met. Are you of royal blood?"

Elizabeth shakes her head. "No. I am only a commoner, like you."

"A king can only marry royal blood."

Elizabeth raises her voice. "He can marry whoever he wants."

Gwyneth smiles. "No he cannot, even if he wants to," she confirms in a calm, steady voice. Gwyneth pushes past Elizabeth and pauses. "I'm sorry, but it's the truth." She speeds out of the entrance, leaving Elizabeth alone with King Martin and the guard.

Elizabeth sits on the chair by Martin's bedside, holding his hand. She turns to the guard. "I will stay here in case he needs anything," she says with tears in her eyes. The guard nods, closing the door behind him.

Elizabeth waits for hours on a wooden chair next to him. The moon hangs in the black sky as Elizabeth's head becomes heavy and her eyelids droop. She yawns, shifting to a more comfortable position on the chair. Martin remains in a deep sleep, his chest moving up and down under the wool blankets. Elizabeth's head falls back and her mouth hangs opens as she leans her back on the chair.

The black sky mixes with swirls of red and orange as the rays of sunlight break the horizon. Elizabeth slowly opens her eyes and notices the side table where a pile of warm wax collects around the final remains of a candle. She raises her head and looks down at Martin's chest where an imprint of her head formed in the wool blankets. She wipes drool off her mouth and sighs. She grabs a piece of cloth off the side table. "Perfect, Elizabeth, drool on the king why don't you? Very lady-like," she hisses at herself. Elizabeth furiously moves the cloth in circular motions along the spot of drool on the king's blanket. Martin slowly opens his eyes. He moves his head slightly, watching her wipe up the spot.

"What are you doing?" Martin asks in a hoarse whisper.

Elizabeth stops cleaning and turns her face to his. "Did you say something?" she whispers back. He smiles slightly. She jumps up and asks, "Do you want a drink? I will get something." She turns again to the side table and grabs the water jug and a silver goblet, pouring him a drink. "Here," she says gently lifting his head and touching the goblet to his dry lips. He chugs the entire goblet. "Are you hungry? I can get you something, too. Would you like some bread, or maybe some mead? I can see what is left in the kitchen for you."

Martin coughs. "Soup," he whispers hoarsely.

"Soup. I'll get it right away." Elizabeth pauses, looking at Martin before continuing. "Right away, *your majesty.*" She winces at her feeble attempt to acknowledge his royalty. It feels weak, and out of place, but she knows Gwyneth is right about her non-royal blood and she should act like the commoner that she is. Elizabeth leaves the bedchamber in search of some soup for her king.

WOUNDED

King Martin frowns and watches her leave. He shifts to his side but winces as the pain shoots up his leg. He watches the candle flicker until he drifts back to sleep.

Elizabeth carries a hot bowl of vegetable broth, lifting the top layer of her smock to wrap around her hands. The guard steps aside and opens the door for her. She nods in thanks and gives him a slight smile. Elizabeth sits on the chair by Martin's bed before noticing that he is fast asleep. She thinks about how Gwyneth told her she will never be queen and her eyes turn teary. She places the steaming bowl of soup on the side table, wipes her eyes and quietly leaves.

Chapter 3
CLOSE CALL

Captain Witter stands in front of the Queen as she lies on the late kings bed, waiting for her to say something in between sobs. "Please tell me what you think happened," she pleads. Witter looks around the darken bedchamber then inhales and clears his throat before starting the story.

"It was an autumn night, and it began cooling off from the warm day as the castle fell into darkness. This would be King Castile's third home, his third castle and his third successful takeover of a much smaller territory in a very long time. The king strolls past the two guards who stood outside his bedchamber, his long scarlet cloak dragging behind him. The smell of smoke lingered throughout the hallway as blazing fires remained lit for the duration of the new night. Two maidens enter his bedchamber, ready to prepare the king for bed. Both women were older, a condition the queen demanded of the king so there would be heirs to the throne. The king removed his heavy cloak and stroked his short beard as he thought about what he was going to do the next

CLOSE CALL

day while the maidens removed his shirt and replaced it with his nightshirt. They removed his boots and warmed up his bed by placing rocks from the Great Hall fireplace under his sheets. Once the king was in bed, the two maidens tucked in the heavy wool blanket around his large body.

As the older maidens left the bedchamber, they did not notice the figure that hid behind the large tapestry in the darkness of the room. The assassin stood as still as he could and took slow, deep breaths in order to remain silent. The smell of the tapestry was musty and old, with a hint of smoke. But he dared to not move.

Soon, the king fell into a deep sleep and began snoring heavily.

The figure tiptoed out from behind the musty tapestry holding a large serrated knife in his hand. He did not shake at the fear of what he was about to do, nor did he hesitate from his duty to assassinate the king. He had done this type of thing before.

The assassin halted to a stop when the king suddenly snorted. He waited in the shadows, listening to the king's breathing until it became rhythmical once again. The assassin continued his stealthy pattern along the wooden floor, avoiding the creaky floorboards. As he got closer to the bed, he saw the king fast asleep in the middle of the large bed.

The king was in a delicate position. He could not put up much of a struggle. But far enough into the center of the bed, he might be able to cry for help. With each step, the assassin thought about how he was going to do what he had to do. Each step was done with caution, making sure no noise could be heard. The twenty-five feet across the bedchamber floor would take more time than most would care for, but the assassin knew stealth was mandatory in order to kill the king.

The assassin stood beside the bed, watching the king as he pulls out his knife. He carefully measured the distance from one side of the bed to the king and realized he could not reach the

THE NEW QUEEN

king without getting onto the bed itself. All of a sudden, the king became restless and rolled over onto his side, close enough for the assassin to now reach his victim. The assassin raised the knife and plunged it straight into the king's neck, blocking him from any possibility to cry for help. A burst of dark blood squirted from the gash and onto the assassin's face. The blood sprayed all over the sheets and soaked the bedspread. The king's eyes shot open, and his hands struggled to grip around the blade when the knife was pulled out and thrust back in with the same strength as the first. Before the blade was in all the way, the king was dead. The problem now was that the king would be too quiet and a curious guard might check on him from lack of snoring.

The assassin removed the knife and wiped it on the king's pillow before placing it into the sheath. Once again but with haste, he moved across the floor being careful not to step on the creaky floorboards. He made his way to the open window slat behind the tapestry and reached out to grab a hanging rope. He pulled himself up to the roof and ran along the top. He moved his way down the unfinished staircase to the main courtyard where he stayed among the shadows. He lit a small fire a few feet from the gatehouse and waited for the guard to notice the fire. When the guard called for help, the assassin raced straight out the front gate and into the darkness."

Witter finished his version of what he thought had happened and watched the queen as she quietly cried with her face in her hands. Witter thought her mourning was over done as it looked like an act by the queen.

Simon watches his king and guards withdraw into the forest until they disappear, leaving their tracks in the mud and slush. He pulls on his leather vest and protects himself from the cool breeze

CLOSE CALL

and dampness of the cold autumn day. He turns back to the castle and shouts for two guards who scramble to his side. The two guards are locals from the area and have been at the castle only a few weeks. "I need you two to go up to the Great Army and ask what their intentions are," Simon commands as he points towards the large hill. "What are your names?" Simon asks.

"I'm Douglas," the taller of the two responds as he tosses back his straight black hair. He is an older man in his late thirties with a finely trimmed beard and cleaner teeth than most people. Unlike Simon, Douglas keeps a two-handed sword strapped to his hip. He wears part leather armor and sections of worn chain mail along his arms and neck.

Simon turns to the next man. "I am Jade from the House of Lancaster, second heir to the crown." He flexes his chest and grins. Jade is a dirty blonde, clean-shaven man with a square jaw. Jade also keeps a single sword strapped to his hip which reflects in the sunlight. His leather armor hugs his bulky body, and a full set of chain mail peeks around his neck, torso, and arms. "You can count on us, sir," he nods. The two guards head out the front gate towards the Great Army.

One of the Black Army guards approaches Simon. "That Jade fellow being an heir to the throne...what do you think of that? I don't like the looks of him."

"Well, he's not the heir to our king, I take it. Most likely the King of England and if so, he has been banished along with the rest of us. Jade appears eager to help, but we should watch him anyways. There's something different with him..." Simon tells the guard, still watching Jade and Douglas as they move towards the camped army on the hill. Simon watches until Jade and Douglas reach the top of the hill and vanish over the other side.

Jade and Douglas walk into the Great Army's camp, passing large groups of men sitting around fires, while puffs of smoke from

THE NEW QUEEN

burning wood fills the air. A fire burns between every third tent, extending throughout the hill farther than the two guards could see. Each soldier continues their regular duties: roasting meat, sharpening tools on stone, grooming their horses and making larger fires. No one pays much attention to them until Jade asks a young man with no beard, "Excuse me, sir, but who is in charge of this camp?" A group of men nearby lower their pieces of meat and stare at them.

A nearby guard stands up from a log, dressed in chain mail and shiny armor covering his hands. He holds a polished bassinet. "Who are you?" the man asks as his breath disappears into the cold air.

"We are from that castle just over the hill, and we wish to know your intentions on this land," Douglas answers, pointing towards their castle.

"Is your castle part of the one that once stood over there?" the guard asks, pointing to the land where Saxton's castle used to be.

"No, sir." The two look at one another. "No, we are from King Martin's castle. His father died in the war when we claimed the right to our land." Douglas shuffles from foot to foot.

The guard squints at Douglas. "Is something wrong?"

Jade interjects. "No. No, sir. We just never saw such a large army up close before." He flashes a smile.

The guard steps back. "Ah, it was once much larger, my friend." The guard pauses and looks around. "Our ships are in the channel to take us home. We mean no harm to you."

"How soon until you are all gone?" Jake asks, flashing another smile.

"Oh, it will be some time. We only have four ships in the channel and forty thousand men. How long do you think?" The guard looks back and forth between both men, making them

CLOSE CALL

uneasy. "Is this land yours that we hunt?" The guard looks out past the two men and slowly draws his sword from its sheath.

Jade and Douglas back away, keeping their hands on top of their swords. The guard moves away from the men. An arrow shoots out of the forest, bouncing off Jade's chain mail and into the snow. The guard yell as several men run draw their swords and scream as they bolt over the large snow mounds and into the surrounding trees. A guard runs from behind Jade and knocks him to the ground, pointing his sword at Jade's face. Douglas draws his sword and knocks the guard's sword to the ground. Jade jumps to his feet and pulls out his sword, his back to Douglas.

"That was a clever diversion to attack us," the returning head guard says to Douglas and Jade. "Your three friends from the forest are now dead and you will suffer the same fate." He points his sword.

"We are not with anyone else. We are from the castle over yonder. We did not attack you!" Douglas exclaims, pointing his sword outward.

"Then why are your swords drawn?" the guard demands.

"You attacked us! You knocked my friend down and put a sword to his face. I cannot help but think that this is an attack on us," Douglas states.

Suddenly, shouting erupts at the end of the camp where Jade and Douglas entered from. The head guard looks over to see a few of his men in some sort of battle. "Keep them here!" he shouts to his two men as he rushes towards the fight.

With just enough light from the setting sun and the overcast clouds, Simon watches as two men stumble and fight down the hill towards the castle. "Archers, stay ready!" Simon orders. "Wait for my command." Simon notices a familiar man in chain mail and a shiny bassinet that had the royal crest painted on it's side racing

THE NEW QUEEN

down the hill with a guard. "Don't shoot yet!" The archers wait and their bows are drawn tight.

The two men race onto the castle grounds, fighting and killing man after man. They look like the two men Simon sent up to the camp but he could not be sure. Impressed by their skill and stamina, Simon watches the one man he knows. It is Prince Simon of England, the prince himself from the kingdom that Simon and King Martin were banished from. Simon was sworn to protect the prince and was instructed to train him in battle, how to fight and how to kill quickly and effectively. The last time Simon had seen him, he was sent off to fight in the Great War, the same war this Great Army was forced to accept as a stalemate between the two kingdoms. Simon orders the archers to lower their bows and stand down. He watches the two men fight until the Prince strikes down the ambushers with one violent blow.

After the blitz attack, Prince Edward returns to Jade and Douglas on horseback. They remain back to back with their swords drawn, facing the surrounding guards. "It was your castle who attacked us, so we will burn it to the ground!"

"No!" Jade yells. "It was not us! We do not want a war with you!"

Douglas adds, "You think we would attack all of you with just a few men when we have thousands at our disposal?"

"Yes, we have tens of thousands of men on both sides of the channel," Jade adds nervously.

The Prince squints his eyes and scrunches his face. "If it were not you, then who would attack us then? Who?"

Jade shrugs his shoulders. "We don't know. All I know is that it wasn't us."

The Prince scratches his chin, staring at the men. He waves his hand and his soldiers lower their swords.

"So you believe us?" Douglas asks.

CLOSE CALL

The Prince exhales. "Well, it would have been a suicide mission for you to walk in here and try to kill a man or two before we would have killed you." Prince Edward dismounts his horse. "We will leave and will not attack your castle as long as you don't lay arms upon us. Will your king accept that?"

"Yes, you have our word," Douglas responds, sheathing his sword.

"Very well, we are in agreement." Edward commands five guards to escort Jade and Douglas out of the camp and to the top of the hill facing the castle. He turns back to the camp.

Simon commands all the catapults the three trebuchets loaded and ready to be fired. They face the hill where the Great Army camps out. "Sir, our men approach!" an archer shouts.

Simon rushes down the stone steps to the front gate. "Who did they kill?" He asks Jade and Douglas.

"What?" Jade asks.

"You know the two men who were good fighters and died trying to get away? Who were they?" Simon persists.

"We don't know. We were almost killed because of whoever attacked the army, though." Douglas responds.

"What happened?"

"They thought we were a diversion and that the main attack was yet to come when I guess the two men who attacked the camp showed up," Douglas explains. "The captain said if we let them pass and use the land temporarily in peace, they will leave us alone."

"I thought the two men were you two and I almost sent some more guards to help them." Simon pointed to where the men lay dead on the hill. "Go out and see if you know them," Simon orders.

Jade and Douglas nod and take a deep breath as they head out to the bodies on the field. Simon watches them bend over the bodies and poke at the corpses with their feet. Jade crouches beside one of the bodies and pats the sides for any valuables before

THE NEW QUEEN

standing back up and walking back to the castle with Douglas. "We do not know the dead men," Jade tells Simon.

"Well, it figures that the only landing place for ships would be directly beside our castle," Simon says to Jade and Douglas. "So if you don't know who those two men are, how do we find out?" The two shrug their shoulders. "Well then, I guess you both can return to your duties," Simon concludes. The men leave as Simon is summoned to the wall-walk.

Over the next few days, thousands of men march down the hill to their ships in small groups. Simon remains along the wall-walk, carefully watching the men pass through Martin's kingdom. On the fourth day of watching the Great Army, Simon summons one of his guards. "Have the Black Army assemble and leave through the far tree line where Richard started his attack, the area at the far end of the farmland. Tell them to stay there. If there is any problem, we won't need them here with us. They are to move around and attack from behind over the hill. They will most likely kill enough of the Great Army before anyone knows they are even there. Understand?" The guard nods and leaves.

Simon stares at the white field, resting his head between two stone merlons in a crenellation. His eyes droop as he thinks about his old kingdom and his mad king; his mad thirst for blood through beheading, including his wife, or banishing people like Prince Martin. Simon closes his eyes and wonders what state his old kingdom is in and if he made the right decision in leaving. Simon catches himself as his head off the side of the stone tower and jolts him awake. He quickly looks around, hoping no one saw him asleep when he was supposed to be on watch. "Time for some sleep," he yawns, heading towards his bedchamber.

CLOSE CALL

Queen Joanna of Castile stands on the stone balcony wearing her gold crown with lots of green and red gems and long scarlet robe to give her speech. The King once stood in this very spot and often gave motivational speeches and important updates to his subjects. The stone balcony glistened from the bit of rain in the dimming sunset as the moon ascends over the hills. Witter watches her raise her hands to quiet the crowd. "Today is a sad day, but a day which we are also reborn. So if we are to be reborn and start a new, we must let the surrounding kingdoms know that we are still very much a force to be reckoned with." The crowd dulls to a soft murmur. "Although we have lost a great King, you now must rely on your Queen to guide you through difficult times such as these."

The Queen pauses and the crowd continues staring at her. "What our king had started, we shall continue and expand our kingdom to take what is rightfully ours. The surrounding territories have changed. No longer does King Richard hold the kingdom to the far north, but an unknown king now does. To our far east, the king was defeated and again we know nothing about this takeover. With such uncertainty all around us, it would be prudent to strengthen our borders and claim more for our kingdom. Today we lost our King, but have faith in your Queen and I will lead us to a prosperous kingdom in the years to come." The Queen bows with a slight smile on her face and waves at the crowd as the crowd cheers and waves back to her.

Witter holds out his hand for the Queen as she steps away from the balcony. He follows her into a well lit room with torches and candles along the walls. The floor made of the finest oak and furniture covered in the most beautiful silks and cottons. At the head of the room stands the royal desk where the King wrote many royal decrees. The desk is made from imported marble and decorated with ivory statues given to him as gifts from a king

THE NEW QUEEN

oversees. Queen Joanna wraps herself in a second robe as dampness sets in the room. She rests in the royal throne behind the desk and looks at Witter. "I want to increase the army. Have as many young men brought into the army as you can get."

"Increase the army to what number, my Queen?"

"Tenfold," she responds.

Captain Witter shuffles from foot to foot. "But how will we pay them, my Queen? This is the reason why the King did not make the army any larger before."

"If they do not sign up, we will take their farms if we have to. They will do their duty as men of this kingdom, or they lose everything."

"But my Queen, how will we feed them? There is not enough food in the granaries either." Witter tries to reason with her.

"We are going to have to protect our borders. Once other kingdoms find us without our king, they will try and attack us, so we must be ready! Once we are in battle, we will lose many men and the food problem will even out then. Now go!" The Queen shouts, furious with all of the questions. She rises from the throne and storms out of the room, leaving Witter alone in the office.

Witter snaps out of it and follows the Queen to the Drawing Room where a large map is painted along the floor. The Queen marches across the map and turns around to face Witter. "Tell me where our men are now and where this king to the east is and where his men are." Witter steps forward and walks to their kingdom on the map. "This is where we are, this other king is here and here," he responds, pointing to several places on the map. "My scouts tell me he is building up his army as well, but they look as if they will be heading north towards King Saxton's realm. There will surely be a great fight. Saxton had a large army, too, and even thought he could take King Richard's kingdom right from under him."

"So these two will be at war for some time then?"

CLOSE CALL

"Indeed, my Queen. Saxton may ask this king next to him that took Richard's kingdom to help him. That will leave him scarce for men and supplies, and a good time to strike to claim the land. By the time they get an army together to try and retake the land, we will have already set up a stronghold." Witter stops and looks up at the Queen. "France helped us fight King Richard so maybe it would be prudent to ask them for help once again?"

The Queen scrunches her lips. "My husband, your King, regretted ever asking the French for anything. They squeeze most of our money from our treasury, and we still have to fight to gain back what we have lost."

"And what about the French, my Queen? We are surrounded by them. We will have to go through their land to get to Richard's kingdom if we are to take it from this new king."

"The French are worried about the English in the far north. The bit of land we will be taking will not be noticed by the French. Besides, that land was ours way before the damned French came along. Richard took it from the French, and now we will take it from this new king."

"That could mean going to war against the French, my Queen."

"It is none of your concern. As your Queen, it is my responsibility to protect this kingdom." The Queen turns away from the Captain and walks around the map where the water had been drawn in. "We will need access to water anyways, so I want to take this small strip of land from the French. Then we will claim up to the channel, and over to the water. This means we will have to take Richard's old castle as well."

"My Queen, that castle was never ours, nor the land on which it rests."

"That land belongs to us," she yells at Witter. The Captain lowers his head. "It was the French that cut us off from what should have been ours in the first place!' She stomps her feet as she

THE NEW QUEEN

moves around to the point on the map where the French owned the land between her kingdom and King Martin's kingdom. She rubs out the line with her foot. "This is now to be considered ours!"

"What if the French do notice us taking the land?"

"I said that is not your concern."

"Yes, my Queen."

"Now, how many soldiers will we have to start our quest?"

"I estimate three to five thousand men currently ready for a battle, my Queen."

"That is a great number, but King Richard had ten times that amount and we held our own. I have faith in my soldiers. I want the increase to be done in the next year before winter finds us a second time. That way this unknown king cannot attack during the winter, and this will give us plenty of time to strengthen our strongholds." Witter takes a long, nervous breath. He knew that they had prepared for King Richard's battle for years in advance, but this would not have the same preparation. "You understand what I want, don't you? I want to take this land back and hold it through the winter so we can strengthen our forces. The march will be strict and it will be tough."

"Yes, my Queen." Witter bows and turns to leave the Drawing Room.

"And one more thing..." the Queen continues. Witter pauses and turns his head to the side. "If you can't get it done, I will find someone who can."

"Yes my Queen."

Chapter 4
NEW FEAR

King Martin opens his eyes to a cold, dimly lit room. The wooden shutters remain closed but the sunlight peeks through the cracks. Nine empty wooden cot beds stuffed with hay remain in two rows along opposite walls of the room. Wool blankets remain folded in a pile at the end of each bed. A thin line of smoke swirls into the musty room from the glowing logs in the stone fireplace. The young king yawns and rubs his eyes and he tosses the wool blanket off with one hand. He sits up and looks down at his naked body. He widens his eyes and scrambles to grab the blanket, flopping back down on his side. The quick movement from falling onto his side causes a surge of pain that pulses through his entire body. The king inhales, fighting the urge to scream from the pain as he holds his leg and clenches his teeth as his eyes tear up. His bruised leg contains a row of sloppy zigzagged stitches and is swollen twice the size of his knee.

"Guard!" the King yells in a hoarse voice. A broad guard rushes in, stumbling on his way to the bed. He dresses in black stockings and a worn leather vest ripped by his shoulders and sides, almost matching his mangled brown beard.

"Yes, Sire?" he responds, reaching the end of Martin's bed.

"Why am I naked?" Martin pulls the blanket closer to his chin.

"Your leg needed tending, and it was the only way to tend to it, sire. Lady Gwyneth had to sew you up and your clothing was in the way, I suspect, your majesty." The husky guard's unshaven face glows from the faint light from the fireplace. The largest hands Martin ever saw rest on the guard's hips, revealing a large, two-handed sword strapped to his back and a large knife strapped to his side. His beautiful leather boots extend up his stumpy legs to his thick, beefy thighs.

"Where are my clothes?"

"Lady Gwyneth took them to mend, sire."

"Why is it so cold in here?"

"The fire's goin' out," the guard replies, stepping closer to the king. Martin raises his eyebrow at the guard and nods to the dimming fireplace. The guard clenches his jaw and steps closer to the bed.

"Let's keep you warm before we get that fire goin'," the guard responds.

The King watches one of the guard's giant hands slide onto his knife. He grasps the handle and the King quickly rolls to the right, tossing the sheet at the guard while the guard stabs at the air. "Guard! Guard!" The King yells for help. The large fat guard raises his knife again and slashes downward, trying to stab the king. "Guard!" Martin cries out again. The King grabs hold of the man's arm with the knife and punches him with his left. "Guard!" the King yells over and over, but no one responds. The large man chuckles a deep, low laugh as he scrambles to pull off the blanket. Martin quickly pushes himself onto the man using his entire body's weight to knock him over onto the wooden floor. The two become

NEW FEAR

entwined in the wool blankets and hemp sheets and roll on the floor struggling with the sheets and each other. Martin jumps on top of the man, punching wherever he could. The man struggles to raise his arms in front of his face, but he remains tangled in the large wool blanket.

Martin falls to the side in pain from his wounded leg, gripping it tightly and shaking from the cold. The King crawls over to the small table, wincing as he grabs the water jug and crawls back to the tangled man, swinging it repeatedly on the man's head.

"You bugger!" the man yells. The King raises the jug again and hits the man over and over. "When I get out of here, I am going to slice your throat!" the man yells. Martin uses all of his strength and smashes the jug onto the attacker's face. The water jug shatters and the man stops moving.

Martin crawls across the cold wooden floor, grabbing an extra fallen blanket beside the bed and he wraps it around himself. "Guard!" the King yells. A tall guard rushes into the room dressed in new full leather, unlike the king's attacker.

"Yes, Sire?" He stops in his tracks at the blood splatters along the bed and floor. He rushes to the king. "Are you alright?" he asks, helping his King to the bed. Martin's body shakes and tears well up in his eyes.

"W-where the h-hell were you?" The King angrily shouts. "H-he tried to kill me!" Martin stutters, his teeth chattering.

"Sire, there is no excuse. I will find another guard right away. You need to see someone right away." The guard scrambles out of the bedchamber. The King looks at his leg. The stitches tore open and blood dribbles down his leg. Martin wraps the sheet around his leg and tightly ties it, wincing at the pain. He lays down on his back and rests his hands over his face to try and relax but continues shaking from shock.

THE NEW QUEEN

Suddenly, the blankets from the floor rise in complete silence, like a ghost rising from the dead. Martin peeks through his fingers at the large blanket standing before him. The King lays still and wide-eyed, unable to yell for help as the blanket grows higher. A hand from under the blanket tugs at the blanket, pulling it away. The sizeable fat assailant stands in front of Martin, furiously glaring at Martin and panting. He searches the floor for his knife as blood runs from his nose and mouth. The large man leaps at Martin, trying to choke him with both hands. Martin moves his injured leg to the side and uses his good leg to push him away. The fat man staggers and thumps to the ground. He wobbles and turns back to the King, drawing his long sword from its sheath. Martin springs off of the bed towards the man before he can aim the sword, knocking the man to the ground. He pulls Martin down with him. Martin's arms are too short to reach the man's throat, so he begins hitting the man's arms in an attempt to break away.

The guard returns with another guard and the two rush in and pull the impostor off their King. The man continues to fight, now on the floor with the two guards, and he shoves one of the guards towards the fireplace. The guard staggers and falls back, impaled by the fire iron. The large man shoves the remaining guard to the side and rolls over. The guard draws his sword and jumps on the back of the large man and plunges his sword deep into the man's back. The impostor swings his arm wildly, knocking the guard to the side as he continues his fight to stand. He slowly gets up and faces the King with the tip of the blade sticking out of his stomach. The man lunges for King Martin when the guard jumps on the man and uses the assailant's lost knife on the floor to slice his throat. Blood splatters across the wooden floor. The two tumble to the ground, the impostor finally dead, and the guard breathing heavily.

NEW FEAR

"Are you alright, Sire?" the guard asks out of breath as he fights to push the large man off his leg. He rolls the dead man to one side, enough for the guard to free himself, then kicks the body in a rage. "Get off me you fat cow!" the guard screams as he straightens out his leather armor around his leg.

Martin sits up on his elbows and cringes in pain from his torn stitches as tears form in his eyes. "It's a good thing you returned in time. Otherwise, I would have been minced meat," he says through clenched teeth as he tries to joke. The King slides himself to the wall and sits up against it. He glances at his leg. "As it looks, I am!" he says with a sound somewhere between a cry and chuckle.

The door flings open and two more guards rush in with their swords drawn. Martin looks up and lets out a slight chuckle as a few tears run down his cheeks. "Well, I guess it's a good thing you two show up even though a little late." he says raising his voice. The guards scramble to the dead body and drag it out of the room, leaving the impaled guard's body by the fireplace. "How the hell did he get in here anyway?"

"We are searching for impostors all through the castle. He must have slipped in and told the guards they were needed elsewhere. I think this time, your majesty, I will stay here with you while I send someone to fetch Lady Gwyneth to sew you back up again," the cleanly shaven guard responds, retrieving his sword from the floor and wiping the blood onto the bloody blanket. The guard walks over to his king and slumps onto the floor next to him. "I think I will sit here, Sire," he says, looking at Martin with a tired smile on his face. "I'm Mark." The young man holds out his hand. Mark is about twenty years old five feet, five inches in height, thin build but muscular, and clean shaven.

Martin takes his hand and shakes it. "I am your King. King Martin," he says shaking violently.

THE NEW QUEEN

In no time at all, Gwyneth rushes into the bedchamber, her long braided hair swinging behind her. She carries a needle and a long piece of thread dangling from her dress. Mark and Gwyneth help their King to the bed where she removes the sheet around his leg and wraps it around his waist. Martin blushes as his eyes meet hers, then he glances away.

"Guard, please leave, then close the door behind you. I must get to work immediately," Gwyneth says. Mark nods his head and closes the door behind him. "Sire, I have already seen everything there is to see since I have sewn you up once already." Martin exhales and unties the rest of the blood-soaked blanket. "You have torn most of the stitches, Sire. I will have to re-stitch the entire thing." She grabs the lamp and brings it over to the nightstand beside Martin. She takes out the needle from her dress and draws the thread through her lips. "I'm sorry Sire, but it's going to hurt."

Martin grips the sides of the mattress and nods for her to continue. "I understand you were King Richard's healer as well." Martin tries to take his mind off of the needle going in and out of his leg. Gwyneth ties a small strap around King Martin's legs and tightens it to slow the bleeding.

"Yes I was, but I never had to sew him, however." Gwyneth continues stitching.

"I was told he liked his ladies in the bedchamber all the time."

Gwyneth looked up at Martin. "He had his conquests, this is true."

"Were you one of his conquests?" Martin asks without thinking.

"Why? Do you want to continue his reign of conquests? Besides I don't think it's any of your business," Gwyneth says without looking up from Martin's leg. "Stop shaking. I cannot stitch you if you keep squirming."

NEW FEAR

"I meant no disrespect, just trying to keep my mind occupied is all." Martin grimaces at the pain as he wipes his nose on the blanket. "I should actually say that I heard he likes beautiful women and that you fall into that category."

Gwyneth laughs. "Why thank you, Sire, but no I was not one of his conquests. Any woman in his bedchamber did not want to be there but what choice did they have? It was that or death." Gwyneth stands up. "May I say, Sire, I have stitched many men but only you talked while I was doing so." Martin looked at her handy work. "We have to wrap it tightly, so no dirt gets into the wound." She leaves briefly and returns with some cloth to wrap the King's wound.

Throbbing pain shoots up Martin's leg. "That was fast. Did you make that dress yourself?" Martin asks through clenched teeth.

"Ah yes. It's my last one made up from all my other dresses since the war," she pauses, "before the war with you, that is, Sire. No new cloth was available, and now there's no money for any." Gwyneth lowers her head.

"Did you lose someone in the war, my lady?"

"My husband died in the first year of the war. I never got to see his body but they sent word, which is a lot better than what most here received. Many others heard nothing when their husbands or children died until the army returned." Gwyneth lowers her head.

"I am sorry for your loss." Martin pauses. "Go buy a new dress and tell them the King will pay for it. It is the least I can do for your service. As a matter of fact, make that three dresses: one for your service, one that you may think of your husband, and one to pick up your spirits." He smiles.

Gwyneth looks up and smiles. She pulls up a blanket and covers him. "Thank you, your majesty, but you will need more cloth for this wound. I will return soon," she says, then leaves. The king flops his head down onto the pillow. Mark returns and closes the door behind Gwyneth.

THE NEW QUEEN

"Do you know where Elizabeth is?" the King asks his guard.

"No Sire. I don't know who she is," Mark says, handing his king a shirt. "This is all I could find right now," Mark pauses, his cheeks reddening, "but I have another man looking for some stockings and pants for you." Mark opens the shutters to the window and the afternoon sunshine beams through the slats. Two guards return to remove the skewered body from the fireplace poker.

King Martin grabs the white wool long-sleeved shirt, and Mark helps him put it on, noticing some scratches on his back from the fight on the floor. "I want you to send someone to get one of my guards who came with me to fetch Elizabeth. I want to know she's alright!" Martin leans to one side as Mark puts his arm into the shirt sleeve.

"I would rather not leave you, Sire," Mark hesitates and stands beside the King's bed. "I feel somewhat responsible. I saw that man and presumed he was a guard. Little did I know?" Mark shakes his head and sighs.

"Even I thought he was a guard, Mark. The mistake was easily made, but I don't want this to happen again! I thought Simon would have been more careful. This can not ever happen again."

"Who is this Elizabeth, Sire, the future queen perhaps?" Mark changes the subject as he asks with a giant smile.

"No, I don't think so. She's sweet, speaks her mind and lets me know how I come across without holding back. She's not a woman, really. More like a man's mind in a woman's body." Martin chuckles.

"Yet you care for her? Every man needs a woman, even if it is to serve him. We still need women."

"Whoever marries Elizabeth will have their hands full. She speaks her mind even when her king tells her to be quiet!" Martin balls up his fists, fighting to stop himself from shaking.

"And you never put her in the dungeon?"

NEW FEAR

"No, I could never do that," Martin admits.

"Forgive me, but that sounds like love to me, Sire." Mark winks at Martin.

"She's too young, Mark. Maybe if she were older, just maybe!"

The door opens and Gwyneth enters carrying a long piece of cloth. "We better wrap your wound properly, your majesty." Gwyneth removes the blankets and wraps the fabric around the King's legs until he can barely move it.

Captain Witter stands in silence and watches as Joanna, Queen of Castile, receives measurements and customization of her new black gown to grieve the loss of the King. The seamstress works furiously on the hem of Queens Joanna's new royal dress, pinning up loose fabric and measuring different angles of the Queen in the candlelit room. "With the threat of war from this new king in the north, we will have to get the lords to come around and support building up the army." She looks down at the girl sewing the hem. "You won't tell anyone, will you?" The girl keeps her head down and shakes her head with a mouth full of pins. "I know they will be here by next winter, wanting to take our land and I know they will kill all of the men and beat the women and children, but what can I do if the kingdom is not behind me one hundred percent?" Witter stares at the Queen with puzzlement on his face, not sure who she is talking to. "We need everyone in the kingdom to give me their full commitment to do what needs to be done. If the lords and barons are fighting with me, we will all parish next winter." The Queen looks back down at the girl, satisfied with the length of her new gown. "That will be all for today. Come back tomorrow, and we will finish up." Joanna waves the seamstress out. The young girl fumbles as she quickly gathers her sewing tools and rushes out the door.

THE NEW QUEEN

Captain Witter walks over to the Queen. "My Queen, where did you hear we are to be invaded? I have not heard such things. When is this supposed to happen?" Joanna turns around from looking at her reflection in the silver mirror.

"Oh, I did not hear such things." She smiles and turns back towards the silver mirror. "I made them up. That little hem maker has the ear to many of the lords and barons. Once she does her lip service to them, they will come and ask if they can do anything to help. She is nothing but a mouth about the kingdom and I am sure she will enlarge the tail spun here. Soon it will be that the kingdom was already attacked and the men were dead, and the women were enslaved or something like that. Either way, they will come to me over the next few months with full control over their armies and their granaries that will feed the entire army."

"But it's a lie, my Queen," the Captain responds. "Surely nothing good comes from speaking in such a tongue!"

"You dare challenge me?" The Queen snaps. Remember what your job is, and I'll do mine."

"Of course, my Queen." Witter bows his head. "How are you so sure this possible invasion will happen, my Queen? I mean there have been no sightings of this new king and no aggression that we know of."

"Because you are going to make it happen and when it does, every last person in this kingdom will beg for me to protect them. They will give me anything I want as long as I protect them!" She walks off the pedestal and raises her hand, signaling for Witter not to follow her into the next room.

Word soon arrives that Elizabeth returned to the other castle. Martin orders his personal guards to meet in the Great Hall and update him about the events from the other castle. The King sits

NEW FEAR

at a table in the main hall dressed in all leather armor. Mark stands at his side while guards crowd around the room, with even more by the doorway. Three of the Black Army members sit across from their king. Martin waves his hand and the small crowd of guards falls silent.

One Black Army guard speaks first. "We know nothing, your majesty."

Another guard chimes in. "There's no news from the other castle as of yet, Sire."

Martin nods his head. "Let's send two or three men to see if they can find out anything. And do we know yet who attacked us on the way here?"

"We think they must be from around here, Sire. They fought in the old ways, and there were many of them, Sire," the first Black Army guard answers.

Martin taps his hands on the table. "Well I toured these lands and claimed them as my own, and no one objected, so I suspect they are not from this kingdom, would you not agree?"

"They may have been from this kingdom, but when you were visiting, they were not around at that time. They could also be from another kingdom, as you know. King Richard was prominent in these lands," a Black Army soldier responds.

"We should send some to the other castle right away and see what is happening. I can't believe you have not done this already," Martin says with a frown.

"Sire, we sent out a small party of four men last week, but they haven't returned yet, and we have not heard anything about them," the Black Amy guard comments.

Martin glances at the men with a puzzled look on his face. "Did we not just get here two days ago? How could you send out a party last week?"

THE NEW QUEEN

"You were unconscious for an entire week, your majesty," Mark speaks up. "You woke up only after seven days passed."

"Who acted on my behalf while I was asleep?" He glances around the group.

"Well," Mark starts, "well, no one. We waited for you to wake up, that's all."

Martin stands and grabs his crutch. "That will be all." The King starts to leave the Great Hall with his head hanging.

Mark jumped up and quickly moves to Martin's side. "Your majesty, you cannot concern yourself with what happens when you were sleeping."

"I was not sleeping! And we need someone to run the kingdom when I am not available, but I need someone who knows what I would want and not cause any treason."

"Who would you trust with such power?"

"There are not a lot of people I trust, perhaps only one or two." The King takes a deep breath before answering. "Either Samantha or Elizabeth. I don't know about Simon. I don't know Simon well enough to trust him with that power."

"Again with this girl, Elizabeth. Who is this Samantha?"

"'They are sisters. Elizabeth is the youngest." Martin starts to walk again, and Mark follows. "Samantha was once married but her husband died in the war. She is quiet and smart. Elizabeth is quite assertive, especially for a woman. She often says what needs to be said. She is not as smart as her sister but sees things in a different angle that most men do not. Together they would make the perfect Queen. Separately, neither could fit such a role."

"If you marry one, will the other not follow their sister? That way you would get them both and together they would make you the good queen you're looking for." Mark smirks.

NEW FEAR

The King raises his eyebrows. "Are you saying that I should marry one?"

"'It may solve many problems, your majesty. You should consider it." Mark helps Martin to his bedchamber and closes the door after him, leaving him to his thoughts.

Chapter 5
Taking the Fight to Them

Simon and Elizabeth stand on the wall-walk at Quarry castle and watch the Great Army step into rowboats to cross the icy waters to their ship.

"They really want to go home, don't they?" Elizabeth asks, her fur coat unbuttoned from the unusually warm morning.

"I would after years of fighting," Simon answers, adjusting his leather vest.

"I remember telling the king not to try and fight them and wait to see if they go away. I guess I was right," Elizabeth says with a grin as she looks towards Simon.

"You seem to advise the king on many things, don't you?" Simon glances back at Elizabeth.

"I think he needs a woman's view most of the time." Elizabeth looks back at the Great Army. "I think he values my council more than yours at times, Simon."

TAKING THE FIGHT TO THEM

Simon shakes his head. "I don't doubt the king likes your advice, but remember his ultimate decision will be made on behalf of the kingdom, not for you." Simon pauses. "The king is bright enough to know whose advice to take and when."

"Should we get the king from the other castle now? I mean, there is no one here who wants to harm him so he should be here, don't you think?"

"Are you asking my advice, Elizabeth, or are you searching for something else?" Simon asks in a sarcastic tone.

"I just think a king should be in his castle. Nothing more, sir," she replies in irritation.

"The king is in his castle, just not this one." Simon moves away from Elizabeth.

Elizabeth looks back. "What are you going to do now?"

"What I am about to do is none of your concern. Why don't you go and feed the men who stay on the wall, guarding this castle?" he commands.

Elizabeth glares at Simon as he continues to walk away. "I do more here than most," she snaps back at Simon.

Simon leaves Elizabeth on the wall-walk and continues down the stairs to the keep. He mounts a horse with a small party of soldiers and they ride out the front gate.

Samantha leans against the wall and stares at the icy waters as she watches her little brother, Andrew, play with other children in the keep. "Oh!" Elizabeth exclaims, when she spots her sister. "I didn't see you there." Samantha shrugs her shoulders and pulls her fur coat tighter around her shoulders.

"Why would Simon leave the castle when there is a big army just outside of it?" Elizabeth watches the group ride across the frosty field.

Samantha notices the four large, bulky men riding alongside Simon. "I don't know, but he took some of the best men with him."

THE NEW QUEEN

"I think the king should be here, don't you?" Elizabeth turns to her sister.

"I am sure he has other things on his mind." Samantha pauses. "I don't think I ever heard you call him 'The King' before." She stares back at Elizabeth with her eyebrows raised.

"I just realized I can never be queen and neither can you." Elizabeth frowns and looks at the floor.

"Yes, I already knew that. It's just not in our blood to be royalty." Samantha places her hand on Elizabeth's shoulder. "I'm sorry," she adds.

Elizabeth shrugs, watching the party of men shrink in the distance. "Where do you think they are going? Simon wouldn't tell me."

"Of course he wouldn't. You're not a soldier, Elizabeth, remember you are no more a soldier than Andrew is, here." Samantha pats little Andrew on the head as he looks up and smiles at her before running away with a smaller boy. "Anyways, maybe they left to talk with that army again?"

Elizabeth shakes her head. "No, they did not turn to go to their campsite on the hill or to the other castle to get the king."

"I don't know then, but I'm sure they will be fine. Are you coming inside?" Samantha shivers as she waves Andrew over to her.

"Soon. It's such a beautiful day." Elizabeth smiles.

Samantha nods and heads back to the keep, carrying Andrew. He waves to Elizabeth and she waves back.

Elizabeth spots a nearby soldier and walks over to him, feeling slightly nervous. "Can I ask you something?" The guard nods, sharpening his slightly rusted sword as he stands on the wall-walk in full leather armor with his shield at his feet. "How long have you served Simon, the Captain of the Guards?" Elizabeth crosses her arms.

TAKING THE FIGHT TO THEM

The man looks up from his sword. "Ever since King Henry was killed."

"And did you know Henry or Simon before that?" she pries.

He squints at her. "No. I only served King Henry for a short time, but Captain Simon served with King Henry since they arrived on this rock." The guard continues sharpening his sword, running the stone down the length of the blade.

"We call this place Quarry castle now, and the other castle is called New Hope. It's much more than a simple 'rock'." Elizabeth turns and walks down towards the heavy iron front gate, not seeing the guard shake his head at her. As she approaches it, the gate swings shut with an echoing crash. Guards flock to the gate and stay posted around the gate, inside and out. She walks up to one of the posted guards. "Why is the gate closed?" she asks, placing her hands on her hips.

"Captain's orders. No one in and no one out," a guard responds as he rushes past her.

Elizabeth watches Simon and his party enter the forest. "Something's wrong, and I'm going to find out what it is." She turns around and rushes into the Great Hall as a light rain begins to fall.

———◆———

A small group of new soldiers march in formation around the courtyard of the kingdom of Castile. Each soldier is fully dressed in their new armor of a breastplate, chain mail skirt, a bassinet, and armor cuisse to protect the thighs. Along with their armor, they carry a bow and a sword. A new white cross covers the bright red breastplate, symbolizing Queen Castile's army. The Queen watches from her balcony, unimpressed by their sloppy formation.

Captain Witter stands next to her, overlooking the soldiers. "They look good, my Queen."

THE NEW QUEEN

"If we are to put on a show of how well we look marching, then yes they look okay for now, but we need fighting men, not dancing fools."

"A soldier has to be able to march before he can fight." The Captain pauses. "They will improve on their marching. We know they can do as they are told, from how to hold their swords to how to use them. Marching is a good way to find out if they can follow instruction, and that's why we practice it, my Queen."

"They are simply marching around my courtyard, nothing more! We only have a year to get ready, and I want to see real progress with my army, not some marching band of idiots! If I don't see them in fighting shape soon, heads will roll!" The Queen storms off, leaving Captain Witter on the balcony overlooking his soldiers practicing their formation.

Elizabeth and Samantha start their day cleaning the King's bedchamber at Quarry Castle in preparation for his return. The old, stale air fades quickly through the opened window slats as crisp winter air fills the room. Samantha tends the bed, folding the blankets into a pile and fluffing the hay underneath. Elizabeth grabs a pillow and whizzes it at Samantha, knocking her in the head. Samantha looks up as Elizabeth leans against one of the four large bedposts, laughing at her sister's shocked face.

Samantha tosses the pillow at Elizabeth's face and a trail of fluff and seagull feathers sprinkles out from the pillow. "Hey!" Samantha shouts, picking up the pillow and whipping it back at Elizabeth. "Knock it off!"

Elizabeth dodges the pillow as it thumps on the floor. She laughs again and places it the back on the bed. She joins her sister as Samantha glances out the slatted windows at two large ships anchored in channel. "What's out there?"

TAKING THE FIGHT TO THEM

"Another ship!" Samantha shouts, pointing to the channel. Elizabeth pushes her out of the way and stares at the dark ships floating at bay. "We better tell Simon!"

"He went away, remember?"

"Maybe he's back! Let's go!" Elizabeth races out of the bedchamber with Samantha trailing behind her, leaving the King's room in a messier state than before. They sprint down the stairs, into the chilly day, and up the stone steps of the wall-walk. Samantha and Elizabeth lean over the wall and squint at hundreds of men marching their way from the hill to the channel landing, which stands beside their wall-walk. The sandy beach is frozen solid with layers of ice and snow. The Great Army marches in rows of four to where the rowboats are anchored off to the shore.

The main gate swings open and Simon's small party trots through with prisoners tied to one another. Their hands tied behind them and a long robe tied to each prisoner around their waist. Each man dragging their feet with each step looking as worn as the cloth on their back that they called a shirt. All of them looking like they needed to wash up with mud spread over them.

Elizabeth races down the stone steps as Simon dismounts his horse. "Simon! Simon!" she yells, waving her arms.

"What is it, Elizabeth?" he asks, alarmed by her excitement.

"There are ships in the channel taking the army away from the hill!" She points towards the channel. Simon looks around at the men with him and points to one.

"Head up to the top of the hill and see how many men are left," Simon orders the soldier.

Simon rushes past Elizabeth and up the wall-walk where Samantha stands watching the men load onto the small boats. "If they don't go now, they will never make it out of the channel in time before the channel completely freezes over! Then they might want to take refuge in our castle!" Elizabeth tells Simon.

THE NEW QUEEN

"They survived four or five years on the battlefield through several winters. I do not think this winter would kill them now," Simon says. He walks along the wall, calculating what was left of the Great Army as he watches his guard travel up the hill in the afternoon sun. "He covered that quickly," Simon says to himself.

"Who covered what?" Elizabeth asks Simon.

Simon grabs his sword and whips around. "Do you have to sneak up on me like that?" He sheaths his sword.

"I didn't sneak. I simply walked up here to see how many men were left." Her curly hair pokes out in all directions and covers part of her face.

Simon looks her up and down. "Did you not sleep last night? You look dreadful."

"I look the same as you always do." She leans over the wall. "I watched the men aboard the ships and sail away last night. It was quite a view. I did not know so many men could fit on one ship. How long is their journey?"

Simon shrugs his shoulders. "It's about a week's sail from here, I guess. It depends on the currants and if the sail is full."

"A week?! They cast most of their food to the shore to make room for more men. One ship even took on water as they fought their way out of the channel. Some ice broke through the ship's hull but they did get out. I heard them shouting."

"Well since you stayed up to watch, is this camp all that is left of the Great Army?" Simon nods his head towards the field.

Elizabeth stares out at the field. "I guess so. Everyone left will not be returning to their homes because they were the 'weak fighters'?" she questions herself, not sure if she heard the soldiers right.

"'Weak' fighters?" Simon furrows his eyebrows.

"Yes, they did not fight nor had other duties, like cooks and builders and such."

TAKING THE FIGHT TO THEM

"How do you know this?" Simon asks, surprised by her knowledge. Both Samantha and Simon turn to Elizabeth.

"Well, a fight broke out about who got on the boats and who didn't. All the soldiers pulled out their swords, willing to kill to get on the ships. The cooks and others grew silent, but then they asked not to be killed and asked to stay in return to live. When the last ship was ready to leave, one of the soldiers told them they would not be coming back for the common folk, and they better be ready to live here."

Simon raises his eyebrow. "Anything else you can tell me about these people?"

Elizabeth shifts from side to side holding her hands for some warmth. "Yup."

"Well out with it," Simon snaps.

Elizabeth shivers. "They plan to ask for refuge here later today."

Simon narrows his eyes. "Well, that's impossible. We cannot take more people since we barely have enough food for ourselves!"

"You are not too smart, or you have not been listening to me." Elizabeth snorts as she laughs. "They went and got the food that was tossed from the soldiers, so they plan to buy their way into our castle," Elizabeth says with a smile.

Simon looks over the wall at the many makeshift tents and smiles. "That will make taking the food all that much easier, don't you think?"

Elizabeth gasps. "Take their food? And what of them? The poor souls, they will surely starve to death! The king will have something to say about that!"

"The king isn't here, is he, child?" Simon hisses.

"I am a woman! I am fourteen now, and you will address me as such!" Elizabeth retorts.

"Oh sorry, *my lady*. You better get some food going, or you will be joining the poor souls you so want to protect." Simon pauses,

THE NEW QUEEN

looking at Elizabeth's horrified face. "I will protect our people, even if that means the death of others. It must be done."

Elizabeth turns back to the army at the shore and watches them load into rowboats one by one.

King Martin and Mark stroll together through New Hope Castle, enjoying the crisp afternoon air. King Martin leans on his walking stick as Mark walks closely beside him for support. "So who is this Elizabeth woman?" Mark asks.

"Oh, Mark," Martin starts. "She has beautiful curly red hair and a great laugh, but beyond that, she is nothing but a handful. She never shuts up, always interrupts, and speaks her mind. She is very pig-headed, even for a man!" Mark smiles and takes a deep breath and tries to stretch his leather armor.

Mark chuckles. "Yet you asked about her as soon as you awoke. She doesn't sound like a no one."

Martin stops and thinks about what to say. "I guess I think of her as a little sister. Annoying, too." Martin pushes hard on the wooden stick and starts walking again. "Now, her sister Samantha, she's nice to look at. She has long brown hair and was married once, but her husband died fighting for our kingdom."

"Is she to be your queen?" Mark asks, holding the King's arm as he struggles to continue walking. "I only ask because I know a king would not marry a widow and that it is beneath his character."

"Why would a king not marry a commoner or a widow?"

"Your majesty, we know kings marry for one of two things. Not for love, but either for power or to stop a war and no commoner has any power to do that. As for the widow, maybe if a king offered his widowed daughter, but other than that, it wouldn't happen."

Martin stops and leans against a wall, placing the stick beside him. "What if a king wanted to marry for nothing but love?"

TAKING THE FIGHT TO THEM

"It would be a waste. Marrying for love won't protect a kingdom, and that is the main duty of a king. A king marries for protection. If a king marries into another kingdom, that kingdom could not attack the other because it would be like attacking your own flesh and blood," Mark explains.

"If the king did marry for love, would he not be happier?"

"No doubt, but that's not a good enough reason to marry as a king." Mark waits for the king to start walking again, but Martin slides down the wall and sits on the grass under an overhang. Mark settles down next to him, taking a deep breath.

"Mark, I don't know if I could marry other than for love." King Martin looks at Mark, and Mark shrugs his shoulders. "You know I did not want to be king?"

Mark turns to Martin. "Oh, no?"

"No. The truth is, I don't know the ways of a king, nor do I know much of anything that a king should or should not do."

"Yes, you were never taught. I understand, sire, but one would have thought you were taught some things, were you not?"

"I was never taught, that's true, but I did not want to be king either, so I was never taught anything. I can barely bow at other royalty. I never know when to wave and when not to. I don't know how to eat properly, and I never accepted a gift without giving something in return. As a king, people always give you gifts, even things I don't want or need."

Mark laughs. "A commoner would trade gifts. Royalty accepts gifts." Mark stops and looks at Martin with a puzzled look. "Why would your father raise you as a commoner?"

"My father thought if he did, I could fit in when necessary. If the kingdom was lost or we had to hear what the people needed or wanted," Martin lies.

THE NEW QUEEN

"I see. What a smart father you had, very smart indeed." Mark picks a long piece of grass from the ground and sticks it in his mouth.

"Where are your parents, anyway? I know very little about you."

"Not much to tell. My father died fighting for King Richard, like so many others. My mother died about two years hence from a fall off her horse. I was already a soldier by then. I did my best to give her a proper send off. I took her deep into the woods and burned her body so no one could see." Mark lowers his head.

"Why did you not want anyone to see?"

"King Richard would not permit it due to a fire attracting the enemy. It would tell them where the castle was."

"I am sorry for your loss nonetheless, but that time is over, and we will send our family in a more friendly way from now on. Now help me up. Let's get back to the main hall." Mark helps Martin up and they walk back to the castle together.

Elizabeth rushes into the kitchen as Samantha makes soup. Tears stream down Elizabeth's face. "Hey, what's wrong?" Samantha asks, placing a lid on the pot as it hangs over the large fire.

"Didn't you hear him? Simon is going to kill the rest of the army outside of our walls, and they are unarmed, I'm sure of it!" She sobs and rubs her eyes. "What can we do?"

Samantha nods. "We will have to tell the King before that happens." Samantha places her hands on Elizabeth's shoulders and pulls her into a hug.

"How?" Elizabeth looks up at her with glossy eyes. "He is at the other castle, and some bad men between here and there tried to kill us last time I was with the King."

TAKING THE FIGHT TO THEM

Samantha gasps. "You never told me that!" She nudges her back but retains her hold on Elizabeth's shoulders.

"The king was badly injured, but he will be alright. That's why he's not here." Elizabeth wipes her nose and sniffles.

"Why would you leave him if he was hurt, Elizabeth?" Samantha asks.

Elizabeth cries again. "I was told I could never be queen!" Elizabeth moves her head into Samantha's chest and begins to weep.

"You are in love with the king and thought he would marry you and then you would be Queen, didn't you?" Samantha lightly pats Elizabeth's back as she holds her.

Elizabeth lifts her head and looks at her sister. "I can't be Queen 'cause I am not royalty, only a stupid girl."

"You're not a stupid girl. You're my strong, intelligent sister." Samantha holds her sister's face in her palms. "How did you get back here if there are bad men in the forest?"

"I snuck over to the channel and crept along it until I saw the castle. It took three days to walk."

Samantha glares at her, then smiles. "You walked three days to get back here? Why?"

After a long pause, she answers. "You're here." Elizabeth smiles as she looks at her sister.

"If we take some horses along the channel, it might take a day and a bit, but we could warn the King together," Samantha suggests. She turns around and removes the pot from the fire. She instructs Elizabeth to fetch some blankets while she packs some food for their trip to New Hope Castle.

Chapter 6
THERE BE DRAGONS!

Martin spends the next day stretching his leg, walking around the castle in between breaks. The day is bright and cold with storm clouds in the far distance to the north. Two guards, Mark and Gus, remain by Martin's side at all times to ensure his safety. Gus is a former Black Army soldier and he carries two swords across his back, a stash of knives dangles from his waist, and he wears knee-high leather boots. His straggly gray hair is cut short and has an unkempt face covered in a wiry graying beard.

"I want to go outside the castle walls," the King tells his guards. They nod and slowly ride to the front gates and across the lowered drawbridge. Martin is surprised at all the fertile, vacant land that his farmers have not started to use yet. "I want to tell the people once spring arrives that they can farm outside the castle walls again. I will direct them with what to grow."

"I don't ever remember any farms out here, sire," Mark tells his king.

THERE BE DRAGONS!

"Never?" Martin asks with surprise.

"Never. King Richard said he wanted to see everything he owned in the castle, so as far as I know, we have never farmed outside the castle walls." The small party continues riding around the large castle, occasionally slowing down in larger areas of stiff, untouched snow.

Martin glances upwards as the tracking archers follow them around the castle wall from the wall-walk. They ride the rest of their tour around the castle in silence as the king surveys the surrounding land for any possible threats. Martin is surprised by how close some trees are to the castle walls and how it could shelter an enemy. Suddenly, the group hears a whistling noise approaching from above as a ball of fire crashes into the tree, engulfing it in flames. A horn blasts from atop of the wall, alerting the castle of the attack. King Martin kicks the horse forward as the two guards unsheathe their swords directly behind their king. Archers fire arrows into the air in the direction of the fire ball as Martin and his guards speed back to the castle entrance.

Another fireball combusts beside Mark's horse, spooking it enough to buck wildly until it knocks Mark off. Mark thumps onto the frozen ground and rolls onto his chest as his horse continues thrashing at the air. Mark watches as another small fireball lands two yards away, shooting fire in the direction of the King. Mark fights hard to stand, but a sharp pain shoots up his rear end and he grimaces in pain. Fireball after fireball shoots from beyond the tallest trees in the distance. Mark crawls over to where the fireball landed and sees nothing left from the blast: no cloth that could have been set on fire and no wood that gives off ash.

Just as suddenly, the fireballs stop. A group of men with large metal shields rushes around the wall and helps Mark back towards the castle. Mark is dragged back around the castle wall to the front

THE NEW QUEEN

gate and into the courtyard, where King Martin waits with a group of guards holding metal shields over his head.

"You alright?" the King asks.

"I was about to ask you the same thing." Mark winces in pain.

"Do you know who was shooting at us?"

Mark shakes his head. The King turns to the wall-walk, searching for someone. He spots a guard and yells up to him. "Hey!" The man looks down. "Who was shooting at us?"

The soldier runs around the wall-walk to talk with his King. "Sire, whoever is shooting at us is beyond the far tree line, too far for our arrows."

"Are they using a catapult then?"

"Doubt it, sire. The fireballs came too quickly one after the other and all from the same spot. Hard to say who they were or what they were using to shoot at us." King Martin clenches his fists and calls for his soldiers to assemble and head for the tree line. They hold a sword in front of them and a metal shield over their heads as they march out of the castle.

King Martin stands on top of a tower, the highest point of the castle and stares at the soldiers move into the forested area. Martin paces back and forth, waiting for the men to reappear. With each passing minute, his pacing grows quicker and more agitated until Mark appeared from the steps leading to the top of the tower. "Sire, they are good soldiers. They will have answers for you when they return, don't worry."

"Why attack us? I don't understand why someone would attack us with something that wouldn't do any damage. Sure, it may kill a man if they managed to hit one, but we were just a small party, and even a good archer could not hit a man at such a distance."

"I don't know, sire." Mark watches the men emerge from the trees, still holding their shields over their heads. The men march in two lines, side by side, and race back to the castle. King Martin pushes past Mark and rushes down the tower stairs holding on to the wall for support.

"Well, what have you?" the King shouts to the entering group of soldiers.

"It's hard to explain, your majesty. There were no tracks to speak of...only a few strange footprints. The thing had only three toes, and his foot was a little larger than both of my hands put together. Never saw a track like that before. The tops of the trees and a small patch of grass are burnt as well. We saw no sign of oil or wood and no catapult tracks, or human tracks, to say the least." The guard remains silent.

"Then what are you saying?" a nearby soldier not from the search party asks.

The same guard clears his throat and continues. "What I am saying is, we cannot find any familiar tracks or anything that could have been used to make fire and shoot at the king."

"That is most peculiar," King Martin comments. "Let's send out a few mounted scouts all around the castle to make sure whatever attacked us is still not here." The guards nod and disperse. Martin looks up at the wall-walk. "Let's double the guards on the wall for tonight," he says to Mark before Mark leaves with a group of guards.

A group of guards run to the south gate and archers keep their bows aimed at the field. The King heads towards the south entrance and is met by Mark. "Sire, the southern watchtower has signaled that there is trouble. I sent a group of men out that way to see what it is."

Martin enters the wall-walk at the southern wall. "Now what?" the King asks Mark. "Is the watchtower on fire?" He squints in the distance.

"No, Sire. That's the signal for an attack." Mark looks over towards the watch tower and slowly raises his head. The smoke

THE NEW QUEEN

thickens and forms giant clouds above the tower. "It may be on fire instead. That's too much smoke for just a signal."

"That doesn't look very good. How far away is the watchtower?" The King asks.

"It was built so we could see the signals in the far distance. It will take the men a quarter of an hour to get there, but like all towers, it is made of stone and only the inside is of wood."

Martin paces once again, limping on his one good leg, and draws both swords out of anger. Martin remains glaring at the forest, waiting for his group to return. He growls and kicks at a nearby stone. A few moments later, the riders emerge from the south with another man on a horse. The King heads for the southern gate.

"Sire, it may not be safe for you here," Gus says to the King. "Not until we know more."

"Tell me what is happening," the King commands. A short, middle-aged man rides to the gate and dismounts, his hair singed and his shirt still smoldering at the shoulders. "And who are you?" King Martin asks.

"I am a farmer, your majesty. My farm was attacked."

"Attacked by whom?" Gus interrupts.

"Not who, sire, what!" The farmer's eyes widen.

"What? What?" Martin yells.

"The reason we could not find any tracks, sire, is because this man says he was attacked... by a dragon!" a guard declares.

Mark snickers. "Dragons aren't real," he announces.

"I once thought that, too, Mark, but everything leads to them being real," the soldier says.

"Everything? Like what?" Gus interjects.

"The fireballs earlier, lack of tracks, the watchtower being burnt down and the men inside lost, and now this man's testimony that he saw the creature!" The soldier points to the man with the burns. Mark moves to the man.

"You saw this creature?" Gus sternly asks.

"It attacked me last night in my house! The fire came from the sky, one after the other. I barely escaped alive!" The man shakes.

"Take him to clean up and give him something to eat. I will talk with him later." The guards take the nervous farmer away. Martin turns to Gus. "Well, what do you think? Were there any bodies at the watchtower?"

"We could not find any, the fire was still burning. Only the insides were lost, the stone still remains."

"Go back and bring me the bodies. There were two men in that watchtower. I want both bodies," the King demands.

"Yes, right away," Gus replies and orders a party of soldiers to retrieve the bodies.

"We should get ready," King Martin announces.

"Yes, I think we will be under attack soon, sire."

"So you think dragons are real now?"

Mark and Gus look at each other. "Maybe, but I have my doubts. I think it is all just fuss," Gus answers.

"You sound like Simon. He doubts everything," Martin comments.

"I am skeptical that there are dragons out there, but there is definitely something out there."

"What do you mean?" Martin asks.

"This is nonsense. I don't believe in dragons," Mark says as he walks away from the castle gate, leaving Gus and the King standing together.

Dusk approaches as light snow powders the land. Half of the total archers are posted along the wall-walk, each with a loaded crossbow and a young armiger for tonight's watch. One of the lit torches around the outer castle falls over. Two archers approach the fallen torch when another falls over down the wall. An archer waves Gus and Martin nearby. "Sir, two torches have fallen over, yet there is no wind." Gus looks out to see a third torch fall over. And another.

"Archers, ready!" Gus yells, and the archers hold their crossbows. A massive fireball plummets towards the wall, whistling in the air. The flaming ball crashes down against the wall, setting the rocks ablaze for a few seconds. "Archers, take aim at the fireball!" Another fireball spirals forward, and two hundred archers shoot their arrows in the direction of the fireball. The armigers reload the crossbows as the archers grab for their second crossbows.

"Is it a dragon?" Martin asks, watching the fireballs explode against the castle wall.

"It must be if the fire starts in the air. If it were anything else, the fireball would start from the ground. The torches were blown over, but there was no wind in the air. I suspect it was from the dragon's wings. It is the most baffling creature."

"When the attacker is unseen, maybe we should shoot around the area instead of at it?" Martin suggests.

"You mean shoot where the fireball starts and not directly at it?" Gus asks.

"Yes, we might have better success at killing it."

Gus commands the new order at the archers and they wait for their next attack. A whistling shoots across the sky as a fireball approaches closer and closer as hundreds of arrows shoot across the darkening sky, all missing their target. After reshooting time and time again without success, the archers begin to question their own skills. Fireballs explode around the castle grounds, creating black, singed soil where they land. Other fireballs attack the castle walls and immediately erupt at impact with the stone.

After a few minutes, the fireballs stop and the sun sets behind the hills. "Is it gone?" Martin asks.

THERE BE DRAGONS!

"It might have moved to attack us from behind." Gus turns and shouts to the archers. "Spread out securely along all the castle walls in case it has changed its approach!" The archers, exhausted and frustrated by their lack of success, remain alert for the rest of the silent night.

The first colours of reds and oranges from dawn break the horizon, yet no more fireballs continued. Gus orders a party to investigate the land.

Mark joins Gus on the wall-walk. "Did you get it?" he asks. "Did you kill this dragon?"

"How can you hit what you cannot see?" Gus snaps back at him. He narrows his bloodshot eyes.

"You need to get some sleep now. You're exhausted. I will keep watch." Martin places his hand on Mark's shoulder. "I will change the archers and send these men to get some rest."

"Wake me if anything happens." Then Gus, too, leaves for bed.

An hour passes when a rider arrive at the castle. The gate slowly lowers to let him in. Mark slowly works his way down to meet the rider, his back throbbing more and more with each step. "And who are you?"

The rider looks up at Mark and dismounts. "I'm Garnet, the King's advisor." His long wool cloak trails after him as a grey wool hat is pulled tightly around his head of thick hair.

"Have you seen the dragon?" Mark asks Garnet.

Garnet smirks. "Dragon? Dragons are made for the night to make sure children stay in their beds."

"Apparently we were attacked by one last night," Mark coolly answers.

Garnet laughs again. "My good fellow, there is no such thing as dragons." Garnet chuckles to himself as he heads to Martin's bedchamber.

THE NEW QUEEN

Three guards remain posted by the King's bedchamber door. One guard opens the door and moves inside the king's bedchamber with Garnet and Martin. The king remains asleep under his wool blanket as a single candle burns on the table across the room from the king's bed.

The guard shakes his King gently. "Sire, your advisor is here to see you."

King Martin opens his eyes and jumps out of bed and onto the wooden floor. "Is the dragon back?" Martin's eyes widen.

Garnet laughs. "There is no such thing as dragons, your majesty."

Suddenly the horn blares through the window slats and a second guard rushes into King's bedchamber. "The dragon is back!"

Martin and Garnet rush out of the room and up the wall-walk. "The dragon is behind the trees again. Our archers cannot shoot that far, so I told them not to shoot unless they see it," Mark notifies Martin.

"Have a few men ride out to see what it looks like," King Martin orders Mark.

"Your majesty, I cannot run, forget riding. When I fell from my horse yesterday, I injured myself." Mark frowns. King Martin nods and orders the soldiers to accompany him to the edge of the tree line to attack the dragon.

"May I come along?" Garnet asks. "I have never seen a dragon before," he asks sarcastically. Garnet follows Mark and King Martin to the party of guards.

The large group of soldiers ride towards the trees, with King Martin in the middle, when they are attacked by a line of fireballs. They swerve their horses out of the way and dodge the blast as the fireballs explode against the castle wall. When the group reaches the tree line, the fireballs suddenly stop. Slowly, the large group of riders makes their way through the trees, swords drawn, and shields held in front of them.

"Ambush!" a guard shouts to the others. The group of guards fall into formation around the king as archers and swordsmen attack from every side. Martin pulls out his two swords as one man barreled through the guards and tramples at him. The King jumps off his horse and holds the two swords together to block the enemy's long sword. The king staggers and strikes the man but is quickly disarmed. The man swings at Martin, making him jump backwards. The assailant drops his sword and grabs onto the King, turning the fight into hand to hand combat, something Martin has no experience in. The man swings his fist at the king, but the King steps forward and head butts the enemy in the chest. The man wraps his arm around Martin's head. King Martin stabs the man's foot. The man screams and hops backward, and the King thrusts his sword deep into the man's chest.

Another man manages to get through the line and charges towards the King with a long sword, knocking King Martin to the ground. Martin rolls out of the way and jumps up as the man attacks him a second time. Martin stabs the man in the back and he falls to the ground. The guard jumps in front of his king and fights the new attacker. King Martin jumps to the side and watches the fighting around him. A fire erupts as the struggle moves closer to the edge of the tree line. The King stays with the guards as more guards arrive to fight. Gus slices a man's neck with little effort and blood whips off his sword as he swings it to another man. The party of guards moves closer to the edge where seven or eight men shoot stones through large slings until the guards shoot arrows into each of their chests. Martin searches for the dragon in the forest, looking for strange footprints and areas of charred leaves.

The king watches as the last man dies on the bloody field by Gus, some hundred yards from the tree line. A group of guards including Gus and Mark walk Martin back to the castle. Mark walks in great pain, trailing behind the party.

"I didn't see the dragon," King Martin says to Gus.

"That's because they don't exist!" From behind the group, Garnet cries out.

"Who is that guy?" Gus whispers to Martin.

"He was the old king's adviser and master architect. He got banished just after we did!" Martin whispers back.

"You should have stayed in the castle, sire, you could have been killed," Gus says with a frown. "Forgive me, but that was very foolish."

"Gus, I know you are right, but I had to lead my men against a dragon. The thought of hiding in the castle while our soldiers challenge such an awful beast did not feel right to me." They continue walking in silence until Martin speaks again. "Gus, I will need to speak to you once we are back at the castle."

"Would your majesty mind if I get some sleep first?" Gus asks as they reach the main gate.

"Yes, I will talk with you tomorrow." Martin leaves Gus and heads for the wall-walk with Garnet following behind. He watches as his guards slowly cross the field. Less than half the guards return. Martin hangs his head. "It's my fault so many died, isn't it?" he says as tears well up in his eyes.

Garnet says nothing.

"I shouldn't be king, should I?"

Garnet thinks about the question. "There have been many kings that should not have been kings, sire." Garnet rests on the edge of the wall-walk, watching the injured soldiers return. "You are not one of them."

"Garnet, you know I am not royalty. I don't know the first thing about being king. I don't even know anything about a castle, never mind fighting. I stand here on the wall looking out at what?

THERE BE DRAGONS!

Land? Land that I am supposed to control? Own? It's not my land, it's everyone's land."

Garnet turns to Martin, the torches flickering above his head. "I can teach you what you don't know about the castle, even royal duties, but I cannot teach you how to fight. I am not a fighter. I can teach you about the past, what has happened and what should have happened. I can be your teacher, but it will take time. It will not happen overnight. It will take months, maybe even years!"

"I almost died today, and no one would have known any better. It was Henry who wanted me to play the prince, but it was the people who wanted me to be their king."

Garnet chuckles. "And how did you get to be King anyway?"

"Oh, it's a long story, Garnet." Martin smiles slightly as he shakes his head.

"Tell me, I want to know."

"When Henry died, not only was he the King's Captain of the Guard, but mine as well. Anyways, when he died, I was a mess. I couldn't help but cry. I mean, he was my best friend and my father's best friend as well. I knew him all of my life. When he died, I was crying in my bedchamber when Elizabeth came in, and somehow she thought Henry was my father and since I was a prince that made him—"

"That made Henry the king so when he died, they thought you were the heir to the throne, so you became king." Garnet finishes. Martin nods as he hangs his head. "Well, you were right, they did make you king. Now it's time for you to start acting like a king, don't you think?"

Prince Martin glares at Garnet. "I have been acting like a king, or do you not remember that I spared your life?"

"You need to be educated and learn how to fight. There are some kingdoms where the kings fight instead of going to war. It's called The Honor Challenge, and it's to the death."

THE NEW QUEEN

Martin looks up. "Then why have an army?"

"Our King never fought any honor fight. He had the Dark Shadows, an army everyone feared. And when you have a military everyone fears, they are not going to challenge you to an honor fight because you would be killed by the Dark Shadows anyway. In this kingdom, those same soldiers are called the Black Army, the very same army that you control. A big responsibility, don't you think?" The king looked at Garnet, puzzled. "As king, you have to control the Dark Shadows and take care of them as well, along with everyone else in what is now your kingdom. This means to feed them and protect them and know what is right and wrong, like dragons. There is no such thing as dragons, and you know that."

Martin kicks a rock. "I'm not so sure. With everything I have seen, I beg to differ."

"That's lesson one." Garnet points his finger into the air. "A king never begs."

Chapter 7
TELL THE KING

Elizabeth and Samantha sneak out of the castle through the side gate, accompanied with two horses Quietly, they lurk among the shadows to avoid the dimming dusk light, changing the sky from red-orange to a swirl of dark blues and grey. A layer of frost covers the crisp yellow grass and hardens the muddy surfaces. Once they reach the channel, they mount their horses and crouch closer to them, staying as hidden as possible. The fresh and salty air fills their nostrils from the almost completely frozen channel. Elizabeth wears her favorite dark green dress with a matching hood to cover her fiery red hair against the dark scenery. This dress was given to her as a gift from the King and she only wears it on important occasions. Samantha wears a black dress and black hood with a yellow ribbon to tie her hair back. They slowly ride past the ships that are anchored on the shore. The five vacant ships are tilted to the side as snow piled on top of them. A light snowfall drifts in the sky, swirling along

THE NEW QUEEN

the currents as the wind howls around them. "Ghosts," Elizabeth whispers to Samantha.

Samantha nods. "Ghosts," she whispers back. She stops her horse and Elizabeth follows. They stare at the large ships and listen to the whistling wind travel through the cracks of the ships and ruffles the snowy sails. Samantha imagines a ghostly man watching her at the tip of the and shakes the image from her mind. "Let's go," she whispers, biting her lip. She flicks the horse's reigns and they march forward out of sight of Quarry Castle.

They move in a silent trot along the snowy shoreline. Their horse slowly disappear as the fluffy snowflakes continue blanketing the frozen land. "By the way, what did you do with Andrew?" Elizabeth whispers.

"The same as always. That old lady, Annie, who has a bunch of kids is taking care of him until we return. I left her with extra food from the kitchen as payment. Andrew was happy to be with his friends," Samantha whispers back.

They travel further along the shoreline in silence until the moon and stars hide behind thick clouds, concealing the moonlight. They decide to stop for the night in the outskirts of the tree line where they pitch a small tent, barely large enough to fit them both. They tie their horses to a log where they are shielded from the snow and wind. Elizabeth quietly moves into the forest, searching for fallen branches and for signs of any intruders while Samantha unloads their small leather bags of small buns and boiled potatoes, and clothing inside the tent. Elizabeth returns with some branches and drops them into a pile in front of Samantha. Samantha looks at Elizabeth's small collection and her face hardens. "No wood? We will freeze if you don't find any wood, Elizabeth!"

"I could not find any! It's all covered in snow, you dumb ox!" Elizabeth hisses.

TELL THE KING

"Dumb Ox? You're the ox! You're the one who was supposed to get the wood, like an ox!" Samantha snaps back and moves closer to her younger sister.

"Are you not afraid someone might hear your big fat mouth?" Elizabeth fires back.

"No, they would hear yours first! Now go get us some wood before we freeze to death!"

"You're not the queen, you can't tell me what to do!" Elizabeth moves closer to her sister until they stand face to face. "You go get the wood!" she snaps.

"Why are you being this way? I set up the tent, so you get the wood!"

Elizabeth glances at the half-made tent, not hardly strong enough to stand up on its own. "That's not set up properly. It's going to fall over on us as soon as we get in. Can you not do anything right?"

"What does that mean?" Samantha says, pulling off her hood.

Elizabeth takes a deep breath. "What it means is that I will set the tent up and you go get the wood."

Samantha places her hands on her hips, then glances at the pathetic tent and sighs. "Fine!" she shouts in Elizabeth's face, then marches away, stomping her small feet in the snow.

Samantha wonders into the forest collecting small pieces of wood, mainly twigs. She bends down to grab a larger branch and hears a crunching sound behind her. Not moving a muscle, she listens as the sound moves slowly and quietly towards her. She hears another branch break behind her and remains frozen. Samantha's heart races and her body trembles as she drops to her knees and crawls towards the edge of the forest where her sister waits.

Elizabeth finishes setting up the tent and moves some rocks into a circle for a fire. She opens her flint box, knowing Samantha would forget hers, and lays out some blankets in the thin tent. Elizabeth realizes that the canvas is bright red and yellow and becomes angry at her sister for not packing a neutral-coloured tent. Elizabeth hears rustling in the forest so she quickly picks up one of the larger branches. "Samantha? Samantha?" She moves closer to the sound, grasping the branch tighter. A shadowy figure emerges from the forest and Elizabeth screams.

Samantha bolts towards Elizabeth, holding the bottom of her dress in her hands. She hears Elizabeth calling out her name and fighting with a creature. Samantha sprints down a hill towards their campsite and trips over a wild boar that threatens Elizabeth. Her knees collide into the side of the wild animal lands on its side. The boar squeals loudly and its hooves flail as it fights to turn itself upward. Elizabeth screams at the sudden appearance of her sister. Samantha lands face first into the hard snow as the boar rolls over and shakes the snow from its five-inch tusks. Elizabeth strikes the boar with the branch, breaking the dead branch over the boar's nose. Samantha jumps up, her face bloody, as she watches Elizabeth strikes the boar a second time. The nearby spooked horses thrash their heads and whinny to break free, kicking wildly side by side.

The boar charges at Elizabeth with its mighty tusks and she is knocked back onto the tent, crashing to the ground. Samantha jumps onto the boar but the large animal bucks and throws Samantha off and charges again towards Elizabeth. Elizabeth jumps out of the way, making the wild animal smash into the tent. The stakes of the tent rip up from the ground and the canvas wraps around the beast's hairy body. The tent moves in circles as the boar bucks and struggles to break free, tearing the tent to shreds. Samantha and Elizabeth rush to their horses as the boar squeals in the entanglement, thrashing its head wildly. Samantha runs behind her horse, nearly missing its powerful kicks as it remains

TELL THE KING

spooked from all the noise. The bloodied boar follows the screams as it charges for the girls hiding by their bucking horses. With one powerful kick, the horse hurls the boar ten feet in the air before landing in a small uprooted tree outside of their campsite. Samantha and Elizabeth stay shaking behind their horses, staring at the unmoving boar in the distance.

Samantha and Elizabeth hold onto each other as they walk closer to the dead boar in the tree. "Help me knock the tree over," Elizabeth asks her sister. They push the dead tree over and the bloodied boar falls to the ground with a thump. A thick branch staked its chest and blood oozes down the tip of the branch. Elizabeth gathers the fallen branches while Samantha starts a fire. They drag the boar to the bonfire and prepare it for dinner, roasting it over the flames.

"Is eating a boar on the king's ground against the law?" Samantha asks.

Elizabeth breaks a large piece of a branch and throws it into the fire. "Who cares? It's our land, too. All I know is in the morning, we will have fresh boar to eat instead of starving." They clean parts of the bloody tent and their faces in melted mounds of snow by the fire and wrap themselves in the tattered, bloody tent and wool blankets. They listen to owls hooting overhead, and the cackling of the wood burning in the fire until they fall asleep under the full moon.

The sun hangs low in the horizon when Samantha sits up, barely able to see from her swollen eyes. Her nose is also swollen and her face is black and blue. Samantha clenches her stomach and hunches over, trying to steady her nausea.

Elizabeth hears her sister moving and opens her eyes. "Oh, Samantha, are you alright?" Elizabeth asks at first sight of her sister. Elizabeth sits up.

THE NEW QUEEN

"My whole face hurts, and I can't see very well." Samantha touches her puffy eyes.

"I should think so, you look dreadful," Elizabeth responds as she stands. She groans in pain.

"What's wrong?" Samantha asks, squinting at her sister.

"It's my legs," Elizabeth whines, pulling up her gown to reveal a large gash in her calf. She tears a piece of the tent off and wraps it around her leg. Samantha stands but remains still for a moment until her dizziness subsides.

"Do you think it's broken?" Elizabeth asks as tears form in her eyes.

"Oh, don't be such a baby. I'm almost blind, and you have a scratch," Samantha responds. "You're fine." They look at each other, both bloody and bruised, and laugh. "If the King could see us now," Samantha adds, laughing and carving a large piece of boar for both of them.

After they eat their fill, Samantha wraps the rest of the boar in what is left of the tent, and the two take turns dragging the roasted boar onto a pile rocks until it is high enough to slide onto the horses. Samantha pushes while Elizabeth guides her until all the heavy pieces of boar are secured to the horses. Samantha helps Elizabeth onto her horse, shifting around until she secures herself on top. "Thanks, Samantha."

"Come here," Elizabeth feels her way over to Samantha's face. "This may hurt."

"What will...?" Elizabeth pulls tightly onto Samantha's nose and pulls it hard to the left. Samantha screams. "What are you doing?!" She covers her face as blood gushes down her nose. "Are you trying to make it worse?"

"No, Samantha. It was crooked but I fixed it. I'm really sorry, but it had to be done." Elizabeth hands her a handkerchief.

TELL THE KING

"I can't even cry because my eyes are swollen shut! My tears will come out my ears for sure!" Samantha holds the handkerchief over her nose.

"Oh, the blind woman who can see out her ears! Well, wouldn't that be a dream for a man!" They both laugh and Samantha forgets about her pain for the moment.

They ride until the next river bend before Elizabeth breaks the silence. "How do you ride so close to me without seeing me?"

"You smell." Elizabeth sniffs Samantha's dress. "The horse knows we are together. It is staying with you by itself, I am just along for the ride."

"Oh, the horse is smarter than the rider today?"

"Shh! Be quiet! We might be heard!" Samantha snaps.

"I'm tired of being quiet! I want to talk," Elizabeth pleads.

They travel a few paces until Samantha responds. "What do you want to talk about?" she says from under her hood.

"Why can't I be queen?"

Samantha turns to her sister. "Elizabeth, we talked about this already. You know you have to be royalty to be queen, and you are not!"

Elizabeth frowns. "But can the king not marry who he wishes?"

"The king can marry anyone he wants, I suppose, but princes marry princesses so they can become more powerful. Sometimes a prince is married off to stop a war or to avert one, but it does not mean that they marry for love. That's why King Richard was so unfaithful."

"I think a king can marry anyone he wants, even me, if he wishes," Elizabeth says.

Samantha pauses. "Are we talking about any king or King Martin? And are we talking about what the King wants or what you want?"

"I fancied King Henry."

THE NEW QUEEN

Samantha smirks. "So you won't mind if I get King Martin to fancy me?"

Elizabeth's face hardens, and she turns to face her sister. "You were already married, Samantha, it's my turn! Don't try and go after Martin!" Elizabeth pleads with her sister.

Samantha laughs. "Oh, don't worry, he sees nothing in me. I think he does fancy you, though." Samantha stops her horse.

"What's wrong?"

Samantha grabs her forehead. "I have a terrible headache. Can we stop for a bit? I want to lie down."

"Yes, of course." Elizabeth dismounts her horse and helps Samantha off hers. Pain shoots up Elizabeth's leg and she limps. She starts a fire along the riverbed and heats up some wild boar. Samantha grabs a blanket off her horse and falls asleep by the fire. Elizabeth lies down in the mid-morning sun, welcoming what little warmth the sun offers.

After an hour of rest, Elizabeth wakes Samantha. "Samantha we have to go, or we will be out here another night." Elizabeth gently shakes Samantha awake, but she does not wake. "Samantha stop playing! Wake up!" Elizabeth shakes her shoulder harder but Samantha remains still. Elizabeth fights back tears as she holds her hand to Samantha's mouth, feeling her warm breath. "You're alive!" she screams and falls back on her hands. "We need to get you to a doctor right away. We aren't far now!" Elizabeth grabs some large branches and ties them together using strips of the tent material until the branches form a stretcher. She rolls her sister onto the stretcher, covers her in a blanket, and ties her arms and legs to it. She rips longer pieces of the tent and ties the stretcher to the back of the horse's saddle.

"You are going to owe me when we get back," Elizabeth tells her sister. Elizabeth rides her horse while Samantha's horse follows behind, pulling Samantha on the stretcher. "Maybe I will marry

TELL THE KING

King Martin, and I will be queen, and you know what Samantha? That will make you a lady, I mean a real lady. I bet you would like that?" Elizabeth looks back at her sister still sleeping. "Are you ok, Samantha? I did the best I could. You will be better when we get to the castle. Think of it, the warm fireplace in the bedchamber, the smell of that awful oil lamp King Richard used to use... Remember when we snuck in, and you almost knocked over that lamp, and then I stubbed my toe on the wood?" Elizabeth laughs, then glances back at her sister once again. Elizabeth shakes away more tears. "You're going to be alright, Samantha, you have to. What will happen to Andrew and me if you leave us?" Elizabeth whispers, kicking the horse to move quicker along the snowy riverbed.

After a few hours, Elizabeth stops and checks on her sister. "Samantha, can you hear me?" she asks, sniffling from the cold. She touches Samantha's cold face and notices that the swelling inflated and the bruises turned darker shades of blue. Elizabeth brushes off some snow and pulls Samantha's hood closer over her sister's face. Elizabeth returns to the horses and feeds them with soft snow out of her warm hands, melting it so the horses can drink. The skies turn cloudy, and thick snowflakes fall quickly. "Samantha, we better go before it really starts to snow out here." Elizabeth fights her way back onto her horse and pushes it to a jog, knowing she can't go fast because it could lame the horses on the rocky ground, or even hurt Samantha.

An hour passes and the horses refuse to move anymore. "Please keep going," Elizabeth begs the horse, pulling on their reins. Elizabeth's hand slips and she lands on her back. She sits up, tears streaming down her face. "Please Samantha, we can't last another night out here. We have to get to the castle." Elizabeth stands up and searches through Samantha's bag that hangs off the side of her horse. "A carrot!" She breaks the carrot in half and gives it to each horse. The two horses devour the carrot from Elizabeth's hand

THE NEW QUEEN

with their warm, slimy tongues. "You can eat all the carrots you want if you can get us to the castle before nightfall."

Elizabeth, too concerned with the horses, does not see a man on a slight hill ahead, sitting quietly on a horse of his own. "Hello?" The man calls out. He is dressed in heavy furs from head to toe and a thick wool scarf covers his mouth.

Elizabeth hobbles back to Samantha. "Please don't hurt us! We just want to get to the castle!" she pleads. The man slowly rides over to Elizabeth. His horse shakes its head side to side, brushing away the snow. The man dismounts and walks towards her, unraveling the scarf from his mouth. At full height, he stands as tall as the horse, and now Elizabeth can see the man's bearded face and sunken eyes. "What's wrong with your friend?"

"She won't wake up." Elizabeth bites her lip and glances at Samantha.

The man moves next to Samantha and analyzes her face. "What happened to her?"

"We were attacked."

The man stands and looks around as the snow falls more heavily under the thick, grey clouds. The man lifts Samantha up in his arms and places her on his horse.

"Stop! What are you doing? Stop! You can't do that!" Elizabeth cries in panic.

The man turns around and looks at her with a stern face. "Ride the horse your friend was with. The other one will follow."

Elizabeth hobbles to the horse, and slowly mounts it, the pain in her leg shooting upwards past her knee. She kicks the sides of the horse and it launches after the man and into the tree line.

"Come on! Hurry! We can't lose Samantha now! She gave you the carrot, you should be her best friend, come on," she encourages the horse the best she can. The wind picks up and blows snow over their tracks. Elizabeth pulls her hood over her head and pushes

TELL THE KING

on, trying to stay with the man. She keeps her head lowered most of the time as the snow pelts her face and piles onto her hood. Elizabeth squints through the storm and makes out the entrance to the castle as the horse's hooves clonk against stone. She looks up as her horse slows into the keep.

The soldiers led by captain Witter march through the blizzard, their heavy wool coats covered with snow. "Let us not keep the Queen waiting...you know how she hates tardiness," Witter yells to his small group of marching men. His clean-shaven face is bright red from the cold, and snowflakes collect on his eyebrows and along a scarf around his head.

One man stops and cries out. "I live just over that tree line. Can we stop for a bit and get some real food?" He rubs his shoulders.

Captain Witter only had twenty men with him and they did not bring food. In truth, he was starving, tired and soaked from the snow. He raises his hand to signal for everyone to stop. Most men bump into each another, not watching up a head. "Go and see if they will feed us all but we have to be back on our way within the hour!" he says to the boy.

The boy smiles widely and races off to home, jumping through the snow. 'The rest of ya take a load off, and we will see if we are welcomed or not.' After some time Witter gets everyone up, and they start their march toward the direction the boy went. The snow grew very heavy, and they could not see where they were going when they find a barn. Captain Witter piles everyone into it away from the blowing snow. 'No fires!" we have a bit of a shelter here. Let's not lose it!' The men break up and sit on bails of hey that are scattered around but huddle together for what little warmth one could get from another. The door to the barn opens, and the boy comes in and is surprised to see them there.

THE NEW QUEEN

'Ma just sent me to make up the barn for you to stay in for the night, she's cooking some mead for everyone and pa's getting ale.' The boy said as soup had frozen to his face.

'We won't be staying the night boy, and you best get everyone some of that soup, or we raid the house and take what we want, got it?' fear cross the boy's face as he turned and ran back into the house.

Elizabeth sits holding Samantha's hand next to her bed. A fire roars in the fireplace that keeps the room warm. Cold water was used to wipe Samantha's face and to help with the swelling. "The swelling is down enough. You can open your eyes now, Samantha," Elizabeth says to Samantha. Samantha remains still.

Martin walks into the room and Elizabeth races over to him. They both hobble while holding each other.

"It's all my fault! She wanted to come with me, but we got attacked by a wild boar, and she tried to save me, and we almost died and..." Elizabeth shakes her head.

"Shhhh," Martin interjects. "She's not dead, just a bad bang on her head, that's all." Elizabeth rubs her eyes. "Why did you leave in the first place?"

Elizabeth shrugs. Martin glances down at the top of her head and notices dry blood on her dress. He holds her away from himself. "You're bleeding," the King says, then grabs her under her shoulder and lowers her onto a cot bed. The tent patch along her calve is soaked with blood. "Wait here," he commands. King Martin yells to a guard to send for Gwyneth right away.

Gwyneth rushes into the room moments later and inspects Elizabeth's leg. "It will have to be sewn up, sire," she announces, still wearing her patched dress.

"I agree," Martin nods.

"Well, I don't! I am not some piece of tattered cloth to be sewn up from a tear!" Elizabeth objects as the fire cackles loudly.

Martin takes her hand. "Elizabeth, it has to be done or you might bleed out. If you don't do this, you might not see your sister alive again. You saw me get stitches."

Elizabeth looks at Samantha, then at Gwyneth, then back to Martin. "I can't," she says between tears.

"Samantha would call you a baby if you didn't. I thought you were a woman and a woman can do this." Martin squeezes her hand.

Elizabeth wipes her tears with the back of her hand. "Ok I will do it, but you can't be here. Just Gwyneth and Samantha."

Martin smiles. "Gwyneth will have to clean it first. I have to go see some men anyway, and if you do this, I will buy you another dress to replace that one." He points at her torn dress. She nods and continues to wipe her tears away. Martin closes the door behind him as he hears Elizabeth cry in pain. He lowers his head and walks away.

Hours later, Martin stands up from his chair in the main hall, discussing with his soldiers about the surrounding land, when Gwyneth walks up to him. "It's done, your majesty. She fought every stitch, but in the end, it got done."

"How many stitches did you give her?" Martin asks, remembering his seven stitches.

"Over twenty, your majesty. The wound was deep, and it had already opened wider than it should have."

Martin winces at the number of stitches. "Where is she now?"

"She's asleep, beside her sister. And sire, her sister…" Gwyneth pauses.

Martin's heart pounds. "Is she dead?"

THE NEW QUEEN

"No, but she may never wake up. The blow was too much. It crushed her nose and pushed it in. The only thing that might have saved her was Elizabeth straightening it out."

Martin nods and dismisses Gwyneth, then slumps back into his throne. "Everyone seems to be getting hurt. Me, Mark, Samantha, Elizabeth, and no doubt Simon as well, with the Great Army at the castle already. That's probably why I haven't heard from him." King Martin bows his head. "Should I ask the Viking leader, Rollo, to help fight the Great Army?"

Mark approaches and interrupts Martin's thoughts. "Your majesty," he says quietly.

Martin jolts up and looks at Mark. "Yes, Mark, how are you feeling?"

"I broke my tail bone, your majesty, so it hurts to walk and I am unable to sit, and of course, riding is out of the question." Mark smiles, holding his hat in his hands.

"That must be terrible. I'm sorry to hear that," the King replies.

"Oh, it is, sire. A real pain in my arse, one might say," Mark chuckles. "But that is why I am here. Gus had asked Rollo to have a few men help parole around the castle for more enemies and *dragons*." Mark smirks before continuing. "Even though there are no such things as dragons, Rollo agreed to help. My concern is that the men may not know the difference between Rollo's Vikings and the enemies."

"Have there been any problems so far?"

"When Lady Samantha was brought in, they almost fired upon them. The only thing that stopped them from doing so was Samantha's body laying across the horse."

"Our soldiers should be told if one man comes alone towards the gate since one man alone is not much of a threat." Martin waits for Mark to say something else. "Anything more?"

TELL THE KING

Mark clears his throat. "I must request to leave the castle to recover. I would like to go home until spring, sire."

"I understand your problem, and that you must recover. I also understand that we need every man available to fight in these times," Martin hesitates before continuing. Mark shifts his weight from side to side to ease the pain. "Mark, you may go home but do return with the first signs of spring. Also, take a goose from the kitchen as payment for your service."

Mark bows his head and backs out of the room.

King Martin paces in the Great Hall alone, talking to himself once again. "What would Henry do?" Martin whispers. He stops pacing. "What should *I* do?"

"That's the real question of any King, isn't it?" Martin jumps, startled by the sudden presence of Gus who slumps in the throne with his legs hanging over the arm.

"I didn't hear you come in. You scared the hell out of me," Martin says as his heart beats wildly in his chest.

"It's one of the things the Dark Shadows are taught." Gus smiles as he looks around the dimly lit room. "A little bird tells me that you want to learn to fight?" he adds.

"Who told you that?" Martin snaps.

"Is it true?" Gus asks, avoiding the king's question. Martin sighs and Gus continues. "There is an old man who was the first teacher. He was exiled by the king years before you and I were and he ended up in a village not far from here. I saw him not long ago and he yearns to teach once again. The trouble is, he cannot teach just anyone. It has to be someone who has a purpose, a purpose that has good intentions." Gus pauses before continuing while twisting a knife between his hands. "He taught most of the Dark Shadows, or should I say the Black Army, at one time or another. I think he might take you on as his student."

Martin shakes his head. "It's not a good time now."

THE NEW QUEEN

"I have already sent for the old man. Do not tell anyone who he is and tell no one, not even Simon, that he is teaching you." Gus stands up from the throne, sheathes his dagger along his belt, and pauses at the main door. "Do not tell anyone," he repeats, then walks out the door.

Chapter 8
ROYAL TRAINING

Garnet, an older man of fifty, with grey hair walks beside King Martin in Castle Hope, wearing a wool hat, sheepskin gloves and a sheepskin cloak. He was the best architect of his time, having designed four separate castles, three different strongholds, and the most durable wall that has yet to be breached.

"Castle Hope has everything: a church, a lumber mill, and even a large blacksmith shop. It houses over ten thousand people, although they have to sleep on the roads." Garnet points and starts the king's lesson. "And what do you call this place?" Garnet asks as they stand in the courtyard of Castle Hope, a large stone wall surrounding a patch of land attached to several buildings and towers.

King Martin places his frozen hands inside his leather gloves and pulls his gray wolf coat closer to his body. The wind blows stronger, tossing his long brown hair. "This is the courtyard, everyone knows that, Garnet."

THE NEW QUEEN

"With all due respect, your majesty, it is actually called 'the bailey.' Some call it 'the ward' in the south, but its name is 'bailey.' You're right, sire, it is a courtyard, but it is more important than that." Martin stares at Garnet, puzzled. "And this wall that surrounds the bailey, do you know what it is called?" Martin shakes his head. "The walls that surround the bailey are called 'the curtain walls' because it is much like a curtain that one might draw to hide another room. Easy, right?" Garnet smiles.

"Easy for you, Garnet. I have no idea why everything has a name. Why do I need to know these things, anyway? I think it would have been easier if I just cut off your head for confusing mine," Martin says with a pout.

"Okay, let's give you an easy one. What do we call the deep ditch around the castle? Now I know most times it is filled with water, so if under attack, the enemy cannot swim across to fight, but what is it called?"

Martin places his hands on his hips. "I thought it was called a ditch, but if it is filled with water, it would be a moat. Are they the same thing?" Martin asks.

"Indeed they are, but one is a dry moat while the other is a wet moat. The dry moats are filled with stakes that are pointed upward. They are also extra deep, you know, to be deadly," Garnet pauses. "A castle can never have too many defenses," Garnet adds with a cheeky grin. Alright...what is that man standing on?" Garnet asks pointing to a guard on the wall.

"He's on the wall, Garnet, can you not see that?" Martin asks.

"No, your majesty, he is not on the wall. I beg your pardon, but the wall is the side of a castle, and one cannot stand on the side of a castle, can he? What he's standing on is called the 'wall-walk,' sire. It is the place a man can walk along the walls of the castle and where you can see most of the kingdom's land." Martin scratches his chin. "Let's try again," Garnet continues. "Can you tell me the difference between a peasant and a serf?"

"Well," Martin starts, scrunching his face. "A peasant is one who works for a lord or an earl and gives all of his earnings to his master, while a serf works the land and pays the lord something, but not everything he earns."

"Close, but wrong. A peasant works for the lord, and the lord owns the peasant, while a serf is a semi-free peasant who has some rights. He works the land and pays dues to the lord because he is allowed to keep some of his hard work: crops or whatever he raises."

"So a peasant is a slave to his lord or earl?"

"Yes, now you're getting it!" Garnet says, slapping Martin on the back.

For the first time as king, Martin feels proud of himself.

Elizabeth hobbles around the small bedchamber in Castle Hope while Samantha sleeps on the cot bed next to her. She adds another log into the cackling fireplace. "Samantha, I wish I knew punching you in the nose would have always stopped you from talking. At least now I get to say what I want, and you can't interrupt me unless you are playing a mute." Elizabeth stops prodding at the fireplace and glances back at her sister. "Samantha, really, please talk to me. I don't think I can take this silence much longer." Samantha remains silent. "Okay, I think I am going to ask the king to marry me. I have it all planned out. I will wear that white gown you got when you were married with some white flowers in my hair, and when he says yes I will shout out for all of the kingdoms to hear me." Elizabeth limps to Samantha's bed. "What do you think?" Elizabeth tilts Samantha's face towards her. "Samantha, please talk to me. Please." Elizabeth kneels by her sister's bed and

THE NEW QUEEN

lowers her head when the bedchamber door opens and Gwyneth walks in. "Gwyneth, please make her talk to me! She won't talk to me! She remains asleep and it's driving me mad!" Elizabeth stands up and her eyes start stinging.

Gwyneth walks across the wooden floor towards Elizabeth and places a hand on her shoulder. "Elizabeth, Samantha may never talk again, and she may not even know who you are. The bone of the nose went so far into her head that it made her senseless." Gwyneth places her hand on Samantha's forehead and adjusts her pillow.

"Samantha is quite smart, you know. If she wants to talk, she will, but I think she's just playing with me, that's all. She is not at all senseless!" Elizabeth pats Samantha's hand and looks away.

Queen Joanna sits on the bed of her late husband in silence. She caresses the scarlet sheets and stares at the pillow where he used to rest. The door of the bedchamber door creaks open and Witter stands in the doorway under the flickering torchlight. The Captain of the Guards watches Queen Joanna in silence as she stares at the bed, lost in thought. "What is it?" She asks Captain Witter with a hushed voice, breaking the silence.

Captain Witter clears his throat. "Our scout has returned," Witter replies with a calm tone.

She keeps her face turned to the bed, staring at the pillow. "And what does this scout say?" She asks in her hushed voice.

Witter steps closer towards his Queen. "He talks about the French who are ready to fight and asks how we will get to this castle without challenging them."

"Why does he care? I am the Queen, and my husband is gone. It may have even been the French who took his very life, who knows? What has this scout brought me in the way of good news?"

ROYAL TRAINING

"My Queen, he tells us that the French army has been ordered to the north, close to where you want to go. Is it possible they want the castle, too?'

Queen Joanna turns to him. "No, they will go to fight the English. They will cut them off before they can reach the castle or else they will lose. Richard fought the French for so long that the castle was forgotten. The stupid king that he was would just keep sending boy after boy to fight while he sat in his castle. This new king, King Martin, has taken what is mine, and I want it back. Once we gain this castle, we will push back the French. The English will think they did it on their own, then we will strike and take every last castle on the sea. No one will leave or infiltrate this land!" The Queen stands up with a flushed face.

"Yes, my Queen," the captain responds as he backs out of the room and closes the door. He hears something smash against the stone wall followed by heavy weeping.

King Martin trains with his two-handed sword, his chain mail armor hindering his movements. A young guard swings his sword around, attacking Martin from the side. Martin tries to block it but the sword pierces through his chain mail and stabs Martin's thigh, leaving a small scratch. Martin drops his sword and cups his hand over the scratch. "Again. You must hold your sword stiff enough that it does not move," the young guard responds, swinging his sword again. The king whips up his sword and almost blocks the attack. The guard's sword taps Martin's chain mail, but not enough to pierce through.

Garnet exhales and walks closer to the two men, blocking his eyes from the bright sunlight. "I can't believe that one man has such little strength in his arms." Martin clenches his jaw in frustration. "Alright, let's try the two wooden swords and see how

THE NEW QUEEN

you fight with them," Garnet adds. Martin tosses the two-handed sword down and takes the wooden sword Garnet holds out to him. "Alright, stand back to back, sword in hand. When I say go, turn and fight," Garnet instructs. The king and the young guard stand back to back, swords at the ready. "Alright? Go!"

The young guard turns around quickly, striking the king hard on his hip, then another strike at his stomach. Martin lurches over and exhales a few times, then lashes out at the young guard with a two-handed swing. The young guard deflects the attack with ease and allows his wooden sword to slide along the shaft and into his hand, causing Martin to drop the sword.

"It's for your own good, you know," Garnet says to Martin. "Pick up that sword and let's start again." After a few hours of training with wooden swords, Martin's body is covered with enough bruises and scratches that he looks like he has been beaten all over again. "I think that will be enough for now," Garnet says. The guard bows towards Martin and leaves.

"Thank you. Any longer and I would have no hands at all."

"You will be late for archery training," Garnet responds, steering Martin towards the archery training area around the corner.

"Archery training?" the tired king asks.

"Yes. A king must know how to defend himself in all areas of combat, sire." Martin follows Garnet's lead and hesitantly walks to the archery training. The area contains three different burlap sacks stuck on a pole and stuffed with hay. One archer, whom Martin recalls seeing a few times in battle, stands before Martin, shooting arrows at the bull's eye of each target. "Welcome, your majesty. My name is Merek," the blonde haired middle-aged man says with a bow. He holds a bow in one hand, two arrows sticking up from his belt a small shield. "It will be my honor to train with you this afternoon. We have much to cover over the next few days."

ROYAL TRAINING

After three hours, Martin has a good understanding of how to set up and shoot his arrow. Merek watches his king shoot arrows in the direction of the target, but each arrow lands on the frozen ground. "With a bit more practice, you will be hitting the targets in no time, your majesty," Merek says with a smile.

Martin re-loads his bow and shoots the next few arrows at the burlap sack, each time getting closer to the target. "Your majesty," Merek interrupts, "it is time for your next duties." A flock of geese honk and fly over the king's head. Martin raises his bow, takes aim and shoots the flock of geese, missing all five of them.

"I see we still have lots of work to do!" Merek comments as Garnet chuckles beside him.

"What do I have to learn now?" Martin asks as he rubs his eyes.

"I have someone I want you to meet first," Garnet responds. Martin and Garnet walk towards the bailey and pass through an opening in the curtain wall. Beyond the curtain wall sits an old man on a snow-covered tree stump, holding a large staff. The old man looks somewhat frail and thin with sunken eyes, a bald head and wearing one long shirt that reaches the ground. A wool blanket hangs over his shoulders as a makeshift shawl. "Your majesty, I would like you to meet Sir Anthony, one of the original explorers and teachers of the Dark Army," Garnet announces.

"Wow! One of the explorers? You mean to tell me you are one of the original men who was commanded to explore other armies and learn their methods of combat?"

Sir Anthony nods his head and grins slightly.

"Sir Anthony, I am honored by your presence," Martin tells the man, extending his hand. "Sir Anthony, I said what an honor it is to meet you," Martin yells at the man, thinking he must be deaf and blind. He still holds out his hand, waiting for Sir Anthony to shake it.

THE NEW QUEEN

The man looks at Martin's face and slowly looks up and down at the king. "I may be old, but I am not deaf, nor blind!" he says, striking Martin's shin with his staff.

The king jumps back and rubs his shin. "How dare you! You best not strike the king if you know what's good for you!" Martin glares at Sir Anthony as Garnet leans against a tree and watches in silence.

"And I am a knight. Do you see me hiding behind my title? I was a knight long before you were a king, boy." Sir Anthony comments.

"What is it you want, Sir Anthony?" Martin asks, narrowing his eyes at him.

"It is you who summoned me."

Martin tilts his head when Garnet interjects. "I asked you to show up, Sir Anthony, to teach King Martin your ways."

The old man looks up at Garnet. "You fool! I am the knight who was taught to defend, not to fight! What good will it do for a king to defend himself without a striking blow to kill his enemies?"

Garnet smiles. "That's what he needs to learn, and he needs to learn it from the very best, Sir Anthony. I cannot help him as well as you can."

"I am truly sorry, Sir Anthony," Martin interjects, "but Garnet has made a mistake. I need to learn how to fight more than to defend myself from someone your age, you see."

"I see, so you wouldn't mind a small brawl between us?" Sir Anthony slowly rises. "Draw your sword," he orders the king.

"No, I will not fight you. One hit and you may die!" King Martin backs up.

Sir Anthony steps forward and smacks the king's shin. Martin hops up and down, holding his shin. "That hurt! Would you like me to hit you?"

ROYAL TRAINING

"Yes, as a matter of fact, I would! And I bet you a lamb you can't even lay a finger on me." The King lunges at Sir Anthony but as he reaches out, Sir Anthony blocks Martin's attempt with the staff. "If that's all you've got, you better go and hide under your bed." Martin tries to strike again but is blocked by the staff. Anthony smacks the king's shin again.

Martin moves back and rubs the side of his leg. "Stop doing that!"

"Draw your sword and show me you are worthy of my teachings, young king."

Martin hesitantly draws his two-handed sword and swings it at the man, only to be blocked by the staff. "You hit like a boy, young king. I could close my eyes and still beat you." Martin side swings at the old man with more force. Sir Anthony blocks it with little effort. "Pathetic," Sir Anthony taunts. Martin turns frustrated and swings the two-handed sword with a mighty swing, but Sir Anthony deflects it. "Keep this up, and you may even strike like a man!" Anthony taunts. The King pulls back his sword and thrust forwards in a stabbing motion as Sir Anthony chuckles at the attempt. "You think I could not stop such a lame attempt to pierce me?" he chuckles again. Martin swings his sword as Sir Anthony braces the staff against his shoulder, allowing the sword to harmlessly slide down it.

"Hold on!" Garnet steps in to stop Martin from losing his temper. "I think Sir Anthony has proven his point," Garnet says, looking at Martin, then turning to Sir Anthony. "And I think his majesty has shown that he is more than capable with his sword." Martin stands still and sheaths his large sword while Sir Anthony slumps back onto the stump, keeping his staff in front of him.

"Very well. Young king, I will train you, but know that getting old has slowed me. My first lesson to you is no matter how strong or mighty your foe is, if you are aware of what he is doing, he will

THE NEW QUEEN

never hit you. I was able to fight up to three men at the same time, and they never hit me, buying me time until it was right for me to strike. Soon I stood alone."

"Is that when you were knighted?" Martin asks.

"Alas, no. That was only a few months ago when King Richard sent some men to take what food we had left in the village where I was staying. No one would stand up to them until I said I would." Sir Anthony laughs. "Were they surprised when I bested their best," he says, slapping his knee and chuckling.

"My king, we still have more lessons to learn," Garnet says. Martin looks at Garnet, tired from the day's training.

"Oh, you old goat, leave the boy. He looks like he's been beaten enough for one day." Sir Anthony laughs under his breath. "If we run him to exhaustion, who will we taunt tomorrow?" He winks at Garnet. Garnet bows to both Martin and Sir Anthony before leaving them alone.

"Walk with me, boy." Sir Anthony walks and leans on his staff. "Garnet is good-hearted, just not a skilled fighter. He's a smart fellow, always thinking. I was like that once." Sir Anthony looks at King Martin. "Young and smart, sometimes I was too smart for my liking. When I was sent out with the others, I was no older than ten. I never knew my way from a stick to a hole in the ground, but I walked. I stole what I needed to survive. I walked for about a year, had a few fights along the way, but I managed to survive one way or another. When I came to a small Shaolin village, it was mostly boys and womenfolk. I approached one boy and he ran out to meet me. The Shaolin boy said nothing to me, even when I asked who he was. When I tried to pass, he used a staff, not much different from my own, and stopped me at every turn."

"Did you fight him?" King Martin pushes.

"No, the last thing I wanted was a fight. When that boy kept stopping me and I did not fight or try to hurt him, he became less and less hostile with me. That was when I simply grabbed the staff from him. He was only trained to stop an attack, not have someone grab his staff away from him." Sir Anthony laughs. "You should have seen his eyes. They opened so wide like he saw a ghost, then he stepped back and went running back into the village." Sir Anthony shakes his head.

"Little did I know that I just broke one of the Shaolin's secret vows, 'Thou shall not give up your defense'." Sir Anthony pauses and glances at Martin. "That boy's name was Tam Sung and he was going to be a samurai, a type of eastern knight. We became almost like brothers and we were inseparable. It was Tam who started to teach me how to defend myself with the staff, and as I got better, one of the monks pitied me and started teaching me properly. Soon, I exceeded Tam and I was teaching him. After many years, the village was attacked, and I watched as Tam was killed by an arrow from a rival clan. The monks did not teach on how to defend against other clans so I picked up a fallen shield and used the staff with the other hand. The monks watched me fight off most of the army, single-handed." Sir Anthony stops and closes his eyes.

"It sounds like you did well, so what happened?"

"The Shaolin monks, including me, took an oath to never fight, only to defend. You see, to save the village, I must have killed about seventy soldiers, and I made it my objective to kill Tam's murderer, too. I put my staff into his neck, crushing his windpipe and killing him instantly. Although I saved the village, I still broke the monk's oath, so they exiled me." The old man exhales.

"Then you came back here?" Martin asks.

"No. I wanted the one thing a man should never want– revenge. I followed the rest of the intruders back to their camp and killed almost everyone. I let a few escape so I could follow them to their village and do what they did to mine. But when I got to their village, the English army had already killed everyone there. I watched as

THE NEW QUEEN

the soldiers who lost everything fall on their knees and cry. I didn't have the heart to kill them so I left them in what remained of their village." Sir Anthony opens his eyes, shaking his head.

Martin frowns. "Then you came back?"

"Yes and no, my young king. I started walking all over again, not having a clear path as to where I wanted to go. I came to another village and they let me rest for a few days. I spoke to one of the village elders and it was him that made me see the ways in how I had done wrong. Revenge controlled me, but it became my new mission to learn to control it. I decided to make revenge my strength by returning to the castle and showing the king that I am better for it."

"Was the king happy to see you or surprised you were alive?" Martin asks excitedly.

"When I returned, the king was mad and not of his rightful mind. He told me to train more men in the ways I had learned, and if I refused, he would have me skinned alive. At first, I did refuse until I saw a man who had been skinned and was barely alive. Needless to say, it changed my mind quick enough."

"So did you teach them everything, then?"

Sir Anthony stops walking and looks carefully at Martin. "I think you may have been listening after all. What would make you ask that question?"

"Well, I know you would not want revenge, but at the same time, you would not want them to know everything in case they tried to attack the village at some point."

Sir Anthony smiles and wrinkles form at the corners of his droopy eyes. "Maybe there is a king in this boy after all."

King Martin leaves Sir Anthony and walks alone through the castle towards his bedchamber feeling hungry, exhausted, and sore all over when Elizabeth rushes up to him. "Martin!" she shouts.

Martin turns around as her fiery red hair almost covers her face. "Keep your voice down!" he hisses. She throws her arms around him. "Samantha is mute now," she says into his neck. "I need you to talk to me. I need to hear someone's voice," she chokes.

"Elizabeth, I'm sorry, but it has been a very long day. I'm tired, and I am hungry, and I do not wish to talk at this time." He stomps his feet to get rid of the snow.

Elizabeth pulls away from her king in disbelief. "Fine!" she yells. "I won't tell you what's going to happen at the castle then!" She turns and stomps away, using her crutch to increase the noise. Martin watches, waiting for her to turn around and tell him anyway like she usually does. Elizabeth walks around the corner, and Martin pauses momentarily before he turns into his room.

Later that evening, Elizabeth creeps up to Martin's room and slowly opens the door. She tiptoes to his bedside as tears slide down her cheeks. "Why won't you listen to me?'" she whispers. She crawls into the high bed and slides her cold feet under the sheets, trying not to wake him. One of her feet touches Martin's leg, and he jumps up, letting out a slight scream.

"Ahh!" He wakes up and finds Elizabeth pretending to sleep beside him. "Elizabeth! Elizabeth I know you're awake. What are you doing here? What's wrong?"

Elizabeth turns over, her eyes still filled with tears. "Samantha is mute," she repeats. "No matter what I say or do, she won't talk. It's all my fault! If I hadn't screamed, the wild boar would not have found us, and it would not have attacked Samantha, and she would still be able to talk!" Elizabeth stops, inhaling before she continues. "Simon is going to attack the army outside the castle!"

Martin sits up. "What? Are you sure?" he asks in disbelief.

Elizabeth nods and holds her hands on her face. "And he went out of the castle and captured some men and started to torture them and there were a lot of them, too!"

THE NEW QUEEN

Martin sighs. "Elizabeth, you're making up stories."

"No! It's true, I swear! Ask Samantha...she will tell you!" Martin sits there in silence, letting Elizabeth realize what she said.

"Oh, right." Her voice cracks.

"I'm sorry, Elizabeth, but there is nothing we can do except wait and hope that she can talk again," Martin whispers to her. He glances at the tray of food left by his bed and grabs a freshly baked bun. He rips a piece and hands it to Elizabeth.

"Thank you." She breathes deeply, then lies on her side facing the wall. The King waits until he hears her snoring before falling asleep himself.

The king awakes in the morning as the bright sunlight fights its way through the shutters. Elizabeth places a tray of hot water and buttered scones on his bedside table. The fireplace is nothing more than embers, and the stench of stale smoke lingers in the room.

"I'm sorry, your majesty," Elizabeth begins. "I don't know what to do. Samantha is mute, Simon has gone to war, and I left you when you needed me. I won't blame you if you send me away." She bows her head.

"Elizabeth, I know you're afraid and worried for Samantha. I also worry for her, but we just have to wait. As for Simon, I just can't believe he would attack the Great Army, especially when I told him not to." Martin grabs a scone and bites into it. He scrunches his face and spits it out. "Did you make these?" he asks, chugging down some water.

"No, I found them already made in the kitchen. The scones aren't good?"

"Have one for yourself. In fact, take them all," Martin says as he hurries her out of the room so he could dress. He just finished pulling on his boots when someone knocks at the door. "Elizabeth, I am getting dressed!" he shouts.

ROYAL TRAINING

"It's me, Garnet, your majesty. Time for your training to begin!"

The king flops back onto the unmade bed with his arms outstretched, already dreading what Garnet has planned for him today.

Chapter 9
Going Home

Weeks pass as King Martin continues his intensive training of sword fighting and archery through rain, snow, and wind. Sir Anthony even manages to break the king's toe with his staff in a thorough one-on-one fight. The snow piles up quickly along the castle, interfering with Martin's practices outdoors. Large mounds of snow collect at the main gate, clogs the insides of the arrow loops, and turning the frozen terrain into an icy tundra.

Mark returns and sighs as he sits with Garnet and Martin at a table in the main dining hall. "We have sent man after man to Quarry Castle, and no one has yet to return."

"And we still do not know the faith of the other castle, whether it has been overrun or surrendered to another power," Martin adds.

"Simon is a good guard, sire. If he were in trouble, I think he would have sent word one way or another." Garnet pushes his pile of chicken bones and half-eaten rolls away from him and pats his belly.

GOING HOME

"I told the king," Mark starts between chews, "that we should send a party of twenty men or so to find out what's going on. They might get ambushed along the way, so twenty men is a strong number that contains a higher chance that at least one guard could escape. Maybe this is why no one has returned yet, because they have been getting ambushed," Mark finishes, grabbing some of the stale rolls Garnet had pushed away.

"And who will lead this party?" Garnet asks.

"I will," Martin says, standing up and placing his bruised hand on the long, two-handed sword strapped to his side.

Garnet shakes his head. "I would be the first to admit that you would be a formidable fighter against anyone, sire, but your life is far too valuable for such a task."

Mark nods in agreement with Garnet, chewing a large bite of meat. "I told you so."

"Nevertheless, I will lead the party. I have had enough training, and I need to know what happened to my castle," Martin retaliates.

"Sire, if I may?" Garnet interjects. "Why not wait until spring? The weather would not be so bad, and one would not be so easily tracked."

Martin shakes his head. "If the castle has been taken, we may need to fight to claim it back. The spring brings reinforcements for them, and they could become more powerful by spring. I want to know what happened and I want to know now!" Martin bangs his fist onto the table, then pulls back and rubs his bruised hand.

Garnet sighs. "Who are we to say that the king is wrong? But, your majesty, I would send a party of five or six ahead of your party, just in case…" Garnet's comment is interrupted as a scream echoes inside the castle. Martin looks at Mark as they draw their swords, and they both rush up the stairs to yet another cry. Mark moves ahead of Martin and runs into a room to find Samantha sitting up in bed, screaming all alone.

THE NEW QUEEN

"Samantha!" Martin yells, moving to her bedside. "Samantha! What's wrong?" Martin grabs her shoulders. Sweat beads around her forehead and soaks her tangled hair as she shakes her head back and forth.

"Where am I?" she whispers in a hoarse voice.

"You're in the castle," Martin replies.

"How did I get here?"

"Elizabeth brought you here."

Samantha's eyes widen. "Elizabeth? Where is Elizabeth?"

"She's in the castle. I will send for her." Martin spots a maiden approaching the bed carrying blankets and an iron kettle of hot water. She places the tray on Samantha's side table, then wipes her hands on her apron. "Find this woman's sister, Elizabeth. She has red hair. Send her here right away." The maiden nods and exits out the door.

"I don't remember anything." Samantha coughs.

"What is the last thing you remember?"

"I remember picking up twigs for a fire, and Elizabeth being bossy."

Martin smiles. "It's okay, save your voice. Elizabeth will be here soon, and we can talk about it then." Samantha nods and closes her eyes. Martin hands her a chalice of hot water, and she chugs the entire cup.

Rapid stomping echoes through the hallway and the door of the hospital wing bursts open. "Samantha!" Elizabeth yells, running to her sister and wrapping her arms around her. "Are you talking now? We have so much to talk about! Why did you not talk to me? It was making me crazy!" Her eyes glisten and Samantha sniffles. "This must be a miracle," Elizabeth adds. Martin smiles and backs away from the bed to let the sisters be together. Mark sheaths his sword, as he leads the king back down the stairs.

GOING HOME

"We will leave tomorrow morning for the other castle. I want a group of five Black Army men to scout ahead of us. Mark, you and the remaining guards will stay here, but I will take ten more guards with me, making fifteen men. We have to know the faith of the other castle before we can do anything," Martin informs Mark. Garnet waits at the bottom of the stairs as Gus follows behind.

"In that case, I think it is only prudent that you train one more time today, your majesty," Mark emphasizes. Martin stops on the last step and reluctantly nods in agreement before following him out to the training stations. The snow had been cleared away enough for the King to continue his training. King Martin holds two swords in his hands as two guards charge at him. He observes their movements and jumps to the left where the leading man charges and imitates slicing his throat before defending himself from the second attack. Martin defends against the second guard over and over again without success. As fast as the king deflects one sword, it swings back and he has to defend himself from it a second time. Finally, the king observes patterns through the guard's repetitive strikes so Martin devises a plan. Instead of deflecting the attack, Martin jumps out of the way, making the men stumble forward and lose balance while Martin strikes a simulating stab deep into the man's chest. Garnet and Mark clap and grin.

"Excellent, your majesty! You are learning how to defend and attack in battle! Keep this up, and you'll be a fine warrior someday," Garnet cheers. Martin takes a bow. Geese honk overhead and Martin glances up. "Now, let's see how good your bow is!" Gus adds, handing him his bow and quills. The king quickly takes aim at one, killing it with the first shot.

"I think that shows that I am ready and I do not require any more lessons from either of you, thank you," Martin comments.

Garnet and Mark glance at each other and nod. "Indeed, it appears as though you are in fact a fair soldier. You have made us

THE NEW QUEEN

proud, my king." Garnet and Mark bow with broad smiles on their faces before leaving the king in front of the burlap target bags

"And what about the training I have done with you?" Sir Anthony asks from the side.

Martin whips around at the voice, not realizing Sir Anthony was watching nearby. "I feel that I will never be ready with you, Sir Anthony. Although I have improved greatly, I could never be as good as you."

Sir Anthony nods towards Martin, leaning against his staff. "It is the first understanding that makes a man great."

"The first understanding?" Martin walks towards him.

Sir Anthony nods. "One must understand that there is always someone better than the best, no matter what one thinks he is the best at."

"So you can never be the best at anything?" Martin pries.

"Yes and no. One can still master the art, but you can never think that no one can beat you. If you remember this, you will be a stronger soldier. You managed to learn this lesson quickly during today's match by not attacking right away. You waited until the precise moment and overcome the combat."

Martin smiles and picks up the dead goose. "So which should I fight with- my two swords or my single sword?" Martin turns around to hear the answer but Sir Anthony is nowhere in sight. He stands alone next to the burlap targets as snow begins to fall.

The snow storm rages on for more than a week, covering Queen Joanna's new kingdom in thick layers of snow and ice. The Queen of Castile rests in her throne in the map room, wearing a white dress with gold trim, reminding her of the fluffy snow outside. She stares at the newly painted map on the floor. The fire crackled behind her in the fireplace, keeping her back warm. She

GOING HOME

rests her arm on the cherry wood arm of the chair and places her chin upon her closed fist. The Queen, lost in her thoughts, doesn't hear a guard approaching from the opposite end of the room.

Knowing the Queen's temper, the guard carefully walks around the map. "My Queen," he says in a quiet voice, bowing to her. "The storm grows worse. I am here to inform you that three more men have died today, and my captain asks to stop training until the storm passes."

She nods. "Very well."

The guard bows once more before leaving her alone in the room.

Queen Joanna takes a small sip of wine before setting the cup on the floor next to her chair. She swishes the wine around in her mouth before swallowing it, never breaking her stare on the map. She moves to the map and sits down on it, gliding the tiny wood ships that symbolize France's navy. She begins to measure the distance from her castle to Castle Hope, thinking about how long it would take to get there. "Guard!" she yells, keeping her eyes closed. A guard appears at the door and bows. "Tell the captain to stop the training and let the men rest for the next three days." The guard bows and turns away. "Wench!" the queen bellows again. Two women in rags scramble to the door. "My wine!" the two women carefully walk around the map and retrieve her wine beside the throne and handing her a full goblet. She takes the goblet and looks at the one woman. "Does anyone understand what is about to happen over the next few months?" The maiden slowly shakes her head and steps back. "We are going to take the land that was once ours years ago when my father ruled this retched land and we will be victorious, and everyone will remember me as the most successful Queen of Castile." She looks over at the silent maiden who stands in the doorway. "Oh, what do you know? You're just a wench. Leave me," she commands, waving her away. The queen

THE NEW QUEEN

closes her eyes and dreams of future victories when another guard enters the room.

"My Queen, a French delegation has arrived and asks to speak with you urgently."

The Queen opens her eyes. "About what?"

"Fighting our common enemy!"

Simon takes pride in his torture technique that he learned when he was an English soldier. The imprisoned man is tied to a wooden chair as Simon swings his axe into the side of it, leaving a deeper cut into the wood each time. "So you ambush the King and many travelers on several occasions so do you kill them?" Simon presses. The man stares at Simon as sweat runs slowly down his face. Simon swings the axe into the side of the chair and the man jumps. "Do you not wish to talk?" The man slowly takes a breath as he stares at Simon in silence. "The chair will not save you, but the truth will set you free from your sins."

The prisoner grins. "The sin is on you."

"So you do speak." Simon walks to the front of the man and pushes the axe under his chin. "Speak, tell me what sins I have and why you continue to attack the stronghold." Simon lowers the axe and continues swinging his axe into the chair when a chunk of wood falls to the floor. "That's the first piece, and you're next. Care to start talking now?"

The man looks down at his exposed thigh from the fallen chunk of the chair. "We own this land! Leave or die!'

"King Martin owns this land, you fool! Now tell me where your people are hiding!" Simon raises the axe once again. "Tell me and I stop!"

"No, no I will not!" The man shouts as Simon swings the axe right onto the man's thigh. Blood squirts onto the floor and pours down the side of the man's leg, exposing the bone. The man screams in pain and he squirms in the chair as blood continues rushing down his leg.

Simon watches the man in agony as he grips his axe tighter. "Tell me."

"No, I won't," the man says in between shallow, shaky breaths. Simon sighs and lowers his axe onto the man's thigh, dismembering the leg. Dark blood gushes out from the stump and the leg as it falls to the floor in a pool of blood. The man continues screaming and writhing in agony as a guard enters the room and drags the lame man out of the room, leaving a trail of blood out the door.

Another guard approaches Simon. "Captain, there is a group of men at the gate wanting entry to the castle." Simon drops his axe and quickly follows the guard out of the quarry castle's small hall and towards the main gate.

A group of thirty men shout and cluster around the main gate. Simon walks up to them. "Who are you and what business do you have here?"

"We are from King Henry' realm. He has dismissed us and we seek to join your kingdom," a middle-aged man at the front responds.

"And what do you have for a tribute?"

"We gots food!" Another man yells from the back of the crowd. "Ye gots food, sire."

"Where did you get this food?" Simon asks. "Did you get it from here?"

"No, ye gots it over yonder at the other castle."

Simon raises his eyebrow. "Now what castle would that be?"

Martin awakes early the next morning to prepare for his trip to the castle. The sun peeks over the horizon as the castle starts

THE NEW QUEEN

to stir with other early risers. The overnight guards switch shifts with the daytime guards as they begin their shift. Martin begins preparing his bag with clothes and weapons when Elizabeth enters his bedchamber carrying a torch. "We want to go," Elizabeth announces. She is dressed in a wolf fur jacket and a grey wool dress under it.

"Sorry, Elizabeth, but we plan to go and come right back. No need for you to join." Martin continues packing his bag.

"We want to go home," Elizabeth begs.

"I will let you return when I know it is safe, but not now. You and your sister will remain here where I know you will be out of danger," Martin reaffirms, strapping his swords across his back.

"I want to come!"

"It's not safe!" Martin moves past Elizabeth and walks down to the kitchen as Elizabeth follows behind. He shoves cold chicken legs, potatoes, corn, and buns into a handkerchief and ties the extra food to the side of the horse that waits by the front gate. Guards by the front gate tie a small wagon to the back of their horses, filling it with extra food, clothing, and blankets. Martin watches five Black Army guards move out before him, crossing the icy land. Martin mounts his horse and Elizabeth pulls at the reigns. "Elizabeth!" he shouts to her, seeing Samantha pull up next to her with another horse.

"We already packed our food, blankets and a tent. I bet you never thought about a tent, did you?" Elizabeth chimes.

"And this time we even have wood to burn." Samantha waves a stick from the back of her horse.

Martin glares at the two women. "You're going to get yourselves killed! I forbid you both from coming. Especially you, Samantha, when your health is still wavering. You are in no position to join us," the king says, mounting his black horse.

GOING HOME

Elizabeth and Samantha jump up on theirs. "Actually, we are," Samantha confirms.

Martin sighs. "I know there will be nothing I can say to keep you from staying. And I'm in a hurry. Stay beside me and keep quiet."

The party heads out on their horses before the full sunrise. The wind is sharp and cold against their faces. Two guards ride ahead while two ride in front of the king, and two more guards ride behind the king. Elizabeth and Samantha ride side by side with two more guards behind them, leaving two guards to ride on each side of the king. The ride across the hills remains quiet. As soon as they reach the entrance of the forest, the frontal guards raise their hands and slows the party. Bloody bodies scatter the path and are entangled in the thickets. A man groans in a nearby bush when two arrows land in his chest and silence him for good.

One of the guards dismounts and checks a body. "It's still warm!" he shouts while the guards reload their crossbows. "That was from our five friends ahead of us, sire," the guard announces, nodding towards the fired arrows. "We should be okay to continue from now on," he adds. Martin nods and the group continues in silence through the forest of English Oaks and pine trees as glimpses of sunlight shine between the branches.

Samantha and Elizabeth trail the end of the party on their smaller horses, weaving between the paths of flattened snow from their fellow comrades. Their horses shake their heads and gallop through the forest, kicking up snow. Elizabeth and Samantha laugh at their playful horses, even when they try to race each other along the way.

Once the group enters a brief clearing in the forest, one of the Black Army men holds up his hand. Martin looks around, seeing a reasonable distance into the tree line and through some of the thickets. Snow blankets the branches and icicles sparkle in the

THE NEW QUEEN

distance. The five Black Army men dismount their horses and weave between the surrounding trees, crunching on the ice and untouched snow with every step. The king and the rest of the group remain on their horses, listening to the Black Army men exploring the area. King Martin rides up to one of the Black Army men circling a collection of nearby trees. "What's going on?"

"There are tracks we have been following to get to the other castle and now they are gone. It's like they vanished... or flew away," the Black Army man says slowly, embarrassed by his answer.

"I heard there were dragons around here!" Elizabeth exclaims, riding closer to the man.

"Maybe they were attacked by dragons?" Martin agrees, looking up to the sky.

Two guards exchange their swords for their crossbows. "Oh, that won't help," Elizabeth starts. "Dragons have tough skin, and an arrow won't go through it. Some dragons breathe fire, and some breathe acid, but both have armor skin." She glances up at the sky.

A guard riding alongside Martin joins the conversation. "Why are we stopped?"

"Dragons might be here!" Elizabeth shrieks. Martin shoots her a stern glance and she lowers her head.

"They have lost the tracks. We are lost," Martin tells him. The guard on the king's side signals to the guard on the other side of the king to search in the tree line. Martin stays sitting on his horse waiting for any word as he watches the one guard search with the Black Army men.

"How far are we from the other castle?" Samantha asks, her horse chewing on some leaves from a wild berry bush covered in snow.

"Still a ways," the guard says.

She tries again. "How far are we from the channel then?"

"Not sure," he responds.

GOING HOME

"If we cut into the tree line and go that way, we will come to the channel and it would be harder for an attack on us there, don't you think?" Samantha asks. Martin looks at the way Samantha was pointing to. A large rustling sound starts in the opposite direction, and the guard returns, crouched behind his horse. The king motions for a guard to meet the other guard and a few minutes later, both guards emerge from the thicket.

"Your majesty," the guard starts. "There is a huge army that camps beyond the tree line. In fact, it is the biggest army I have ever seen!" he whispers.

"Who is it? Do you know?" Martin asks.

The guard shakes his head. "Not a flag to be seen, sire."

"How big is this army?"

"As far as the eye could see, sire. They are camped in a small valley."

"Tell everyone we will take the channel route until we get to the castle. It may take longer, but we will be out of this army's way. Until we know who it is, we are not to let this army see or hear us," the King orders. The guards nod and the Black Army lead the way to the channel, taking most of the day to get less than halfway to Quarry Castle.

After some time in the trees and thickets along the channel, they stop to make camp before nightfall. Martin knew they did not travel far because he still recognizes parts of his land: the same path they used before, the same dead tree and the same salty smell from the channel.

"I hope there are no wild boars around," Samantha says to Elizabeth as she hangs her linen tarp from a thick branch. Elizabeth nods, shivering at the thought. They tie their horses to a tree under the tarp while the horses nibble on berries from nearby bushes.

THE NEW QUEEN

"I think we could have walked to the other castle by now," Elizabeth whispers.

"It's the snow, Elizabeth, it slows everything down. It's hard to walk in it, even for the horses," Samantha explains.

Three guards scout around the campsite and return shortly with a deer. "I think that's the first deer we have seen around here in some time," a guard comments.

Elizabeth and Samantha prepare and clean the deer for dinner. The men gather wood and prepare small fires by each tent. They huddle around each fire and roast the deer meat, taking their time chatting and eating. Martin yawns as he stands up. "Let's keep the fire going through the night. We are so deep into the trees that no one should be able to see us. I want everyone to get some sleep while two guards keep watch at every hour of the night. Alternate amongst you all, and keep your crossbows armed. If a threat approaches our camp, yell," he commands before crawling into a smaller tent.

King Martin opens his eyes to the sounds of birds chirping and the sound of a fire cackling nearby. In the tent next to him, he hears ruffles from Elizabeth and Samantha folding their sheets and giggling. Martin leaves his tent and stretches, the crisp morning wind blowing through his knotted curly hair. He walks over to the fire and slumps on a log in front of it and wraps his fur tightly around him.

Samantha exits her tent and hands Martin some hot water infused with berries. She cooks some of the deer and pulls out some bread that she baked. "Here you go," Samantha says to the king, handing him a handkerchief of deer and rolls. Samantha turns her head and sniffs at the air, wrinkling her nose. "Do you smell that?"

"Yes, I believe it's one of the guards. We are starting to smell like pigs," Martin confesses, sniffing the sleeves of his shirt. Samantha turns away and leaves Martin to eat.

Martin finishes eating and decides to explore the land before continuing their journey. He lights a torch and carries his sword in the other hand, backtracking the path they walked the previous day.

The guard outside Martin's tent quickly joins his side. "Is someone out there? Did you see something?" he asks.

"Just thought I would look, that's all," Martin says, keeping the torch in front of him. The men take a few more steps when they hear a snap between some trees. Martin looks at the guard, and the guard looks at the king, placing a finger on his lips. The guard moves in front of the king, his sword at the ready, and squinting his eyes to see anything at all.

Another twig snaps from their side. Martin puts the torch out in the snow, realizing whoever is out there may be able to see them more clearly than they can see him. Another snapping noise occurs from the same side and then the strain of a bowstring being pulled back. The guard lunges at his king and knocks him to the ground. They lay still on the frozen ground until they hear the sound of an arrow zooming past them and landing on the trunk of a tree. Martin signals for the guard to go one way while he moves the other, flanking the shooter. They nod and crawl in opposite directions, staying as close to the ground as possible and listening for any other sounds of movement.

The eerie silence of the early morning sends shivers up Martin's back. He peers into the darkness of the forest, unable to see more than ten feet in front of him. He carefully crawls towards the direction he believes the arrow was fired from. Then he hears another snap behind him, this one closer than before. Martin places his back to a tree in the middle, turning his head from side to side where the two snaps came from. "There must be two

THE NEW QUEEN

attackers," he whispers. Martin picks up a nearby rock and throws it towards the first attacker's direction. An arrow flies in another direction, opposite where Martin hunches. Suddenly, a twig snaps right behind Martin. The king whips around, swinging his two-handed sword and out of the corner of his eye, he sees a figure and tries to kill it. He misses the figure and slices a deep cut into a tree.

The figure screams and on a closer look, the shape emerges with fiery red hair. Elizabeth shakes and clasps her hand to her mouth, falling to the floor to avoid Martin's blade. An arrow whizzes by her head and lands in a tree behind her. "Shhh!" Martin hisses, too angry at her to say anything else. Men shout and rush into the forest, swords clanging and arrows flying. "Stay here and don't move!" Martin orders Elizabeth.

The king weaves his way between the trees as the large dark figure shoots arrows aimlessly into the darkness. Martin sneaks up behind the figure and places his sword on the man's shoulder. "Drop the bow, or you will die," Martin says through clenched teeth. The archer freezes and slowly moves his hand out to his side still holding the bow in his right hand. "Last chance," Martin adds. The archer turns around furiously, knocking Martin's sword down. The man lunges for his own sword still strapped to his side but Martin knocks it out of his sheath. "Nice try but that won't work here," Martin affirms, pushing his sword firmly into the man's large chest. The man releases a slight yelp and tries to reach for his bow and arrows. Martin lunges at the man, forcing his sword into the man's chest. The archer gasps and grabs onto the sword with both hands, falling to his knees. He looks up at Martin, wide-eyed, before collapsing onto the icy ground. The king rushes back to where he left Elizabeth by the tree. "Get up now," he whispers, while they rush back to camp, sticking close to the shadows of the trees.

GOING HOME

The guards watch Martin and Elizabeth rushing into camp and they scramble to his side. "Your majesty, are you alright?' the guards ask as the sounds of battle intensify in the forest.

"We have visitors," he says, nodding towards the forest. The guards nod, unsheathe their swords, and rush towards the forest. Then he turns to Samantha and Elizabeth. "Wait in the camp, and for goodness sake, don't move!" He looks straight at Elizabeth, giving her a stern look, then leaves to find more guards.

Elizabeth and Samantha take down each tent and put out each fire while Martin hears shouts and fighting heading closer to their camp. "We have to go! Pack up everything and let's get out of here, now!" Martin shouts, throwing as many belongings onto the horses as possible. "Hurry, hurry!" he cries. A man stumbles out of the forest running away from two of Martin's guards. Both guards impale their swords in the man's back and he falls, his head cracking on a large boulder.

One guard runs over to the horses where Elizabeth and Samantha stand and prepares them. "Get on your horses and get the king to the castle right away. Don't stop for anything!" he says, pushing Elizabeth and Samantha onto their horses. He runs over to a crossbow leaning against a burned out campfire, loads it with a fallen arrow, and gives it to Samantha. "If anything attacks the king, shoot it," he instructs her. Samantha nods and Elizabeth straps her crossbow to her back. "Protect your king!" he shouts to them as another enemy rushes out of the trees towards him, slicing the enemy's throat. He turns to Martin. "Your majesty, you must go," the guard pleads. Martin looks at the two women on separate horses, weapons attached to their hips and backs, and agrees to leave. He mounts a horse and holds the reins with one hand, and his large, two-handed sword in the other. Martin kicks the horse into action and the three head into the break of day, leaving the destroyed camp and increasing battle behind them.

THE NEW QUEEN

They race out of the forest in the direction towards Quarry castle, Elizabeth sniffling loudly. Martin and Samantha slow their horses to a gallop. "It's over," Martin says between breaths. "We got away. No need to cry, Elizabeth."

"You have to be quiet or else they will hear you!" Samantha hisses. All of a sudden, a man jumps out of the trees and raises his sword over his head, spooking all three horses. Elizabeth screams, and Samantha sloppily fires her crossbow at the man. The arrow pierces the top of his shoulder and pins him against a tree. Elizabeth takes out her crossbow and aims at the pinned man, shooting her arrow above the man's head. Samantha reloads her crossbow and shoots right at the man's chest. A pool of blood soaks the snow around the tree. Martin looks at the dead man and then back at Samantha, her eyes hard and unmoving. Elizabeth whimpers and closes her eyes at the sight.

"We better keep going," Martin says, pulling on the reigns of his horse. The farther they travel, the less of the camp fight they could hear, but Elizabeth still flinches and whimpers at the sound of the screaming men. Martin glances at Elizabeth– her skin so pale, and eyes so empty that Martin thinks she might have died, too. After traveling on horseback past a few more snow banks in silence, they reach a clearing, and Martin dismounts. "Stay here. I will see if it is safe to cross the clearing," Martin says. The sisters nod and steady their horses. Martin walks between trees, looking for any tracks or signs of life, leaving Samantha and Elizabeth alone. Samantha rides up beside Elizabeth and grabs her arm.

"Elizabeth, if you want to be queen someday, you better start fighting like one. If someone comes at Martin, or at us, then shoot or else there will be no king to marry!" Elizabeth continues staring blankly ahead, not looking at her sister. Samantha sighs and tries in a softer voice. "I have to know that you will defend your kingdom, including us."

GOING HOME

Elizabeth blinks and looks back at her sister. "I'm scared, Samantha."

"Me too." Samantha pauses. "We need to stick together, okay? This is our battle, too." Samantha grabs Elizabeth's hand. "We wanted to join on this journey because we can handle it, right?" Elizabeth squeezes Samantha's hand.

Martin returns in a jog, clonking through the mounds of snow. "It looks good," he starts as he reaches the sisters. "Stay close, and we will move quickly across the open before the sun fully rises." He mounts his horse and they each tug on their reigns, moving the horses forward. They race across the opening on the side by the cliffs of the channel as the morning sun casts oranges and reds across the all-white landscape. Martin leads his horse towards the tree line instead of cutting across the open fields.

"Why are we going into the trees?" Elizabeth asks. "We are not that far from Quarry Castle now."

"Staying in the trees will conceal us from any further attacks." They move just inside the tree line, keeping the channel in their site as they are guided back home. Martin looks up at the sky. "It's going to get real horrible soon," Martin says to himself.

"What? Do you see someone?" Elizabeth asks raising her crossbow as she sits up on her horse and squints into the distance.

"No, the sky is red," Martin concludes.

Elizabeth and Samantha exchange glances. Samantha shrugs her shoulders. "What does that mean?" she asks.

"When I was young, I was on a ship to fight in a war with my father. A sailor told me this saying. 'A red sky at night, sailor's delight. Red sky in the morning, sailor's warning.' It means there's a storm coming."

"I think you're mad. It's winter time, there's always a storm," Elizabeth jabs.

THE NEW QUEEN

"And what if the sky is blue?" Samantha joins in, intrigued by Martin's sayings.

Martin smiles. "If the sky is blue, the course is true."

"Rubbish. I have never heard any of those things. Are you sure you're not just making them up?" Elizabeth asks.

The cold wind picks up and thunder crashes beyond the channel. "We better move into the trees, they will protect us from the wind," Martin says, leading them deeper into the trees. "Elizabeth, do you know how much further we have to go?"

Elizabeth bites her lip. "No, not particularly. I don't recognize anything besides the channel, same as you."

Martin nods. "Well, we need shelter anyways. The storm is already heading our direction." Elizabeth and Samantha look towards the channel as dark grey clouds swirl into the red-orange sky, slowly blocking out the sun. The horses fight to continue galloping through the snow and slippery patches of ground. The wind whistles between the trees, cracking the branches and blowing the snow into a flurry. Thick snowflakes fall heavier until they can barely see a few feet in front of them.

"Martin? We need shelter now!" Samantha shouts to him as the thinning trees no longer provide any shelter from the snow.

"I see the end of the forest and I think I see the channel through the opening!" Martin shouts back. "Come on!" The group arrives at the end of the tree line covered in snow. Martin squints through the snow. "Come this way! I see a few large buildings right by this bend!"

Martin pushes his horse forward as Samantha and Elizabeth tail behind him, keeping their heads down against the wind and snow. Martin dismounts in front of the wall and finds a wooden door. He kicks it a few times and bangs along it to crack the ice around the ledges. Samantha and Elizabeth dismount, pulling their horses towards the door. Martin rams his shoulder into the

GOING HOME

door, and it swings open, a trail of snow blowing in. They pull their horses inside and slam the door closed.

The small room is filled with hay and cots hang from the ceiling. Boxes and crates of all sizes line the walls, and a stale stench of salt lingers in the air. Elizabeth reaches into her travel pouch around her horse and pulls out a flint, steel, and homemade torch. She rubs the flint and steel together until the sparks ignite and catch on her homemade oil torch. She holds it up, and they look around at their new surroundings. "This looks familiar somehow," Martin says as he scans the row of cots and mounds of hay. Torches mount the walls between the cots and a small pile of folded linen are stacked in a neat pile.

"It smells, too," Samantha says, wriggling her nose.

Martin walks towards an opening in the floor in the corner of the room. Elizabeth holds the torch beside Martin and Samantha follows behind. He wiggles the rusty handle and pulls the trapdoor up. It creaks and groans under the force, and Martin coughs at the dust that falls from the top of the door. He looks around and sees the timber in a cross section and shutters closed tightly in order to keep water out. Martin recognized where he was at once.

"We're in a ship!" he shouts.

Chapter 10
THE WINTER STORM

Simon awakes after a sound sleep on a pile of hay in Quarry Castle, next to a passed out drunkard holding a chalice next to his chest. He stands and stretches, feeling well-rested and ready to start the cold winter day ahead. The passed out man snores with his mouth open as a piece of hay flutters above his mouth. Simon readjusts his twisted leather armor and brushes off the hay that clings to his leather boots. A guard walks past Simon and chuckles at the hay stuck in Simon's hair. Guards around him begin cooking and eating breakfast over small fires, drinking ale and belching loudly. The drunkard remains snoring, and a pig sniffs at his knotted hair.

The stable door creaks open, and Jade scurries in covered in snow. His cheeks, nose, and forehead are bright red, and his wool scarf covers his mouth and bottom half of his face. He stands at the door and brushes off snow from his fur coat and stomps his leather boots.

THE WINTER STORM

"You look like a snowy beast," Simon says with a smile. "Are you not the man whom I sent to talk to the Great Army?"

"Very funny," Jade responds, untying his scarf. A collection of snow falls on the stable floor.

"What's it like out there?" Simon asks.

"We won't be leaving anytime soon, that's for sure. The snow is really falling down."

"Well, it would look odd falling up, wouldn't it?" Simon jousts with him.

"Alas, I won't grow old of your wit," Jade smirks. "What I mean to say is that it's so bad out there, we might not be able to open the doors to this stable, even. I could just barely get through now." Jade walks over to the fire to defrost.

"Perchance I shall check it out to be sure," Simon responds. He walks over to the door and pushes on it but the door remains unmoved. He pushes harder, and the door opens just enough for him to fit his head through. The entirety of the castle is covered with snow, and the sky swirls different shades of grey as the storm rages, blowing thick snowflakes in a flurry. Simon sighs and pulls the door back until it locks.

Jade grabs the chalice from the passed out man and drinks the remainder of ale, then belches. He carries the chalice, walking between other men and asking for more brew.

Simon notices Douglass by another fire, staking a piece of dried meat. "Hello, Douglass. Once you are done eating, I need you to get some brooms and keep this door clear of the snow. We do not have enough food or supplies to be trapped inside the barn." Douglass nods and shoves the meat into his mouth. He wipes his hands on his leather pants and searches for a broom. "You are the other guy I sent up the hill with Jade, right?" Douglass nods with his mouth full of meat. Simon sits down next to Jade.

THE NEW QUEEN

"Did you find out anything from the man you tortured?" Jake asks Simon.

Simon hesitates before answering. "He was with a group who claim that they are the rightful heirs to Richard's kingdom." Simon shakes his head.

"Does it really matter now that we beat Richard in war? I don't see this heir raising a new army after what Richard did. I mean, he forced his men to fight to the death, and threaten that their home would be taken away. How much worse can you be?" Jade asks.

"If there is an heir, they would have to challenge this kingdom to claim it back, but you're right, I don't see that happening anytime soon," Simon agrees.

Within Quarry Castle, Gregory struggles to manage the snowfall as it piles up and threatens to trap the kingdom inside. Gregory assigns peasants at each entrance to sweep the snow and mop up the puddles until most of the kingdom collect at the entrances, working together. Once the buckets are filled with snow, they would either be used around the castle as a water supply or be dumped through the arrow loops in the stone walls. Instead of burning so much wood, Gregory assigned the people to wear extra layers to preserve the wood for cooking. "This storm could rage for another few days, even weeks, so we must spare the wood! Anyone who is seen burning wood for heat other than the designated fireplaces in the main rooms will face severe punishment!" Gregory shouts down the halls and the keep where people are working.

Gregory leaves the warm castle and treks his way into the blowing snow to the stables where Simon and some men occupy. He pulls on the door, prying it from its icy seams until the ice cracks and the door swings open. Simon gets to his feet quickly, startled by Gregory's appearance. "Something wrong?" Simon asks.

"Nothing. I just want to let you know I am going to make my rounds," Gregory answers.

THE WINTER STORM

"Start with the towers since you can see the farthest from the outpost." Gregory bows and leaves for the tower. After Gregory climbs up the spiraling staircase, he rests on the top step, watching a flock of owls perching by the arrow loops.

"Hello," a boy says from behind Gregory. "What's your name?"

Gregory jumps and spins around, staring at the small, pale boy. "Gregory. What's yours?"

The boy walks towards Gregory and leans opposite from him, staring at the snowy field. "I'm Andrew, Andrew the 'king killer'. I killed King Richard," the boy says with a smile.

"And how did you do that?" Gregory asks.

"You haven't heard? King Martin was very pleased," Andrew beams.

Gregory looks at the boy with both amusement and confusion. Andrew continues. "Where were you when we were at war?"

"I was in the war fighting behind the tree line."

"I was standing on a bale of hay on the wall. I saw King Richard, and I shot my arrow at him, and I hit him in the neck, and he died." Andrew smiles wider.

"Ah, yes, so you're the king killer?" Gregory taunts the boy.

"That's right. And who are you?"

"I told you, I am Gregory."

"No, not your name. I mean who are you? Just Gregory? Or Sir Gregory from the Black Army?"

Gregory folds his arms. "And what do you know about me, Andrew, the 'king killer'?"

"Well…" Andrew sits beside Gregory, focusing on the owls. "I was told that you are from the Black Army and that's why you're in charge. Is that true?"

Gregory smiles at the boy. "Does that frighten you?"

"Nothing frightens me. I've killed a king."

"That's right. Well, I did belong to the Dark Shadow once."

THE NEW QUEEN

"Are they killers, too?" Andrew looks at Gregory.

"As a matter a fact, they are, and they are even stronger than the Black Army!"

Andrew shakes his head. "Nothing is stronger than the Black Army."

"Oh, they were better and scarier than the Black Army in every way you could think of," Gregory teases.

Andrew thinks of what the man has said. "Can you throw a knife and kill a man?"

"No," he lies, not wanting to scare Andrew. "But I can sword fight!"

"That's alright, sir, I can sword fight with my friends," Andrew tells him, then stands up and skips down the stairs.

The kingdom of Castile undergoes war preparations as the impending blitz attack on Hope Castle quickly approaches. The blacksmiths vigorously continue making swords, shields and crossbows for every soldier in the kingdom of Castile. Queen Joanna has wagons of food and supplies from her hardworking farmers and peasants prepared for her large army. She seizes a halt on the granaries to strictly grow grain for the soldiers only. Any commoner caught stealing grain for their families would quickly be beheaded. She orders for half the army to attack Hope Castle while the other half remains to defend her kingdom. The soldiers secretly question her war plan amongst each other, knowing that only a large army together can infiltrate and capture such a strong castle as Hope Castle. Out of fear of being beheaded, no soldier dared to speak up about their concerns. Behind her back, word quickly spreads and Queen Joanna becomes known as 'The Mad Queen' amongst her kingdom.

THE WINTER STORM

Captain Witter enters the map room where Queen Joanna spends her days scheming and planning her attack against King Martin. "My Queen, two months ago King Saxton was killed..."

Joanna raises her head. "And who claims the throne?"

"No one as of yet, my Queen. It is not known if he had any heirs."

Queen Joanna taps her chin. "That kingdom touches ours, does it not?"

"It does. It touches our most south-eastern side, but only by a small farm or two at most."

"Send out word to the castle that I, Joanna, Queen of Castile, is the rightful heir to the throne as sister of King Saxton." She looks at Captain Witter with a large smile.

Witter shifts from side to side. "Unfortunately, my Queen, when the kingdom was attacked, there were no survivors. The army killed every last person." The man lowers his head.

"Old Saxton was not a stupid man. He must have had another castle somewhere in his kingdom, perhaps to hide."

"I believe it might be in the southern region of the kingdom. I am not sure where though."

"Assemble the army, the entire army. We are going to take Saxton's kingdom for ourselves! Send out a few scouts to find that other castle...I want it for my own! Make sure that anyone we meet along the way to the castle knows that I am the rightful heir of Saxton's kingdom, and I am to claim what is mine!" She bangs her fist on the desk.

Witter clears his throat. "But my Queen, you are not related to Saxton in any way."

"Those people are too stupid to know that, and by the time they figure it out, it will be too late. They will have to bow to me and fight for me, and then we will take this new kingdom from the young king!"

THE NEW QUEEN

"What about food for the soldiers? It will take more food than what we have in the wagons."

Joanna thinks for a moment and taps her hand along the desk. "Take the food from the workers. Tell them we need it for the soldiers who fight for them. Anyone not willing to give up their food will be made to march alongside the army and will only get what they find along the way." Queen Joanna stands up. "From this day forward, I am King Saxton's last standing relative and next heir to his throne! The Kingdom of Castile will thrive."

Captain Witter bows and leaves the Queen alone in the map room where she continues planning the expansion of her kingdom.

Smoke fills Elizabeth's nose and she jolts awake. She coughs and squints in the semi-darkness for her sister, moving her frizzy hair out of her face. Elizabeth gasps, choking on the smoke and falling out of her hammock, closer to the fire. She grabs a long pole from the wall and pushes on the ceiling vent, unable to open it. She coughs again, but neither Martin nor Samantha awakens from the noise. She drops the pole and pushes on the front door but it stays frozen shut. Her eyes start to water and she coughs again, bringing her linen nightgown over her nose and mouth.

"Wake up!" Elizabeth yells at Martin and Samantha, throwing a clump of hay at her sister in the corner. Samantha jumps awake and coughs at the soot around her. Martin sluggishly sits up and pulls his linen long sleeve shirt over his nose and mouth. He points at the door. "It won't open!" Elizabeth shouts. Elizabeth spots a wooden bucket full of water and tosses the water on top of the fire.

"No!" Martin shouts, jumping off his hammock towards the front door. Martin runs towards the door, slamming his thin body against it. He bounces back and falls on his backside. "We have to get the door open!" he shouts, then coughs. Samantha and Elizabeth rush to his side, all three pushing against the door, opening it enough to see snow piled as high as the door itself. "Push!" Martin encourages and the three push again, moving the door enough for Samantha to stick her hand outside and wedge a piece of wood into the opening. Martin grabs the pole and forces it between the piece of wood and the door. He pulls hard on the pole, opening the door wider. All three stick their heads through the opening, heaving in the crisp winter air as smoke wafts out the door above them.

"Grab another piece of wood," Samantha orders Elizabeth after several deep breaths.

Elizabeth scans the room, finding only small twigs that they had brought with them. "I can't find any!" Elizabeth shouts, panicking. "We're going to die!" she yells, going through the piles of hay.

"My sword!" Martin shouts back at her. Elizabeth grabs the king's two-handed sword leaning against the wall by his hammock and rushes back to the front door.

"Here!" she shouts handing Martin the sword. Elizabeth takes Martin's spot holding the door open and moving to a wall beside the door. He plunges the sword between two planks of wood in the side of the ship and wedges his sword up and down. With the handle of the sword, he bashes the plank on one end until the plank falls free and Martin can wiggle his hand through the new opening.

"Push that side!" he shouts to Elizabeth. She pushes the plank, but it remains unmoved. Samantha joins her and the two push the plank as far as they could reach, but it still would not break free. Martin moves to a lower plank and wiggles it free. The snow sifts into the new opening, filling it quickly. "Hold them as far out as you can!" Martin orders them. They nod and struggle to hold the heavy wooden planks, heaving, under its weight. Martin crawls out the side of the ship, falling into the waist-deep snow.

THE NEW QUEEN

"Are you alright?" Samantha shouts, not seeing where he landed.

"I am not hurt, but I am stuck in snow up to my waist!" he shouts back, rolling to one side to free himself from the snow bank. He crawls towards the vanishing door as snow piles up the door. The King chips away at the snow mounds in front of the door until Samantha squeezes through the opening.

"I thought we were dead!" Samantha shouts, throwing her arms around Martin. Elizabeth follows and hugs them both.

Elizabeth smacks her sister on the arm. "You arse! You were supposed to open the vents during the night to release the smoke! You agreed to do it!"

Samantha clasps her hands over her face. "It was an accident! I was exhausted from our travels, and I passed out! You know I usually wake up during the night, but I just didn't this time!"

Martin sighs. "That's enough, it is over now. We will just have to be more careful next time." The sisters nod. "Samantha, clear the top vent so we can air out the cabin. Elizabeth, make sure the fire does not go out." Martin leaves the cabin and struggles through the waist-high snow towards the tree line.

The King moves more easily in the woods, as the branches protect the forest floor from the heavy snow. King Martin chops off small, dead branches with his sword until he has a large armful of firewood. The cold wind blows settled snowflakes off branches into a sprinkling of snow that coats Martin. He carries the branches back to the ship, stepping in the same steps he made towards the tree line.

Samantha jumps off the top of the ship from the vents and wipes her blackened hands on her nightdress. "Why do we need more wood? The castle is not a far walk from here, I thought?" Samantha asks, grabbing all of the wood from Martin.

THE WINTER STORM

"Samantha, we still do not know if the castle is under siege or has been taken over. I am going to go to the edge of the trees that lay before the castle and look for a sign of some sort. The wood is to keep us warm in the meantime. When I return, we will either be staying here or moving into the castle, but stay warm until I return."

Elizabeth rushes through the door. "What if you don't come back?" She frowns.

"You will wait a day for me, then get the horses out and walk them back to the other castle. Take everything with you- wood, food, everything! Understand?"

Elizabeth glares at him. "No," she starts. "You are the king, and you should not put yourself in any danger. I will go. I saw you and Samantha together so if I die, at least you will have each other!" She rushes past Samantha, her eyes stinging and starts to climb down.

"Enough!" Martin yells. "I am the king, and you will do as I say! Now get in the cabin of the ship before I have your head!" the King commands, pointing vigorously towards the ship. Elizabeth immediately stops and turns back towards Martin, her jaw clenched. "We don't have a lot to keep warm during the night, so I did what I had to do to make sure we all survive. Now keep that fire going and quit acting like a child. I will be back, one way or another." Samantha and Elizabeth do as they are told and carry armfuls of branches into the room and close the door behind them. Martin straightens his leather coat before heading for the forest that separates the ship from the castle.

Martin heads for the tree line again, following the same path he took earlier. He heads towards the channel, following the salty scent of the cliff side. He stops in his tracks and sniffs the air. "Pork?" the king turns around and raises his nose up into the sky and sniffs again. "Bacon! Where did they get bacon?" Martin starts

THE NEW QUEEN

back towards the ship. "The castle isn't going anywhere, anyway, and no one will attack us in this snow," he says, climbing aboard the ship and brushing off the snow from his wet leather pants. The King opens the door and looks in. "Where did you get bacon?"

Simon walks with difficulty through the snow accompanied by six other men towards Saxton's old castle. Simon wanted to see for himself who and what was left of the palace. Everyone was in their leather armor with their swords sheathed and heads bowed as they fought the wind. Simon tried a few times to look ahead to see where they were headed without much success. Out of the corner of Simon's eye, he catches one of his men slipping on something, but he quickly gets up and marches onward.

After some time, they reach Saxton's kingdom. The large castle was burned almost entirely to the ground. No stone was left in place and no bodies or people are anywhere to be seen. Simon orders a man to start a fire and to pitch the tent they brought with them to dry out somewhat. Three of the other men set up stations around the camp for protection. Simon and the last two men search the rubble for anything of value.

"It feels eerie finding a silver platter," one guard says, holding the platter over his head. Simon glances but says nothing. He walks through what he remembered to be the main hall; nothing but stones laid about as he finds the large stone fireplace that was once the centerpiece of the room. It still stood, slightly damaged, with char marks and covered in debris. Beside the fireplace is a large pile of firewood so he carried it to the tent for firewood.

A loud crash sounds from the castle and Simon drops the wood and charges back into the castle. The fireplace rests on its side, large chunks of stone missing around the frame. He looks

THE WINTER STORM

around the fireplace and notices large footprints in the snow. "So someone is here?" Simon asks, as his men follow behind Simon.

A bush moves and Simons' eye catches it as he turns and heads towards it. An arrow flies by Simon's shoulder as he takes cover behind some stone rubble. The falling snow blocks Simon's view ahead and he squints through the flurry. "Head that way." Simon points then turns to see his man lying on the ground, impaled by the arrow that nearly hit him.

Simon moves beside his guard, pulling a fallen table closer for cover. The man lays on his back, shivering, as blood surrounds the arrow in his chest. "You will be alright," Simon repeats as the man dies in Simons' arms. Simon slowly lowers the body to the ground and raises his sword and shield. He races towards the area where the arrow was shot from, jumping over what was left of the fireplace. Simon lands on both feet and searches for someone aiming at him but saw none. He turns his attention to look for footprints and starts to run in their direction. As the snow continues falling, the snow quickly hides the tracks of the assailant and Simon loses the trail. Simon stands up straight and takes a good look around but sees no one. Another guard appears in view from the direction they were heading. "Did you see anyone?"

"No. I was barely able to make you two out in this snow," the guard responds.

"Someone shot at us and..." Simon looks back at the dead man. "And he got hit." He pauses for a moment. The guards lower their heads for their fallen comrade before spreading out to search the rubble for anyone who might be there. Simon walks back over to the dead man and kneels down beside him. He studies the arrow and notices that it was made by an amateur. The shaft was twisted with small signs of twigs all over it. Simon yanks the arrow out and looks at the tip. It was made of rock and shale with a piece of twine to hold it in place. Simon had never seen anything like it before,

THE NEW QUEEN

besides the iron tips he's used to seeing. It must have been a lucky shot by the looks of the shaft alone. No one could shoot straight with this shaft. He looks around once again. Maybe a child? Like Andrew, the king killer. Simon lays the arrow on the man's chest and crosses his hands over it as if holding it in place.

A guard approaches beside Simon. "There's no one about anymore, sir." The guard looks around at the carnage. "With this many thick boulders and stones, one could build another castle."

Simon stands and looks around at the same boulders and stones the guard referred to. "Yes, we could." He pauses and stares at the stone. "We will have two men on guard all night. It's too bad we never brought any crossbows with us."

"Are we staying the night? We are not far from Quarry castle, sir, we could make it back before long."

"We have someone hunting us. Simon pauses as he looks around, making sure what he is saying sinks into the guard so he will pass it along. "Best not be moving in the open, for they would have a clean shot at us and we don't have anything to shoot back with. We stay and pull a few stones close to the tent for protection. I think two on each side of the tent should make them high enough." Simon retreats into the tent, leaving his guards to transfer and disperse the stones around the campsite.

Chapter 11
SEARCH

Mark wakes up with his face in the snow. He slowly lifts his head and looks around at the snow-covered trees around him, the smell of pine filling his nose. He slowly rises and a dusting of snow slides off his body. A sharp pain jolts throughout his lower body and he hunches over, grabbing at his tailbone. He looks around in the forest but sees no one else. The thick, overgrown bushes block out most of the sunlight where he stands. He searches for his sword, finding it only a few feet away from where he was lying. He sheaths his sword and walks towards the bushes when he spots someone in the distance. He takes cover, crouching behind the bushes.

Mark waits until the man turns away before sneaking closer to the stranger, dashing behind wide trees. Each time the stranger looks away, Mark shuffles closer, remaining in the shadows of the trees. Within fifteen feet of the stranger, Mark pulls out a small knife from his boot and waits for the stranger to turn away again, when suddenly another man joins the target.

THE NEW QUEEN

"You think this king will help us?" the second man asks the first.

"Why do we need his help?" answers the first man. "We are supposed to be the best army in these here parts. I think we should just forget this king and move around to fight the French. They will still believe we are in the North but we can march all the way around like the king said, and we will take Paris without a war, and the French will have to surrender." The two men walk away as the echoes of approaching voices sound over the hills.

Mark rushes behind a bush closer to the army to get a better look. The large army prepares to leave their camp: rolling up tents, packing equipment onto horses and wagons, and diffusing their campfires. Mark's heart races as he tries to remember what happened before he passed out. "Wait, we were ambushed. I remember fighting and sending the King with Samantha and Elizabeth." He pauses, thinking about what happened next. "Then I woke up here...but where is here?" He peers through a small opening from the treed area, studying the army. "English!" he surprises himself. "These men are English. Did they ambush us?"

Mark quietly retraces his path from the army and towards the channel. He travels along the channel towards what he believes is the way to Quarry Castle. The wind grows stronger and colder. It is only now when Mark realizes just how wet and cold he is. Mark's pants and vest turn stiff from the dampness as each step becomes harder to move in. His freezing hair slaps the back of his head as his cheeks and nose start to bleed from the frost. Mark becomes dizzy. He staggers and falls to one knee but fights to stand, using his sword to lean on. Snow begins to blow, blocking his sight as the clouds cover the sun. Mark shoves his sword into the frozen ground and kneels in front of it, holding the handle with both hands. He closes his eyes as the snow whips his blistering cheeks, nose and lips.

SEARCH

"Mark?" a voice calls out.

Mark turns around and squints at the approaching figure through the snowstorm.

Gregory wakes in the early morning to survey how much damage the snowstorm during the night has caused on the castle. He walks to the front gate and takes a deep breath before stepping outside. Snow piled up as high as the gate itself, nearly impossible to get through. He searches for an opening in the snow where he can have someone start clearing the frozen mess. Gregory sighs and starts to climb up the staircase to the wall-walk. He slips up the frozen stairs, holding onto the ice-covered walls for support. He slips and falls several times before reaching the top step, panting and hunched over. He steps onto the wall-walk and slips, landing on his back. Snow sprinkles onto his rosy face.

Gregory crawls along the wall-walk with his sword dragging beside him, until he stands above the front gate. He looks out towards the tree line and the snow-covered fields, untouched by any prints of any kind. The snow camouflages the open land and the channel, creating an illusion of one continuous blanket of snow, but Gregory remains familiar to the land, knowing where the field and channel start and end. Pleased that no signs of life have traveled the land, he makes his way back into the castle. Before landing on the second step from the top, he hears the crunching of snow and a breaking of some wood echoing off the castle walls. He rushes back and scans the white landscape: around the castle, the front gate, the wall-walk, and the staircase, but all he sees is snow. At once, he carefully makes his way down the slippery steps, waddling and gripping the wall with each step.

He finally reaches the bottom and exhales a sigh of relief before shuffling through the deep snow to the front door. As Gregory

THE NEW QUEEN

reaches the front door, it swings open, almost knocking him back. "You!" he shouts to the guard, catching his balance. "Get five guards and go to the tree line on the north side. See if you can find any tracks."

"In this snow?" the guard asks in disbelief. "With all due respect, but that is nonsense! Any tracks made are already covered."

"Don't make me ask again. I saw something out there, and we need answers." Gregory lies.

"Like what?" the guard asks, shifting from foot to foot.

"That's what we need to find out. Now hurry!"

The man turns away and does as ordered, gathering five men and exiting out the side gate into waist-deep snow. Gregory stands at the side gate with a few archers, and one man watches above from the wall-walk. Gregory watches the small party as they battle the piles of snow towards the tree line. He was relieved that the small party finally make it to the tree line, where less snow was piled under the trees. They stomp on the ground in their leather boots, shaking off the clumps of snow that stick to their bodies. They draw their swords and search the forest in silence, staying close to each other. Moving out of sight of Gregory. The frozen ground of leaves, twigs, branches, and mud, untainted with snow, hides the men's footsteps and from any trackers. They moved towards the northwest, near the end of the tree line when they hear a noise coming from that direction. One man crouches down and creeps his way towards the edge of the tree line, lurking among the larger trees for cover. A snow drifts piled as high as the man himself, blocking his view beyond it. Instead of climbing the dune, he scampers to a large tree nearby and quietly climbs the thicker branches until he is high enough to see over the dune. A large army packs up to move out of their camp, an army he does not recognize. Their campfires are reduced to ashes, and animal bones scatter the ground. The vast army, as many as there are, march in silence,

SEARCH

seeming to know the land and invasion strategies only too well. The guard, wide-eyed, quietly lowers himself from the branches and heads back to the four other men. He stops in front of the wandering men and waves them over to a substantial collection of bushes. He quickly whispers what he saw. "There's a large army just over that dune who just packed up their campsite. I don't recognize this army, but there are several men. Do you think they would march against the castle, even in this deep snow? I mean, they could lie down, and no one would see them. You could move right beside the castle, and no one would know." The men stare at each other with wide eyes. Realizing this could be the army's plan, they scamper back to the castle moving as quickly as they can through the deep snow.

Martin pushes through the waist-high snow in the tree-line, where the snow piles higher than any snow hill he has ever seen. Martin uses fallen branches, large flat slate, and his sword to chip away at the blocks of ice and snow. He scoops away the debris with his hands, protected by leather and wool-lined gloves. He digs upward on a diagonal until he breaks the side of the snow hill where the sunlight meets his gaze. He pokes his head through the side of the snow hill, and Martin pauses there for a moment, heaving and wiping the sweat off his forehead. He grabs the stick and uses it to pull himself out of the hole.

Off to the side, near the end of the valley, he watches a collection of soldiers heading towards the castle. Martin ducks down. "Are they running to attack the castle or to take back the castle? I can't tell who they are..." Martin rushes down the side of the hill towards a group of trees to follow the footprints of the unknown men. The sound of snow crunching and the murmur of people talking starts ahead of the path. The murmur grows to a rumble, and the

THE NEW QUEEN

multiple voices confirm that a large army marches their way up the path towards his castle. King Martin backs further into the thickets.

"Did Simon keep these men at bay all this time and could not send for help because they stood in the path?" Martin whispers. He watches the army march and sing in good spirits, patting each other on the back and playfully punching each other on the shoulders. He listens to the army sing war songs Martin has never heard before. His heart races and he backs up even farther until he reaches the end of the tree line and races back to the tunnel he dug. Flustered and panicked, he crawls back into the tunnel to think in peace. He crawls quickly through the tunnel and pokes his head up to look around. "No soldiers?" he asks, searching the barren landscape. The king sits atop the tunnel, folding his arms across his chest. "Why not attack the castle here?" Martin asks himself. "Richard camped on the other side of the tree line in the west, so perchance this army is doing the exact same thing?" A scratching noise echoes from his tunnel, inching closer to him. He squints into the black hole and draws his two swords strapped to his back.

"Martin is that you?" someone whispers.

Martin squints in the tunnel. "Elizabeth, is that you?"

Suddenly, Elizabeth's giant red hair emerges from the tunnel as her flushed face meets his gaze. "I told you to stay with your sister!" Martin hisses with both relief and frustration.

"She did! We are both here," Samantha answers him, squeezing next to her sister. She looks around the tunnel. "Are you building some type of snow fort?" Samantha pushes on the tunnel walls.

Elizabeth joins in. "You should have invited us if you just wanted to play in the snow."

Martin slips back into the tunnel, sitting with his back against the snowy wall to face the sisters. "You two should have stayed in the boat!" Martin hisses in a louder whisper.

SEARCH

"We thought something might have happened to you," Elizabeth answers. "And what would be done with us if we let you get captured or killed?"

Martin clenches his jaw in frustration, then places a finger to his lips. "Look," Martin starts, "there's a large army not far from here, and I think they are going to march against the castle. I saw some men running towards the castle, but I can't tell if they are our men or not. Now please, you two have to go back now. It's too dangerous for you both, and I need to figure this out."

"We will go back if you come with us. What if someone finds us?" Elizabeth asks.

"And what if another boar comes? You know what happened to me the last time I came across one," Samantha adds.

Martin remembers the way Samantha looked when she was attacked by the boar and shakes his head. "Alright, I will go back with you two, and we will stay the night in the boat and figure out what we should do."

Elizabeth claps her hands and they all crawl back through the tunnel with Samantha leading the way. Before crawling through the tunnel, Martin quickly pokes his head out through the opening one final time to check for the intruders. The fields remain barren. With a sigh, he follows the sisters through the tunnel back to the ship.

When they arrive back at the ship, more snow piled in front of the door. They each chop away the chunks of snow and ice with sharpened sticks and Martin uses his sword. Martin notices that the sisters patched up the roof when they had pulled away the planks to allow the smoke to escape. Inside the room rests a large pile of dried firewood which the sisters already collected.

"Where did that come from?" Martin nervously asks, wondering if it belonged to someone else.

THE NEW QUEEN

"Elizabeth found a few logs in the trees, and we cut them up for firewood," Samantha tells him.

"You think we are incapable of getting firewood?" Elizabeth snaps back, holding up the two-handed sword she used to cut the logs, now with a few nicks out of the blade.

Martin shrugs. "Where are the horses?"

"Oh, they were stinking up the place, so we moved them to their own boat. After all, there are five boats here, you know? They poop out more hay than they eat," Elizabeth says as she starts a fire. "And I made a small shelter to keep the snow away from the vent on top so we can have a fire all night now."

Samantha moves a large piece of meat above the fire as she hangs it from the top of the boat. "This large rabbit will be done by nightfall," she says with a smile. "We followed its tracks near the tree line." Elizabeth places a log under the rabbit.

Martin takes his two-handed sword and shakes his head at the damaged blade. He pulls out his sharpening stone and sits with his back against the wall, facing the fire, and begins running the stone along the edge to sharpen his sword.

Elizabeth widens her eyes. "Do you think the castle has fallen? Will they head to the other castle now? Should we stay here or even try to go back? What if they capture us? They did capture the five Black Army men we had leading us, remember? I think we better stay here for safety." Elizabeth stops, noticing Martin's soaking wet clothes and bright red hands. "You're all wet, Martin. If you don't get warm, you will surely get sick with a fever and die. You must get closer to the fire right now." She kneels down to help him move closer and feels that she too is wet. Her cold, wet clothes cling to her body, as the fire melts the ice. "We are all soaking," she says out loud. "Samantha, we better get closer to the fire, too."

"We are not going to die from being wet," Martin says, shaking his head. He moves closer to the fire anyways.

SEARCH

Samantha returns with some bread she made with Elizabeth back at the castle. She pours Martin some ale. "It's all we have," Samantha says, handing Martin the chalice. Martin smiles at her and takes a drink, even though he hates ale. Martin surveys the tiny boat to see how the sisters have made use of the space. The room is divided into smaller sections: a portion for a kitchen, another portion like a bedroom, and a portion for storage to pile goods as they dry out meats and hang a cauldron filled with a stew. "It's mostly meat and some potatoes and spices that I brought with me from the camp," Samantha says, noticing Martin eyeing the cauldron. Samantha slumps beside Martin, holding his ale while he eats.

"So who do you think they are?" Elizabeth asks.

"I don't know," Martin pauses, "but they spoke English, so they can't be the French or the Romans," Martin replies with a mouthful of stew.

"So we have no idea who they might be?"

Martin swallows. "Elizabeth, I have no idea! I told you that!"

"Are they from England?" Samantha chimes in.

"Yes, they must be!" Elizabeth yells out. "They have come to get the men left behind in Saxton's castle. All of the cooks and the other men that are outside of our walls. Maybe they came to take over the castle just to give their men a place to take shelter."

Martin nods. "I don't think they would go to war just for some cooks and maidens, but it could be the English, that's for sure."

"We should talk to the English and ask what they want," Elizabeth suggests.

"We?" The king asks.

"Yes, we. You, me and Samantha." Elizabeth takes a swig of ale.

"No way, keep me out of it," Samantha says, waving her hand in the air.

"If I decide to talk to that army, it will be me and me alone."

THE NEW QUEEN

"You know you need me there to support you and help you reason with them. You just do as they want."

"That will not be happening and you will remain with your sister, and not interfere with any negotiating that I must do," Martin clarifies, staring at Elizabeth. He stands up and hands Samantha his empty bowl. Martin leaves the fire and lays on some blankets in the far corner to sleep.

"I will go get more wood for the fire to keep me busy," Elizabeth says, picking up a crossbow and walking out the door before Samantha can object. She races outside and makes her way towards the channel with her hood pulled over her head. Once she finds the opening of the trees, she dashes through it. "Look for wood...what dumb person would look for wood in this storm, anyways?" Elizabeth shoves her way through the snow towards Quarry castle, following the footprint-covered path. "I have to see if the castle has fallen so I can tell Martin and then he will see that I am worthy to be Queen." Elizabeth pulls her hood tighter and pushes through the wind.

Chapter 12
A Witch Among Us

Simon and his party of Black Army soldiers returns from his usual scouting trip around Quarry castle, searching for a rumored army camped out nearby. Simon wears his leather armor as his normal everyday wear, well the black army soldiers wore their black heavy leather armor cloaks over their chain mail armor. Gregory awaits by the front gates for Simon and his party to arrive. Gregory, along with every man in the castle dresses in full armor while every archer remains positioned on the frozen wall-walk. Simon enters through the front gates and Gregory rushes over to meet him as he dismounts his horse. "You were not gone long. What's out there?"

"The man I interrogated spoke the truth... there's a huge army, indeed. At least five thousand men, well-armed but not trained at all. I sent two scouts to keep watch over them so if they plan to attack, we will have some notice."

"How do you know that the army is not well-trained?" Gregory asks taking, the reins from Simon's hands.

THE NEW QUEEN

"The men march well together, but they lack discipline. They drag their swords and shuffle their feet...some even use their swords as a staff while walking."

"Disciplined or not, do you think they can fight?" Gregory pats the horse while Simon turns and yells orders for hot water to melt the ice on the wall-walk.

"Any man can fight, but something tells me we would have a winning chance against them." He looks up at the men on the wall-walk. "Be sure that we do not light the torches tonight. Best to be hidden from sight as much as possible." Simon adds, leaving Gregory in the keep.

Mark rests in the forest surrounded by a few prisoners and what remains of the king's guard from the small battle they had. Scouts remain searching for the King, despite the heavy snowfall. Mark is second in command after Simon, and his duty is to guard Hope Castle, where he is also the king's guard.

"Sir, the scouts returned with no news about the missing King," a guard reports to Mark.

"Do you think they made it to the castle?" Mark asks.

"That army was between the castle and us...I doubt very much that they made it anywhere safe with this storm holding us here." The guard warms his hands over the fire. "Maybe they turned back towards Hope Castle...I mean, if the large army was here and they could not reach Quarry Castle, then maybe they turned back?"

Mark walks over to the edge of the forest and looks out at the clearing. Snow continues falling and the temperature drops. Some of the soldiers begin building walls with the snow in hopes of blocking in some of the heat from the small fires.

A WITCH AMONG US

Mark looks towards the channel as the snow flurry intensifies. "The channel! They would have crossed the channel and looked for safety with Rollo!"

"Rollo?" the guard asks.

"He is the chief of the Vikings. King Martin and Rollo are allies. Rollo would have taken him in. We will have to find someone to go and see if his majesty is there." Mark looks back out at the falling snow. "But for tonight, we rest." Mark turns back to his camp and sees the rest of his party sleeping on blankets around the small fires. The snow walls block out the light from the fires, so the party remains hidden in the dark. Mark scans the area once more for intruders before falling asleep next to some guards.

Simon approaches the channel shores in search of enemy scouts when he hears the horn from Quarry Castle. He looks back at the castle then to his party of twenty men. "Quick, everyone into the forest!" he orders. The group fights their way through the deep snow and into the forest, not one hundred yards from the castle. "The horn means they are under attack, but I don't see anyone," Simon announces.

One guard walks towards Simon. "On the far end of this forest are our old ships that we can use for shelter in case of an attack."

Simon nods. "That's a good idea. Have five men go and scout it out to be safe, then have one other guard to make the trip back to the castle to report what is happening."

Five men travel through the forest towards the ships when they catch a glimpse of someone nearby. They fall silent and split up to capture the stranger, staying among the thick trees. As they slowly approach, they hear humming from the hooded stranger. One guard jumps out when the girl turns around and aims a crossbow at him.

THE NEW QUEEN

"Drop your sword," she demands.
"Lady Elizabeth?" he asks with surprise.

King Martin returns after looking for Elizabeth and warms his hands by the fire. "Where has she gone? I cannot find any trace of her!" Martin shouts angrily.

"She can be quite stubborn at times, but she will return, eventually. I remember when she ran away from King Richard... father had promised her to the king for some food and a deer, and my, was he surprised when she returned home. Father gave her a good beating and that's when we had to leave. If we didn't, then King Richard would have thrown us all in the dungeons or beheaded us all!" Samantha lowers her head.

"Did your father give you away to your husband?" Martin asks, drinking hot water.

"Yes, but only after he caught my husband snogging me, though. He chased Paul away using the horsewhip, then he turned and gave me a few of my own. He told me I was no good after a man snogs me, especially before marriage." She sighs. "I guess it doesn't matter. Paul never got to see me after we were married. He went straight to war and never came back. My husband was a fine man; caring and thoughtful. He even brought me flowers once, but I had to tell father I picked them for him." Samantha wriggles her nose at the memory, then grabs some ale and bread from a handkerchief on the table.

Martin frowns and clears his throat. "I'm worried she could be hurt or captured by the army." He stands up and looks through the holes in the wood when he sees a Black Army soldier approaching the door. Martin rushes to the door and opens it.

"Your majesty, I have orders to escort you back to the castle." The Black Army soldier coughs and waits for Martin's response.

A WITCH AMONG US

The king looks back at Samantha. "Pack up, we are going home."

The soldier enters the ship and warms his hands by the fire. His hands are wrinkled, and his fingernails are yellow and blackened around the edges. Samantha looks at the man, then at Martin, and shuffles around the room to gather their belongings.

"We will have to find Elizabeth before we can leave," Martin tells the soldier.

"No need, sire. She is safe," the Black Army soldier confirms.

Samantha clasps her hand to her mouth, and Martin sighs with relief. "As long as she is safe," Samantha pushes.

"She is. We found her or its more like she found us. She took a guard by surprise but either way she is safe now." the Black Army soldier responds.

After a long, silent walk with their horses through the deep snow and ice, the castle emerges in the distance. Martin notices the trampled snow around the front of the castle with the drawbridge lowered. The king wonders if it was the army they saw that trampled the snow or his own men. He looks around towards the treed area and sees more trampled snow but not answering his question to himself. Simon stands on the bridge, waiting for his King to approach.

Elizabeth glances at the shivering scout as he rubs his hands along his arms. She walks to the side and bends over, pulling out some dry branches and enough flint for one more small fire. She rubs the flint together until some sparks shoot out and catch fire on the branches.

The scout turns around at the smell of smoke and approaches Elizabeth and the small fire. He moves quickly over to her. "You started a fire?"

THE NEW QUEEN

"Yes, you looked cold so I started a small fire so we can warm ourselves before continuing," she lies. They both warm their hands around the fire when Elizabeth grabs a small twig and draws circles in the snow as she waits for the scout to warm up. Elizabeth notices something shimmering in the snow. "Look!" She crawls over to it and pulls a sword out of the ground.

The scout stands up and walks over to her. "How did you see that in the ground?"

Elizabeth shrugs. "I just saw it under the leaves and mud and pulled it out from the snow."

"You can see under the ground?" The scout asks, his eyes widening.

"No! I saw the handle sticking out of the ground."

The scout shakes his head. "I was right here beside you and there was no sword in the ground. How did the sword get there?"

Elizabeth glares at him. "I didn't pull it out of the air. It was right there, and you didn't see it, but I did. Is this sword worth something?" she asks, turning the sword over.

"There is no decay on the sword. No damage, and it looks new, so who would leave a new sword in the ground?"

Elizabeth studies the sword and places it back on the snow. She shrugs. "It was probably left here after a fight." Elizabeth picks up the branch again and continues drawing designs in the snow.

The guard shakes his head. "There was no battle here or nearby...so tell me, how did you make this sword come out of the ground like that?" He places his hand upon his knife strapped to his waist.

King Martin rides into the small courtyard. "Is everyone alright?" he shouts to the small crowd.

Jade rushes to help the king off his horse. "All is well, sire. We saw a man on a horse and overreacted by sounding the horn, but that guard now knows better."

"And the Great Army on the south wall?" Martin asks.

Jade walks over to Samantha and takes the reins of her horse. "My lady," he bows. Samantha hops off the horse and curtsies to Jade. He bows again.

Simon approaches Jade. "Hey! Go and feed the horses. Have Douglass give you a hand." He waits until Jade leaves before speaking to the king. "How are you, Martin?"

"It's been awhile, Simon. I sent many men to see how you were doing, but none ever returned." Martin frowns.

"No one ever arrived, sire. I would have sent word but there were two large armies not far from here and I did not want to risk it. Most of Great Army have left by ships at nightfall."

Martin nods. "Two armies? Who are they?" He pauses and looks around the castle.

"There is a lot to tell you, sire. We are not under attack, so do not worry. I am sure you two are hungry, so let's get you some food." Simon looks from Martin to Samantha.

"It seems so small compared to Hope Castle now," Martin notices as he examines the courtyard.

Simon leads them into the Great Hall and seats himself at a nearby empty table. A few maidens sweep the floors and wipe the tables while some children run between them, chasing one another.

"Are you sure Elizabeth is alright?" Samantha asks, taking a seat next to Martin.

Simon hesitates before answering. "I've been told she was seen doing magic."

Martin and Samantha glance at each other. "What kind of magic?" Martin asks nervously.

THE NEW QUEEN

"Yes, what was she doing exactly? She's not even good at cooking, forget magic," Samantha adds.

"She was playing with magic, using it to start fires and even making a sword out of nothing! She had a wand, your majesty."

"Are you saying that my sister is a witch?" Samantha glares at Simon.

"I know she's your sister and a friend to the king, but I cannot argue with what my man saw. That big army you saw...she just made them leave for no reason. They saw her, then got up and left."

"You're lying," Samantha hisses, her eyes full of angry tears.

Simon sighs. "I'm sorry." He stands up and leaves the room.

"She's no witch!" Samantha yells at him, then turns to Martin.

The king sighs. "We will have to know more." Martin places his hand onto Samantha's shoulder.

"She is not a witch! I will place my life on that!" Samantha claims, smashing her fists on the table. She shakes the king's hand off of her. "He's lying!"

Martin shifts uncomfortably in his seat. "Simon's guard has evidence and he would not just cause blasphemy."

Two maidens carry trays of roast duck and boiled potatoes, and two goblets of ale. The king and Samantha nibble at the duck and poke at the potatoes in silence. Samantha sniffles and stands up. "I need to be alone for a bit. Maybe there's something in the kitchen I can do." She leaves her almost full plate of duck and exits the Great Hall.

Martin slumps on the bench and pushes his plate away. He walks upstairs to his bedchamber, thinking about the accusations against Elizabeth. He pushes the door open and finds six children asleep in his bed. The fire blazes in the fireplace, crackling and spewing sparks along the stone floor. Martin grabs a wool blanket folded at the end of his bed and places it on the ground next to the fireplace, wrapping half of the blanket over himself. He listens to the crackling fire, thinking about Elizabeth, until he falls asleep.

A scout returns from Mark's small party as they cross the frozen channel through the cold wind. "Sir there's another army moving away from Quarry castle. It's not as large as the first one we saw, but still a good size." The scouts hesitate before continuing. "I believe them to be Spaniards."

Mark stops his horse and turns around. "Why would the Spaniards be so far North? They would have had to travel through the French territories as well." The scout shrugs his shoulders and Mark continues. "Are you sure they were Spaniards?"

"They wore Spanish clothing, spoke Spanish, and carried Spanish shields."

"If the Spanish and English are here, then Quarry Castle has little hope of surviving." Mark turns his horse around when a sudden pain shoots up his back. He falls off the horse and lurches over as the nausea intensifies.

"Sire, are you awake?" Douglass asks, shaking Martin's shoulder. Martin opens one eye and looks at Douglass. "There is much to talk about, and things you need to know."

Simon walks into the room. "Douglass, get the king some breakfast before he starts his day." Douglass nods towards Simon and leaves the room. Simon turns back to Martin and raises an eyebrow. "Why are you sleeping on the floor and not on your bed?" Simon asks, glancing at the empty bed.

THE NEW QUEEN

"Children were already sleeping in it when I arrived and I didn't want to wake them." Martin stretches and lifts the blanket off of him.

Simon kicks the bed frame. "Blast these guards! Don't they understand that no children are allowed to just go where they please? I'll make sure these kids don't get in your way again."

"It's really quite alright, Simon. I don't mind." Martin yawns and tosses the blanket back on his bed. "Any news about Elizabeth?"

"None, your majesty. I will ask one of my men to have her go through a trial before sentencing her." Simon hands Martin his boots by the bed. "We can't have a witch about, now can we?"

Martin grabs the boots and looks away. "Yes, that is true," he answers slowly. "Is there no other way, Simon? I mean, I know there are witches, but Elizabeth? I know her well."

"Have you ever seen a witch?"

"No'" Martin says in a quiet tone.

"The next thing you need to know this morning is that there are two armies about our castle. One of the armies is not well trained and the other, I know nothing about."

"I see...well that's good," Martin says, distracted by the news about Elizabeth. "Where is Elizabeth now?"

Simon frowns. "Did you hear anything I just said?" Martin nods. "You need to have your priorities in check, sire." Martin paces the room and Simon sighs. "I had her taken to the other castle so that she cannot put any spells on you. But by the looks of it, I think she might have already."

Martin stops pacing. "What do you mean?"

"I mean a love potion of sorts. It's blocking you from thinking like a king."

Martin folds his arms. "I never loved her, Simon, at least not like that. Maybe as a sister, but that's about it."

A WITCH AMONG US

"I believe that's how love potions start, sire. You think of her as a sister, then you slowly fall for her. The next thing you know, you cannot think of anything or anyone else except her, until you are eventually under her spell and you are taking orders from the witch. Don't you see what she's doing to you?" Simon widens his eyes with concern.

Martin rests on the bed and places his forehead in his hands. Between the news of the Great Army and Elizabeth, Martin turns anxious. "I need to think of a plan," Martin whispers, more to himself than to Simon.

Simon stands by the fire, his arms folded across his chest. "Okay, here's the plan," Simon starts. "I will ride to Saxton's old castle to see if there is anything left there that we might use. I will be leaving henceforth, and I will be taking the best Black Army men with me, whomever remains."

Martin nods in agreement. "Very well. Let's start there."

"I heard that the other castle may have been attacked, but I cannot be sure if it is true or not," Simon mentions before leaving the room. He slows his pace as he passes Douglass carrying a tray to Martin's room. They stare at each other, then Simon shoves Douglass against a wall. Simon glares at him, his face inches away from Douglass. "Not a word to him, or I will have your head."

Douglass remains still against the wall, clutching onto the tray, until Simon exists the hallway. He clears his throat and exhales before walking into Martin's room. He smiles and opens the door as Martin changes into a clean shirt. "Here you go, your majesty," Douglass says with a dry mouth. He places the tray of quail meat and a glass of hot water with mint leaves next to the king then quickly closes the door. "Sire, a lot has happened since you left," he whispers.

"Yes, and I have a story for you, too," Martin says, rubbing his leg.

THE NEW QUEEN

Douglass shakes his head. "No, you don't understand. Someone has betrayed us!" Douglass whispers.

"What do you mean?"

"Someone wants Elizabeth to be a witch so she can't get close to you, or they want her out of the way," Douglass confesses, unsure of what to say. "Whatever the case, it is untrue!"

Simon enters the room and gives Douglass a stern look before turning his attention to the king.

"Lady Elizabeth has been accused of being a witch, and I believe what has been said," Douglass spills out.

"I want to go and see Elizabeth today to talk with her, and ensure that what you both speak is true," Martin says looking from Simon to Douglass.

"You doubt me?" Simon asks, frowning at the king.

"Not that. I just cannot believe that Elizabeth is a witch," Martin responds.

Simon nods. "Let me get the guards and we will head straight for Hope Castle, so you can see what we see." Simon turns to Douglass. "Go and gather a small party to escort us to the castle." Douglass nods and leaves the room before glancing at Martin one last time.

Martin agrees to the plan and he heads down with Simon to gather his horse. The king joins the group of guards and they start their way towards Hope Castle. The group slows their horses once they cross the fields.

Martin rides up next to Douglass. "You're very quiet," Martin says, breaking the silence.

Douglass looks around, making sure he is not being watched. "I do not believe Elizabeth is a witch. I think someone has something against her." He pauses and looks around once more before continuing. "It might even be Simon," he adds in a quieter voice. Then he rides his horse ahead of Martin and joins the other guards.

The king rides in silence, thinking about what Douglass said, as his guards continue surrounding him. Simon notices Martin alone and joins him, slowing his horse to fall back from the other guards.

Martin turns to Simon. "Do you really think Elizabeth is a witch?"

Simon looks straight ahead at Hope Castle. "I have seen a witch before. She, too, said she was not a witch, but the guards knew better and proved her to be one."

"You did not answer the question. Do you think Elizabeth is a witch?" Martin repeats.

"The man that came to me has been very loyal to us, and he was quite frightened by the events. I have to go by his word."

The king pushes his horse forward and the party rides most of the day to get to Hope Castle. Martin keeps a distance from Simon and Douglass, but not far enough for Simon to notice. Martin becomes lost in thought as he debates between what Douglass and Simon both told him.

Once the party reaches the castle, Martin finds Douglass and Jade already waiting by the front gate, having ridden ahead of everyone.

"Take the King to the Great Hall. I will bring Elizabeth to you," Simon says to Martin as he dismounts his horse. Martin nods and some men escort him to the Great Hall. He slumps into the large throne while maidens serve him cured beef and beans.

The doors swing open and Simon drags Elizabeth to the throne. Her shackles scrape along the stone floor and echo through the hall. Dirt covers her face and dried tears leave streams down her cheeks. Black Army members march into the room and stand on either side of Elizabeth and Simon.

THE NEW QUEEN

"Martin," she whispers falling to her knees.

A soldier whips her back and Elizabeth screams. "Quiet!" the soldier yells. "Speak only when you're spoken to, witch!"

Martin jolts up and raises his hand. "There will be no need for the whip in here!" He walks closer to Elizabeth. The guards pull hard on her chains and her head hangs downward. Simon grabs a fistful of her hair and pulls her head back, exposing her face.

"See, your majesty. The witch tried to change her look to look like her older sister. She said you are in love with her sister and she wants to control you!"

"That's not true!" Elizabeth yells. "I look the same as I always do!"

The guard yells and whips her again on the back. "Don't speak, witch! I told you!" the guard shouts, then gives her a second lashing. Elizabeth screams, but Simon ignores it.

Martin looks at Simon with anger on his face. "If she is whipped once more, you will get one as well!" Martin shouts.

"Can't you see her spell is working, sire? Her face already started to change when we stopped her." Simon continues to hold her hair in his fist, and he pulls harder.

Martin walks slowly around Elizabeth and looks at her closely. Her face is darker, her eyes are blackened, and she looks more frail than usual. "She seems smaller somehow?"

"It takes a lot of energy for her to cast a spell, your majesty, and since we stopped her in the middle of casting one, her energy is low," Simon adds.

Tears well in Elizabeth's eyes. Her lips are chapped and cracked. "I am not a witch! You must believe me, don't you?" she pleads.

Martin leans in closer to her. "If it were anyone else accusing you of being a witch, I would dismiss it, but it's Simon. I trust him." Martin says in a hushed tone then backs away from Elizabeth.

A WITCH AMONG US

"Please, please I am not a witch! Martin please, I am not a witch!" she cries as they drag her out of the hall. The doors close and Martin is left alone with Simon.

"I am sorry Martin," Simon says, placing his hand onto Martin's shoulder. "If I did not see her in that state, I would have not believed her to be a witch. Now I am certain that she must be," Simon assures his king. Martin blinks away his tears. "We must have a trial and test her to be sure that she is a witch," Simon says.

Martin looks at Simon. "What tests are there?"

"We tie weights to her feet and have her thrown into the water. If she sinks then she's a witch, but if she floats then she is not. We can also burn her at the stake, and if she burns, she is not a witch, but to be sure, we must cut off her head before we light the fire."

Martin sighs. "Is there no other way Simon? I mean really that sounds terrible," Martin says, facing the floor. "Schedule the trial for next month, that way if there is any way to save her, we can."

"As you command, your majesty." Simon bows and leaves Martin.

"Everyone out!" the king yells. A guard waits by the door as the last servant leaves. Martin looks up at the guard. "You, too. Leave me." The guard bows and closes the door, leaving Martin to quietly weep in his throne.

Chapter 13
TO BE FREE

Martin awakes in his bedchamber at Hope Castle. He kicks the damp blankets off his sweaty and tense body. He rubs his dry, red eyes and rolls out of bed, a pang of pain shoots u his leg where he was recently cut, not long ago. A musty smell mixes with the scent of oil from the oil lamps burning throughout the night. He wipes his nose on his sleeve and changes into a new outfit that Gwyneth had laid out for him on a chair beside the bed. He wears new cotton trousers with extra leather on the thighs, a loose-fitted cotton shirt, and a leather vest underneath a fur-lined tunic.

The room is lavished with gold trim along the stone fireplace where large velvet tapestries of heroes in violet and royal blue hang along the stone walls. At the end of his bed, a new pair of black leather boots replace his old, worn out pair. He slowly slides his feet into them, and they instantly block out the cold. The soles are extra thick and padded with layers of cotton fabric. He straps his swords to his back and the long sword at his side. He opens the bedchamber door where four soldiers remain guarding the entrance, staring straight ahead. They nod and escort the king down the slate stairs to the courtyard; two in front of Martin, and two behind him.

Martin steps outside and takes a deep breath. The scent of flowers lingers in the gentle breeze, and the sun shines in the clear sky. A few pages walk some horses around the castle, children chase each other along the fields, and women hang wet laundry on clotheslines between the trees.

"Where's Simon?" Martin shouts to a guard on the wall walk.

"Your majesty, he has gone back to Quarry Castle," the guard responds.

"Why would he go back to Quarry?"

"We know," Jade responds, pointing to himself and Douglass.

"Sire, may we speak to you in private?" Douglas asks.

The king nods and they head back to the Great Hall, Martin approaching his throne and slumping into it. The two guards stand before him.

"Well," Douglass starts, "we were with Simon when he was told about Elizabeth performing magic."

Martin leans forward in his throne, eyes widened.

"We were with Simon when a soldier told him that he saw Elizabeth doing magic. She found a sword where there was none, and made a fire with her foot," Douglass explains. "She made the sword by waving her wand in a pattern in the snow."

"A wand?" Martin asks.

"Well, not really a wand, more like a branch she had found," Jade clarifies.

"Then why would Simon say she is a witch?" Martin pauses. "Is he so threatened by her that he would want her out of the way?"

"Is that just sinking in now?" A voice starts from behind the men. "You are a slow learner, aren't you?" Sir Anthony says as he approaches the guards, shaking his head. He wears a long black robe and leans on his staff.

"I just have a hard time believing Simon would condemn Elizabeth without proof," Martin says in a hurt voice.

"He is not a knight. A knight would risk his life to maintain honor. He is a man trying to survive, that's all. The man who speaks such blasphemy is a nobleman, so his word is to be taken as truth. You must speak with him," Sir Anthony declares.

"And say what?" Martin asks as Douglass and Jade stand in silence.

Sir Anthony turns away. "Sometimes honor is more important than survival." He slams his staff on the ground, and King Martin jumps up. "You still react, even though I am not close to you. Your training hasn't been wasted." Sir Anthony smiles and strolls to the entrance, slower than usual. He leans on his staff and arches his back, almost hopping on his right foot.

"Isn't there something to be done about this?" Jade asks.

"I don't know, but I will have to fix this somehow. Was there anyone else that saw this magic from Elizabeth?" Jade and Douglass shake their heads and look down. Martin paces the courtroom, studying the carvings on the stone walls of two ravens surrounding a boar, each raven facing each other. The boar stands on its hind legs, its front legs outright to one side. The connecting wall details the boar's face with large eyes, large ears, and small teeth. The eyes stare at Martin, at first with kindness, but at a second glance, they turn to fury. Martin looks away. "Do you know anything about these carvings?" the king asks, disturbed by them.

Jade shrugs his shoulders. "They were here before I was, your majesty. What does it have to do with Lady Elizabeth?" Jade answers.

"Nothing. What can you tell me about this castle then?" Martin tries again.

Jade clears his throat and talks slowly, gathering his thoughts. "Well, your majesty, it was built fifty years ago or so, by slaves." He pauses. "It took twenty years to build, I am told, and then King Richard killed the slaves instead of freeing them." He inhales, then continues. "When I was growing up, I was told that King Richard told the slaves he would free them, just not how they would be freed." The boar's eyes glare at Jade.

"He freed them by killing them... is that what you're saying?" Martin clarifies.

Jade nods, staring at another carving. The carving depicts two men standing side by side.

Martin shakes his head. "I believe the world is better without that man, don't you?"

Jade nods.

"Yes, your majesty."

"I will need to speak to Simon and see what evidence he has against Elizabeth. He did tell me that there was another man who saw her do magic, but if it does not add up, I will release her. If this accusation has some honor in it, I will unfortunately have to test her as a witch." Martin hangs his head.

"Do you think she is a witch, your majesty?" Sir Anthony asks from the doorway. "What do you feel in your heart?"

Martin looks at him carefully, not sure if this is another one of his tests. "Simon told me she has put a spell on me to make me fall in love with her."

"And are you in love with her?" Sir Anthony presses.

"Like I told Simon, it is more like a love for a sister. He said that's how the spell starts. So I have to be careful because if I am under a spell, who knows what I could do."

Sir Anthony walks towards the king, gently thumping the staff onto the cobblestone with each step. "One thing comes to my mind," he pauses as he looks about the room, "how does Simon

THE NEW QUEEN

know so much about a spell? I have been in faraway lands, and I have heard many things, but never of a witch or spells. How does such a young man like Simon know more than an old man such as myself?"

"Why would Simon do this if it were not true?" Martin questions him.

"That's something you will have to ask him. While you are asking him things, ask him where the girl is. Do you know?" Martin shakes his head. Sir Anthony looks at Douglass and Jade, and they too shake their heads. "Get your head out of the mud and stand up for what you believe in. Never cease questioning what you do not understand!" Sir Anthony walks out of the room, and all three let out a sigh of relief.

Martin turns to Douglas. "Lets go back to Quarry castle, I have had enough of this place."

The army looked well trained, well fed and well suited for battle. The late winter day cast a calm over the kingdom.

"It has taken much too long for this army to come about," the Queen of Castile says to Captain Witter. "We know it will take three to four weeks to march because they did it during the winter, the fools. They marched right into the enemy's territory and almost got themselves caught." She turns and looks over the massive army of ten thousand men. "All of them have a sword?"

"Yes, my Queen," Witter answers.

"A shield?"

'Yes, my queen.'

"And all of the catapults are made with all of the bow and arrows?"

"Yes, my Queen. As ordered, all has been carried out as you have said." She looks over the army from her bedchamber balcony

TO BE FREE

as each man holds perfect formation. She takes a deep breath and smiles.

"They sure look fine. Start the soldiers marching toward the castle I want it in the next five weeks!"

Captain Witter impishly raises a flag and waves it back and forth until the large army marches in unison.

"War is coming, and we are going to win it this time," she says, walking back into the bedchamber.

Captain Witter spends the next few days rounding up his young soldiers, fourteen year old boys and up, and preparing them for the invasion. At the early signs of sunrise, Captain Witter leads his army on the first day of the invasion. Witter remains uneasy by the scarcity of supplies, food, and finding safe places to camp. The soldiers remain in good spirits for now, and that's all that mattered to Witter. If he can satisfy his army, then they can all focus on the greater mission of overthrowing King Martin. Witter and Queen Joanna know that very few of their men had even seen a battle, most only heard of battles and tales told to them from friends and family. Most of these young men were to be married while others wanted their family's inheritance. Most have a girl whom they are sweet on, and tell tales to each other of the girl waiting for them back home. In good spirits, they march on.

Samantha cries at the steps of the tower where her sister is locked away. Her gown remains soiled where she sits, and tears dampen the cloth in her hand. Her hair is pulled back and braided. "Please let me see her," she begs the guard. The guard ignores her, looking ahead. "Let me at least give her food," Samantha begs as she lies on the ground in her torn, yellow dress. Her braided hair bounces with each movement of her head as she sobs.

The guard ignores her, pushing her away with his foot.

THE NEW QUEEN

"It's no good. The guards have their orders," a voice behind her says.

Samantha turns around at an old man standing behind her. "She's not a witch, and I don't care what anybody says." Samantha slams her fist on to the stone walkway, scrunching the cloth in her fist.

"If you had seen the things I have seen in my life, I don't believe you would think anyone could be a witch!" Sir Anthony leans on his staff and walks to Samantha and he stands in front of the guard, pulling his robe to one side. "Now, let her see her sister or will I have my way with you?" he says to the guard.

The guard smiles then lets out a slight chuckle. "No offense old man, but you are not in any shape to fight." The guard chuckles again.

Sir Anthony smirks and stubs the guard's foot using his staff. The guard yelps and hops around. The guard advances towards Sir Anthony, arms outstretched towards Sir Anthony's neck. Sir Anthony ducks out of the way and pulls out his leg, tripping the guard as he lands flat on his stomach. He tries to stand up, and Sir Anthony lashes his staff violently across the guard's torso. The guard remains on his back, unconscious.

Sir Anthony leans on his staff once more. "The way is clear for you to see your sister, but I cannot let you set her free," he says with sadness. "Not yet, anyways."

Samantha nods in agreement as tears stream down her face, then she jumps up off the ground. "Thank you, good sir," she says, then runs up the steps of the tower, taking two steps at a time. When Samantha reaches the top of the tower, an old, rotting door faces her. She pulls on the handle and pushes the door, but it remains locked. "Elizabeth," Samantha calls, banging her fists on the door. "Can you hear me? Elizabeth!" Samantha screams, placing her ear against the door. "Elizabeth!" she screams again, even louder. The air remains silent. Samantha falls to her knees and peaks under the door but only sees darkness. She panics and breathes heavy, gripping the rusty door handle as her tears drip onto it. "Elizabeth?" she whispers to herself. She rubs her eyes and reluctantly starts down each step.

"Did you see her?" Sir Anthony asks, leaning against the wall next to the passed out guard.

Samantha frowns. "No, there is another door at the top, and it is locked. I couldn't get through." She wipes away a tear. "Thank you for trying, though." She walks away, staring at the ground.

Sir Anthony stands upright behind her. "We will have to find the key first, then. Maybe later tonight after the guard changes? No doubt another fool will take this one's place. Then I can have a proper fight, so make sure you come." Sir Anthony chuckles. "Meet me at the tower tomorrow evening. Don't be seen by anyone."

Samantha turns around and wipes away a tear. "Why do you want to help me? You might get into trouble," Samantha says, turning to where Sir Anthony stood. She looks around in the dim lighting, only seeing the guard on the stone floor.

Mark received word that King Martin had made it safely to Quarry Castle. Mark and his men were three days into the Viking kingdom and felt uneasy. He did not now the land or what to expect when he meets the vikings. Mark walks his horse most of the time, due to his injured tail bone. Most of the time he felt sick and tired to the point that he had to stop and find a bush, which slowed down his travel time.

After walking back towards Quarry castle, Mark knew things were not right with him. He waves over a guard who rides up to him. "Tell the king I have gone home, and I am sorry for not being at his side. I am very ill and cannot serve his majesty in my state."

THE NEW QUEEN

Mark mounts his horse and rides away from the small band of soldiers.

※

Samantha awaits in the kitchen until the courtyard empties before heading back to the tower, as instructed by Sir Anthony. She changed into her dark green gown to be more hidden in the shadows. As she tiptoes between pillars, peering between each one, someone pulls her back into a darkened room.

"Shhh!" the voice hisses.

She turns around and faces Sir Anthony. "You scared me half to death!" she hisses back in a loud whisper.

"Wait here until I get you," he says, and quietly leaves Samantha standing in the doorway. The old man quietly walks around the corner, keeping his staff raised, as he heads towards the tower where Elizabeth is held.

Two guards stand in front of the staircase, yawning. Sir Anthony slowly approaches, but trips on a crack in the floor, and the sound echoes down the hall.

"Who goes there?" one guard calls out, lifting his head. Torches line the walls, and Sir Anthony walks opposite them, staying hidden among the shadows. The guards pull out their swords at the emerging shadow. Sir Anthony raises the hood of his black cloak and jogs quickly, hiding his staff in one hand behind his back. The guards brace themselves and hold their swords outwards, but Sir Anthony strikes them both across their legs and they stumble to the ground. Both men attack him from opposite sides and Sir Anthony swings his staff one way, knocking the first guard in his stomach, and swings the staff back around his front to attack the second guard, hitting a solid blow over his head.

The first guard bounces back, determined to continue fighting, his sword raised over his head and charging at Sir Anthony. The sword crashes down on Sir Anthony's staff but doesn't damage it. Sir Anthony chuckles and twists the staff between the man's legs, flipping him backward onto his stomach. His head bangs on the stone floor, and he remains there. "I thought I would have had a challenging fight this time around," Sir Anthony comments, cracking his neck from side to side. He peeks his head down the hall for intruders before sneaking back to Samantha.

"All is clear," he whispers to her at the dark doorway. "Just a couple of jesters," he teases. "Follow me." Samantha follows him, holding her gown up as they move promptly down the hall, passing over the unconscious guards sprawled along the steps to the tower.

Samantha turns to Sir Anthony and frowns. "I still do not have a key to the door."

The old man holds out his hand with a key dangling from a piece of rope. "As I said, I was dealing with a couple of jesters." He winks with a smile.

Samantha smiles and takes the key, rushing up the stone stairs as fast as the first time, skipping over every second step. Her shaking hands shove the key into the rusty keyhole and she twists the key. The door swings open and reveals another staircase. Samantha's heart pounds as she continues up the second set of stairs. One torch flickers at the top of the staircase, and she rushes towards it. At the final step, she grabs the torch from the wall and peers down a hallway with many closed doors along each side. She paces slowly down the hall, lowering the torch as she looks through each slit in the doors.

At the fourth door on the right side, she sees a familiar limp figure curled up in a ball. Elizabeth lies on her side, her back facing the door. Her dull red hair in large knots and dirt covers her pale, bony arms and legs. A filthy grey smock covers her weak body with rips and dried blood along the front and back. A large, black rat races across the room. "Elizabeth!" Samantha shouts, staring wide-eyed at her. Elizabeth stays curled up, and Samantha's palms turn sweaty. "Elizabeth, it's me, Samantha," she tries again, blinking away her tears. Out of her cloak, Samantha pulls out a boiled duck and a half loaf of bread and pushes it through the tiny hole. "Here's some food," she whispers as it drops to the floor. "I can't stay, but I will be back soon. I promise." She weeps, holding her face in her hands before moving away from the hole.

Samantha sprints down the hallway, placing the torch back in the socket and down the staircase, locking the door behind her. She races down the spiraling staircase, and down the lit hallway, searching for Sir Anthony. He emerges from the shadows in the corner and waves her over. They move in silence until they reach the courtyard. They stand against a wall under a staircase. "Did you see your sister?" he whispers, clutching his lower back.

Samantha's eyes sting. "Yes, but she is not moving."

Sir Anthony pauses. "We may have to get her before it's too late."

"You mean to break her out?" Samantha sniffles.

"If that's what it takes," he responds, turning away.

Samantha watches him cross the dark courtyard until he disappears into the night.

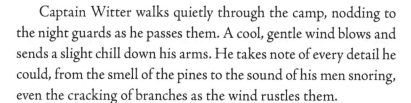

Captain Witter walks quietly through the camp, nodding to the night guards as he passes them. A cool, gentle wind blows and sends a slight chill down his arms. He takes note of every detail he could, from the smell of the pines to the sound of his men snoring, even the cracking of branches as the wind rustles them.

A small man emerges from his tent and walks around to the back of it. The man did not stop, and kept walking toward the surrounding forest. Captain Witter follows the man, tip-toeing around the tent as he tries to keep the man in sight. The soldier walks hastily past the trees and through to the opening, far from the camp. The man had no thought of danger, for he did not carry a sword or even have a knife in hand.

"A wild boar would soon make a meal out of you," Witter says quietly to himself.

After what seemed like an hour, the man finally stops and sits on a log. Witter hides behind a large tree and watches the mysterious man. The man crosses his legs and holds his hand out from his side with his thumb touching his middle finger. Witter looks around for anyone else but no one else approaches. The man starts humming, and lays on his back. Witter watches him until the man quickly falls asleep. Witter rests against a tree and slowly nods off.

Captain Witter is startled when the man shakes him awake.

"Captain? Captain are you alright? Where are we?" the man asks. Witter jumps up and pulls out his sword, looking around.

"What, where?"

"Captain, we're fine. I found you sleeping here. I awoke just over there," the man points towards some trees, "and I found you here. Where are we, how did we get here?"

Witter realizes he had fallen asleep and sheathes his sword. "I followed you here. Why did you come here?"

"I was asleep in my tent and woke here, the same as you, sir," the man tries to convince him. The sun breaks through the trees.

"Come on. We better get back to camp before they leave without us." Witter starts in the direction they came from, but the land looks different from night and day. After following some trees for a bit longer, Witter knows he is lost.

Simon watches the last of the Great Army set out to sea, the ship sailing towards the horizon until it disappears out of sight. He turns back and rushes down the stone steps towards a

THE NEW QUEEN

scout dismounting his horse. "Did you find something?" he asks nervously.

With bloodshot eyes and drooping eyelids, the scout staggers towards Simon. He takes a deep breath before answering. "As I was told, I rode for four days without stopping, except when I walked the horse, that is." The scout glances to the guard beside Simon. "I made it to the French border, that's where I saw this huge army of at least five thousand men. Heavily armed and were well-trained. They could be at war with the French, but they were not heading that way, as far as I could see. It looked like they were heading in our direction. They traveled with catapults and thousands of horses, too, but most were walking."

Simon taps his chin. "How sure are you that they are coming here and not going to France?" The scout stares blankly at Simon and shrugs his shoulders. "Find another scout and send them to watch this army. Make sure we are ready in case we end up in some territorial battle of some kind. Have the catapults and trebuchets loaded and ready."

Simon returns to Quarry Castle when a horn by the main gate goes off, signaling the kingdom that someone approaches. Simon rushes to the main gate where he notices his scout riding closer to him. The scout stops his horse, his face red and eyes wide. "What is it?" Simon asks.

The scout dismounts and hops off the horse. "An army grows close."

"Yes, I know. We have had news of it coming. It will be here within a week, I am told." Simon places his hand on the scout's shoulder.

The scout shakes his head. "No, they will be here today, or at Castle Hope by nightfall! Is the army you speak of made from farmers and noblemen?"

Simon widens his eyes, and turns back to his surrounding soldiers. "Destroy the symbol and the rest will fall! Send word to

Castle Hope! We need reinforcements!" Soldiers take out their weapons and dart in different directions around the castle. "Two armies approach! Send out another scout to see who they are and what they want before it is too late!"

The day slowly turns to night, and the torches light the perimeter around the small castle. "If one goes out, we know they are here," Simon speaks aloud. Simon walks down the stairs of the wall-walk, mumbling to himself. "We cannot beat any army with what we have, and I know we do not have the resources to be of any challenge to any army..."

"Who are you talking to?" Gus, a former Black Army soldier, interrupts Simon's thoughts.

Simon looks up at Gus. "How do we stop a war before it begins?"

Gus thinks before answering. "We would have to scare the approaching army into rethinking their attack."

"And how do we do that? We have not one, but two armies approaching."

"If we have the larger army, any army would stop and rethink their plan. They will want to avoid a mass slaughtering of their people."

Simon jolts up and looks at Gus. "That's it! All they have to do is see the army, not fight them!" Simon calls for a scout when he sees the first scout approaching the front gate.

The scout notices Simon and furiously rides over to him. "Sir, one army will march against Castle Hope tomorrow. They are camped not far from the castle."

Simon grabs the scroll from the rider and scribbles a note. "Take this to Castle Hope. Make sure you do not get caught and stay in the shadows as much as possible." The scout nods and grips the reigns. Simon shoves the note into the horse's saddlebag then smacks its backside, and the horse leaps to a run.

Chapter 14
INTERVENTION

The morning sun brings the smell of spring, as shoots of grass sprout between melting piles of snow. The bird had returned and fly above the castle. The castle buzzes with activity as the kingdom prepares for battle. Men outside use mules to plow the melting snow, creating several paths around the castle and through the fields. New huts spring up for the farmers out in the field to have a place to sleep in during the crop season.

Scouts from Quarry Castle cluster in the courtyard, dining room, and kitchen. Hundreds of men joke with one another, shooting arrows at targets for fun, sword fighting, and moving the wood to different rooms for fires. Sir Anthony and Samantha, like other onlookers, stare at the goofing men with annoyance, keeping away the children who try to sneak into the training grounds. Gus and Douglass rush to each group of men, trying to make them take their training seriously.

INTERVENTION

Douglass stands in full armour holding his bassinet in his hand. Sweat beads along his forehead from the heavy suit and the warming weather as he wipes the inside of his bassinet with a cloth. The soldiers taunt his sweaty appearance, calling him a 'knight in shining armor,' because of his polished, unscratched, and unchallenged armor, unlike the soldiers' armour.

Gus walks over to the targets and shows off his knife throwing and archery skills. The men cheer him on before attempting his techniques themselves, all missing their targets entirely. Gus looks outwards to the field of men trying to hold their swords with one hand but failing. "We have a long way to go," he mumbles, before heading towards a group who have trouble marching in sync with each other, laughing and pushing others.

At the other side of the castle, Gwyneth remains in the resting wing, teaching women of all ages how to sew soldiers' garments in a perfect way so that from afar, all the men would be uniform. She also teaches the other maidens how to sew the kingdom's flag, a lion pinning down a phoenix, with her goal of completing fifty flags before the war. Each of the five rooms are filled with women hunching over tables covered in different fabrics, sewing vigorously.

Out on the fields, Sir Anthony walks with Samantha towards each training station. "They look like fools," Sir Anthony comments, watching some men failing to hit a target with their knives. "We look like fools," he corrects himself. "The entire kingdom does."

Samantha stands beside him and watches the training. "It's not going to work, will it? And we are all going to die if the army decides to attack anyway."

Sir Anthony looks at her blank face. "I wouldn't take it that far, but I don't think the idea of training a large amount of men will stop war just because they think there are too many men to fight. That won't stop anything if the other army already has intentions of fighting."

THE NEW QUEEN

"It doesn't matter anyways, none of it does," Samantha says gravely. "Soon, Elizabeth will be hung until she is dead." Her eyes well up with tears. "Why won't Martin just say she is not a witch? What is he afraid of? Instead, he is nowhere to be found while the life of my sister draws close!"

Sir Anthony frowns and leans closer to Samantha. "You must have faith in this king, my dear. I know he is young, but he is very smart for his age. I doubt he has forgotten about her."

Samantha shakes her head and looks away from him. A horn blows from the wall, and the playful mood falls silent. All heads turn upwards to the wall-walk where the horn repeats its call in slow, deep blows. Gus runs to the wall-walk and looks out to a small approaching army under an unfamiliar dark flag. Gus orders the archers onto the wall-walk as the small army stops before the fields in rows. The first row contains archers pointing their bows at the castle's entrance and at the wall-walk.

"That army is fairly small in size," Douglass says behind Gus.

"True, but we don't have many soldiers either, and they outnumber all of our real soldiers by three to one, I would say," Gus estimates.

"I think it's great timing, don't you?" Sir Anthony challenges Gus.

Gus glares at him. "A great time for what, to surrender? I will never surrender this castle!"

Sir Anthony smiles. "A great time to see if your army has the power to change events before they happen."

Gus clues in to what Sir Anthony means and orders the men to move in perfect formation outside of the castle wall. Archers kneel in front and load their arrows while soldiers stand behind the archers, pointing their spears forward with their shields covering the archers for protection. The army takes so long moving out of the castle, scared and stressed out about acting like soldiers, that

INTERVENTION

the small army retreats into the forest before all the men can make it outside.

Gus looks at Sir Anthony in amazement. "I would have never believed it if I hadn't seen it with my own eyes."

"I thought you said they were going to attack Quarry castle?' Gus chuckles and orders the men back into the castle. "Our plan worked here, so it should work with the other army, too." The soldiers head back into the castle before they break into whoops and hollers, skipping around the courtyard with ale in their hands. The gates close behind them, and the men carry out their festivities, celebrating their first battle without losing a single person.

"What's your name, son?' Captain Witter asks the man whom he followed into the woods with. Captain Witter leads the way through the woods.

"John, sir. Are we lost?"

Witter glances back at the man. "Why did you come out here, anyways?"

"Well, I walk in my sleep, sir. I mean I am not taken over by a ghost or anything, at least I don't think I am, but sometimes I just wake up in funny places, that's all."

The two find a clearing and stumble across their camp where the army stands around and awaits orders. "Hurry and get your things," Witter says to the man before turning to the camp. "Pack up. We are heading to French territory as soon as possible!"

Elizabeth lays on the cold, damp floor, listening to the faint cheers echoing down the hallway and through the opening of an arrow loop. As the guard comes by to give her daily beating, as

THE NEW QUEEN

ordered, she tries to ask him about the cheering. He unlocks her cellar door, and she backs away to the wall. "Please, sir," Elizabeth starts, her body shaking. "Could you tell me what the cheering is about?"

"Quiet, witch! No questions from you. Witches only get beatings from me, nothing else." The burly man spits by his foot, gritting his rotting teeth. "Now get to the wall and spread your arms, you know what to do." He takes out a cat's tail whip, a weapon made of nine leather ends to imitate the feeling of nine separate lashes all at once.

"Please, not today," Elizabeth begs. "I'm still in so much pain from yesterday." Tears stream down her face. "Please." Her voice cracks. "I'm so weak."

The man advances at Elizabeth, whipping the ground. She hops out of the way and screams. "I won't ask you twice." The man's voice fills with anger.

Too weak to fight back, Elizabeth places her shaky, thin arms against the stone wall covered with her own blood. She rips a piece of fabric off her sleeve and shoves it in her mouth. The first lash burns along her back and she bites down on the ball of cloth, screaming. Her lash scars break open, and she feels the warm blood run quickly down her cold, shaking body. She cries harder. "Just hang me already!" she screams to him in a muffled voice.

"You will be, soon enough," the man chuckles. He whips her again, and Elizabeth drops to the floor, falling into unconsciousness.

King Martin remains in his bedchamber at Quarry Castle, thinking of how to convince Simon to free Elizabeth. The king paces back and forth across the bedchamber floor when he hears a loud noise against the castle wall growing louder with each thump. Martin opens the slats to look outside when a hand appears at

INTERVENTION

his ledge. Martin jumps back with fright, pushing his body flat against the wall. He grabs his two-handed sword from its sheath and positions the blade flat on the ledge and waits. The intruder moves closer, his huffing breath shooting faint swirls into the air. The other hand stops in front of them, and it grips an unlit oil lantern. He swings his hand back and forth, preparing to throw the lantern through the slats to break them open. Martin waits until the man's face is centered with the ledge, and his eyes lock with Martin's. Martin shoves the blade hard towards the man, making the intruder jerk out of the way. He loses balance and slips, falling off the wall and landing on the rocks below to his death. The guards rush into the room, hearing the man's frightened scream.

Martin waves his hands and points out the slats to the ground. The guards crowd the slats and look down. "All is fine," Martin starts. "There was an intruder but he is taken care of now. I need you all to go find that body and bring it to me," Martin commands, following two guards out of his bedchamber.

The two guards walk across the drawbridge and wait until the body floats closer to the platform while Martin stands at the gate with Sir Gregory. The body broke through the thin sheet of ice and floats on top of the water, bobbing its way to the drawbridge. Within a few minutes, the body is close enough for the men to grab.

"Where is Simon?" Martin asks while watching his guards pull up the corpse.

"I believe he has gone to explore battle options, sire," a guard replies as he drags the soaked man over the drawbridge and into the keep.

Martin and Sir Gregory circle the body for a closer look. Sir Gregory peers into the dead man's green eyes. His black and silver hair harden into thick coils around his pale face.

THE NEW QUEEN

"I know him!" Sir Gregory says, the old man breaking the silence. "He was one of the Black Army members. We used to call him 'Goat.' He never said much, but he could always climb the hardest cliffs." Sir Gregory pauses for a moment. "So what made him fall, I wonder?"

A small group of people gathers around the body. Mothers escort their children away from the scene, but the fathers and older children stay to watch. Martin looks at the body, then at Gregory. "How many more are like him?"

"He was an eccentric, never taught anyone his skills. He stayed separate from the others, but he was a good soldier, always followed orders and was one of the first to always complete tasks," Gregory adds, still staring at the body.

"He was going to throw a lamp into my bedchamber. I guess he leaned out too far and lost his footing," Martin lies.

"A pure tragedy, but at least you are still safe," Sir Gregory announces and the small crowd cheers in agreement.

The king briefly smiles then tugs on Gregory's arm to leave. "What would setting my bedchamber on fire accomplish?"

"Well," he pauses scratching his head, "it would have possibly destroyed the main castle, and everyone would feel that they have no place to safely rest. After that's gone, a few arrows into the main courtyard would set it on fire and then no one would be left."

Martin nods. "When did you last see Goat?"

"He returned to our kingdom and he just came with us but was never banished, as far as I know."

"You think the king sent him?" Martin asks.

"Maybe, it would make sense," Gregory answers, peering towards the trees.

"Would Goat have come alone?" Martin asks.

Gregory shrugs. "Maybe."

"Would there be more Black Army?"

INTERVENTION

Gregory thinks for a moment. "Not likely, but the king might have sent more men, maybe even the small group we scared away."

"What group?" the king asks, surprised by the sudden news. "If a group of men or an army is about to attack, I need to know about it."

"Well, I do not know for sure, your majesty. But s a former Black Army member, I know they travel together, never alone," Gregory explains.

"If they thought my bedchamber was on fire, would they show themselves?" the King asks with a slight smile on his face.

"Most likely. The soldiers could be anywhere."

"Good! Then I have a plan!"

Minutes later, archers secretly line the castle walls, crouching or sitting along the floor of the wall-walk, all aimed at the hill. From the courtyard, all the women and extra men hold large buckets of water and snow as Martin starts a fire in his bedchamber's fireplace. He closes the flue, and the smoke travels back down. The King feeds the fire wet wood and fans at the fireplace, spreading the flames. Martin stays by the closed door by the guards in case he passes out. After a few minutes of coughing, Martin shoves his mouth and nose in his shirt, waiting for more smoke to fill the room. Almost choking from the heavy smoke, Martin rushes back to the flue and pulls it open. A giant smoke cloud travels through it and releases into the cold air outside. The archers on the wall, along with Gregory, notice a small fire just beyond the hill and they wait, keeping their bows aimed at the hill along with two catapults and a trebuchet.

Thirty men pour over the hill, running towards the castle with lit bows and arrows. Gregory watches them run until they reach a shooting distance. He counts to ten before he orders the archers to fire. "Fire!" Gregory yells to the archers, and at once, they all rise and fire their arrows at the approaching men. With nowhere to run

THE NEW QUEEN

or hide, most of them are killed or hit instantly, dropping their lit crossbows onto the melting snow, extinguishing their flame. Two of the men from the back row escape the air raid, hiding behind a hill, out of range from the archers, but not the catapults. The two catapults fire into the air well beyond the escaping men. Gregory points them out and sends a small party to capture them. The intruders await behind the hill, planning an escape in silence, not realizing that five of King Martin's men already made their way to the survivor's hiding place, armed with crossbows. They surround the two men, their crossbows raised and ready to kill.

"Drop your bows and give up, or die," a soldier say to the intruders.

The two intruders stare at each other. They then drop their bows and raise their hands in surrender. The guards tie their hands in tight knots and march them back to the castle where the King waits for them at the entrance. The two approaching men are the same height with short blonde, choppy hair and blue eyes. Smears of dirt cover their faces and both dress in full leather armor. The men push the two intruders forward, and they stop in front of the king.

"Why do you attack us?" Martin asks, getting straight to the point.

"Why does anyone attack another?" The clean-shaven man asks in a thick, unfamiliar accent.

"We want more land, and when King Henry's army returns, we will have an army you will be unable to stop. Surrender now," the bearded man continues.

"Who's idea was it to attack us, then?"

The two say nothing but smile. "You won't hurt us, you won't even fight back. You'll do anything you can do avoid a fight. Some leader you are."

INTERVENTION

Martin clenches his jaw and belts the side of his face, knocking him to the ground. "That's true, I do have a hard time hurting people, but that's why I gave Sir Gregory full authority over you both. He isn't as understanding as I am."

Sir Gregory takes his sword and slices a deep scratch down one of their legs. He cries in pain as the other tries to break from his bond.

"You heard the king! I can do whatever I want with you until you tell me what we want to know," Gregory tells the men, punching the other hard in the stomach. "Now, where is your army camping?"

Mark walks his horse up a small hill towards the village of Ansure where he grew up. The yellow flowers were in bloom as they stood higher in the lush grasses. People he once knew waved at him; some gave him a hug while others just stared. He reached his family home where his brother, his mother, and father had all passed away. The grass around the house had been chopped down, but the house remains standing. The wood had faded greatly in the one year he has not been back home. He pushed open the door, and it swung slowly open into the darkened house. He carefully stepped inside and looked around. Nothing had changed, and everything was where it should be. Mark walks to his mother's bed and lays down, quickly falling asleep in his full leather armor, happy to be home again.

Elizabeth leans against the cold wall of her cell to numb her back from the swelling and bruising. She sits quietly, ignoring the flares of pain that shoot up and down her back. As she fades

THE NEW QUEEN

in and out of sleep, she hears the long moan of the creaking door downstairs. Her heart beats faster as panic sets in, knowing that another whipping approaches. Her eyes fill with tears as she listens to the approaching footsteps that stop outside her door. Keys jingle and clang against the lock and she moves to the far corner of her cell to the small hole in the wall and hides in the shadows. She weeps silently as the door swings open. "Please," she begs, "not now. I'll do anything to avoid it right now. Please."

An old man in black cloak steps into view. "Are you Elizabeth?" he asks in a soft, calm voice.

She nods and struggles to stand, accepting her time to be hung.

He moves towards her and turns her around. She grimaces at his touch, keeping her head low. He stares at her bloody gashes down her back. "Follow me. I will get you out of here and take you to your sister, Samantha," he whispers. "But you must be quiet."

Elizabeth looks at the old man with confusion and amazement, too overwhelmed to move. The old man studies her gaunt face and cracked lips before pulling out a small wine sack for her to drink from. She takes the wine sack with her shaking hands and gulps loudly. She pauses for a large gasp, then continues the rest of the cold water. The old man grabs her hand, avoiding her raw wrists, and walks ahead of her, pulling her along. Elizabeth almost falls down the stairs, her legs too weak to support her body.

On the fourth step down, she trips and stumbles from dizziness, nearly knocking down the old man as well. Sir Anthony, too weak to support her weight on his own, places her arm over his shoulder. She leans on him and he leans on his staff. She holds out her free hand and sets it on the wall for extra support.

After a few more steps, he locks the door behind them, and they enter the torch-lit staircase. Samantha waits in the hallway with a wagon filled with hay, hiding in the corner of the hall among the shadows. The door swings open and Samantha rushes

INTERVENTION

down the hallway to the limp, female body draped around Sir Anthony. Samantha's eyes instantly burn at the sight of her sister's body, but she holds her tears back to help Sir Anthony. She takes Elizabeth's free arm and walks her to the wagon, helping her squeeze in the back with the bundles of hay and notices Elizabeth's bloodied back. Elizabeth lays on her stomach, her back exposed, as Samantha wraps her sister in a thin white linen sheet to avoid the sharp texture of the hay. Sir Anthony lays beside Elizabeth on the opposite end, placing his staff between them.

Samantha readjusts the hay and covers both bodies until they look like lumps of hay. "Make sure she stays quiet," Samantha whispers. "She cannot say a word until we are safe."

Elizabeth whimpers under the blanket as each bit of hay presses onto her bloody back, feeling like small knives stabbing her over and over. The old man reaches over and covers her mouth. "You're almost home," he whispers.

Samantha pulls the wagon and it jerks forward. Sir Anthony and Elizabeth remain silent, feeling the rattling wagon travel over the stone castle floor, occasionally hitting a small hole. Sir Anthony steadies his breathing and calms his heartbeat, hoping Elizabeth can't hear or feel his stress. Elizabeth grows drowsy, her eyelids drooping from the silence and the feeling of safety and warmth. As soon as Samantha exits the tower hallway and enters another, Elizabeth passes out and does not wake up, even when Samantha pulls the hay away and carries her into a small stone cabin within the castle's keep.

Simon rides his horse around the outskirts of what was once Saxton's castle. Him and his eight men have scavenged everything they could in the ruin. "Mount up and let's continue searching around here," he orders, looking for some clue as to why King

THE NEW QUEEN

Saxton was so powerful. It had been three days since they left Quarry Castle, and each day they came back to the burned ruins, but today Simon thought to travel.

Out of the corner of his eye, Simon notices someone rustling in a nearby bush. He motions to his guards as they guide their horses towards the bushes when the man jumps out, half-naked and wearing only torn clothing. It did not take long to grab hold of the man as he mumbles about a great army attacking him. They tie the distressed man to a tree and set up camp before questioning him through the night.

King Martin and Sir Gregory slump at a far table in the Great Hall, away from other families nearby. The two men talk in whispers, clutching goblets of ale and Martin's preference of hot boiled water. Sir Gregory takes a large drink of ale before retelling Martin what he needed to know about King Henry. Martin, surprised, learns through Gregory's torture that the two men did not plan the attack on the castle, but planned to force Martin into joining King Henry's kingdom once again. Sir Gregory informs his king that each earl and baron will have their own army in this kingdom. "I think King Henry will take the castle by force, leaving you in need of defending this kingdom."

King Martin looks down at the table, sipping his hot water. "If King Henry attacks us, we will not be able to hold them off for very long," Martin says with a frown. "He has a large army at his disposal."

"I know. That's why I think we have to search farther to get some type of help." Gregory taps the sides of his goblet.

"Who? Who will help a small, new kingdom without wanting to take it for themselves?" Martin asks, shaking his head.

INTERVENTION

"I have been thinking about that, too." He pauses. "The French," Gregory says with a smile.

Martin shakes his head. "The French will surely attack us."

"No, I don't think so. We are not in English territory, nor are we in the French kingdom. We are in a neutral area surrounded by the French, English and the Spaniards. The French won't attack because it might upset the English, and the Spaniards won't attack because it is too close to the war between the French and English. The English would rather have us join them instead of attacking us. If they attack us, the French will see it as the English wanting to expand their hold on the area, so the French will protect us as long as we do not take sides," Gregory explains.

Martin scratches his head. "And why won't the French attack us?"

"They have an agreement not to expand towards the Spanish."

Martin grins and his eyes widen. "Excellent! But does that mean the French will protect us?"

Gregory's smile turns into a frown. "Only if King Henry's army gets here first. They will want this kingdom before the French get it, but if the French gets here first, they will not take it because they will want another ally against the English."

Martin stares at Gregory. "Gather the horses, we leave at once!"

King Martin, Sir Gregory, and Jade ride out the front gate towards the direction of Paris in a great hurry, and all wearing dark cloaks. Although the sun dips just below the tree line, and the horizon swirls into oranges and reds, the three men continue riding hastily, knowing the ride is more than a week away.

They ride until the semi-darkness ascends, before the men dismount and set up camp near a collection of boulders in the west. Martin starts a fire with a stone splint and dry wood while Gregory and Jade set up the individual canvas tents. Jade and Gregory drag over a fallen log in the forest and place it around the fire. The three

THE NEW QUEEN

sit side by side as the fire grows, providing enough light and heat for the night.

Jade holds his hands over the fire, clears his throat, and says, "Not that there's anything to be done, and I trust your judgment, your majesty, but I don't understand why we did not bring more men with us?"

Sir Gregory answers for Martin. "The least amount of men, the better. No one will suspect the king to be so unprotected, right? If we were to be spotted, we would be overlooked as enemies or intruders since there's no way we could possibly pose as a threat with just three men."

Jade nods. "So that's the same reason we don't carry the flag as well?"

"Yes and the reason we wear our armor under our cloaks," Gregory says as the wind picks up. Martin shivers and heads into his tent. "We can rotate watches, but I am too tired right now," he calls through the closed tent.

Gregory turns to Jade. "You take first watch. Wake me when you need sleep." Gregory tosses his canteen of hot water to Jade and heads into the empty tent beside Martin.

Gus and Douglass start to march their army of farmers from Hope Castle to Quarry Castle, bringing with them enough food to last a month, sacks of cured and smoked meats, barley, oats, potatoes, corn, and salted fish from the channel. Each wagon carries clothing, and one uniform that the maidens created with Gwyneth's guidance. The growing number of soldiers reaches ten thousand men, yet only few hundred have any soldering experience. Gus and Douglass, overwhelmed by the vast gap between amateur and professional, try to think of more efficient ways to do basic training in large masses.

INTERVENTION

The morning of their march remains aggressively colder than the entire week, but the men stay in high spirits from their previous victory. The massive army walks their way to Quarry castle, a good day's worth on foot instead of a half a day's travels by horse. They walk together in long lines, some horses scattering along the way with as many parcels and bags strapped to them as possible.

Across the fields, on the outskirts of the castle, Gus notices a small army camped out where they need to travel through. He raises his hands and at his command, the army marches in groups of parallel rows, as a professional army would. The men readjust the bags and items they carried to make their swords more prominent. They puff out their chests, hold their heads high, and march together, starting with the right foot. They march all the way across the field to the campsite.

Gus rides ahead to the campground, his army stopping behind him in rows. Gus walks up to a black haired man with a mousy face. A thick mustache coats his upper lip and short black hair hangs above his ears in a chopped fashion. The man steps forward and faces Gus, while the rest of the campsite drops their belongings and stands up. "Why do you camp here? Has the king given his permission for you to be here?" Gus asks with authority in his voice.

"And who might you be?" The small-eyed man with the thick mustache asks.

"I am the Captain of the Guards to King Martin, the land who you stand upon. Why are you here?"

The man had not looked past Gus until now, and he gulps at the sight of the fighting formation that the army stands in. "We are with the Earl of Saxton, land and kingdom of King Henry, King of the United Kingdom. What kingdom do you serve?"

Gus tries again. "I carry the flag of King Martin. These men are here to protect his kingdom, and if you do not leave now, I will

THE NEW QUEEN

order my men upon you and your band of bandits!" The mustached man shifts uncomfortably and backs away towards his men. He shouts at them to pack up and leave. Gus smiles. "You will have to be marched out." The man nods and clears his throat, leaving Gus to help dismantle the campsite.

Gus walks back to the army and orders them to stand in two lines, one on each side of the group of campers. They march silently in the two rows back to the campsite, standing on each side of the group of men, and the two armies march up the hill and out of the kingdom. Gus' men avoid eye contact with the real army, too nervous to blow their cover by looking terrified. The small army reciprocates the feelings, keeping their heads held high as a distraction to hide their nervousness.

Once they reach the top of the hill, Gus turns to the mustached man. "Now, if you ever come back to this castle, it better be in peace. Otherwise, we will have a war." The man turns away, trailing after his small army of a few hundred men as they march down the hill. Gus turns around and walks the men back in perfect formation the rest of the way to Quarry castle.

Once arriving at the tiny castle, the tents left by the Great Army still surround the small castle, creating a sea of yellow, red and white. "It looks like we're having some sort of celebration, never mind there being a large army here," Douglass comments to Gus as they walk around. A man juggles short swords, dropping them all on the ground. He stomps his foot, picks them up, and tries again.

Gus watches the man juggle. "That's it! If we make it look like another army is here for fun, King Henry won't attack for months since he will think that more than one army will be here celebrating together! By the time he decides to attack, we will have time to get help."

Douglass looks at Gus, confused. "Why won't King Henry attack?"

INTERVENTION

"If he did, he might be attacking as many as ten armies together. Even King Henry's army could not defend against such great numbers."

King Martin awakes to the sun shining through the walls of the tent. He sits up, completely dressed in his clothes from yesterday, and steps out of the tent. Small embers dance and crackle along the firewood and Jade sleeps in front of it, his head against the log. Martin walks closer to Jade and notices the tip of Jade's brown leather boot has been charred black. Martin grabs a large log behind Jade and tosses it into the pit of tiny embers, sending them flying into the air with a tiny puff of smoke. The loud sizzling starts a quick flame engulfing the log, the sudden brightness waking Jade. "What? I'm awake!" he yells, sitting up straight.

"Did you stay out here all night?" the king asks.

Jade stretches his hands over his head and yawns. "Yeah, I guess I did," he replies through the yawn. "Who knew a log could be so comfortable?" he says, standing and rubbing his head.

"Get some food from the horse bags. They are in the tent."

Jade makes his way into the tent and rummages through the leather bags, finding some dried meat and dried apples. He grabs a small pot with water and heads back to the fire pit, placing the pot of water over the fire. He peels the apples and tosses the meat into the pot.

Sir Gregory walks out of his tent, finding Martin and Jade eating around the fire. "We best not stay here too long. We don't even know who owns this land. We still have quite a trek to Paris." Gregory grabs the water and chugs the entire canteen, then tosses the empty container to the side.

THE NEW QUEEN

"You should eat. We might not get time later on to stop," Martin responds to Gregory, handing him some meat.

After they finish eating, they toss snow on the fire and disassemble camp. They travel through fields of yellow flowers, across a collection of slow-moving streams, and down a forested hill until a small stone house peeks through a clearing of trees. The small stone house is wrapped in vines and stands beside a small stream running down the forested hill. The slate stone roof of the house slopes upward into a point where a matching stone chimney puffs out smoke. Six wooden shutters, two on the front and sides of the house, remain closed. Dead vines cover the wooden door, and a cobblestone path leads towards the field. Near one side of the area stands a large, old wooden barn where a few horses flick their tails while grazing in the field.

"Well, your majesty, you are in France now," Gregory announces, overlooking the field.

A thin, blonde girl walks up the worn path in a long white dress carrying a bucket of water. She looks up at the three men, pauses, and continues walking up the hill towards them. She places the full bucket in front of the wooden front door and walks towards the men, smiling. "Bonjour!" The girl curtseys.

"Hello," Gregory answers.

The young girl bows towards Martin. "Your majesty," she says in a French accent.

Martin looks at her with bewilderment. "Why would you think me royalty?"

"Vous n'êtes pas le roi?" she asks in a soft voice. Martin looks around, not sure what she asked.

"She asked if you are the king," Gregory translates.

"Why would she think I am a king?" Martin asks him. Gregory translates the question.

She giggles. "On m'a dit que vous devez venir."

INTERVENTION

"She said she was told you would be coming," Gregory says.

Martin hesitates before asking the next question. "How old are you?"

"J'ai dix ans!" the girl responds, holding up her ten fingers.

"And who told you that a king would be coming here?" Martin asks, and Gregory translates.

"Saint Margret told me," she responds in English.

"And why would Saint Margret tell you I was coming?"

She answers in English. "She said a great king was, uh, going to pass by on his way to Paris and I would, uh, meet you."

"But how did you know I am a king?" Martin asks. The little girl stares at him, blinking as Gregory translates the question for her.

"She tells me what you look like and that the king carries trois swords," she responds, pointing at his two-handed sword sheathed on his side, and the two handles protruding from his shoulders.

"And what is your name?" Martin asks.

"Joan. My father is Jacques d' Arc."

"Well, Joan, when you speak to Saint Margret again, thank her for me. It was a pleasure to meet you," Martin concludes with a smile.

Gregory translates and she giggles before curtseying again.

The group continues past the girl, but she runs in front of them, holding her hands up. "You cannot go to Paris!" she shouts in English to them, her eyes wide. She turns to Gregory and speaks fast in French, her voice squeaking with excitement.

Gregory frowns and translates to Martin. "She said if you go to Paris, you will be assassinated by a man who works for a powerful earl."

Martin clenches his jaw, wondering who would want him dead. "And did Saint Margret tell you this as well?"

THE NEW QUEEN

The girl shakes her head as Gregory starts her translation. "It was Michael, the arc angel. He talks to me the most. He told me you will do great things and bring peace to the land. You will face many enemies along the way to your greatness. I am to tell you that you must believe in yourself and be the king that lies inside you."

Martin's heart pounds faster and his mind races with questions, unsure of this vague prophecy. Before he can ask her a question, she continues in French.

"I cannot let you go to Paris. Do you understand, your majesty? Your life is in my hands."

"Joan, does your father know you have a gift from God?" Martin asks.

"He wishes I do not," Joan answers in English.

"Thank you, Joan. Goodbye," Martin says, clasping the girl's hand and kissing it.

"Au revoir, King Martin!" She waves, skipping back to the bucket and carrying it inside her house. Martin mounts his horse and turns it towards the direction they came.

"Where are you going?" Jade asks, confused.

"Back to the castle." Martin whips the reigns and the horse moves forward.

"You're not going to believe a little girl, are you?" Jade asks, following closely behind him.

"That little girl knew I was a king and she knew we were going to Paris and we did not tell anyone of our plan, yet she knew. I cannot ignore that," Martin responds firmly.

"Wait!" Joan shouts after them. The men stop and turn around. "I, uh, almost forgot something!" She says in English, turning to Jade. "I know you will be a good knight."

Jade smiles and nods at the girl.

INTERVENTION

She turns to Gregory and speaks in French. "And you and I will meet in heaven soon enough." Joan turns back and skips down the hill to her house.

The men stay silent, staring at the house. "What does 'de' mean, anyway?" Martin asks Gregory.

"It means 'of'," he pauses. "Her name is Joan of Arc."

Chapter 15
FRIENDS MAKE ENEMIES

Simon awakes and walks out of his tent to an early morning sunrise. He tugs at his leather armor and straightens his vest before moving towards the fire to cook breakfast of eggs and boiled potatoes. His prisoner is tied to a tree, sleeping quietly as the ropes hold him upright. A guard hands Simon a slice of tree bark with eggs and potatoes on it. Simon grabs it and takes a generous bite.

"The prisoner told me that the Great Army attacked him two days ago," the guard tells Simon.

"The crazy man told you that? It's not possible... I saw them leave on their ships just the other day. They did not have time to attack anyone before that." Simon breaks the potato and dips it into the egg yolk.

"Could there be more of the Great Army than the ones that we saw leaving?"

FRIENDS MAKE ENEMIES

Simon swallows his bite before answering. "I guess it could have a few more men, but what good would they do in attacking a deserted, burned down castle?"

The guard shrugs his shoulders and starts to eat his own food. Simon looks back at the man and studies him closely. His torn leggings and shredded shirt show signs of a struggle. He also walks barefoot, mud clinging to the soles of his feet. Simon stands and walks over to the prisoner, tossing a pan of water onto the man's head.

The prisoner jolts awake. "Ah! What?" he shouts, shaking his head.

"Tell me why you attacked us," Simon demands, waving the empty pot in the man's face.

"You attacked us! We are just some farmers, nothing more! We are under King Saxton's rein, and when we came to ask for protection, we find the castle burned down and you scavenging through the king's treasures." The prisoner glares at Simon.

"We just got here, and King Martin has claimed the kingdom for himself. We know King Saxton had no heirs, but you were right in presuming that the Great Army destroyed the castle. They destroyed it but they left it, so in the name of King Martin, we claim it."

"Ha! The barons and the earls will have plenty to say. As a matter of fact, they are planning to combine their forces and take your castle. That little thing isn't worth the land that it sits on, but it will make this kingdom larger and more people will serve our king." The man laughs.

Simon leans closer to the man's face. "And who is this new king you speak of? As I see it, your barons and your earls will fight among themselves before they group together. Who will lead this army?"

THE NEW QUEEN

"I do not know, but they were to attack the other castle before they take this one, just to prove that they can!"

"So you plan to attack Hope Castle before you attack Quarry Castle?' Simon asks with his eyebrow raised.

"Yes," the man says more quietly.

Simon orders his group back to Quarry Castle.

Elizabeth, wrapped in a wool blanket, hunches over a rickety wooden table holding a roasted sheep's leg in one hand, and a loaf of bread in the other. In front of her rests three more loaves of bread, a bowl of drippings, and two casks of red wine. Sir Anthony and Samantha sit across from Elizabeth and silently watch her devour everything in sight.

"Elizabeth, slow down. You will make yourself ill by eating so fast," Samantha coos.

Elizabeth looks up, drippings around her mouth and on the tip of her nose. "You go days, even weeks without proper food, then tell me to stop." She stuffs her mouth with more bread after dipping it into the juice in the stone pan. "Where is Martin? I want to know why it took so long to get me out!" Elizabeth says through a stuffed mouth.

Sir Anthony shakes his head. "The king does not know you have escaped his tower. In fact, no one but us knows, and we must keep it that way."

Elizabeth glares at him. "Why? I've got nothing to hide. I need to speak with him. I think Simon plans to take over Saxton's castle to claim as his own!"

"Not so fast," Sir Anthony chimes in. "If we just jump into this without any proof, we will be hung for blasphemy and treason. We need to find someone who the king will listen to and not be accused of being too close to you or Samantha. And I know just the person." Sir Anthony smiles while nodding his head.

Simon and his group of soldiers ride into the Great Army and stop as three guards ride to intersect them. Simon cannot believe the size of the army and that he did not see them earlier. He feels trapped and insecure knowing he ran into one of the largest armies ever established.

"Who are you?" a guard in full armor asks Simon.

"We are from King Martin's kingdom, ally to King Henry. We helped your men board their ships to safety."

"And who is this king you speak of? I do not know him," the guard presses.

"I am sure a great man as yourself knows many great leaders. King Martin made sure your men boarded their ships safely," he says as he looks at the mass of men marching by.

"Where is this kingdom you speak of?"

Simon points in the direction that they march. "The castle you will see is a friend."

The guard looks ahead. "If this is so, they have nothing to worry about." The guard rides off with the army. Simon lets out a long sigh and starts riding quickly around the Great Army, the longer way towards the castle.

Sir Anthony rides alongside his friend, Garnet, dressed in a dark brown robe, as they head towards Quarry castle. Garnet is best known for being a great architect and teacher, and Sir Anthony values his opinions. "I know who the king is, who he was, and I think he will make a good king if he gets the proper guidance and

THE NEW QUEEN

time. Since he has been here, he has been to war at one time or another. What do you think?" Sir Anthony asks.

Garnet stares at the horizon in the west. "I knew the king when he was just a boy, and he was an excellent siege weapon maker, but a king? I don't know. His father made the best catapults ever made, and when Prince took over, he made them as well but they did not stand up as good as his father's did."

"Prince? He is the King, remember?" Sir Anthony says, surprised by Garnet's mistake.

Garnet laughs and almost falls from his horse as Anthony reaches out to help him stay upright. "No, no. Martin's real name is Prince. Did you not know that?" Anthony looks at Garnet as if he were not in his right mind. "It's true his name is Prince Martin, but he likes to drop Prince altogether. Anyway, I just don't know about him being real royalty."

"I have seen boys become kings, and girls become queens. Some are good leaders, while others are cowards. What matters the most in being a leader is time. Every person needs time to grow and learn about what being a king or queen is all about."

The two ride into a small village while chickens scurry out of the way of the huge horses. Men in the fields sow the ground, turning over the soil and some women hang up their laundry along the walls of their houses. "Excuse me" Garnet yells to a woman in the garden. "Can you tell me where we might find Mark guard to the king?" the women points to the next house. Garnet rides ahead and stops at a small wooden house. He dismounts his horse, leaving it with Sir Anthony. He walks to the house's front lawn and shouts, "I am looking for Mark, Guard to His Majesty, King Martin!" Mark opens the door in a long shirt.

"And who are you?"

FRIENDS MAKE ENEMIES

"I am Garnet I serve the king and he wishes you to return. Now." Mark nod and closes the door to get dressed.

Mark, Garnet and Sir Anthony watch in horror as the Great Army marches towards a bridge made to infiltrate the Viking's land. The army pulls out siege weapons from small bushes left behind by the soldiers who marched ahead of them.

"Why are they marching towards the Vikings?" Mark asks as he adjusts his leather pants as sweat runs down his pale face.

Garnet shrugs. "We best stay out of sight. The last thing I want is to be fighting." Garnet moves his horse back into the tree line. Sir Anthony remains still on his horse, watching the large army march towards their target.

"Are you coming?" Mark asks brushing his long hair out of his eyes.

Sir Anthony turns his head towards Mark. "That is not the Great Army I once knew."

"Are you sure it's not the Great Army that King Martin talks about?" Mark asks.

Sir Anthony stares at the marching men, furrowing his eyebrows. "It has the right colors and the right flag, but it is not the Great Army that I know."

Garnet dismounts his horse and walks to Mark and Sir Anthony. "I sense that you think something is wrong."

"The Great Army was always ready to fight. We would have men on the outside of the march in order to see an ambush coming," Sir Anthony reminisces.

"Who in their mind would attack such a large army?" Mark asks.

"One bee may sting you, then fly away. It may bother you, but it won't hurt for long. If many bees sting you, you feel the pain. It

THE NEW QUEEN

is only when the bees return time and time again that they will kill you slowly," Sir Anthony almost whispers.

Mark huffs. "So one ambush won't do much damage, but many will kill the army? Are you nuts? The first time you ambush the army, they will hunt you down and kill you. You wouldn't live to ambush them again."

Sir Anthony still stares at the men. "Unless you have another ambush for the ones who are tracking you, then they die trying, and you live to do the whole thing all over again."

Mark pauses, thinking over Sir Anthony's words. "You slowly take them down, little by little, until they are manageable enough to fight all at once." Mark smiles widely, envisioning an attack on the Great Army. The two turn their horses back to where Garnet had started moving.

"Can we be on our way now?" Garnet asks, annoyed.

"Yes, but we can only go as far as the trees will take us. The Great Army will still be marching past for another day, I suspect," Sir Anthony comments.

Garnet and Mark glance at each other. "How are we going to get past them to warn King Martin?" Mark asks, looking back from where they came from.

Sir Anthony sits silently on his trotting horse, thinking of a plan. "We have to go around them. It may take longer, but not as long as waiting for them to pass will. Follow me."

The three men ride as fast as they can through the tree line, riding deeper into the thickets near the middle. They slow their horses to a trot, interweaving between the pine and spruce. The shadows from the trees darken their path as the sun slowly moves towards the west. A chilly wind blows between the trees, rattling the branches and twirling leaves off the ground. They continue riding in silence, watching the darkening area around them until they arrive at the end of the tree line, staring at the small castle in the distance. In front of the castle, marching in a straight line, remains the Great Army. The line stretches as far as the men can see.

"How big is this army?" Mark asks in amazement.

"I remember there being twenty thousand men," Garnet informs him, staring at the perfectly synced marching men.

"The entire army is over a hundred thousand men, strong and well-trained, but I heard that King Henry is fighting with France in small skirmishes just south of here," Sir Anthony corrects Garnet.

"Where did you hear that?" Garnet asks.

"I have lived here for some time. You hear things."

"What would happen if we just simply walked across the field to the castle?" Mark asks.

"You can't break the line. To do so would mean death," Garnet tells him.

Mark moves closer to the edge of the tree line and squints against the setting sun, seeing a field of colorful tents camped outside the tiny castle. He notices that the army marches as one unit, but there are no men on horses watching for an ambush.

Mark moves back to Garnet and Sir Anthony. "I think the castle has been taken already; there are tents everywhere."

Garnet frowns. "If the castle has fallen, then all is already lost."

"What about the king?" Mark voices his concern as sweat drips from the tip of his nose.

"You two jump to conclusions without any facts. King Martin may have invited them to stay the night for safety, for all we know, or somehow the king had made peace with King Henry. Just stay here until we can get safely to the castle and only then will we know if the king is safe, if we are all safe," Sir Anthony commands, dismounting his horse and searching for firewood.

THE NEW QUEEN

Samantha remains asleep in a wool blanket on the stone floor hidden in the Hope castle, while Elizabeth paces the room wearing an old gown of Samantha's. Her hair is in tangles and caked with dirt and blood, hanging in large knots. Elizabeth, still upset and hurt by Martin for not defending her, realizes she sheds no more love for him, and that scares her. Being locked in a prison tower for weeks drained all of her happiness, and her peace, replacing it with a hardened soul. Elizabeth, lost in deep thought, stumbles into a wooden table, waking her sister.

Samantha rolls over and opens her eyes. "Why are you not asleep yet?" she asks, looking up at Elizabeth.

"Why are you sleeping during the day?" Elizabeth retorts.

"Because I stayed awake rescuing you from the tower," Samantha snaps back. "Are you not glad to be out of that place? I risked my life to save you," she whispers.

"Of course I am grateful, Samantha, but…"

"But what?" Samantha sits up and pulls strands of hair out of her mouth as she stares at her sister.

"But I thought, I was hoping, it would have been the king to save me, not you."

Samantha's eyes turn glossy and her mouth hangs open. "You ungrateful sot! After I risked my life to save you, you would think you'd be happy to even be out of there alive, given the condition you were left in. I stopped my life to nurse you back to health, and all you care about is why the king didn't rescue you!"

Elizabeth stares at the floor. "I am not ungrateful Samantha, truly I am very grateful for your bravery. I had much to think about all alone in that dreadful place. It just hurts to think that everything we have been through with the king wasn't enough for him to think I was important enough to save. After a few weeks, I realized he wasn't coming for me, and with every lash I got, it was really him that was whipping me. My only thoughts were how bad he was, not how good you are to me."

"You cannot go on blaming the king for things out of his hands, Elizabeth. His entire kingdom is being overthrown, and he must tend to that before all else. You wouldn't be worth saving if it meant the entire kingdom would end up being destroyed anyways."

Elizabeth stares at her sister as one, weak tear slides down her cheek.

"You're still in love with him, aren't you?" Samantha asks.

"No. The King is evil just like everyone else. I would never put anyone in there, then whip them and destroy them piece by piece and leave them to be forgotten!" Elizabeth breathes heavy. "I wish he were dead."

"You don't mean that."

"Yes, I do. He's awful."

"Elizabeth, remember who put you in there in the first place."

Elizabeth clenches her hands into fists. "I haven't. I will kill Simon myself."

"You're no killer, Elizabeth."

"I am now," Elizabeth whispers to herself.

Gus and Douglass watch as the Great Army marches past their tents outside of Quarry Castle. Douglass places his hands over his eyes to shield the sun from them. "I think I can see the end."

Gus follows Douglass' gaze. "No, I don't think so. They are just coming over the hill, that's all."

Douglass shakes his head. "No, I see the last soldier and there are none after him."

Gus moves closer towards Douglass and places his hand on his shoulder. They intently watch the end of the line, hoping that the end of the long march is within sight. The last man finally

THE NEW QUEEN

marches over the hill and out of sight. Gus and Douglass let out sighs of relief.

"Tell the men to suit up in full armor and stand outside of their tents and be ready to eat before we start this charade. Make sure they act like soldiers and make sure they eat a good meal. Have the cooks prepare lots of food. I want these men ready as if they were going to fight," Gus commands.

Douglass goes tent to tent delivering Gus' message to the soldiers. After a short time, Douglass arrives beside Gus and stands beside him. Gus turns his head and sighs. "What's wrong?"

"I'm just not sure we have seen the last of them," Gus pauses before continuing. "I do wish the King was here. It would have been easier if he talked with them and made sure they left."

"The Great Army marched right past us and did not even think of attacking us. I think that's truly amazing, don't you?" Douglass asks.

"I just think that it's not over, that's all." Gus looks back towards the tents to see some of the men joking around.

"Hey!" he yells out, startling Douglass. "You are soldiers now, so act like it!" The soldiers wave away Gus and continue their jokes.

Gus rushes up to the disobedient men. "Hey! I said get back to your tent and wait for your food."

One man turns to Gus. "The army is gone. Don't be such a grouchy old man."

Gus draws his sword and points it at the man. "Care to reconsider your words?"

The man also draws his sword and points it at Gus. Gus smiles slightly and taps the man's sword. The man takes a full swing at Gus but Gus redirects the man's sword away, then slashes the man's arm. The man swings again towards Gus, and again Gus redirects the sword but is met by the man's fist and knocks Gus off his feet. The man watches as Gus stands up, swinging his sword

FRIENDS MAKE ENEMIES

around. The man swings at the sword when he is impaled deep in his stomach. Gus moves in close and looks at the man face to face. "I said I wasn't joking. Maybe your death will remind the others how serious this really is." Gus slowly pulls his sword out of the man and watches him fall to the ground, dead. Gus looks around at the gathering crowd. "Let this be a lesson to each and every one of you. This is for life and death. Don't ever forget that!" Gus waves over two men from the crowd. They reluctantly march over and stay silent. "Bury the body, but don't mark the area. I don't want anyone to find the body." Gus leaves the bewildered crowd as Douglass timidly follows behind.

Chapter 16
LIFE

eeks pass since the Great Army marched near the tiny castle, and since then, word arrived from a scout that Hope castle is doing well. Sir Anthony left to return to Hope castle only after asking Martin for a pardon on behalf of Elizabeth. The King granted the release only after Sir Anthony suggested that Simon's witch theory might have been a ploy all along as a distraction so he could concentrate on the surrounding armies.

King Martin enters the courtyard and Garnet approaches him with a cheerful smile.

"Beautiful day," Garnet says, wrapped in a dark cloak with its hood bouncing behind him.

"Yes, it is!" Martin replies, blocking the sun with his hands as he stares at the wall-walk.

"I think if we were to build the main wall out all the way to the tree line, then you could have farms inside the castle. That will be good in times of siege, but it will take a long time to build though," Garnet suggests, studying the stone walls.

"The small castle did not take long to build because we had everyone working on it day and night. All of this," Martin holds out his arms and turns in a circle, "took only four months," Martin announces proudly.

"Just thinking," Garnet starts. "One good, well-placed catapult would cause half the wall to fall down."

"Do you think we would have to replace the entire curtain wall?" Martin asks.

Garnet scans the wall-walk. "It will have to be re-enforced, but not replaced. I would want to have it thicker, maybe another two feet, just to be sure."

Martin turns to Garnet. "That would make it five feet think, Garnet. I know we are on the quarry but, it would easily take another four months to do that. I'm not sure we have that much time."

Garnet shakes his head. "If we do it right, we can have the walls redone, and the new walls done in about three years."

"Three years? For the entire castle? That does not seem right."

Garnet nods. "I think it can be done in three years and don't worry, we will have a few defensive towers along the way, in case of trouble."

Martin taps his chin. "But how will I pay everyone?"

"Similar to the taxes, one in seven, except this time, you get everyone from your kingdom. That's a few thousand men and even more if you count the women. Let me show you something." Garnet leads Martin through the front gate and points ahead at the tree line. "That's where we have to build past and cut all those trees down. It's just a barricade."

Martin squints at the trees. "I want to see what's on the other side of that tree line. Since I arrived here, I have never gone

THE NEW QUEEN

beyond them. I mean, I have gone to the other castle and traveled to Saxton's castle, but never past my own tree line."

Garnet nods and leads the way towards the tree line. Four guards leave the front gate and follow behind the two men. As they continue walking through the wet fields, ten mounted guards ride out on horses, forming a horseshoe around them. Each mounted guard dresses in full chain mail armor, carry a loaded crossbow strapped to their back, and a long sword at their hip as their shields hang on the side of the horses.

The group arrives at the tree line as a few guards dismount and walk ahead, exploring the forest for any signs of danger. They turn back and wave Martin and Garnet over. The king's boots slosh through the mud and puddles as he approaches an even muddier, beaten down path. Different tracks scatter the path—horse's hooves, shoe prints, deer tracks, and rabbit prints—all the way down, leading to the direction of King Richard's old castle. A rusty sword rests between two fern plants, and torn red flags entangle in a nearby mulberry bush. Martin continues walking up the path, realizing this forest must have been where King Richard's men hid out before he attacked the castle.

"Halt!" a guard shouts, holding up his crossbow. Martin and Garnet immediately stop and they unsheathe their swords. Another guard joins the one that yelled, and raises his crossbow, walking side by side. More guards surround the king, some on foot, others on their horses, and all with their swords drawn. They remain silent as a breeze blows through the trees.

The two guards with crossbows emerge from a thick collection of pine trees. "We found a body, then a few further on. It looks like they have been dead for some time."

"Are they our men?" Martin asks.

The guards shake their heads.

LIFE

"Very well, let's move on then." Martin sheathes his sword and continues up the path.

A few guard rush before him, looking up at the trees and far into the shadows of the forest for intruders. They walk quietly in a group, looking for anything out of the ordinary until they reach the other side of the trees.

"I never realized those were so large a group of trees," Martin starts. "When Richard attacked us, I truly thought my trebuchet could reach the other side of this forest, but now I don't think so. This forest is misleading." Martin turns to the open fields at the end of the forest. He walks to the edge of the field and crouches down, pulling up a blade of grass and scraping his finger in the dirt. "It looks good for tilling," he comments, holding a clump of dirt.

"This will be great if we can get the castle walls around the trees," Garnet says, scratching his chin.

Martin throws the clump of dirt aside and stands up. "Now that will take a long time."

Garnet nods. "Yes...it might be six or seven years."

"If I can get enough men, we can build the towers all at once and then fill in the walls. If we work all day and night, rotating in shifts, I think we can do the entire thing in two years at most," Martin says.

"Doubtful at the two-year estimation, but it would be incredibly impressive if you manage that." Garnet takes one final look at the field, then turns back to the forest with Martin following behind him. "Where is Simon?"

"I have been thinking about that a great deal. With the Great Army fighting the Vikings, I don't think Simon will be back anytime soon. He is exploring Saxton's kingdom, I understand," Martin explains.

THE NEW QUEEN

"I thought it was a great idea to have the men march like soldiers and fool the army that camped by the castle. It was truly brilliant," Garnet comments.

"Yes, Douglass is one smart man, and it worked out in the best possible way. If they only knew how fooled, they were, I think they would want to attack now." King Martin smirks.

"I agree. We need a similar plan to show King Henry that we are not afraid of him or his army. The only way to do that is to have a bigger army that he can see is well-trained and ready for battle, but we don't have an army like that."

Martin leads Garnet through the trees, stepping over fallen logs and ducking under low branches until they find an opening that faces the castle. "I remember when I was a kid, the king had this big fair and I got all this sugarcane to eat." Martin chuckles. "What a great time we had...everyone seemed happy."

Garnet stops walking and stomps his foot on the grass, trying to rid his boots of the mud. He looks up and smiles at Martin. "The only time a kingdom would have a fair is if there were no threats. That way, no army would attack because every ally would be there. To attack at a fair, you would be attacking every kingdom at once."

"That's it!" Martin exclaims. "We will have a fair. We will invite the French, the Vikings and our kingdoms to celebrate with us. Once King Henry sees we are having fun, he won't attack... he might even think that his chances are gone."

"But what if he does attack?" Garnet asks.

"He won't, he's no fool. Besides, we will have the French here as well, and the last thing King Henry will want is to have the French entrenched in this land. Plus, we will have all the landowners here with their soldiers which will surely outnumber his army." Martin stomps his boots along the grass and grabs a long stick, scraping the dried mud off the tops of his boots.

LIFE

"This might work, but you will need to send someone to the French now for them to arrive in time during the next few months. Bringing an army that large requires several months of planning, sire."

Martin stops scraping the mud off his boots and turns back to Garnet. "Months? I want this to start in four weeks. It will take our man five days to get there, and five back. That will give the French three weeks to decide if they want to show or not and we can even have our men wait in their kingdom for an answer before they arrive back to us."

"And what if the French don't come?"

The king thinks for a moment. "You're right, we will have to persuade them somehow. Let's have them bring their bakers to bake goods for the festival, that way they won't be worried about the food. I heard before that they don't like our cooking much anyways."

Garnet nods. "We will need lots of meat to feed all of these armies: boar, deer, even bear, if we can get it. Anything we can hunt, we will need." Garnet taps his finger on his chin. "We should be okay with the crops, but the granaries are in short supply of flour, and there must be bread. Where can we get enough flour in less than a month?"

"That's one reason to bring your own baker—they bring their own flour as well," Martin says with a smile and pats Garnet on the back. "Get a man to go to the French right away and once he returns, have the hunters start hunting. We will know how much they will need to hunt when he returns. And when the man gets back from the French, get a few men to go out and start telling the kingdom. I want as many men as possible to participate in this

THE NEW QUEEN

fair. Also, send word to Otto, the Viking leader. Make sure he is invited, too. This might turn out to be a large treaty party!"

Simon and his band of soldiers travel on a longer path around the channel, crossing paths with another large army heading towards Hope Castle.

"This army must be close to whoever they are going to attack," a soldier says quietly to Simon.

"I thought that as well, but they have not stopped marching. We have been following this army for three days, and they pull those heavy catapults all the way. We will continue to follow them and keep well out of sight. I need one of you to get to Hope Castle and tell them trouble is heading their way." Simon pushes the man's head down as a soldier looks towards them, then turned away. A young soldier volunteered and heads back to Hope Castle on horseback.

The evening starts to set, and the sun grows bright red in the sky, turning the tree color from deep green to a black when Simon spots a man quickly walking through the camp. Simon watches carefully as the guard pulls out something from a sack. Simon recognizes it right away. It is a hand-woven handkerchief from Gwyneth, belonging to the soldier he sent ahead. Not long after, the soldier drags the guard's limp body and drops it in front of the captain. The captain walks around the body and he plunges his sword deep into the guard. Simon's head falls to the ground as he takes a deep breath. "It is war," he says to himself, as the captain leaves the dead body in the middle of the camp.

LIFE

Sir Anthony accompanies Elizabeth through the gardens and hallways, avoiding the busy courtyards and the Great Hall. Elizabeth's blush dress hangs loosely off her shoulders and back, allowing the cool air to relieve the pain from her backlashes. The dark bruises and scabs crisscross down her back, dark enough to be seen through the blush material. Specks of blood dot the back of the dress where some wounds cracked open. Elizabeth stops walking and leans her shoulder against a pillar, breathing heavy, tears welling in her eyes.

"I need to take a break, please," Elizabeth pants. Sir Anthony nods as he stands beside her, eyeing the budding garden. Behind them, shouts echo through the hallways followed by the sound of racing horse hooves and the clang of metal. Sir Anthony turns around and grabs Elizabeth's arm, pulling her with him. "Where are we going?" she asks. Sir Anthony continues to pull her with him but says nothing. "Stop! Stop! I can't move this fast!" Elizabeth pleads.

They stop beside a small hut where women make yarn and hide in the shadows of the side of the hut. Guards run towards the gate and move quickly up the stairs to the wall-walk. Sir Anthony lets go of Elizabeth's arm and places his finger over his lips. He sneaks up to a guard who pauses to load his crossbow.

"What are you doing?" Sir Anthony asks the guard. Elizabeth remains hidden to the side of the hut.

"A scout saw a large army heading this way. We are to be ready for an attack. I think it's a great army. I hope it is the Great Army so we can fight them and in!" The young guard looks up at Sir Anthony with excitement in his eyes.

"If it is the Great Army and you have to fight them, just remember they outnumber you a hundred to one. You could not shoot them all if they just marched into the castle. They would kill you before you got three, maybe four shots off." Sir Anthony places his hand onto the boy's shoulder. "Be careful, my boy, and good luck." Sir Anthony watches the young soldier rush off to the others and Sir Anthony joins Elizabeth next to the hut. "Well," he starts, looking at her, "an army approaches and if it is the Great Army, we won't hold out long. I just hope that they sent for help from Quarry Castle."

"Samantha and I could go and get help," Elizabeth offers.

"No, we need to stay here and let the men do their jobs. I am sure they have sent someone already." They watch as the guards barricade the front gate. "Ah, perhaps we should inform the King after all..."

Several days pass since the messenger left for France. A massive spring storm rages through the kingdom where King Martin paces in his bedchamber, watching the violent thunderstorm rip through the fields and rattle the walls of the castle. The wind shakes the branches of the trees as lightning flashes across the dark grey sky.

"Your majesty," Mark starts, bursting into the bedchamber. "Should we send out some hunters when the storm dies down? That will be a perfect time because the game will be looking for food after the storm."

Martin nods and taps his chin. "Has the messenger returned yet?"

"No, your majesty."

Martin sighs. "Very well, send some men to hunt. It doesn't hurt to have some extra food."

Mark nods. "We have also received word that a scout has sighted an army four days away. They seem to be cutting through the kingdom."

"Are they any threat to us?"

LIFE

"Not at the moment, sire, but if they turn even a little, they will be."

Martin thinks for a moment. "Have a few scouts track this army and send word if they are going to attack us."

Mark nods and leaves the room.

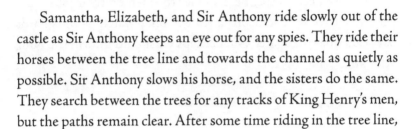

Samantha, Elizabeth, and Sir Anthony ride slowly out of the castle as Sir Anthony keeps an eye out for any spies. They ride their horses between the tree line and towards the channel as quietly as possible. Sir Anthony slows his horse, and the sisters do the same. They search between the trees for any tracks of King Henry's men, but the paths remain clear. After some time riding in the tree line, they stop at a fallen tree trunk to eat.

They tie their horses to a nearby tree as they graze around, eating leaves and patches of grass. The air is filled with moisture and the soil remains softer than the rest of the forest, signs that they are not far from the channel. Elizabeth sits on the log and gives each of them a small loaf of bread from her leather satchel. Samantha unravels smoked deer, thinly sliced and charred. Sir Anthony brings out his leather canteen of peppermint infused hot water that hangs around his neck. He slides off the log and onto the damp soil, resting his back against the wood. The girls quietly stand up and unwrap some blankets tied around the horses. Sir Anthony's head hangs back, and his mouth gapes open as a low snore escapes his mouth.

"Should I wake him?" Elizabeth whispers.

"Elizabeth, I don't know, he's old! He must get tired faster than we do. Just let him sleep, I guess. There's no one else here right now."

"If someone comes," Elizabeth starts, picking up Sir Anthony's staff on the ground, "I will teach them a lesson in manners, won't

I?" Elizabeth giggles. "Yes, I can see you now," she continues, sidestepping quietly and pointing the staff in front of her. "Now draw your sword, and I will stab you with this stick. It may not look like I know what I am doing, but let me tell you, I don't!" The two laugh quietly at her rendition of a battle and Elizabeth finishes her speech by twirling the staff between her hands.

Sir Anthony moves slightly, and the girls stand in silence. Samantha studies the man's face, as the deep creases around his eyes look darker and his thin lips almost look grey. She notices a large scar across his forehead that she did not see before. Another large scar extends up his neck and disappears under his wool sweater across his shoulder. His chest rises and falls in a steady rhythm that matches his inhaled snores. A fly buzzes around his nose, and he sneezes, jolting up. Sir Anthony stares between the sisters and blinks at them. "I must apologize. I tend to nod off every now and then...is everything alright?"

They nod and stand side by side. "Yes, everything is fine," Samantha answers.

Sir Anthony glances up at the tree branches and Elizabeth notices the stretched scar down his neck. "Where did you get that scar on your neck?" Elizabeth blurts out.

Samantha nudges her sister. "We better get the horses some water, Elizabeth," Samantha interjects. She pulls her sister towards the horses. "I can't believe you."

"What? It's just a question," Elizabeth answers.

"To ask a man something so personal...you're lucky he doesn't slap you for your behavior. I mean really, Elizabeth, he's trying to help us, and you test him any way you can," Samantha hisses in a whisper.

"I'm not!"

"You are! You never ask a man about his past! Did father not teach you anything?"

LIFE

Elizabeth rolls her eyes. "The only thing father taught me was a question never asked is a question never answered."

Samantha sighs. "You ask too many questions, Elizabeth."

"So I've been told." Elizabeth grabs the horse reins.

They gather the horses and walk them over to the tree log. Sir Anthony stands holding his staff in his right hand. "We better get going," he comments, pulling the sweater higher up his neck.

"Well?" Elizabeth says, looking at Sir Anthony.

He turns to her. "What?"

"The scar on your neck." She moves closer to him and motions towards him. "You know how I got mine, now tell me how you got yours?"

He turns away, stepping over the log. "In a battle during training." He moves towards his horse as Samantha slaps Elizabeth on the back of her head.

"Hey!" Elizabeth shouts while grabbing the reins from Samantha. Elizabeth turns back towards Sir Anthony. "Where was this battle? Did you win? I mean you must have won since you are here. How long ago was it?" She asks, following closely to Sir Anthony.

Sir Anthony stops and turns to Elizabeth. "It was when I was training to fight. I was a boy fighting another boy. One of us was to be killed. It was training, and I survived, that's all. I do not wish to talk about it again." He turns away and Samantha once again slaps her on the back of the head. They all mount their horses and continue riding through the forest, Sir Anthony riding ahead of the sisters.

After clearing a thicket, a bush ruffles off to the far side. Sir Anthony stops his horse and raises his hand. He dismounts while Samantha and Elizabeth raise their crossbows and hold them at the ready. Sir Anthony slowly walks towards the bushes when two men come rushing towards him, wielding their swords. Elizabeth

THE NEW QUEEN

shoots her crossbow at one man, wounding his left arm and making him drop his sword. The other man attacks Sir Anthony who deflects the sword away and whacks him across his knee. The man falls to the ground in pain. Sir Anthony looks at the other man wincing in pain from the crossbow wound. Then he turns and approaches Elizabeth. "You should not shoot so quickly. If you had missed and there were more of them, you would not live to tell the tale." He grabs her crossbow and reloads it. "A good soldier will wait and get a kill shot. One less man to fight, you see?" he says, handing her the crossbow. "But I thank you anyways." He pats Elizabeth's shoulder and mounts his horse once again. They continue riding through the forest, leaving the injured men on the ground.

Chapter 17
ENEMIES FROM THE DARK

The stars from the clear night sky provide light for Simon and his guards to sit quietly among the tall grass, watching the army's movements. "We have to keep out of sight and watch their movement and we will tall the king soon. This grass is good cover."

"Do you know where we are, sir?" a guard asks Simon.

"I was just thinking about that. I know we were deep into what was Saxton's kingdom. We are south, about a three days ride or so from Quarry Castle. We had to travel away from our kingdom another four, maybe five days ride west." Simon points eastward with a stick. "Which means we are still in our kingdom, the part that King Richard owned at one time."

"Do we know who these guys are yet? Are they French? I mean, they came from that way right?" the guard also asks.

THE NEW QUEEN

"The French and English carry large blue flags. The flag that this army carries is unknown; I have never seen before. Their flag is yellow with a red stripe from one corner to the next, and it had like birds on it, too." Simon continues watching the guard of the army pacing back and forth. He hears an approaching noise from some trees, and Simon draws his sword when one of his scouts appears.

"Captain," the scout says quietly.

Simon sheathes his sword. "What do you have to report?"

"You are definitely right. The guards are not well-trained. Most of the army is inexperienced, but some have training. The men are tired of marching and were told they are almost at their destination. I'm thinking their destination is Hope Castle. I think a few good men could kill most off but whoever fights them will just tire out before winning the battle. There is a bunch of lowlife swine to fight," the scout concludes.

"With the Great Army to the east and this army in front of us, we have no way to send for help and I don't want to risk losing any more good men either. We don't have any guards at the castle."

"We might be able to get into camp to kill a bunch and get out before we are noticed," the scout suggests.

Simon shakes his head. "That would be a great idea if we were all from the Black Army, but were not. I think all we can do is follow them until we can find a way to the castle and have them prepare the defenses." Simon walks over to his party, the scout following closely behind, and schedules the nightly shifts before turning in for the night

Martin gathers a group of guards near the edge of the granaries to create a new game for the fair. The sunshine warms the group as they gather around Martin, watching him set up the new game. The king lays out two sticks, ten paces apart, on either end of the

field. "It's easy," he starts, "all you have to do is get this ball between your opponent's sticks." Martin holds up a lumpy, patchy ball made of pigskin and stuffed with grass.

"This doesn't seem very challenging...I can just throw it in from here?" one of the larger guards asks.

Martin shakes his head. "One player will stay between the sticks to guard them, so you can't do that. His job is to stop the pigskin."

"Can we carry the pigskin?" a different guard with curly hair asks.

"Yes, you can carry it, kick it, and even throw it." Martin tosses the pigskin in the air and catches it with both hands.

"What kind of game is that?" the large guard asks.

Martin smiles. "If your team does not have the pigskin, you must stop them from getting it between your two sticks."

"How?" the guard strokes his beard.

"Any way you can!"

"Can we kick them?" a shorter guard asks.

"Yes," Martin responds.

"Can we punch them?" a blonde guard asks.

"Yes," Martin repeats.

"Can we bite them?" a boy asks, clapping his hands.

"If you want, yes. You can do anything to them as long as the opponent has the ball, but, if they do not have the ball, you cannot touch them. If you do, you will be removed from the field, and your team will be short a man to defend the sticks and get points."

"So it is better to get rid of the ball before the other team attacks you?" the blonde guard asks.

Martin nods.

"What is this game called?" the boy asks, jumping up and down with excitement.

Martin stares at the field for a moment. "Soccer!"

THE NEW QUEEN

"Soccer!" the boy repeats. The men nod in agreement with smiles on their faces.

Martin walks with the men out to the middle of the field and divides them into even teams of six players each: one group with shirts on and the other without. He tosses the ball into the air and the fight begins.

Elizabeth waits at the top of a hill under some shade with the horses while Samantha and Sir Anthony travel in opposite directions to search for water. Samantha and Sir Anthony quickly disappear into the forest. She waits in silence as the horses flick their tails and graze behind her. Elizabeth hears a branch snap off to her right, and she sits up, squinting into the darkness. "Samantha?" she calls out. She dismounts and walks towards the noise, gripping her pocket knife. As she passes the fourth set of trees, she hears a growl. "Samantha?" she repeats, her voice quivering. A lower, deeper, closer growl responds.

Elizabeth scrambles out of the forest towards the horses, slashing her pocket knife at the branches and foliage in front of her. Behind a bush of red berries, a pair of yellow eyes and gnarling fangs block her path. Elizabeth stares at the black wolf, paralyzed with fright, feeling her heart pound in her chest. The wolf hops over the bush and creeps towards her, each thick paw leaving a track in the moist ground. Behind the wolf's shoulder, another wolf emerges from the shrubbery; a thinner grey wolf with matching yellow eyes. It bows its head and snaps its teeth, following its leader. Slowly, the wolves pace around her, inching forward. They snap at her, both growling and baring their teeth.

Elizabeth keeps her knife outstretched, pointing it back and forth between each wolf. She feels the hot breath of the grey wolf as it snaps its jaw near her thigh and she backs away from it. She

ENEMIES FROM THE DARK

backs into a tree and the black wolf charges at her. She ducks down and the wolf lands on its side. The grey wolf dashes forward and Elizabeth slices its face with her knife. It yelps as Elizabeth pulls her knife back, dripping in blood. A long gash from under its left eye to its jaw oozes blood, and the wolf shakes its head. The black wolf sprints towards her when Sir Anthony emerges from the side and stabs the wolf with a sword. It yelps and rushes beside the grey wolf, standing side by side. The wolves, both bloody and tired, whimper and back away before disappearing into the trees.

Sir Anthony stands over Elizabeth, his sword in one hand and the other outstretched to help Elizabeth up.

"Where did you come from?" she asks.

"I am where I am needed, never too far." He hands the sword to Elizabeth and he grabs his staff leaning against an oak tree.

"Thank-" Elizabeth starts, but Sir Anthony cuts her off.

"Never you mind, beasts are everywhere...we are in the forest after all." They walk through the thickets towards the horses. "I found a small stream near the bottom of this hill and I filled up both wine sacks," Sir Anthony adds.

Samantha stands by the three horses, her hands on her hips. "Where have you two been?" she snaps. "Elizabeth, I told you to stay here while Sir Anthony and I find water. You're lucky the horses didn't run off somewhere."

Elizabeth looks up at her sister but says nothing. She walks straight for her horse and mounts it, Sir Anthony helping her shaking body onto it. "You're alright now," Sir Anthony says to her.

"What's over? What happened?" Samantha asks, staring into Elizabeth's blank eyes. She waits a minute for an answer before placing her hand on Elizabeth's thigh. "Please tell me what happened."

Elizabeth kicks her hand away, tears welling in her eyes. "Wolves." Her voice cracks. "I thought I could kill them on my

THE NEW QUEEN

own." She shakes her head. Samantha clasps her hand over her mouth. "I'm fine," Elizabeth says, wiping her eyes. "Come on, we need to get out of here before we are found." She whips the horse's reins and she shoots forward, racing down the hill.

Samantha rides alongside her sister as Elizabeth stares blankly ahead. "Elizabeth? Elizabeth, what happened?" Samantha pries, keeping her horse at the same speed as Elizabeth's. Elizabeth stares ahead. Samantha, desperate for answers, pushes her horse closer to Sir Anthony's. "What happened to Elizabeth, to the both of you? Why won't she talk?"

Sir Anthony looks at her. "Perhaps she realizes that she isn't as strong as she thought."

Samantha frowns and she glares at him. "That doesn't explain why she won't talk to me," Samantha starts. "Did you hurt her? Did you force your way with her?" Her voice cracks.

Sir Anthony stops his horse, and so does Samantha. He clenches his jaw and slaps Samantha across her cheek, leaving a red streak. "How dare you! To even think such a thought of me." He quickly inhales and exhales, his heart pounding. Samantha winces as she rubs her cheek, the pain already subsiding. She stares at him again and he exhales, then frowns as the wrinkles around his mouth fold closer together. "You truly have insulted me, Samantha." She hangs her head, hiding her watery eyes. He whips the horse's reins and heads towards the castle.

Samantha trots over to her sister and they ride together in silence.

Rollo, the leader of the Viking village, watches the approaching English army from behind a collection of young oak trees. The long history between the two had always been in conflict, due to the English wanting to rule the Welsh. Rollo crouches in the grass as

ENEMIES FROM THE DARK

his long red beard scrapes the ground. The English wheel their catapults and ride their war horses towards the Viking village. Rollo's heart pounds as he watches the invading force, knowing that the village does not contain enough soldiers compared to the overwhelming amount of English that keep arriving. Rollo rolls his large body over and looks up to the sky. "Forseti, God of Justice, let there be justice today, and I pray to Oden, the Father of all Battles, to protect us. Protect our clan from the English." He watches a large group of old farmers volunteer as soldiers, attacking the English with swords and axes that they own. Rollo knows they are outnumbered and their weapons are weaker compared to the English.

As the English approach the point of ambush, hundreds of their men fall into Rollo's trap— a manmade trench that surrounds the south end of the village. He watches as the grass caves in from the weight of the Englishmen and the trench quickly fills up with bodies. The trench barricades the English temporarily, allowing the Vikings more time to plan a strategy.

"We need to stay here longer," Rollo says to his nearby Vikings as they spy on the English. "If we attack now, we won't do much damage to them, but they will destroy all of us and take our land, too. A night attack will be more in our favour." Rollo's old soldiers murmur in agreement, trusting Rollo wholeheartedly.

Soon enough, the trench fills with the bodies of the English cross over it safely. They set up camp, not ten feet from the ambush point, just beyond the trench. Stars glimmer in the black sky.

Rollo and his men stay hidden among the trees as the English night patrols pace back and forth around the campsite. "Once night falls, I will give the word to attack," Rollo commands. He crawls to the trench, followed by his men. They reach close to a collection of tents and wait until all movement inside the tents stop for the night. He points towards the tents, and once the patrols walk in

THE NEW QUEEN

the opposite direction, his men rush over to the tents and kill the English in their sleep. He watches as they swiftly move to the other tents, rushing in and out in silence.

A guard slumps on a rock and yawns, his eyes drooping. Rollo, with an axe in one hand, rushes up behind the man and slices his neck. The head hangs to the side as the body falls forward with a slight thump. A waterfall of blood gushes from the wound and down the guard's armour. At that time, hundreds of other Vikings from the village move into the campsite, rushing in and out of each tent. Rollo retreats into the woods to spot the next lookout guard and stalks him while his men disappear inside the tents of their enemies, some wiping the blood on the tents as they exit.

Rollo's men circle the campsite once more in each tent, making sure every Englishman was dead before leaving. He orders twenty of his men to look out for any more English soldiers that might be wandering around. They spread around the campsite staring at the darkness and listening for any movements. The men pillage the tents of any valuables—gold, weapons, food, and clothing—before they gather the bodies in a pile and light them on fire. Across the land, small bonfires of bodies break the darkness as dark smoke rises in the air, blending with the night sky. Rollo orders for any useless items such as wooden weapons and remaining catapults, to burn in a separate bonfire. As the fires die down, the Vikings leave the campsites and return to their village with a large hull of gold, food, and weapons.

King Martin and Mark walk around the field, carrying canteens of water when a young boy rushes over to them. "That was a great game," the blonde boy comments with a grin and his forehead sweaty.

"Do you think it would be good enough to play at the fair?" Martin asks him, watching the game continue.

"Oh, yes! I want to play it all the time now!" the boy responds, skipping alongside Martin.

"Yes, why don't you play it when we have the fair?" Mark nags, throwing his shirt back on.

"I might," Martin responds. "Wouldn't it be funny to see King Henry running with the ball?" Mark chuckles. "I would like to get the ball from him. I would make sure he paid for each step he took, that's for sure," Martin adds.

"I would bite him!" the boy shouts.

"It might be hard to tell which one is the roundest—the pigskin or King Henry," Mark adds.

Martin watches two men carry a boy off the field, his leg bent strangely. The boy screams and cries as blood gushes from the leg. They carry him across the field while two more men join the field and the game continues. "It is a rough game...good for toughening up a boy, that's for sure," Mark comments.

"Yes, but I hope no one would get hurt like that at the fair. Can you imagine how busy the maidens would be if they had to mend all those bones?" Martin says.

"Maybe you shouldn't play it during the fair?" Mark answers.

"We will see, I just don't know yet." Martin walks close to a crowd that stands along the side of the field, watching this new game. A woman near the end of the crowd points at the forest and screams. Martin, with the rest of the crowd, stares at a fully grown bison emerging from the forest. The crowd turns and rushes to the castle, while Martin and some guards stay behind.

The bison huffs and charges towards the crowd. Guards rush towards the massive beast, swinging their swords. One guard swings his sword as the bison bows his head and charges right at him, tossing him straight into the air before crashing to the field. Another guard tries swinging at the beast's neck but the wild animal tramples the man, crushing him. The giant beast shakes its head and charges at Martin as guards shoot their crossbows at it. The bison takes many arrows on its side but has little effect as it continues its rampage. Mark draws his sword. "Run, sire, run!" he shouts, standing in front of Martin.

"Everyone, back to the castle now!" the king orders. Arrows fall around the beast, guards swing their swords in the air, and some men without weapons throw rocks until the bison changes targets and heads for the boy with the broken leg. He cries for help, and Martin tries rushing towards him, but Mark stands in his way.

"We can't help him, your majesty," Mark says as the bison catches up with the boy.

Men with crossbows fire their weapons at the animal, many of them bouncing off the animal's horns. Martin grabs a crossbow from a guard and looks at Mark. "Make sure everyone gets into the castle," he orders, then runs towards the giant bison. Martin waves his hands over his head in an attempt to distract the animal, but it continues crushing the remainder of the boy and the two men who carry him. The large, mad animal catches a glimpse of Martin, roars, and charges for the king. Martin's heart pounds as he sprints towards the forest with the bison tailing behind. He listens as the large hooves of the animal approach faster. He changes directions and follows the ruts made by the plows. If he can run across the furrows, the bison might break its stride and slow down, giving the king some time to reach the forest. Martin makes a sharp turn and the animal quickly follows.

Martin hears the animal approaching closer, knowing he will not make it in time to the forest. He stands to the side, pulls out the loaded crossbow, and takes careful aim at the charging beast. He waits until the animal is almost in front of him before taking the shot, aiming right at the animal's leading leg. The bison groans and

ENEMIES FROM THE DARK

trips to the ground in a fit of rage before slowly rising. Martin's eyes widen, and he sprints towards the forest, throwing the crossbow over his shoulder. He hears the beast huffing close behind, the arrow still sticking through its leg. Blood gushes every time the animal steps on the ground but it maintains its speed. The king makes it to the forest and sprints through it as leaves and branches whip him across the face. Martin rushes into the woods as he hears a group of men shouting nearby, led by Mark. They call out to the animal as a distraction, but the bison maintains fixated on Martin and roars in anger.

Martin cuts behind larger trees, but the animal barrels through them and uproots some of the smaller trees. The king stops behind a large tree and watches the animal slow its pace as it fights through the thick branches. The beast shakes its head back and forth, breaking branches and toppling trees in rage.

The bison stares directly at Martin with its black eyes as blood drips down its raw, pink nose. It lets out a loud, angry cry and stomps the ground with its hoof, ready to charge at the king. Martin sprints to a nearby oak tree near the edge of the forest and pulls himself onto a few of the low-hanging branches. The bison repeatedly charges into the tree trunk, shaking Martin and the tree with every forceful push. Martin holds the branches and the tree trunk tighter as he climbs higher and higher. The beast cries out again and stands directly beside the tree, looking up the branches for its prey.

Out of the distance, Martin's men approach closer, yelling for their king while rustling through the tree branches. The animal turns its head to the direction of the approaching men then back at Martin's tree. The beast quickly circles the tree, huffing, then charges towards the approaching men.

Martin's heart pounds as he scrambles down the tree branches to help his men battle the bison. As he lowers himself onto each

THE NEW QUEEN

branch, he hears men screaming in pain. The king panics and jumps off the branch he stands on, landing onto the soft grass below. He slices his hand on a fallen branch as he quickly pushes himself up and sprints towards the sounds of the attack.

By the time he reaches the men, the giant bison lays dead in the middle of the group, while two crushed bodies sprawl on the ground off to the side.

"Sire!" one of the guards calls out to him as he approaches closer. "Are you alright?"

Martin nods, wiping dirt off his upper lip and clenching his shirt with his bleeding hand. Guards sheath their swords and others strap the crossbows back on. He paces towards the creature and analyzes it. Foam pours out of its broken jaw and arrows portrude from its side. Blood forms around each wound and flows out of the moose's nostrils, dripping onto the ground in a pool.

Mark approaches Martin, standing beside him. "Why would it attack like that?"

Another guard nearby steps forward, staring at the answer. "Witchcraft, perhaps, sire?"

Martin shakes his head. "No, it was sick...mad with fever." Martin crouches down beside the animal's torso, looking closer at the arrow wounds. Yellow puss gathers around some of the arrow entries, while others remain dark red. Patches of missing fur expose its leg, covered with scars from animal bites. "Burn the animal here and right away. It is not to be used for meat or clothing. I don't want disease running ramped in the kingdom." Mark motions with a simple nod to another guard to burn the animal and he walks back beside the king to the castle.

Chapter 18
RETALIATION!

Sir Gregory barricades the King's bedchamber door to study the Great Army's map from his tent raids. He lights an oil lamp and places it on top of the fireplace beside the bed. Gently unrolling the torn map, Sir Gregory places it on the bedside table and slumps onto the bed beside it, staring at the detailed drawings. "Hmm," he starts, looking at the unusual markings across the map. He analyzes the map and matches the coloured markings with the legend in the bottom left corner. The red markings symbolize the lords and barons with the most land, while the blue-green markings symbolize unclaimed land. Many of the claimed lands are circled in red, and Sir Gregory scratches his chin trying to think of the meaning behind it. Some groups of villages, including Saxton's kingdom and the villages to the far East of King Martin's kingdom, have dark smudges around them. "This can't be a war map, can it? The king of the Great Army was never at war with Saxton, or whoever owns the land now," Gregory comments, studying the trail of smudges. "Perhaps it's a war map of the Great Army? It would make sense; however, the king of the Great Army would not have known where King Richard's land started or ended...but how would they know about the wealth of all the villages?" Sir Gregory asks himself. The map shows the detail of the entirety of the land— from the village layouts to the detail of the terrain itself; where cliffs start, where the largest rivers run, and the safest routes of travel between kingdoms.

Sir Gregory traces the frayed edges of the map, following the markings down the sides. At the beginning of a forested section, where a safe route is drawn through it, the drawing abruptly stops. He traces his finger down the rough edge where the parchment is ripped. "The rest of the map is missing?" he says aloud, flipping the map over in the search for a name. The backside is blank. One of the markings on the map resembles letters of a foreign language and are written around a village close to the castle. "Time to visit that village and search for answers," he comments, rolling up the map and placing it in the breast of his leather vest.

Sir Gregory rides outside the castle's main gates and pauses as he determines the direction towards the village when Gus walks up behind him.

"Where are you going on this morning?" Gus asks.

"I just have to run an errand, that's all," Sir Gregory responds flatly.

Gus frowns. "Something tells me that's not all of it."

Sir Gregory looks away and nudges his horse to take off. Gus frowns again, then races to the stables for a horse to catch up with his friend.

Gus follows Sir Gregory's tracks at a safe distance, keeping hidden behind the trees and bushes. He follows the trail of mud prints, recognizing the galloping pattern of Sir Gregory's horse. Gus backtracks and turns the corner behind a spruce tree while he sees Sir Gregory rest along some boulders. He dismounts and

RETALIATION!

ties his horse next to a small stream where it grazes nearby. Gus slumps against the tree and drinks water from his flask. He closes his eyes and listens to the chirping birds and squirrels scurrying up some trees. The soothing noises soon drift him off to sleep as his mouth hangs open. Sir Gregory approaches the snoozing Gus and taps him on the shoulder. Gus jolts up and swings around, holding his sword to Sir Gregory's throat.

"Hello to you, too," Sir Gregory says.

"You scared the hell out of me!" Gus sheathes his sword.

"What are you doing here? I said I had some things to do alone."

Gus shrugs. "It was the way you said it, and how little you said. I figured you could use some help."

"You're right, I could use you for some help. Come on," Sir Gregory says, waving his hand towards Gus.

Gus unties his horse and they walk back up the path towards the boulders. Sir Gregory clears his throat and reaches into his vest, taking out the rolled map. "I found this," Sir Gregory says, handing Gus the map.

Gus unrolls the map and stares at all the markings. "Is this a war map?"

"I thought so at first, but it shows nothing about strength or defenses."

"What's this?" Gus asks, pointing to the same mysterious letters that Sir Gregory noticed.

Sir Gregory smiles. "That's what we are going to find out."

Following the detailed map of the land, they take the marked safe routes around forests and avoid major rivers until they reach the village. Sir Gregory looks around carefully, looking at the simple buildings and architecture. A few fields surround the village, the land tilled and ready for crops.

THE NEW QUEEN

Gus dismounts and walks over to a peddler, leaning against a stone house. Sir Gregory follows behind. "Can you tell me how many people live in this village?"

The short man looks back at Gus but does not reply. He blinks his wrinkled eyelids and crosses his arms. The rolled up torn sleeves of his wool shirt reveal dirty, wrinkled skin underneath. His silver-brown shaggy hair hangs past his ears. Sir Gregory stands beside Gus and asks the same question in French, yet the man remains silent. They leave the peddler and continue through the village.

The men pass several houses and a barn until Sir Gregory spots a monk in the distance. The monk strolls up a path heading in their direction. He wears a long black robe that ends right below his ankles, and a black wool hood hangs off his small shoulders. Sir Gregory nudges Gus to follow him. They slowly approach the monk and the monk looks up at them. His soft brown eyes widen at their sight, and he quickly stumbles behind a house. Gus and Sir Gregory quicken their pace after the monk until they round the same corner of the house. The monk whips out the end of a sickle from his breast pocket and charges at them, his hand shaking.

"We only want information, nothing more," Gregory says, trying to reason with the man. "Do you speak English?"

The monk swings at Sir Gregory and he knocks it away with his sword. Sir Gregory asks the same question in French, but the monk still does not answer. "I think it's time we end this," he says, lunging forward and grabbing the sickle. Gus jumps in and they disarm him. Gus pushes the monk backward against the wall. Sir Gregory tosses the sickle to the side and takes out the map. He kneels beside the monk and points to the drawn village on the map. The monk shakes his head, his eyes widened and chest heaving. Gregory sighs and stands up, offering a hand to the monk.

RETALIATION!

The monk is pulled to his feet, and they leave him standing alone behind the house.

"What language do you think they speak?" Gus asks.

Sir Gregory takes a few steps before answering. "They might be from Prussian."

"Do they look like Prussians? Why would they be here then?" Gus asks.

"I don't know what they look like only heard they might be coming this way. It's the times we live in. Like us, everyone is at war. England is at war with Wales because the English think they own the land. The Vikings are at war with England and so on. The Prussians just want to be left in peace, so they are residing in neutral land. That's my guess," Sir Gregory comments.

Gus glances at the map in Sir Gregory's hand. "What about the map then?"

"When I showed the monk the map, he stared at it for a bit, then looked away. That means he understood it but did not make it."

"Any idea who did?"

"Well..." Sir Gregory stops midsentence and watches the monk run into a church, slamming the door behind him and closing both shutters. A stone cross mounts the roof of the stone building and a few gravestones line the field behind it. Sir Gregory walks towards the church and Gus follows, still waiting for him to finish his answer. Sir Gregory knocks on the wooden door. The door unlocks and slightly swings open as the monk pokes his head between the small opening. The monk glances at the men before slamming the door but Gus wedges his foot in front of the door before it can fully close. They both push against the door, forcing it back open. "Hey!" Sir Gregory shouts at the monk who retreats to the back of the room. Sir Gregory reaches into his pocket and retrieves a gold coin, tossing it to the monk. The monk catches it in

THE NEW QUEEN

his hands and places it in his pocket. Gus sits in a pew and makes the sign of the cross, staring at the monk.

"We wish to talk with the leader," Sir Gregory says slowly, pointing to his lips. The monk motions towards the pews for him to sit, then he leaves.

"So, if it is not a war map, then what is it?" Gus asks again.

"A war map would have recorded the strength of the villages and the number of men, different strategies like that. As far as I can see, this one does not," Gregory whispers.

"Is it just a map of the area, then?" Gus whispers back.

"Could be, but for whom it is for and in what language is it written? That's what we need to find out." They sit quietly in the room until a large man walks in with the monk following behind. His bald head shines, and his piercing green eyes stare at the men as he steps closer to them. His shirt remains unbuttoned and reveals his built figure, where a scar runs over his heart.

"I understand you have our map," he says in broken English.

"Is this your map?" Sir Gregory asks, holding the map up.

"Da," he replies, shaking his head.

"What kind of map is this, anyway?" Gus interjects. The man stops in front of them, smelling of incense, as oil glistens along his arms and chest.

Sir Gregory hands the man the map. "We found this map in a campsite of a great army."

The man looks at the map. "Da, this is my map. It was stolen from us when this army you talk about raided our village."

"The Great Army raided your village?" Sir Gregory asks.

"What kind of map is it?" Gus asks again.

"It is a map of the area, nothing more." The man turns to leave with the map.

Sir Gregory stands up. "But why would the Great Army raid your village?" The man turns back around. "They only raid a

RETALIATION!

village when they have been threatened by it," he adds. The man looks between Sir Gregory and Gus, then shrugs his shoulders and turns away.

"Are you sure…" Gus starts to ask when a monk strikes him and Gus stumbles over a pew, landing on his head. He remains knocked out in the pew.

Sir Gregory draws his sword and blocks the monk's attempt to knock him to the side as well. The man rushes to the back of the room where he retrieves bow and arrows, loading the weapon. Before Sir Gregory finds cover, the man shoots two arrows into his chest, penetrating through his armor. He stumbles back as he stares at the arrows protruding from his chest. His vision blurs, and he falls to one knee, wavering. He swings forward, landing face first onto the stone church floor.

"Have you seen Sir Gregory today?" Martin asks Mark as they stand near the soccer field.

"No, your majesty," Mark responds, turning towards Douglass and Jade holding crossbows. They shake their heads. "Do you wish me to send someone to find him, sire?" Mark asks as sweat runs down his pale face.

"Yes. Search the castle and ask around; I wish to send Gregory on a quest," Martin responds, looking at Jade. Jade swings the crossbow onto his shoulder and leaves the group of men, heading inside the castle. "Are you feeling alright, Mark?"

"I am fine, your majesty. What are you looking for on this quest?" Mark asks nervously.

"I am trying to imagine the castle walls all the way out here," Martin points to the field directly north of the castle wall, "and around those trees." Martin points at a collection of pine trees. "I

THE NEW QUEEN

wonder what we will need for this expansion." He taps his chin and stares at the empty area.

Mark's eyes grow wide with excitement. "A blacksmith for sure. Then we will need a lumber mill and a few men to cut trees. With all these men, we will need more hunters and…"

Martin holds up his hand to stop Mark. "I get the picture. But it is still hard for me to see everything together…" Martin trails off and forces his way through the muddy northern farmland as Mark and Douglass struggle behind to keep up.

Mark glances ahead to the right and spots three horses emerging from the far tree line. He nudges Douglass then calls to Martin. Martin turns his attention to the horsemen and stops walking. Mark looks back at the archers on the wall-walk and waves at them, drawing their attention to the horsemen. All the archers load their bows, waiting for a command or signal from Martin to attack.

Jade rides out of the castle towards Martin with his crossbow outstretched. Mark rushes towards the three horsemen, who wear the same armor as Martin's army. They give a quick wave to Mark and the other men before continuing their walk along the field and into the castle. The archers drop their crossbows and return back to their original posts around the wall-walk.

Martin, Mark, and Douglass retreat to the castle as the sun begins to sets. Jade joins them and Martin informs Jade of his quest.

"I need you to go to the other villages nearby and find out where Sir Gregory and Gus went off to. I was told they were seen leaving the castle together, but they have been gone for several days and have not returned yet," Martin tells him as they return to the Great Hall.

RETALIATION!

Jade nods and leaves Martin with Mark and Douglass when Elizabeth exits the kitchen, spotting Martin. She glares at him and stomps towards him.

"How dare you!" Elizabeth shouts.

Martin stops mid-sentence and stares at her, remaining silent.

"You left me there to die! You knew they beat me day after day, lashing me and beating me like I was nothing!" A small crowd gathers around Elizabeth and Martin as she continues shouting. "You thought I was a witch, didn't you? You believed that treacherous liar over me, over what you already knew!" Elizabeth pauses, then takes a step closer to Martin and lowers her voice so only Martin can hear. "I knew you would switch allegiances, all kings do, but at least they could think for themselves. You're just a coward." She stares into his scared eyes, then turns around and storms down the hall, leaving Martin dumbfounded.

Jade finds the trail of Sir Gregory and Gus near a collection of boulders, midway to the first approaching village. He follows a pair of horse tracks leading from the castle to the rocks, hoping they were from his fellow soldiers. He dismounts near the flattest, largest boulder and notices the scrap chicken and deer bones, the pile of ashes and torched branches, and sets of footprints. He crouches lower, following the footprints and their trail through the tree line to the next village. He mounts his horse quickly and pushes it to ride fast, not wanting to be caught inside the forest at night. Jade glances at the ground, following the trail of hooves outside of the woods until he spots an abandoned village. He dismounts and creeps through the deserted village, peering into the shutters of dark rooms and opened doors of homes. He reaches a barn and glances inside, smelling stale droppings and hay. "They must have all left recently," Jade murmurs to himself, picking up a handful of hay. He returns back to his horse and it eats the entire handful before shaking its head with joy. Jade rides out of the village, not wanting to waste anymore time.

He rounds the end of the village and follows a path up the hill when he spots a bumpy cross at the top. Jade rides towards the odd figure where he notices Gus tied to the wooden cross. Gus' head droops, and multiple stab wounds mark his body. His bare feet, covered in dirt and mud, are nailed together on the cross. Jade quickly dismounts and pulls the nail from Gus's feet with his bare hands. Blood trickles where the nails were, and Gus rolls his head to the other side. Jade places one arm around Gus's bloodied torso and chops the ropes that hold his arms up. Gus falls onto Jade and Jade carries his body as his legs drag along the grass. Gus's eyes remain closed and his body still.

Jade surveys Gus's body, noticing that the stab wounds are shallow and have already started scabbing over. His chest rises and falls from each breath and his mouth hangs agape. Jade stares at Gus's legs where one bump protrudes from the baggy pants, just above his knee. Blood circles the area and Jade knows his leg is completely snapped. He whips out a small wine sack of ale from his waist and pours it into Gus's mouth, hoping it will wake him.

Gus spits up some of the ale, and wheezes. He opens his eyes halfway, looking at Jade. "Jade, you best run," he says in a scratchy voice, grabbing his shoulder. "They attacked us...they are going to wage war." Gus coughs again and groans.

Jade takes off his leather vest and places it under Gus's head for support. "Who did this to you?"

"The villagers!" Gus shouts, his eyes tearing up. "They killed Gregory! Their arrows went straight through his armor...we couldn't even fight back before it was all over. I woke up, and then they showed me his body being dragged up this pathway...they told

RETALIATION!

me they will tie him to a tree to show everyone that they own this land..." Gus coughs again. "They have a war map, too."

"Your leg is broken. I am going to put you on my horse, and then I will cut Sir Gregory down and bring him back for proper burial. I want you to send some help and a few horses...we cannot all go on one horse." Jade struggles to lift Gus onto the horse, and Gus screams out in pain from his broken leg. Jade places Gus on the horse, straps a few swords across his back, and smacks the horse to move forward. Gus moans in pain as the horse gallops down the path and out of sight.

Jade swings the heavy quill full of arrows across his back and holds out his crossbow straight ahead as he continues on the dirt trail. He zigzags up the trail to a higher ground, keeping lookout for Sir Gregory.

Jade stands atop a weed-covered hill that overlooks the village and out to the west where Hope Castle remains in the far distance. Bushels of lavender grow between the weeds, almost as high as Jade's knees. He turns his attention to the path and watches as a small party of twenty men dressed in burlap pants and cream colored shirts with no armor on, riding in ten rows of two, towards a forest. The final man drags a limp body behind him while he rides, holding on to a rope that is wrapped around the dead man's neck. Jade clenches his teeth and hands, glaring at the two men who drag his friend's body. His heart pounds in his chest and he races down the steep hill, sliding down some of the ways. As he reaches near the end of the hill, he draws his crossbow up to his eyes and aims at the man dragging the body. The arrow impales the man's neck, and a gush of blood squirts out the other side. The man turns his head and opens his mouth to scream before slumping forward on his horse.

Jade quietly moves behind a berry bush and loads the crossbow once again. He takes aim at the farthest man in the next row of two, behind by half a horse in length. This arrow pierces in the lower neck of the man who quickly falls forward onto his horse, as if sleeping while riding. The horseman beside him does not see a thing. He rushes to the next collection of bushes to keep up with the slow-moving group of men while loading his crossbow. He watches as the men dismount near the entrance of the forest and look up at the trees to find somewhere to hang Sir Gregory's body.

Jade makes a target out of a man still on his horse. He takes aim and shoots the man right in the chest, directly penetrating his heart. The man falls off his horse, still conscious, but unable to shout for help. Jade creeps to a closer group of bushes before backing up the hill, holding tree roots to pull himself up faster. Once at the top, he loads half of the longbow arrows, ready to strike. He aims at the first man at the head of the group, a large, bald man with a scar over his chest. The arrow deflects off a man wearing no armor behind the leader, piercing his lungs as the tip of the arrow sticks out the opposite side of the man's chest. The man arches his back before falling dead off his horse.

Horsemen shout at the fallen comrade and search around for the unknown archer. Some load their bow and arrows while others unsheathe their swords while Jade already climbs his way up the steep hill, pulling on the roots. Halfway up the hill, three riders search the tall grass and bushes directly below him. Jade remains still. They mutter and split up around the area, leaving Jade alone, hanging on the hill. He scrambles to the top, crouches behind the camouflage of the tall grass and loads the crossbow.

Two riders dismount and make their way up the steep incline towards Jade. Jade grabs for his longbow as the men approach the top of the hill. Jade releases two more arrows at the men's chests, then continues along the hills. He follows the dirt path down below, searching for other members from the group. He takes out

RETALIATION!

his loaded crossbow and slings the longbow over his back, still glancing at the empty path below.

Suddenly he hears a group of men talking and stepping on fallen branches as they approach closer. Knowing he is outnumbered, Jade jumps part way down the hill and finds a thick bush to hide under. He crouches, holding the crossbow at the ready as the three horsemen walk by, carrying swords and a mace. He stays silent until they pass by before he scrambles down the hill near a large tree. Its branches grow against the side of the hill, interweaving between the tall grasses and lavender. Jade sprints to the tree, jumping onto a low, thick branch and up its large trunk. He tiptoes along the branches until he spots four men standing with the group of horses. He aims at the closest man, shooting the arrow right in the man's back. He falls to his knees while the remaining three men rush to his aid. Jade draws another arrow, but the arrow wobbles and falls to the ground beside the injured man. The men scramble to load their arrows and aim at the direction of the tree, but Jade shoots another arrow which sticks straight through one man's neck and into the other man's chest, killing both with one swift shot.

The remaining man backs away and sprints down the path, leaving the herd of horses. Jade tries to shoot at the fleeing man but misses twice. He jumps down from the tree and mounts one of the horses, holding his sword in one hand and the reins in the other. He kicks the horse and it gallops down the path back towards the castle. As the horse races, he glances along the top of the hill as a man shoots an arrow, missing him by just inches. Beside the archer, five horsemen approach, yelling and swinging their swords at the sight of Jade. Jade pulls hard on the reins, stopping the horse and turning it around. He looks towards the top of the hill and scans the path ahead of them. Jade guides his steed up the hill to a smaller path as three riders approach him. Jade raises his sword and deflects the first strike, then the second strike. Jade raises his

THE NEW QUEEN

sword with one hand as if to strike, holding the cross bow with the other hand he shoots his crossbow and kills the man as he flies off his horse. The dead man and the spooked horse block the pathway for the two riders as Jade makes a quick escape. Jade glances behind him, seeing the men farther back but still in pursuit. Jade steadies his horse, loads the crossbow under his arm, and jumps off the horse, rolling on the ground. He rolls down the hillside, hitting his limbs along the roots and branches of trees, and kicking up clumps of dirt and mud as his body flails down the side until he reaches the bottom. He catches his breath and struggles to his feet, staring at the riders atop the hill.

Jade sprints away from the men and hides in the thick forest for an hour in the dark before reaching the opening of the path. He falls to his hands and knees and slowly crawls towards the dirt path out of sight. After crawling a far ways up, he hears whispering down the path. As hard as Jade listens, he does not understand what the men say to each other. From behind him, Jade hears leaves muffling and branches snapping as nearby men approach. They talk in low tones and whispers as Jade watches two men pass by near a row of trees. The men camouflage each other with mud and leaves before disappearing into the forest, leaving Jade unsure of how many are left to kill and if Gus is still alive.

Chapter 19
THE BEGINNING OF CHAOS

Gus chokes and jolts awake in the darkness, almost losing his balance on top of the galloping horse. He clears his mouth from the gag of a loose rope that was wrapped around his torso and the horse. The groggy rider coughs and spits, using his free hand to untie some of the knots around his sore body and numb hand. He slows the horse to a trot to untie the finer knots around his wrist before realizing his horse made it all the way back to the castle without guidance.

Gus readjusts himself upright on the moving horse as he spots hundreds of tents lit by perimeter lighting for what appears to be miles long. He leads the horse around the campsite, until he finds a safe, clear path that leads directly to the front gates of the castle. He pushes the horse at full speed, the pain from his broken leg and hunger intensifying with each gallop.

THE NEW QUEEN

Four guards on each side of the entrance step forward to greet Gus, holding their lanterns in front of them. "Halt!" a guard shouts as Gus pulls up on the reigns.

Gus groans in pain as the horse violently jumps to a stop, jolting his leg. He waves a guard over. "Who is in charge of the guards?" Gus asks in a wheezy tone.

"Hey, I know you!" the guard remembers before continuing. "That would be Sir Gregory, but he is not here at the moment. The last thing we were told is that he left with you. Where is he?"

"Lead my horse to the castle and fetch the king. I must see him immediately," Gus demands.

The guard calls for a page to inform King Martin of the visitor. The guard grabs the horse's reigns and escorts Gus inside as the page runs off. The castle gates close behind them as the guard helps Gus off his horse inside the courtyard.

King Martin and Mark bolt across the courtyard to Gus's side. "Gus? What's going on?" Martin asks as Gus is placed on some bundles of hay.

"Your majesty, we were ambushed and outnumbered. They shot Sir Gregory straight into his chest! I was knocked unconscious, and when I awoke, I was tied to a cross. If it wasn't for Jade, I would be bird food by now," Gus says, his heart racing.

"Where is Jade and who did this?" Martin asks.

Gus frowns. "He went to retrieve Sir Gregory's body, sire."

"Where is Simon?" Martin pries.

Gus immediately spits. "I do not know. You see, Sir Gregory found a war map, but not one of Simon's, your majesty. It was a war map from someone we know nothing about—a bald, giant man, over six feet tall! Never heard of his people or of their tongue before, but they are of large stock. And as you and I now know, also deadly."

"Men do not grow so large, Gus," Mark interjects.

THE BEGINNING OF CHAOS

Before Gus could retaliate, Elizabeth rushes out of the castle with Samantha following behind. "What happened to you?" Elizabeth asks, bending closer to Gus.

"Get him inside. Send a man to get Gwyneth right away." Samantha barks orders at the men. Four men scramble towards Gus, including Mark, who all shoo Elizabeth away. She backs away towards her sister, and they watch the men lift up Gus and carry him towards the main hall.

Elizabeth sees Martin heading towards his bedchamber. "Oh no you don't!" Elizabeth snaps, pulling on Martin's shirt. "You can't just leave now! You are getting ready to have a fair. We have been pitching tents for days, preparing enough food to feed everyone, and forget all the cleaning inside and outside the castle. We have calluses on calluses and I never saw you helping, either. I assume you are abandoning your kingdom, too?"

Martin takes a deep breath and grabs Elizabeth's hand, pulling her into the castle. "Where do you think you are taking me?" she snaps. Martin remains silent and continues pulling her hand. The more he pulls, the more she fights with him. He drags her up the stairs to his bedchamber. "Why don't you answer me?" she shouts.

Martin lets go of her hand as they reach the top of the stairs. "I will only talk with you in the safety of my bedchamber," Martin responds. He whips open the door and storms inside. Elizabeth follows him and stands in the middle of the room, crossing her arms. They both remain silent. "Elizabeth," Martin starts after pacing in front of the shutters. "Henry thought you would be good for me."

"What?" she yells. "Good for you? I never... I would never!" Elizabeth stumbles over her words. "You're a terrible, good for nothing..."

"Silence!" Martin yells, standing in front of her. "What I mean to say is that Henry thought you helped me control my impulse...

THE NEW QUEEN

he told me you made me think slower. Why one would want to think slower, I don't know, but that's what he said anyways."

Elizabeth glares at him. "Is that what you need? A woman to slow you down?" she almost spits. "You think that because I am a woman, I slow you down?"

"Stop!" the king yells back at her. "You're twisting my words! What I am trying to tell you is that there is so much going on at once, but I cannot concentrate on one thing at a time." Martin pauses. "I need you to help me be able to …"

"And why should I waste any more time with you?" Elizabeth interrupts.

Martin exhales and looks at her. "I am not your enemy," he says as tears form in his eyes. "King Henry is attacking my allies, and I cannot help them. You are not a witch, and I never ordered you to be tortured…I was tortured instead!" Martin says, pointing to his chest. "I could not bear to see you tortured, because I know what it's like, and I would never give the order to have you killed!" Martin walks to his bed and sinks into it. "I can't do anything alone. My best friend is dead, my Captain of my Guards is missing, you're mad at me, and now the first man I ever knighted is dead." Martin buries his head in his hands.

"If you forced me in here to pity you, then you are mistaken. Snap out of this mood you have and start being a king!" Martin raises his head and stares at her with glossy eyes. "People expect you to lead them, and you can't do that with your head down." Martin wipes his eyes and stands up. "You need to be able to deal with problems right away, not allow them to pile up. For example, who killed this knight of yours?"

"I don't know, but Gus says Jade is going to fight them," Martin responds, clearing his throat.

"Then for goodness sake, send Jade some help!" Elizabeth waves her hands over her head. "Send your army to show these

THE BEGINNING OF CHAOS

people who we are and avenge your knight's death! Secondly, if Simon retreated, so be it! At least we know he can't betray us a second time! Right now, all you can do is prepare for this fair. As far as me being mad at you, I think my scars are reason enough. Maybe next time you won't believe every word you hear."

Martin sulks towards his bedchamber door. "Thank you," he whispers, looking back at her, "and I'm sorry." He opens the door and straightens his posture. "I really am, Elizabeth." He hurries down the staircase to initiate his plan of sending Jade some help.

The gate lowers and twenty knights whip through, riding at full speed to find Jade and Sir Gregory. Each man carries every type of weapon the kingdom has: swords, crossbows, axes, and longbows, with orders to return with Sir Gregory's body and avenge his death.

Martin orders to double the men to be stationed along the wall-walk as lookouts for a possible, pending attack from whomever killed Sir Gregory. The clear night and bright moon help the men see in the distance, almost up to the tree line. Fires crackle along the walls for warmth and light as all men fight their fatigue during the long, still night.

Suddenly, a guard yells out that a man approaches the gate at full speed. Ten archers line the wall, ready with arrows when some guards point out that the man is one of their own. He carries the crest of the kingdom on his shield. "It's the messenger from France!" a guard shouts, and the archers lower their bows. Other men scramble to the main gates to let the tired messenger through while other guards send for Martin.

King Martin bolts out of his bedchamber in his nightshirt and heavy wool socks. He meets the fair-haired messenger in the courtyard. "Well, what have you?" Martin asks the man as he yawns.

THE NEW QUEEN

The messenger pats his horse and takes off his gloves. "They can come, but only a week later, not at the time you requested."

Martin frowns. "Then I will have someone tell them that the fair will begin a week later. We need them here."

The messenger smiles. "I figured you would say that. Never you mind, I already told them, your majesty."

More men gather in the courtyard as Elizabeth overhears the noise and rushes into the courtyard in her nightgown. "What's happening?" she asks.

Martin answers with a smile on his face. "The French are coming."

"Why would you invite the French? Are they not the enemy?" Elizabeth scratches her head.

Martin shakes his head. "If the French are here, King Henry will not attack."

"But King Henry is at war with the French, so why would he not also attack us?"

"Because there will be more than just the French here." He turns to the group of men that stand around him. "We will have all of the barons and landowners from all around, making a formable army if attacked. It would be the largest army that anyone around these parts will see. King Henry, or anyone else, would have to think twice before trying to attack our kingdom!"

The men join in cheers before dispersing back to their posts. Martin heads back to his bedchamber, ignoring Elizabeth who trails after him in silence. When the king reaches his bedchamber door, Elizabeth stands behind him. "What is it you need, Elizabeth?" Martin half asks, not wanting to talk with Elizabeth during the late hour.

"A word, your majesty," she responds sternly, forcing him closer to the door. The guards look at each other and raise their eyebrows at Martin.

THE BEGINNING OF CHAOS

Martin shakes his head and sighs before walking into his room. He closes the door after Elizabeth. "What is it?"

"We never had a chance to talk about what happened when I was in that prison cell. It's only fair that you know since you were part of the reason I was left there," Elizabeth says.

Martin sighs. "Elizabeth, I told you I have lots to deal with, but I did not forget about you. I thought about you every day, but I did not know what to do. Remember this: Simon was gone, Henry is dead, and I did not know if I could trust Sir Gregory or not. Any move I make could end this entire kingdom, and I always have to keep that in mind. I really don't know what else I can tell you."

Elizabeth shakes her head. "If you loved me, or even cared about me at all, you would have done something about it." Martin's mouth opens, but before he can speak, Elizabeth continues. "Was it easier for you to think I was a witch so you would have a reason not to love me? Were you that afraid of your feelings that you left me alone in the tower, hanging on for life? Yet after everything you put me through, I am still here in front of you."

Martin places his hands on her shoulders, but she shrugs them off. "No, that is not why I am here." Elizabeth turns around and lowers the top of her nightgown. Martin steps back, confused. "Time for you to face another problem. I want you to see what you did to me." She pulls her red hair to one side and straightens her back.

"That is not necessary, Elizabeth. This would not look right," he says, taking another step back and looking away.

"Look what you did!" she shouts, her shoulders rising and falling. "Look at me."

Martin slowly turns his head and faces her. Long, scarlet lashes mark her entire back in all directions, like a spider web of blood. Chunks of skin are missing and others are peeled back exposing raw tissue underneath. Red scabs cover some of the smaller lashes,

THE NEW QUEEN

but most remain open and waxy. The skin around each wound protrudes and forms swollen tracks down to the base of her spine.

Martin grabs his stomach and swallows the rising vomit. "I did not know," he whispers, closing his eyes. "I thought they just locked you up. I did not know they did this to you, I swear." Martin rushes to his bed and sits on it, his palms covering his eyes.

Elizabeth pulls up her nightgown and turns to Martin with tears in her eyes. "Even a big brother, like you said you are to me, would not have let this happen to his sister." She takes one final look at Martin, blinks away her tears, and leaves his room.

Martin tosses and turns in his bed, haunted by the image of Elizabeth's back. He opens his eyes and sits up, leaving a pool of sweat on his sheets. He dabs at his forehead, throws on a long cotton sleeve and rushes out of his room to the courtyard. The night breeze cools his sweaty body and Martin slumps against the stone wall near the front gate. The archers watch his every move as Martin remains against the wall for several minutes, his legs pulled tightly to his chest with his arms wrapped around them. He stays in that position for a long time until Mark notices and joins his King along the wall.

"Elizabeth blames me for her imprisonment and her whippings," Martin says, lifting his head up to Mark. "I did not tell anyone to beat her, and I would never tell anyone to whip her, that's for sure."

Mark sighs and looks down at Martin. "In a certain way, you did."

Martin slides his legs down and crosses his arms across his chest. "What?" he asks looking up at him.

"You took the facts you were given and based on those facts, you made a decision to either stop a witch or have one free in your castle. Your decision was her imprisonment. But I doubt you would have put her in that tower if you knew what was going to happen

THE BEGINNING OF CHAOS

to her." Martin nods in agreement. "She clearly loves you, sire, but she is heartbroken that you believed Simon over her."

Martin shakes his head and frowns. "Henry told me that she makes me a better man, and I don't doubt that. I can't lose her, too."

"It's clear that you love her, but you need to decide in what way. I think you are more confused than you admit."

"Maybe you're right. I don't know, and now I can't get that image of her injuries out of my mind." They both fall silent and stare at the stars.

After several minutes, Mark turns to Martin. "What else is bothering you?"

Martin sighs, still staring at the stars. "Simon."

Mark nods. "You are worried, that's an easy one. Anyone would feel the same. Did he disappear? Did he turn his back on you? Did something happens to him?" Mark stops for a moment. "You and Henry have both been betrayed by him in one way or another, but I cannot help but think that he is hiding something.

"Perhaps, but losing Simon has made me question everyone's loyalty... I don't know who to trust anymore," Martin admits.

Mark raises his arm. "You have my loyalty. I think what we all need is something to bring us all closer together, like a common goal."

Martin taps his chin while he thinks. "Maybe after the fair, we should make the expansion of the castle our goal." Mark nods. "Garnett said we should expand to beyond the forest and across the field. What do you think?"

"I think it's your decision. Do what you think is best." Mark stands up and leans against the wall. "My tailbone still bothers me, and I have a temperature all of the time." Mark rubs his lower back.

Martin nods. "So what should I do about Elizabeth?"

"As I said, sometimes it's better for you to make that decision on your own." Mark yawns and heads towards the staircase to the wall-walk. "I know you'll figure it out soon." Mark disappears up the staircase.

Martin rests his head against the wall and watches the twinkling stars, wondering if he just lost Elizabeth for good.

Simon crouches down, forming a semicircle deep within the forest with the seven men left in his party. The trees bend and creak as the wind moves them.

"We have very little food left, and we cannot ration it anymore," one of the guards says.

"Cook everything, let's eat until we are filled," Simon orders. "We know that they plan to infiltrate Hope Castle and we only have one plan of attack." Simon pauses before continuing. "I believe we can kill more than half of them before we are overcome. That will give the castle enough time to send for help."

"I have been thinking about your plan and I know it will be our end, but if we can separate a group from the main party, we might be able to last a bit longer and kill off a few more," another guard adds.

"Are we sure they are as untrained as you think? I mean if they are any good, we might not last long at all and even if they are untrained, how long can we kill them before even we grow tired?" The party all nod in agreement.

"I assure you they are untrained...I have seen it myself. Maybe they will even turn and run away instead of fighting us," Simon adds.

"We can divide into two groups and send one man out to have them chase him deep into the forest, then we ambush them. That way, we keep the surprise attack and the upper hand, too," another guard chimes in.

THE BEGINNING OF CHAOS

"Great idea, we will do that. Once we have killed the first group, we will try and draw another in right after. We will cut them down, hopefully before they reach the castle. But first, let's get some food into us so we will have the strength to continue fighting." Simon stands, and the party disperses to their current duties.

One guard walks away, having his turn as lead scout. Simon moves quickly over to him. "How do we really know they are going to attack Hope Castle?"

"Well," the scout starts to explain. "They have all the makings of a war army because they have a few catapults and everyone is heavily armed, too. Most have some armor, but not all of them."

Simon watches the scout staring ahead. "What is it? Do you see something?" Simon whispers.

"Maybe," he whispers back, and with a wave of his hand, Simon has all of the men into the wooded area, the war has begun, and the catapults are secured with wooden steaks hammered into the ground to keep them from moving.

Elizabeth and Samantha lie down on some hay in the castle's stables. Horses eat from their troughs nearby. "Why are we out here, Elizabeth?"

"I just thought it would be nice to sleep outside like we used to," Elizabeth responds.

"We slept outside because we had to. We were always running away from someone, remember? Who are we running from now?" Samantha asks.

"No one. I just want to look at the stars with you."

"I cannot believe the way you talked to the King."

"I just told him the truth, that's all. He needs to know because he is blind to it."

THE NEW QUEEN

"You are lucky he did not have you beheaded! I could not believe you said those things and after all he has done for us!"

Elizabeth glares at Samantha. "He put me in a tower, don't forget."

They lay in silence with their arms tucked under their heads. "You know he loves you," Samantha says.

"No, I don't think so."

"Oh yes he does! He wanted to talk with Simon and tell him he was going to release you, no matter what he said, but then Simon disappeared."

"You're making that up."

"It's true, I would not lie to you."

Elizabeth sits up and turns to Samantha. "My heart is hardened, like the scars on my back. I cannot love Martin anymore."

"I remember mother telling me it's easier to forgive than to hold malice in one's heart."

"What does that mean?" Elizabeth asks.

"It means you need to forgive Martin. Remember, he did not put you there and yet you blame him. Sure, he could have come to see you, but he is the king, after all. He had royal things to tend to, like protecting our kingdom, don't forget. Besides, if you truly forgive him, just maybe you can become Queen someday."

Elizabeth lies down thinking, about what Samantha had said. "I don't think I will ever be Queen. Besides, I don't want to. My dreams of being Queen died in that tower when he left me there." Elizabeth turns to her side and hides the tear sliding down her cheek.

Chapter 20
RETALIATION

Jade awakes to the rising sun, long after the embers of his fire had burned out. The morning dew layers his leather armor, making it damp and heavy. He wipes some of the dew off his arms as he lays in some tall grass against the sand bar in the middle of the forest's dry creek, soaking up the solitude of the moment. As he breathes in the fragrance of some wildflowers, his stomach reminds him of hunger and with reluctance, he sits up to start the day ahead. He remains crawling to avoid being spotted by the still rampant army dispersed among the kingdom. He stands up and crouches between the bushes to the main road back to his kingdom.

As he continues moving between the trees and bushes, as he catches the scent of a fire and puffs of smoke swirling into the air. His stomach growls from the roasting meat and he stops to peek between a bush, spotting a campfire. He watches some men cooking over the fire, just between the shadows of some trees. He quietly assembles and loads his bow, still watching the men around

THE NEW QUEEN

the fire. The three closest men to Jade all have their backs to him and across from them is the yawning cook. Jade kneels and slowly draws his bow at the cook. The arrow shoots through the air, killing the man on the other side. He falls off the log as the arrow protrudes in his chest. Jade quickly shoots another arrow at one of the three men, but the arrow misses the man's back. One man jolts up and turns towards the bushes where Jade hides behind, whipping out his sword. Before he takes another step, Jade lands an arrow in his stomach and he too falls to the ground.

The last two men scramble around the fire but before the men can call for help, Jade lands two more arrows in their chests then walks up to the fire. He circles around the campfire, bow at the ready. Satisfied that no one else seems to be in the area, Jade places the bow and arrow beside the log and sits down at the fire to warm his hands. Jade grabs some bread in a handkerchief, next to some smoked meat, and devours half the loaf. He grabs the hot eggs from the cauldron over the fire with his bare hands and shoves them into his mouth, ignoring his burning mouth.

He sits closer to the fire, warming his hands and feet before feeling a different kind of coldness, of someone watching him. He grabs his sword and stands up. Jade leaves the fire and walks between the trees around the fire, finding no one. His annoyance turns to anger, knowing that other men who killed his friend are still alive. Jade kicks the dead bodies a few times. "Damn you!" he curses. Jade searches the bodies and takes a little gold and weapons of knives and bows. Jade abandons the looted campsite and starts back through the forest.

Simon and his guards squats behind a sapling as part of an ambush, as one of his guards is chased deep into the woods. The ten men chasing his guard quickly find themselves in a battle for their lives, and they are unprepared for the ambush. All ten fall as fast as

RETALIATION

they ran into the wooded area. Simon drags the fallen men into a small crevice and piles them together. He throws some leaves and foliage to disguise the bodies. The next guard strips his crossbow and hands it to Simon. "Good luck," Simon says as the guard walks towards the army ready to do the ambush all over again.

The ambush works a second time with similar success, as each time Simon and his men kept a fair distance from the real army.

"A few dead and missing men will not stop an army," a guard says to Simon.

"True, but if we can keep this up for a while, then a few hundred men will and we will still be alive," Simon answers.

"We need a bigger group...more men to kill faster," the guard suggests.

"We have to be careful. I know we need to kill them a bit quicker, but we need to stay alive at the same time. Instead of talking, come up with a plan that we can use."

"What about a stake pit? You know, we make a bunch of stakes facing up in a pit to impale the soldiers falling into it?" the guard explains.

Simon shakes his head. "It will take too long to make all of the stakes and to dig the pit." Suddenly, Simon hears his guard running nearby with a few men chasing behind. Simon and his guards quickly take cover behind the bushes until the right moment for their surprise attack. One of the men turns to fight Simon, slicing his arm in the process. Simon winces in pain and struggles to defend against the soldier until one of Simon's guards stabs the soldier in the back, and he falls to the ground. Simon realizes that he cannot keep up the pace much longer, for his arm struggles to hold the sword, and the bodies quickly pile up around them. Soon there would be no place to dispose of the bodies. Simon looks at

THE NEW QUEEN

the same guard beside him and says, "Gather everyone together, we are going with your plan."

Rollo, one of the Viking leaders, is covered in enemy blood as he carries his bloody sword and battle axe while marches his injured, tired men back to their village after a victorious battle. Despite the rivers of blood during the nighttime, the morning sun brightens the day ahead, leaving a golden tint along every bit of land around them. Surely Thor smiles upon them this day.

As Rollo first exits through the forest closest to his village, he sees ashes and torched huts where the village once stood. He bolts towards the ruined village as the rest of the Vikings stumble after him, shouting in anger and fear. At the entrance of the village, the Vikings stop and stare at the smoke leaving the wooden buildings, the charred stone walls, the caved in roofs, and all the debris that litter the dirt paths and crop fields. The Vikings stare in silence, walking between the debris with pale faces and wide eyes. Others weep and mourn for their families, while others curse out loud. Rollo rummages through the destroyed village with tears in his eyes as he searches for any sign left of his people. After hours of searching, not a single Viking turns up from the rubble.

Suddenly Rollo hears loud crying behind a small hut at the edge of the village. He sprints towards the sound as a small group of Vikings follow him. His axe bounces along his back while the ropes rub around his neck, turning it raw. Standing in front of the men, in a tattered dress and braided hair, is Gisela, Rollo's wife. She cradles her crying daughter, wrapped in a blanket. Gisela tears up as she rushes to him and throws her arms around his neck. Rollo kisses his daughter's forehead and hugs his wife again. Around them, other Viking villagers poke their heads through a small storage area disguised as a small hill. Piles of grass, mud,

RETALIATION

leaves, and hay create the shelter's roof, disguising the refuge as a mound of hay for the stables nearby. Children and wives rush out from under the shelter in search for their husbands and fathers among the approaching Vikings. Some fathers toss their kids in the air, laughing with pure joy at the warmth of them, while others stay in long embraces with their families.

Rollo notices a young, thin lad, with shaggy, unkempt hair standing alone. "Oi!" Rollo shouts at him, waving the young man over. The boy walks over, wandering between the embracing couples until he reaches Rollo. He wears winter boots of fine bear skin, and cloth pants underneath his leather coat and fur vest. "We need to know where the English are. Go and find Fulla the who leads us, and see what he knows."

The young man shifts from one foot to the other. "I'm sorry, sir, but our leader is dead... I walked by his home not too long ago."

Rollo glares at the young man. "It's time we take the fight back to the English!"

Jade peers through the thick, laden bushes at the path where the battle began. The air remains silent and the pathways, clear. He quietly moves around where the horses were once tied but sees nothing—no new tracks from people or animals. He stands up and starts along the path back towards the castle. He keeps his bow loaded in front of him, carefully studying the trees and the path ahead. He remembers yesterday's fight, where he killed many men, and thinks about the bodies. They should have been left scattered along the ground where Jade killed them, but the bodies have been moved.

Jade heads for a small village, not far from him, just past a collection of hills at the end of the path. He might find a ride back to the castle, or at least some more food in the village. After

THE NEW QUEEN

walking for over an hour, Jade's path becomes blocked as a group of emerging soldiers on horseback walk towards Jade. Jade darts to his left, where the trees are thin and far apart, not able to conceal him. On the other side of the path, a cliff too steep to climb. He panics and retreats back down the path, hoping the soldiers did not already see him.

Jade sprints down the path and turns around the bend before hearing shouts from the men behind him. He turns and draws his bow as the horsemen charge at him, picking up speed. Jade fires one arrow at the first man behind him, but he is met by four arrows back. Twenty horsemen in full armor gain on Jade, releasing shots as Jade slightly misses each one. He fires another arrow and sends the man flying off his horse, and over the cliff. Two more men gain towards Jade, swinging their swords. Jade ducks between the horsemen and each man stab the other, their horses swaying to a halt. He pulls the injured men off the horses and stabs them both before they can fight back.

Emerging from the thinning forest to his left, a group of Martin's men emerge on horseback through the trees, swinging their swords into battle. They surprise the enemy as both sides start sword fighting, occasionally sending a man off the side of the cliff.

Jade ignores the battle behind him and focuses on one particular approaching man he had seen the day before and wanted to kill, but escaped too quickly. He knew it was the same man by the braided hair and the blood stain on his shirt. He charges towards Jade, swinging a large metal ball with spikes, held by a chain and attached to a wooden staff. The mace swings in a giant circle on the side of the horseman. Jade runs out of arrows and relies on his sword to fight against the mace. As the man approaches, Jade jumps to the opposite side of the horseman, making him switch hands to bring the mace to attack him. Jade charges the horseman

RETALIATION

and slides along the ground to avoid the mace as he watches an arrow knock the man off his horse. The man falls heavily to the ground, still holding the mace in his hand.

Jade starts towards the injured man as he jumps to his feet and starts swinging the mace all over again. Jade blocks the mace with his sword, but the mace wraps around the sword and pulls it from Jade's grip. Jade rushes towards the man as the mace rises in the air and he leaps onto the man, knocking him to the ground. The man releases the mace and the two roll around on the ground, punching and kicking the other. Jade throws a few punches, but the man tosses Jade to the side, and they both jump to their feet, bloodied and bruised. Jade bolts at the man and punches him in the chest, but his chainmail protects him from the assault. He tackles Jade to the ground and the two tussle in the mud. The attacker struggles to get on top of Jade when Jade reaches for the mace and whips it into the man's face, cracking his skull wide open. The man falls to one side as a pool of blood gushes out of his head, his bloody eyes still staring at Jade.

Jade watches the thinning of men as the battle continues, many of the enemy retreating on horseback up the hill. He slowly stands up, exhausted and blood-soaked from his enemy's wounds. He watches as his king's guards fight a handful of enemies that quickly ends in the kingdom's favor.

A guard rides over to Jade having already put Sir Gregory's body on his horse. "I believe these were the men who killed Sir Gregory?" Jade says leaning against the man's horse and nods. The man reaches down and grabs Jade's arm.

"Want a ride back to the castle? I cut the body off the cross." Jade jumps onto the horse, and the two gallop back to the castle, followed by all of the remaining guards.

THE NEW QUEEN

Captain Witter has the army ready in a parade to show the castle their large number in hopes of intimidating the castle into surrendering with no lives lost. Witter had divided the men into sixty different groups, and each group with a group leader whom he would communicate and give orders to.

One leader rides his horse over to Witter. "Sir, group twelve is missing."

"What do you mean 'missing'? A whole group cannot go missing...so where did they go?"

"I do not know. I have been keeping track of my men. Some of my men have gone missing as well, sir. I sent a small group into the woods a ways back but they have yet to return." The man thinks for a moment before continuing. "You see, I think group twelve went to search for the intruder on their own."

Witters' eyes open wide. "Why did you not tell me we were being attacked?"

"With all due respect, sir, one man is not an attack."

Witters' face turns red. "One man no, but when no one comes back, then they are ambushing us in the woods! Take two groups and search the woods and kill anyone who you find!" Witter recalls this battle strategy from when he fought King Richard. His army used this technique to reduce an army's size quickly and without being noticed.

"Sir," the man interrupts, "that's over three hundred men...just to kill one man?" Witter glares at him, his face becoming deadly. "Uh, yes sir, I will get two groups and we will go back and search the woods as you command." Witter watches the soldier approach some group leaders as they form small groups and march back the way they came.

RETALIATION

A day passes since King Martin sent his small party to avenge Sir Gregory. Since then, King Martin has ordered for the farmers harvest their crops, while others make way for the tents of the French army and their king. Villagers and barons from the kingdom supply fruits, vegetables, grains, and drink for all, while hunters gather piles of game for the cooks to prepare.

Martin stands along the wall-walk when he sees the small group emerging from the trees with the kingdom's flag raised. The king rushes down the wall-walk and out the front gates towards the group of soldiers. Jade jumps off the horse and rushes to his king. "Sire, Sir Gregory has fallen," he says, falling to one knee and staring at the ground.

"Your majesty, Jade fought and killed many of the guilty and brought justice for us all. He killed over ten men on his own," the guard who shared his horse with Jade tells the king.

Martin turns to Jade. "Is this true?" Jade nods as a guard dismounts, pulling Sir Gregory's body on a makeshift cart of logs and rope. "Was justice served?"

"Thanks to Jade, it was, your majesty," the same guard responds.

Martin draws his sword and Jade looks up at his king, his heart pounding. Martin lays his sword on Jade's shoulder. "Repeat after me, Jade. I will serve King Martin in life and death." Jade repeats it. "I will protect the innocent, the lame, and the unfortunate," Martin says. Jade repeats it again. "I will not steal, or beg, and will be loyal to only King Martin for the rest of my given life," Martin continues. Jade repeats it as told. "Now rise, Sir Jade, for you are now a sworn knight of this kingdom. All hail Sir Jade!" Martin faces Sir Jade. "Sorry it's not much of a ceremony." Jade smiles and looks at the king.

THE NEW QUEEN

"Thank you, your majesty, this is truly an honor. I don't need a ceremony anyway. I will not let you down." Jade begins to walk towards the castle then stops.

"What's wrong?" Martin asks.

"Did that little girl not say I would be a knight?" Jade asks, referring to Joan of Arc.

Martin nods. "Yes, now you're a knight. Maybe she knows things that we don't?"

"We should ask her what will happen next," Jade responds. He walks through the gates of the castle to the Great Hall, leaving the group of celebrating men with Martin in the courtyard to tell their war stories. Martin waves a guard over.

"Lets give Sir Gregory a proper send off. Prepare a raft to be burned."

Simon waves his men to ready their bows as they hide behind a few large trees deep in the forest. He has never seen so many men look for a single man before. Simon takes a deep breath and jumps out from behind his tree, pulling the bow tight and shooting the arrow. The arrow hits its target and instantly kills the man whom Simon who acted like he was in charge. Simon hoped killing the head would make the rest react to attack Simon instead. Simon runs deeper into the forest as the invading army pursues him, only to fall into the very trap that Simon's group had prepared. The sounds of men splattering onto stakes and cries of pain echo through Simon's ears.

There is only one safe way through the trap and Simon rushes through it as men follow him into the trap around him. Some men who also run through the safe path of the trap are quickly shot down by crossbows and longbows. Once out through the other side, Simon bolts towards the remaining twenty-four soldiers

RETALIATION

who managed to get around the sides. The soldiers raise their swords against Simon but are no match for Simon's well-trained guards. His men follow Simon towards the soldiers, ensuring no one survived their rampage. Silence soon falls in the forest, and Simon looks back at the collection of bodies that litter the forest floor. Simon's guards move from body to body as they scrounge the bodies for valuables.

"I guess five hundred bodies...not a bad start," a guard says to Simon.

Simon just looks at the man before answering him. "Great, now all we have to do is the same thing about twenty more times and hope we are successful each time." Simon smiles and plunges his swords into the ground as he plops onto a soft patch of leaves. He looks around, amazed by the sheer amount of men they had killed. "You know, we won't be able to do this again. They will get more and more cautious and may even send more men the next time. We need help." Simon looks at the guard. "Tell the King that Hope Castle is under siege!"

Chapter 21
A Guest

The mid-morning sun peers through the clusters of clouds as the people of King Martin's kingdom continue preparing the castle for the arrival of the French King, King Louis IX. Knights stand guard along the hills and tree lines around the kingdom to provide maximum protection for the thousands of tents set up along the fields to house King Louis IX and his army. Chefs stay in the kitchen preparing all day and nights, even creating cots using potato sacks and linen tablecloths along the perimeters of the kitchens. In the hastily constructed hospital wing, made entirely of wood and hay, maidens continue constructing kingdom flags, practicing their stitching, and creating clothing under Gwyneth's instruction. Several groups of maidens wash thousands of bed sheets and pillowcases, clothing, and towels along the shoreline, beating the linen against large rocks and wooden boards.

Martin paces around the castle, nervously checking in on the cooks, the farmers, the soldiers, the hunters, and the maidens, all

A GUEST

working as quickly as possible to please their king as he awaits the arrival of King Louis. As Martin approaches the courtyard, a horn sounds in the distance. Martin's heart pounds as he races to the wall-walk where Elizabeth and Samantha already stand, peering out the fields in their most elegant clothing.

Elizabeth wears a royal blue, corseted floor-length gown with a lighter blue petticoat underneath. White lace trim covers the bottom of the dress and at the cuffs of the sleeves. The dress collar is raised around her face, trimmed in delicate lace. Elizabeth's long red hair is pulled back into an intricate braided bun as two ringlets frame her freckled face.

Samantha's dress, a peach-toned corseted floor-length gown, dips down her back as a long pink ribbon circles her waist in layers, tied together in a bow at the back. Her hair rests in wavy curls down one side of her shoulder, exposing half of her back. She holds hands with Elizabeth as they talk and point at the fields until Martin interrupts.

Martin approaches in an elegant red robe, leaving a train as he walks. His white stockings match his white poufy-sleeved undershirt with a crisp black leather vest on top. His curly shoulder length hair is sleeked back with oils, holding the curls tightly in place. Atop his oiled hair rests a hastily-made crown of iron and gold and diamond all around it. The gold crown rests heavily on his head, forcing him to walk with a stiff back and shoulders so it won't fall to one side.

"You look ravishing," Samantha calls back with a smile. "Come, join us." She holds out her hand to him. Martin takes her hand with sweaty palms as he stands between the sisters. "You will do fine," she adds.

Martin turns to Elizabeth. "Hello," he says. "You look lovely." She smiles. "Thanks, so do you."

THE NEW QUEEN

Martin sighs in relief at her friendly words. They all watch the French army emerge through the tree line on horseback, holding up French flags had three fleur de lis in gold color on a blue back gound. Martin's people separate alongside the walls and fields as the French army marches between them. Martin grabs hold of both women's hands, and they escort him down the staircase towards the courtyard to greet their French guests. Martin's palms turn sweaty and his heart pounds. Samantha squeezes Martin's hand, and she briefly smiles towards him. By the time the three walk to the gate, the King of France still remains somewhere within the tree line, as hundreds of his men march through the crowded courtyard. Martin releases the women's hands and stands outside the main gates to nervously wait.

"I don't think we have enough tents," Martin comments as he watches the soldiers ride into the tented fields.

"We do, don't worry," Elizabeth tells him from behind.

More horns sound from the tree-line just as an extravagant painted carriage was painted blue with real gold trim and painted gold fleur de lis on the sides, emerges near the end of the army, guarded by a full group of soldiers. Martin's men cheer at the emerging army, chanting and clapping to welcome their guests. The French guards smile and wave back at the people, some even accepting flowers of yellow daisies, lavender, and pink clover from the young widows in the crowd.

The knights dismount in the courtyard, and the young squires take the knight's horses for feeding and brushing, not far from the tented fields. Martin shifts from one foot to the other, anticipating King Louis to dismount from his carriage. He swallows hard, exhales and stands tall.

Elizabeth, noticing Martin's nervousness, tries to calm him. "I could greet the king as your lady, if you want."

A GUEST

"No," Martin snaps. "Say nothing unless you are spoken to." Elizabeth rolls her eyes. The carriage approaches and Martin straightens his posture, adjusts his crown, and smiles as two guards open the doors for the King of France.

"May I announce King Louis IX, King of France," one knight boldly announces.

The crowd applauds as young King Louis steps out of the finely painted carriage. His straight brown hair hangs right under his ears, framing his clean-shaven face as a tall, gold crown rests on top of his head. Emeralds and rubies rim the entire crown, standing almost double the height of Martin's crown. King Louis extends his hand towards Martin with his palm downward, expecting King Martin to kiss the back of his hand. Martin raises his eyebrow in confusion, so Elizabeth jumps in and kisses the king's hand.

"It is custom to show your guest a gesture of good will. Lucky for you that your queen was around," Louis says, looking Elizabeth up and down.

Martin chuckles, and quickly follows Elizabeth's lead. "It is an honor to have you here with us. Welcome to my kingdom. I hope you'll enjoy your time here," Martin says with a bow. Samantha quickly jumps to Martin's other side, bowing and kissing King Louis' hand.

Louis smiles at Samantha and slowly pulls his hand back. "I think one cannot show too much gratitude towards one's allies," King Louis adds, locking arms with Samantha as they approach King Martin. Samantha giggles. "Your majesty, I must say how impressed I am at your kingdom thus far. Two beautiful women at your side, both doing duties as a queen...but I must ask, which one is your queen?"

Martin smiles, his arm locked with Elizabeth's, as the two couples head towards the front gates. "I am so pleased you could make it, your majesty. I have many events and games planned for you and your people's entertainment, but first, I have a feast prepared for you in the main castle and a few boars roasting for your men, too. I also acquired some wine...I heard you are particularly fond of the red."

Martin leads King Louis into the Great Hall. All the smaller tables create one long table down the center of the room, covered with an even longer red tablecloth that the maidens created for weeks. All the torches along the walls remain lit, and matching red tapestries line the walls. Down the center of the table lines different platters and trays of game, fish, loaves of bread, gravy, and vegetables: potatoes, carrots, and corn. Matching silver chalices, plates, and cutlery gleam under the torchlight.

The two kings sit across the table from each other on cushioned chairs as two servants race to the empty fireplace, tossing some logs to start a fire. Martin turns to one of the servants. "Music, please." The servant nods furiously and begins to sing.

King Louis grabs a chicken wing and bites into it. "Are you not eating, Martin?" Louis asks as he swallows the chicken.

Samantha notices Martin's stress and answers before Martin can. "The king was worried you might not show up, so he feasted while waiting for you."

King Louis frowns. "Did my man not tell you I was on my way?"

"Your majesty, none of your men came before you."

Louis stares at Martin then shrugs his shoulders. "No matter, I am here now." He bites into a pork chop and shoves a fresh roll into his mouth.

Martin leans over to Elizabeth and whispers. "Have the guards search the area and see if there are any signs of his man. Tell Mark to do a check of the outposts as well."

Elizabeth stands and bows at King Louis. "Enjoy your meal, your majesty. Pardon me."

A GUEST

Louis smiles with a mouthful of food, and waves her away like a peasant. "So, Martin, where do you stand with this new King Henry?"

"Well, I can tell you that we are not close and he has been through my land without my permission. He has also taken a few of my soldiers through bribery." Martin stomps his fist on the table.

"He's a bold king, I will give him that. He attacked one of my outposts a few weeks back. My army at the time was too far to send protection against him, but he never took the outpost. Anyways, my men were too good for him. His men are not that smart, you know? They tried to burn down a rock structure!" He bursts out laughing, and it echoes off the walls. "Can you imagine that?" he shouts, slapping his hand on the table. King Martin smiles and nods his head, and Samantha forces herself to laugh.

Elizabeth quickly returns and Martin raises his eyebrows at her. Elizabeth catches his eye and gives a slight nod, signaling that his request was made. Martin grabs a baked potato and starts eating.

King Louis swallows his second helping of pork and continues his conversation. "What a nice castle, but why would you have the fair here and not at your main one where Richard stayed?" Martin begins to answer when Louis raises his hand. "Wait, I know. The smell of the old man overwhelms the castle, right?" Martin starts to answer when Louis speaks over him. "It's nice over here. The men can really get into their root of savagery for the games. What games are there and when do they start?" Martin waits, not saying anything. King Louis looks at Martin and raises his eyebrows.

"I have a few new games to play, as well as some old ones. I have also prepared a field to pitch tents, so no one has to go without. There is a stream that runs right through the tented area

THE NEW QUEEN

so your men will have fresh drinking water and the channel for your leisure."

"Leisure? I do not know this word," the French king asks.

Elizabeth jumps into the conversation. "At your own time, your majesty."

Louis smiles at her, then finishes eating a cob of corn. "I wish to sleep," he says, yawning. Martin stands up and motions over a guard to show the king to his personal bedchamber. "And I wish her to come with me," he adds, pointing at Samantha.

Elizabeth opens her mouth to speak, but Martin cuts her off. "These women are spoken for," he answers quickly.

"You are a better man than I, King Martin, to have not one, but two ladies in waiting," King Louis says before leaving. Martin, Elizabeth, and Samantha watch as the king is shown his way to bed by the singing servant. Martin grabs both Elizabeth's and Samantha's hands to show the King they are taken.

"The nerve of the man!" Elizabeth blurts out.

"It is going to be quite the challenge for me to not brand his arse," Martin spits.

They all laugh and leave the Great Hall. Servants rush to the table and start their long night of cleaning and preparation for breakfast.

The double edge blade of the battle axe swoops down upon the Englishman's head, splitting it in two. Rollo straightens his back and lifts the axe over his head, searching for his next opponent. Rollo blocks the enemy's sword away with his axe, but the Englishman still manages to slice into Rollo's fur coat, slicing a section off. Rollo knocks the soldier with the butt end of the axe. The Englishman staggers from his attack as Rollo swings his large axe again, slicing the man's torso. The man drops to his knees,

A GUEST

his chest gushing blood, as the Viking raises his axe and finishes the man.

Rollo stands still, listening to the battle in the distance. He hears the war cries of men screaming in pain as Rollo heads left towards their shouts, swinging his bloody axe. Barreling his way through the tall grass and bushes, he stumbles upon a small group of Vikings crouching between the thickets, analyzing the fight ahead. He creeps over to the group and motions for them to follow him. One by one, the small group of warriors work their way through the grass and over the odd dead viking body.

One of the Vikings kneels briefly over the bodies, and thanks to the god Freyja for their victory in battle as the remaining men continue forward. He leads the group up the trampled grass in search of a clear path for a surprise attack. The trail leads them to a cleared area and he stops this men. "I think this may be a trap," he whispers. He taps his chin, then sends three men to each side of the bushes and leads the rest to follow up the mysterious path. The men hold their axes outwards, some even walking sideways to look out for the group. Rollo holds up his hand and the party stops once more. He inhales deeply and smells something puzzling, something rotting. The party smells it too as they fan their hands in front of their noses. Suspicious of the strange smell, he leads the party off the made path and into the tall grass where they meet up with other Vikings. Without a word, Rollo motions the three men to move farther away. He pulls one man close to him and whispers, "Get the men and lead them around to flank the English. You should be coming straight at us and be careful!" The man responds with a single nod and moves back the way they came.

"Stay in a line and follow me," Rollo whispers. The group forms a line and follows Rollo's lead. The Vikings move quietly to their right, having their axes at the ready. They reach the far end of the field where he spots a small group of Vikings huddled

THE NEW QUEEN

together, watching a large group of English soldiers as they tend to their wounded. "Half of you move around the English and flank them, then the other half will join in, and we will attack from both sides," Rollo commands in a low voice. He watches as half of his group make their way through the grass to the other side of the English until they disappear. His group waits until they hear the others attacking, then they charge at the English, hacking their way to the injured men and their stronger comrades. As they clear through the tall grass, they notice they are outnumbered by the English, almost ten to one. Rollo cannot swing his axe fast enough at the overwhelming number of men; as one falls down, another takes his place. He effortlessly blocks their feeble attacks with his axe, confusing the English of how the double-bladed axe works. Although the Vikings have the weapon advantage of eliminating the English, the English have the army advantage, and soon, the Vikings grow tired from the constant battle.

None of the English soldiers wear any armor, and most of their thin clothing contains large holes and blood stains. Rollo stops his men from fighting and stands at the ready. The English stop as well, staring at the Vikings with fear. The two armies stand with their swords and battle-axes raised at the other. Shouts sound at the far end of the English, and Rollo takes a step backward, still unsure of who attacks the English.

Whoever fights the English kills them quickly as they move closer to Rollo and his men. Some of the English turn around and face the attackers, while others stay facing the Vikings. Rollo glances ahead, behind the English and notices the familiar furs and pelts, the long braids and bushy beards, and double-edged axes from another Viking village. "Thank you, Odin," Rollo says as he charges back into battle, killing the men in front of him as both Viking groups close in around the English.

A GUEST

As the trampled grass soaks up English blood, the two Viking groups stand face to face among the scattered corpses. Rollo extends his arm to the blonde Viking leader who faces him and the two embrace. "I didn't know you were near," Rollo says to the blood-covered Viking. He gets cut off as an Englishman rises to his knees without a sword, begging for mercy. The blonde Viking glances at the man and swings his axe across the man's neck without thought or looking where his blade would land.

"I am Borghild, and these are the men from our village." Borghild points to the Vikings behind him. "You and I are the last of the leaders," he says to Rollo. "The English tried to take the castle, but we managed to hold them off for now. We know they are planning to attack it from the channel that leads them home."

Rollo looks up to the sky asking for help from his god. "If Aegir will command the sea, we might be able to stop them." He looks back to Borghild. "How many men do you have?" Rollo asks.

"I have all the remaining men from the castle...around a thousand or so."

"We leave now then," Rollo says. He calls over one man. "Tell King Martin what has happened and ask him for help in battle." The Viking turns and leaves the two leaders, disappearing into the grass.

King Louis stomps down the stairs, dressed in lavish furs and giant ruby rings, as his gold crown shines on his head. Two guards follow behind him on either side, glancing at the staring crowd down below.

"Good morrow, your majesty," Elizabeth says with a curtsy. She greets him at the bottom of the staircase.

"Oh, thank you, my lady," King Louis replies.

THE NEW QUEEN

"Why are you wearing your crown? Everyone knows who you are." Elizabeth walks alongside the king.

"That may be so, but I don't get to wear it enough," he responds with a wink.

Elizabeth smiles, then walks with him towards the Great Hall. "I know King Martin would never ask you directly, but how is the war with the English?"

King Louis whips his head at her. "Why would a lady ask such a question? Those are concerns for soldiers and kings."

"As I said, sometimes King Martin has issues asking about such information, so I try to supply it to him when I can."

Louis moves past Elizabeth. "I do admire your conviction, but I would never talk about such matters to a lady, not even a Queen."

Elizabeth snickers. "It is I who got the king to invite you here, not just for information, but for entertainment and to take the king's mind off other troubles. The same could be said for you, King Louis. Do you not feel more relaxed knowing you are at a fair and not at some stuffy castle discussing a battle plan?"

The king stops walking and stands in front of Elizabeth. "King Martin is a lucky man to have such a lady with a talented tongue." He pauses before continuing. "Since you seem to have him all figured out, what does King Martin want with such information?"

"King Martin has reason to keep the English at bay, for the good of his kingdom."

King Louis snorts. "You are not talking to some commoner who is easily persuaded by conversation, so I ask you again, why does King Martin want to know how my battle goes?"

Elizabeth crosses her arms. "King Henry has made certain threats to the kingdom, and Martin needs to know if his attention will be set upon us."

King Louis thinks for a moment. "King Martin told me that King Henry took some of his men with bribery."

A GUEST

Elizabeth nods. "Yes, he did."

"So I ask you then, dear girl, what makes you think I would not do the same?" King Louis turns to Elizabeth.

Elizabeth's heart pounds and she gulps in fear. "Surely such an honorable king would see the injustice in such an act? King Martin would be best as an ally, don't you think?"

King Louis smiles and chuckles. "A talented tongue indeed! You choose your words well, my lady." Elizabeth gives a small smile and curtsies. "If I am to tell you anything, you must only repeat it to your king."

Elizabeth nods.

"The fight is heavy with blood. The Romans watch our every move, but they don't join either side, even though we offered a great reward for their assistance. That is what worries me, whether or not they plan to fight us after the battle is over."

"Who is winning the war?" Elizabeth asks.

King Louis sighs. "Well, we are. If we were not, I would not still be fighting."

Elizabeth nods. "Does King Henry not think the same thing, your majesty?"

King Louis scoffs and speeds away from her. Elizabeth heads the opposite way towards the kitchen, knowing she angered the king. She moves through the hallway when she finds Samantha balancing a platter of scones.

"Samantha, where do the Romans come from?" Elizabeth asks.

Samantha furrows her eyebrows. "What do you mean?"

"What country do you they come from, the Romans?" Elizabeth asks again.

Samantha stops and thinks for a second. "Well, I suppose they would come from Romania."

Elizabeth smiles. "That makes sense, Romans from Romania. Would they attack England, do you think?"

THE NEW QUEEN

Her sister frowns. "So many questions! What are you getting at, Elizabeth?"

"King Louis told me that the fight against the English is being won, but the Romans are watching them closely. Do you think they would attack England before France, or would they attack us?"

"Romania has a large army, so I suppose they would not want to fight, either. A good army waits until their enemy is tired and then they would attack. It would also depend on who wins the battle between the French and the English, but they would not attack us. We are too far away."

"I think Martin would like to know if the French are our allies or if the English intend to fight with us...or even with the Romans for that matter."

"Yes, I guess you're right, Elizabeth. Now please, I must get these scones to the king and his knights before they get cold!" Samantha brushes past Elizabeth, leaving her pondering alone in the busy hall.

Simon and the men he had left waited in the forest edge not sure if they could continue the fight. He could see one of his men had gotten into the castle to help it get ready for the siege. He is confused that the gates had remained open until his man had them closed. "What's the plan now?" A guard asks Simon.

"Well," he sighs before continuing. "Getting our man into the castle was a big win for us. At least he can get them ready to fight or shoot a few arrows."

"We could get a few more into the forest again." One of the men says to Simon.

"I don't think that is an option anymore," another guard interrupts. "The army is sending men around our back so I expect them to start an attack after they get there. Our time is limited."

A GUEST

Simon gathers his men in a circle. "We need a plan that we can make quickly...any ideas?"

"It's too bad we could not make the pits work again. That's at least five hundred to our credit," a young guard says.

Simon smiles as an idea crosses his mind. "Get the spikes from the pits as quick as possible. We might not be able to dig a pit, but we can hide the spikes under something and pull them up when the time is right."

The guards rush towards the pit to pull out all of the spikes they implanted earlier. They remove the impaled bodies and toss them into a pile, preparing them for a fire.

Chapter 22
TO BATTLE!

King Martin settles in his throne at the end of the Great Hall among King Louis IX and his men. Everyone seems to be in excellent spirits. The frenchmen are joking with one another and Martins men are singing in the corner of the room. At a table across from Martin men are talking about the game and how they plan to win. Martin flattens his crinkled leather pants and minx furs given to him by Rollo, the Viking leader, then places his hands in his lap.

Elizabeth walks over to her king but says nothing to him. King Martin looks up at her, studying her mysterious face. "Something wrong, Elizabeth?"

"I want to check the boats after we play the game. Meet me in front of the channel after the game," Martin whispers back.

Elizabeth bows and strides away, just as a guard approaches Martin.

"Your majesty, time to start the games," a guard announces.

TO BATTLE!

"Thank you," Martin rises from his throne. "Welcome, my friends, to the first day of the fair!" He waits as the men finish cheering. "There are several different games planned for your enjoyment, but right now, I ask for you all to join me to the fields as we make our way to the first game." The crowd erupts into cheers again. Martin follows his guards towards the crowded field as King Louis and his men follow Martin. They pass by small crowds and jesters, vendors in wooden mobile shacks selling ham legs and roasted corn on the cob, even decorated horses with long braids and flowers entangled in their manes. A handful of pages and pipers play their flutes as both kings and their parties pass by. The castle's grounds pack with people, all dressed in their most elegant gowns, headpieces, and pressed garments, waving at both kings and handing them freshly picked wildflowers.

As they reach the field, both kingdoms wait to play the new game, soccer. A wooden stand rests on the side of the field for the kings and their guards to sit and watch the game. The stands contain ten rows of benches at the top of a wooden staircase, covered with a linen roof. Individual cushioned chairs stand at the top row of the benches for both kings, overlooking the field. The kingdom's flags flutter side by side at the tip of the linen roof in the warm morning sun.

Martin stands in the center of the field, surrounded by the fifteen men on each team as they eagerly listen to Martin explain the rules. People from both kingdoms—men, women, and children—crowd around the field as they cheer their kingdoms on, some snacking on the treats from the vendors. After his explanation, Martin makes his way to the stand where King Louis already awaits, holding a roasted turkey leg and a chalice of red wine. One of Martin's guards stand in the center of the field between both teams. He waits for silence, throws the pigskin into the air, and races to the side of the field. The ball lands on the ground with

THE NEW QUEEN

a thump and both teams race towards it. A French player jumps to grab the ball while Martin's player punches the man in his stomach, causing him to drop the ball and fall to the ground.

King Louis leans into Martin. "Is that a rule?" he asks, keeping his eyes on the game.

"Did he have the ball?" Martin asks in reply.

"Of course he did," King Louis responds, taking a bite out of the turkey leg.

"Then the rules allow you to do anything to the player when he has the ball," Martin tells the king with a large smile on his face. "This game will show the fear in men or their bravery," Martin adds.

King Louis nods. "Yes, I see who is afraid to be hit!" King Louis frowns at his team as one of Martin's players grab and trip the legs of the French player kicking the ball. The crowd cheers. The French man trips and falls, landing face first with a bloody nose. Martin's man jumps on top of him while another of his players kicks the ball away, pelting it towards the French net. Another French player jumps in front of Martin's player and punches him in the face, knocking him backward. He pushes back and continues with the ball, kicking it into the goal posts as a French player jumps in front of the pigskin. The crowd erupts into cheers again.

"Aargh!" King Louis shouts, tossing his turkey bone towards the field. King Martin smiles.

The French guard shakes his head and throws the pigskin into the field as both teams fight for the ball, bruising and bloodying each player along the way. Some men start limping, holding their limbs or sides while spitting blood as they jog. A jester rushes onto the field waving a yellow flag.

"Is this another part of the game?" King Louis asks, his eyes still carefully watching the game.

TO BATTLE!

"No, it means we are halfway done the game. Each team gets a break for ten rotations of the minute glass," Martin explains.

"I see...so who is winning?" King Louis asks.

Martin smiles. "There is no score yet. Someone needs to get the ball between the two posts to score."

King Louis frowns. "How can they do that when your men attack them as soon as they get the pigskin?"

"That's why it's such a good game. Your men have never played this game before, yet the game is tied. This shows that anyone can play and win, whether you played before or not." Martin pauses and turns to Louis. "Well done with your team so far...they sure are brave." King Louis smiles and nods.

The game continues until one of King Louis' men from the crowd kicks the ball and the jester rushes onto the field, stopping the play. Both teams leave the field for a water break, leaving the jester and the French player alone on the field. As a jester explains the infraction, the French man punches the jester.

King Martin immediately stands. "Your men cannot attack the jester!"

King Louis stops his conversation with a guard and turns to Martin. "Does he have the ball?"

"No! He is not playing for either side, he is the rule keeper!" Martin rushes towards the field, squeezing past the crowds of people.

King Louis stands up and waves a man over, shouting in French and pointing at the fight on the field. The man jogs over to the men and breaks them apart, screaming in French. The bloody jester lays on the ground, still wanting to fight. More men rush onto the field from both sides, shouting at one another. Martin pushes through them and waves his hands, plunging his sword into the grass. A sign that a line has been crossed and could mean war. Everyone stops fighting and drops onto one knee. King Louis shows up

THE NEW QUEEN

beside Martin with a stern look on his face. "Gentlemen, I call the game a draw. Congratulations on a good game!"

"What good is a game if there are no winners?" King Louis frowns. The crowd murmurs.

Martin pauses. "It shows that both teams are of equal skill, your majesty."

"What a stupid game if you cannot have a winner," King Louis concludes.

"Most games have a winner, your majesty, but this time there is none." Martin glances around at the men, most with swollen eyes and bloody faces.

"Let's get some food," Samantha interjects, and motions to the tables of wine and food.

The groups of teams and their kings move to the adjacent field where rows of benches and wooden tables remain under large linen roofs. The tables, similar to the first feast in the Great Hall, lines with silver platters and plates of roasted meats, fresh fruits, and vegetables. A separate tray of freshly caught salted fish remains at each of the five long tables.

Martin watches the teams, relieved to see his men laughing with the French and discussing the game instead of arguing or fighting.

"That was a new game I have never seen before," King Louis finally comments.

Martin looks at him and picks up a chalice of wine off the table. "Yes, I learned it as a child. If you don't want to get hit, I find it best to kick the pigskin. It makes the men stand out, don't you think?" Martin sips the wine.

"All the men were standing," King Louis answers.

Martin shakes his head. "What I mean is that the game shows the real men from the boys. It is a game of honor and bravery for their kingdom."

TO BATTLE!

Just then, one of the French soldiers moves towards Louis and whispers in his ear. King Louis stands up straight and clears his throat. "Your majesty, I regret having to say this, but we must return to France first thing tomorrow morning. The Pope wishes an audience with me."

Martin frowns. "Oh, that is an honor, your majesty."

"For a man so close to God, I find him annoying to talk with." Louis scowls then he takes a seat next to Martin at the head of the table, both kings surrounded by their guards.

"Your majesty," Martin starts, "let's talk a bit about this new King Henry."

"Do you think he is a threat to you?" King Louis asks.

"I believe, if left unchecked, he is a threat to both of us. Does he not fight with you in the North?" Martin asks, grabbing a platter of salted cod.

"You have been speaking with your lady, I see," King Louis starts. Martin, unsure what he means, nods to keep the conversation moving. "I know I told her that we were winning the war, but in truth, both sides are evenly matched, much like your game. It takes Henry time to sail across the sea and time for my men to march up the coastline. By the time either gets there, it is about the same amount of time." Louis grabs a roll and a pork chop, swallows a piece of pork, then continues. "You say he took some soldiers from you?"

"Yes, I believe my Captain of the Guards and he was a good friend of mine, too, so I don't truly understand." Martin drinks from his chalice.

"Gold can be your best ally or your worst enemy. It can buy things you could never imagine, like your best friends. But know that once they leave, they may never return. No loyalty can be gained by returning."

THE NEW QUEEN

"Yes, you speak the truth," Martin says with a frown. He bites into a roll and wipes his mouth along his sleeve. "Have you ever heard of the Dark Army or the Shadow Army?"

King Louis thinks, slowly chewing a piece of fat. "No. What kind of army hides in the shadows, anyway?"

"No, your majesty, they do not hide in the shadows…" Martin stops and realizes that they do. "I mean, they do, but they hide, so you don't see them until they attack." Louis nods his head in understanding. "Anyways, most of the army was disbanded, but the few that were left went with my captain. It is these men that concern me most."

"If they are any good, King Henry will use them elsewhere. You would not be his main concern." Martin shifts uncomfortably in his seat. "How big was King Henry's army when he moved through your realm?"

Martin thinks for a moment. "I would hinder a guess of three thousand men or so."

King Louis leans to his guard beside him. He speaks in quick French as Louis' eyes widen. He turns back to Martin. "I am afraid we will be leaving today. With these many men at Henry's side, they could attack my kingdom. With most of my men here, my castle is left in a fragile state for a fight. Surely you understand."

Martin frowns. "I understand, and I would like to say that I have enjoyed your visit, your majesty. Please come visit again, but at least stay to finish this fine feast with me."

King Louis sighs. "The Pope wants to see me. If it is not a want for gold, it will be for a war to defend the church. I do not think we will talk anytime soon." Louis finishes his pork chop and wine, then stands up.

"Can you not stay for a day or two?" Martin asks.

"The Pope is next to God, so when he calls, one has to answer the call or God himself might go against us. I cannot stay, I am sorry. The only way I would not answer the Pope would be if my kingdom were in peril." King Louis looks around the room and gives a slight nod to his guard, who round up the rest of the French army. "Thank you, King Martin, for your hospitality. I believe you to be an ally with France." Martin bows and shakes King Louis' hand. Louis turns and walks away, leading his men back to France.

Martin slumps into his cushioned chair, watching the French army march away, waving at Martin's people. Samantha approaches Martin with Andrew holding her apron strings. She sits on his right side. "Do you think Simon is gone?" she asks him.

"Simon might have been captured or killed and we don't know about it yet, so I'm still not sure. Thank you for reminding me to meet your sister...I did forget."

"What's your plan?" Samantha asks.

"I want to know where King Henry's attention is. I am told that he is trying to get money for his brother to take the throne in Sicily," Martin answers.

"What about that Great Army of his?"

"Some fight the French in the North while others stay behind at the castle. That would spread the army thin," Martin says. Andrew climbs up on a chair and sits quietly, watching Martin. "I will have to be careful what I say to King Henry, but I need to know his intentions."

"Will you not say goodbye to King Louis?" Samantha stands, grabbing Andrew's hand.

"I will, I just want to see the channel first." Martin leaves Samantha and Andrew and joins a small party of guards. They sneak across the field towards the tree line. The guards move swiftly behind Martin while the remaining kingdom clusters inside the castle to send King Louis and his men off. Martin looks up and down the clear channel, then glances at the incomplete foundation of the stronghold across the channel. "Do you think King Henry has moved his boats through this channel before?"

"I suppose," a guard answers, eyeing Martin suspiciously.

"If he does, do I charge him like any other merchant? Or do I let him move freely without any hinder or reimbursement?" The king looks around. "Where is Mark?" The guard shrugs his shoulders. Martin picks up a small rock and tosses it into the water, watching the ripples fan into the current. "We best get back to say goodbye."

Elizabeth watches as all the French soldiers rush around the castle, gathering their belongings in sacks and packing any food left in the kitchens. "Where is everyone going?" she asks Samantha.

"I'm not sure." Samantha looks up at the wall-walk as the archers remain at ease.

"You don't think Martin said something, do you?" Elizabeth frowns.

"Like what?"

"King Martin is not reliable with conversation, that's why I tag along with him most times. I bet you he said something wrong, something he misunderstood. I better see what he thinks." Elizabeth scrambles between the flock of people towards the main gate looking for King Martin or Louis. She spots one of the bruised French guards who played in the soccer game and rushes over to him. "Why are you leaving? The fair goes all week, and we have much food to be eaten and wine to drink." The French man stares at her, blinking, not understanding English. He shrugs his shoulders and continues stuffing his pouch with dried meats and berries. Elizabeth sighs and rushes through the front gate as she spots King Louis approaching. She runs towards him as a French guard stops her. "I must speak with the King! There has been a misunderstanding!"

TO BATTLE!

The king sees her and shouts for the guard to let her pass. He steps aside and she moves quickly towards King Louis. "Sire, is everything all right? Did King Martin say something wrong? I will apologize for him immediately."

King Louis chuckles. "No, my lady, your king has not offended me. Something needs my attention right away."

"Is it so important that you must leave? Do you not value King Martin as an ally?"

King Louis squints at her and his jaw hardens. "I would hold your tongue before you continue to make a wedge where one should not be."

"I apologize, your majesty, but…"

"Tell me, does your kingdom fear attack by King Henry?"

"Um, well, that is a hard question to answer, your majesty. We don't fear attack from King Henry himself, but we do fear attack from someone else."

Martin and his small party approach from the right, heading back from the channel. Martin glances at King Louis talking with Elizabeth and he rushes over to them. "Elizabeth, your majesty, what's going on?"

"Nothing, your majesty, I was just leaving." Elizabeth backs away and moves towards the castle.

"What did she want?" Martin asks with a frown.

"She has a silver tongue…you best watch her."

"What did she say?"

"She was misinformed and thought I was leaving due to something you might have said. I assure you that this is not the case. In fact, I have enjoyed my time here, but royal duties call us back home… unless you have said something that I should know about?" King Louis stares at Martin.

"You think Henry is going to attack your kingdom," Martin confirms.

THE NEW QUEEN

Louis nods at Martin and walks away, his party following behind. Martin crosses his arms and leans along the castle wall, watching the remaining crowds of people trickle into the castle. From across the fields, he sees Sir Jade approaching on horseback. King Martin heads towards him as Jade slows his pace and dismounts.

"Where did you go?" Martin asks.

"I went to look for the messenger sent by King Louis, as you ordered, sire."

"And did you find him?"

"In fact, I did. He fell victim to the same men who killed Sir Gregory. I found his head among several others in the village. He must have gotten lost and wandered into their village. The poor soul did not have a fighting chance."

Martin shakes his head. "I will inform the king. Have you been riding long?"

"Not too long, sire."

"Good. I have another task for you and your men. I want you to track King Henry's last movements through the kingdom. Make sure he did not take what did not belong to him. Think of it as a royal visit without collecting any taxes. Also, see how many men we can get to start expanding this castle. We will need to build a stronghold between both castles in case we need to stop halfway among our travels."

Sir Jade nods. "We will grab some more food and weapons and be on our way, your majesty." Martin follows Sir Jade inside the busy courtyard to prepare for his next journey. He locates Samantha carrying a tray of baked biscuits, and handing a few to a group of French soldiers. The soldiers take them reluctantly and mumble their thanks. Sir Jade grabs a handful of the hard biscuits. "Thank you most lovely lady." he says bowing towards Samantha making her blush. She moves on to another group of soldiers as Sir

TO BATTLE!

Jade bites into a biscuit. He wiggles his nose at the sour taste and Martin smirks. They head towards one of Martin's guards and he greets them with a smile. "Here, I got you some food for our next trip." The guard tosses Jade a sack of salted cod and buns.

A horn sounds along the wall-walk from a guard facing the channel. Both armies below look up at the longhorn that signals a threat, then they scramble outside the castle in marching formation; both armies lined side by side. Sir Jade stops his men from leaving, and they rush to the wall-walk instead. Martin rushes to the side of the wall-walk where his guard waves him over, pointing towards the hills. A large army of thousands of men line the horizon, their bodies in perfect formation.

Martin shouts for his men to stand in battle formation against the army as King Louis barks orders for his men to join Martin's. "Get all the women and children inside!" Martin demands as he skips down the stairs. His men scramble to round up the terrified women and screaming children. They race back to their own homes within the castle's walls, leaving behind whatever they hold as they race with their children for shelter.

Martin sprints around the castle wall towards the channel as Sir Jade follows closely behind. They watch as a large man approaches in a small boat from the other shore towards Martin's kingdom. As Martin paces back and forth along the coast, King Louis meets Martin in a fury.

"I cannot have my men fight here, Martin! We do not have enough men for a battle. Whoever this enemy is, I cannot have as well!" King Louis' forehead beads with sweat as he wipes his face along his sleeve.

"I understand," Martin replies, keeping his eye on the growing figures along the channel. King Martin moves closer to the approaching ship and notices the braided red hair at once. The ship anchors near the shore and the Vikings pack themselves on the rowboats, loaded with spears and axes, heading towards Martin. Rollo leads them in the first approaching rowboat as other Vikings surround him.

Martin and Louis back away as their guards step in front of them, their crossbows pointed at the Vikings. "Why do you bring your army against me, Rollo?" Martin shouts as the man sets foot on shore.

"You have a new army, Martin!" Rollo points at Louis.

"They are the French, here at my invitation!" Martin shouts back.

"Are you here to attack?" Louis directs at Rollo.

Rollo looks at Louis, then turns back to Martin. He nods at his men and the Vikings lower their weapons. Martin's men do the same. "My men surround your kingdom, Martin, but they will not harm you. We split up to ambush you if there was a threat, but by the good god Kvasir, you are here." Rollo pauses. "Martin, the English have attacked us. They have many men and are heading towards your kingdom along the coastal waters. They will be in France within the week and annihilate your kingdom along the way. They have already killed many men and women in my land, burning down villages as they go. We were able to stop some of them, but I fear there will be many more to come."

"How soon until they reach Martin's kingdom?" King Louis asks.

Rollo sighs and looks back at the channel. "I fear a day or two."

"If they plan to get more men to fight, they will have to come through the channel. I will stop them here, but you will have to stop them at my border," Martin replies, talking to both men.

King Louis shakes his head. "I cannot fight for you, Martin. I have my own battles."

Rollo purses his lips at King Louis' answer.

TO BATTLE!

"Henry intends to march down the coastal waters, straight to your kingdom and then once there, who knows what he will do. Your only chance is to take the fight to him at my border, that way all three kingdoms can fight him together. It's the only chance we have in ending this war once and for all." Martin places his hand on Louis' shoulder to show his sincerity.

King Louis taps his chin. "I understand what you are thinking, but I do not have enough men to fight a large army. It would be prudent for me to return home and make previsions to fight there."

"With Rollo's men and your men, you can hold them there while my men try and stop them here at the castle. If I can stop them here, that will mean no supplies for Henry's men and no reinforcements either," Martin insists.

"Maybe if I had some of my men from the frontline up north, then we might win, but I cannot see us holding the English," Louis says, staring at Rollo.

"I can have my men send for your men to help us. They could be here in a week, maybe two," Rollo tells the French king.

King Louis scratches his head. "Do you think you can hold off an attack by the English at this time?"

"We held off Richard," Martin stands firm and pauses before continuing, "and won the war!"

King Louis paces between the men, staring at the ground. "I see no option but to fight, whether it be here or home..." He looks up at the men. "We will fight!" King Louis tells them, then walks back to the castle, leaving Rollo and Martin along the shore.

"I thought he would never give us the answer," Rollo says with a grin. "Looks like we are at war once again!" Rollo watches Louis walk away, scratching his head. "Do you think he has lice?" King Martin ignores Rollo, thinking of battle strategies. Rollo shrugs and heads back to his ship to tell the Vikings their plan.

THE NEW QUEEN

King Martin waves at Sir Jade, already dressed in his dented suit of armor. "Yes, your majesty?" He slows his horse.

"We need to prepare for war, and our job is to stop anyone moving through the channel. I need three catapults set up on the other side of the channel. Build a wall so no one can shoot back, one made of stone facing the channel and one made of wood on the landing up there." Martin points at the cliffs.

"Yes, sir."

"And Jade, one more thing." Jade turns around. "I need it done by tonight."

"Y-yes sir," Jade repeats with less confidence and rides away up the hill.

Samantha rushes out the gate and spots Martin near the channel. She barrels down the hill and flings her arms over him.

"What is it?" he asks her awkwardly patting her back.

She looks up at him with glossy eyes. "Please, Martin, don't go to war. I already lost my husband at war and if you die, where will we be? I beg of you, please don't go."

"Samantha, I will not be going to war. Great kings send their men to fight for the kingdom while the king stays behind to plan the attack. Now you must go back to the castle, it's not safe out here." Martin pulls her away and looks at her with concern.

"Yes, your majesty," Samantha says with a smile. She beams and hugs Martin again, kissing him on the cheek before running back to the castle. Her waist-length wavy brown hair bounces in the wind, swaying down her back. Martin watches her until she arrives safely in the castle.

"I think she is quite fond of you, sire," Rollo says as he returns, eyeing Samantha. "She is quite pretty. I like long hair."

"That's Elizabeth's sister. You know, the redhead? Their younger brother, Andrew, is the one who killed Richard with his arrow."

TO BATTLE!

"Ah, well then, I best stay clear of him." Rollo laughs, and they make their way onto the castle grounds.

"Your majesty, we better have those ships at the ready. We should send a few men to prepare them and keep them guarded. I guess that King Henry will be trying to get them for himself," a guard advises as they climb the staircase to the wall-walk.

Elizabeth pushes through the armored men along the narrow path and stops in front of Martin. They look at each other and Elizabeth wraps her arms around him. He hugs her back. She looks at him one more time, then disappears among the growing group of men.

Rollo rubs his forehead and squints at Martin. "Does everyone in that family do that?"

Martin ignores Rollo and turns to watch Jade and a group of guards make their way out of the gate on horseback, leading the French up the steep, rocky wall of the channel. Suddenly, another horn blows from the castle. King Martin looks at Rollo with a puzzled look.

"Now what?" Martin asks as rushes back to the main gate. A guard runs down the stairs from the wall walk.

"A horseman is riding this way, and it's one of ours." Guards walk with King Martin towards the main gate when the rider, comes riding in and almost falls off the horse. "Its one of the men that were with Simon." The guards rush to help but the man is wounded and in need of a drink.

"What now? The King says.

Chapter 23
IT'S A TRAP!

The King orders for the remaining of the kingdom to help with the construction of the castle walls. To every ten men cutting the stone, one lays it in place. Martin organizes for over one hundred men to cut stone at the same time. All of them hammering away with chisels. He has already set two of the four trebuchets to face out to the channel while two small catapults are being assembled on the other side of the channel. Garnet remains in charge of the double wall construction, watching the men fill in the gaps of both walls with dirt. The dirt acts as a cushion and promotes better insulation throughout the seasons. Garnet walks up to King Martin with crossed arms.

"This is moving very quickly. I am impressed with your organization skills."

Garnet nods. "Even though we are building this quickly, we won't be done until next summer if all goes well."

Martin shakes his head. "I do not think I can get any more men, and this needs to be completed sooner."

IT'S A TRAP!

"Adding more people would not matter. The men we have now are already tripping over one another."

Martin taps his chin, staring at the men filling the walls with dirt. "Let's get the smaller kids to help dig the ground and move the dirt...that might keep things moving quickly."

Garnet nods and leaves Martin as Jade approaches from across the courtyard.

"The boats are in the channel, but one sank. We are going to try and repair it, but I told them not to worry about it right now. The men are almost done the stronghold across the way, but I fear if it finds any fire, it will be lost." Jade hesitates. "It is made mostly of dried timber and grass."

Martin glances up towards the stronghold. "Can it withstand a catapult?"

"I can only say that I believe so." Sir Jade hesitates. "Your majesty, what about Castle Hope? It is under siege by now...do you have a plan?"

"That will have to do then. Have the guards scout up the coastline and see if any ships are coming. That is all." Jade bows and rushes towards the front gate.

Elizabeth approaches Martin and stands silently beside him. "Martin, I thought you might want to talk. I know how talking helps you think sometimes...and I want to make sure that your decisions are the best for the kingdom."

"Elizabeth, I'm fine, just a bit tired is all." Martin continues watching the men.

Elizabeth continues. "Okay, but if we stop King Henry's ships from coming through here, will he not send more ships to deal with us later? And if he does, how will we stop him and the Great Army?"

Martin raises his hand to silence her. "We will deal with one thing at a time, but the important thing now is to stop Henry's men from crossing our border. If we stop him there, he will have to

THE NEW QUEEN

decide what to do there. We are too small of a kingdom compared to the French. Henry will surely keep his eyes on the French, especially since the Vikings are now siding with France, too."

"What about Castle Hope? And what if Henry beats Rollo and the French? What are you going to do?"

"I don't think that will happen. The French have been fighting the English for years and they are evenly matched. I think Rollo and King Louis will be victorious just from the sheer number of their men."

"The army that passed by here told me it was at least thirty thousand men."

Martin whips his head to her. "How do you know this?"

"I heard some men talking, you see..." Martin's stomach growled in hunger. "I knew you were hungry, you don't look well. I set out some soup for you with fresh bread, but don't eat all the bread." Elizabeth pulls Martin towards the Great Hall for a quick break as the kingdom buzzes around him, carrying stones and buckets of dirt. Garnet's voice fades in the distance as Martin enters the Great Hall, his stomach rumbling again.

A guard walks into Mark's bedchamber and finds Mark laying silently in bed. "Sir, the king, is looking for you," the guard announces. Mark does not answer or move. "Sir, the king is looking for you!" he almost shouts out. Again, Mark does not acknowledge the guard. The guard takes a deep breath and moves over towards the bed and rolls Mark onto his side. Mark's gaze remains unmoving and his body is as stiff as a board. The guard searches the body for any wounds of any kind before running out of the room to inform the king. The guard runs down the stairs as quickly as he can and finds the king eating next to Elizabeth.

IT'S A TRAP!

King Martin sees the guard. "So what have you?" the King asks, looking up from his soup.

"Your majesty," the guard pauses, before delivering the news, "Mark is dead."

Martin drops his spoon into the bowl and lifts his head. "What? How?"

"I checked his body and there are no wounds about, your majesty. I think he may have been poisoned!"

"Oh, I don't think so. I had the soup and so did everyone in here and we are all fine.," Elizabeth assures him.

"Where is the body?" Martin asks.

"In his bedchamber, sire."

Martin stands up and the guard escorts the king to Mark's bedchamber. Martin holds his hand next to Mark's mouth and nose and waits for warm breath, but his hand remains untouched. The King looks around the sparse room. "Where are his things?"

The guard looks around the room. "This is all that was here. Nothing has changed, sire."

Martin opens Mark's mouth and looks for lesions and burn marks, but finds nothing. "Bury him and tell no one. The last thing we need is everyone looking for a killer among themselves." Martin looks around the room. No one says anything about this understand? The guards nod and pick up the body wrapped in the bedsheets.

Sir Jade travels through the tree-line, searching for any movement or signs of intruders. After stopping over ten times to scout different areas, Jade stops once again and hears movement and low murmurs up ahead. He crawls behind some bushes closer to the noises and finds one of his scouts impaled in a pit. Jade sinks closer to the ground, his heart pounding in his chest at the sight before him. He glances around for signs of any other men before rushing over to the pit.

"I can't get it out!" the scout hoarsely whispers to Jade.

Jade looks at the stake pierced through the scout's shoulder and knows he will have to cut off the bowed end to remove it. "I have to cut off the end to get it out. Stay quiet." Jade cautiously cuts the end off and pulls out the stake. The man cries out in pain as Jade lowers the man onto the ground. He rips off a piece of linen from the man's shirt and presses it onto the wound.

"This is better than standing like I was," the man says.

"Have you seen any other scouts?"

The scout holds the linen to his wound, breathing quickly. "No, have they not returned either?"

"No, I cannot find any others besides you. What's going on here?"

"This pit is a trap. The stakes were covered with branches, and I thought I could just cut through the pit instead of going around."

Jade picks up the cool, dark soil around the it. "It looks like this was dug recently."

"I thought the same thing," the man says as Jade helps him back to his feet. They find their way out of the pit and Jade stays with the man until they reach the tree-line by the castle.

"You can make it from here, tell the king what has happened. I will look for the others and hopefully they are still alive." Sir Jade leaves the scout and heads back into the forest towards the pit. Jade creeps and stops again, listening for any movements. He hears nothing and continues past the pit, only to spot another one close by. He spots another scout with a stake through his leg, asleep and groaning in pain. Jade approaches the scout and wakes the man, holding his hand over his mouth to keep him quiet.

IT'S A TRAP!

The scout opens his eyes wide and jumps. "It's a trap!" the man hisses. "Get out, now!"

The evening remains silent and clear as Rollo and the Vikings set up camp in a thick collection of trees to stay hidden from the near by French. A small fire flickers between the Vikings as the forest hides their flames. Rollo's scouts locate the French campsite nearby and keep watch of the campsite for any movement. Rollo shoves a bun into his mouth, then quickly spits it out. "Who made this rock?" he asks, tossing the bun into some bushes.

"That's the food from King Martin's castle," one Viking responds. The men break out into laughter.

"Maybe Martin should build his castle with those buns...no rock could break through it!" Rollo adds. A scout returns to the camp and informs Rollo of an approaching ship in the sea. Rollo leaves with the young scout to see the ship in the sea. The night hinders Rollo from seeing how large the ship is, but Rollo has an understanding of its size from the faint light of lanterns around the ship. "Stay here and tell me if the ship comes towards the shore," Rollo commands. "If morning comes and the ship is still there, don't let anyone see you, understand?"

The first rays of the morning sun break over the horizon as the young Viking quickly opens his eyes to the sea, where two ships became five, and one is sailing to shore. The boy rushes through the grass back to camp where a few Vikings stand around the fire while others continue to wake up around them. The young Viking tells Rollo and King Louis of the news and soon both groups head to the shore. Rollo and King Louis walk together in the centre of the two groups. "I do not think King Martin held back the English. We cannot count on him anymore," King Louis comments.

THE NEW QUEEN

Rollo looks to King Louis with anger on his face. "If Martin let them pass, then his castle would not be standing. I would trust him with my life. He is an ally."

"Then how do we explain these Englishmen? What's all that about?"

Rollo shakes his head, not knowing the answer. Suddenly, the Vikings stop and kneel, while looking through the tall grass. The French stand behind, waiting for the order to march out and fight.

One Viking approaches the leaders. "There are about sixty men on shore and I do not know how many are still aboard the ships."

"You!" Louis shouts at one of his men in French. "Take two groups around to the other side and surround them. We will attack from here after they start fighting you." The soldier nods and rushes off.

"What did you tell him?" Rollo asks.

"We will handle this. My men will attack from the other side, then we will attack after they start fighting." The French wait in silence for the other group to start their attack. Rollo watches as the English load materials and supplies on their ships.

"Are you not going to attack?" Rollo asks.

"I think my men might have been ambushed, which means there are more English than we thought," Louis responds.

Rollo sends his men to check that they are not being outflanked. While he organizes the Vikings, a large ball of fire crashes down on the men in front of King Louis and Rollo. Blazing balls of flame quickly launch one after another from the ships as the English load their catapults towards the armies.

"Charge!" King Louis yells and his men rush towards the Englishmen. The Vikings charge to the rear of the English and ambush them as they attack the French. Rollo catches up with his men and joins the French in combat with the English along

IT'S A TRAP!

the shore. Rollo orders some of his Vikings to wait while the ship bombards the French on the other side with the tremendous force from the catapults.

"Get half of the archers into the tree line while the other half approaches around the ship as close as possible. We will send three volleys at the ship, wait for them to turn their catapults towards us before you send yours." Rollo watches half his men disperse and head towards the ship. The French attacking in the front quickly die off from the catapult explosions and Rollo decides to attack the English so the French have time to retreat.

The Vikings charge towards the English, jumping into the open pit and swinging their axes at the English. Rollo and the Vikings use great force with their axes, easily decapitating the English while the catapult attacks continue exploding around them. The Viking archers attack the ship, hoping to change the direction of the catapults to them. The rest of the Vikings make their way through the English, with their powerful axes doing more damage than the English swords. Blood pools along the shore where dead bodies scatter about, including the English, the French, and the Vikings. Rollo quickly kills as many English as possible, knowing that one accurate shot from the catapults could kill them all.

Sir Jade slowly pulls his sword from its sheath. He quietly moves around the open death pit where the next scout lays injured. Jade moves on his belly towards a small thicket of bushes where he thought the enemy could be hiding. Sir Jade holds his sword in one hand while in the other he grips his knife. Within yards of the small thicket, Jade spots a man picking at the grass. Grabbing handfulls of grass then throwing them into the air and watching them fall to the ground. Sir Jade briefly sees the man's figure but cannot make out his face behind the thick bushes. Off in the distance, Jade sees brief movement from behind a group of trees, knowing that this man is not alone.

Sir Jade follows the man who has no armor on one a cream colored shirt and burlap pants, until the man rests on a rock. He places the sword down and grips his knife as he sneaks up behind the man. Jade wraps his arm around the man's face and slits his throat while his free hand covers the man's mouth. Jade lays the body down on the rocks, then places smaller rocks to prop the body into a slouching position. Jade then crawls behind the tall grass towards the area he saw movement in, and spots another man eating a root on a nearby log dressing in the same attire as the one before. Jade approaches the man from behind and silently slices his throat, the man falling dead. Jade positions the second body along the log, as if fallen asleep. Sir Jade takes as to who the men could be, all he cares is that they could have been there watching the trap that might have killed the castle scouts. He crouches behind the grass and retreats back to the tree line, remaining close to the ground when a knife is suddenly pressed against his throat.

"Now I think you best be very quiet and drop those weapons you have, lad!" a mysterious voice demands. Jade drops his weapons and the man pulls on Jade's hair, jerking his head back. "You are very good at killing the guards, and quite quietly, but I am better."

"Are you here to brag or to kill me?" Jade asks, ready to grab the man's arm at any sudden movement.

"I wouldn't do that, lad," the man says as he feels Jade's tighter grip on his hand. He pushes his blade closer into Jade's neck. "I already know what you're trying to do."

"Well are we going to stay here all day then?" Jade asks, trying to provoke the man.

"Where are you from?" the man asks.

IT'S A TRAP!

"I am from King Martin's castle," Jade responds through clenched teeth.

"We used to be a part of it...do you know of Henry?"

"I did."

"We left with him. He said we could live in peace, but all there has been was war after war. We left the last kingdom because the king wanted us to do nothing but fight. I am tired of fighting."

"Henry is dead...have you heard of the Black Army?" Sir Jade asks. Jade feels the pressure of the knife lessen on his neck.

The man pauses before answering. "I have."

Jade smirks and takes a deep breath. "Were you one of them?"

King Martin and Elizabeth sit in silence on the wall walk as they watch the sunset. Martin exhales. "You know, I did not want to be king."

Elizabeth turns to him. "Why? Being a king you get everything you want. People will always serve you and give you whatever you need."

Martin looks at her and shakes his head. "Is that what you think? Do you see people falling over me, wanting to please me with every breath they take?"

"King Louis of France respects you," Elizabeth quickly responds.

Martin smirks. "King Louis only came to evaluate the kingdom, and nothing more."

Elizabeth glares at him. "How can you say that when he is out there fighting for you?"

"He is fighting for his kingdom because if the English get past my kingdom, he will be fighting on his own land."

"But was it not you that made him see that? King Louis surely understands that you pointed that out to him." They sit quietly for

THE NEW QUEEN

a moment before Elizabeth continues. "For having such insight, you can be quite blind sometimes."

"You know, I planned this entire kingdom years ago. It was once a dream of a poor boy, yet here I am as a King of my own kingdom." Martin pauses. "I cannot enjoy my place as king because we are always at war, fighting day after day. I have to send men and even boys into war who die fighting, and for what? A made-up kingdom."

Elizabeth exhales and shakes her head. "There you go again. You have something great, yet you put yourself down. Look around you." Elizabeth opens her arms towards the farmlands and the channel. "You had saved many people from a life of tyranny from the English. You even saved me when my own father tried to sell me off. You started this kingdom for the people who were left to die. You saved everyone here."

"I did what I had to do to survive and to save these people from a massacre. I am not royalty."

Elizabeth cuts him off. "What I understand is this: you beat King Richard in a war where he had the upper hand with experienced soldiers, but you, King Martin of Quarry Castle, won that war against all odds. Do you not think God smiles in your favor?" Martin opens his mouth only to be stopped by Elizabeth's finger quieting him. "So whether I understand or not, I see things in you that you have not been able to see in yourself. I think you have been sitting here thinking more about what to do with the design of the castle than the fight ahead of us." Elizabeth stands and straightens out her dress as the twilight darkness touches the kingdom.

"You know you are the only person I would ever let talk to me that way," Martin says with a blank expression.

Elizabeth gives Martin a smug look. "That's because your father told you I would be good for you, but he did not say that you would be good for me." Elizabeth walks away, leaving King Martin speechless in the dusk.

Martin stands up and watches the torches light up the area where his men work furiously to build the castle wall. He thinks about what Elizabeth told him and hopes that she is right.

Chapter 24
THE ENEMY WITHIN

Sir Anthony and Douglass stride in the fish market, wearing long black robes to conceal their armor underneath. Sir Anthony stops in front of a coy fish stand as the morning sun reflects off the fish's scales in a rainbow pattern. They continue walking to each vendor, avoiding the other commoners as they continue their shopping. Sir Anthony leans on his staff with every right step he takes. "What have you?" Sir Anthony asks in a low voice, avoiding eye contact.

Douglass looks ahead, and answers Sir Anthony in an even tone. "We are under siege."

Sir Anthony stops in front of another fish stand and chops down a large coy that hangs from the beam above. He tosses a few silver coins to the man behind the stand and drapes the fish over his shoulder. Douglass walks in a different direction and Sir Anthony thumps behind. Sir Anthony glances at the few soldiers on the wall-walk, pacing and scanning the kingdom. Douglass follows Sir Anthony's gaze at the minimal soldiers.

THE ENEMY WITHIN

"Not many up there," Douglass says to himself.

They continue walking between each fish stand, heading towards the fruits and vegetables. They stop at an open pit fire and Douglass warms his hands, rubbing them together. Sir Anthony pierces the floppy fish with a shaved wooden spear beside the fire pit and roasts it above the flickering flames. "What do you think we should do?" Douglass whispers to Sir Anthony.

Sir Anthony nods and leans in. "We must find out who the intruders are and carefully eliminate them."

"I believe there are too many of them," Douglass whispers. Sir Anthony slowly turns the fish on its raw side, using the spear as a spit. Douglass inhales. "That sure smells nice," he chimes, thrusting his hands in his pockets.

"It's mine! Go away, you can't have any," Sir Anthony responds, stepping away from Douglass.

"Alright, I'll let you be then," Douglass responds, leaving the fire pit and heads towards his room. He follows the cobblestone shortcut between a few bakeries. Off the stone walls of both bakeries projects two large shadows following him. Douglass speeds around the corner under a long tunnel, pulling out his knife once he positions himself in its shadows. He waits in the darkness.

The two men wear long leather robes and a cotton shirts with leather boots, sneak into the tunnel, the glimmer of sunlight reflecting off their pocket knives. They creep along the walls in search of Douglass. Douglass pushes himself further against the tunnel wall, knife outstretched, waiting for the intruders to reach an arm's length distance from him. The first man, just around the corner where Douglass hides, tiptoes closer to him, and he pounces. He lunges at the man and instantly slices the man's wrist. He shrieks and drops his knife, falling to his knee in pain. The second man rushes to his accomplice's aid, raising his blade to

THE NEW QUEEN

Douglass, but Douglass turns and sprints down the tunnel towards his room before the second man can reach him.

Sir Anthony finishes the rest of his fish, tossing the bones and the head into the fire as he heads towards the wall-walk. Along the wall, Sir Anthony spots a soldier carving a carrot with his knife. Sir Anthony approaches the man, recognizing the throwing knife the soldier uses to slice the carrot. "Black Army," Sir Anthony whispers to himself. "A dull blade does not stick," Anthony says out loud.

The man looks up at Sir Anthony. "Did you say something, old man?"

"I said a dull blade does not stick." Sir Anthony points to the man's blade. "Those are throwing blades, not carving knives!"

The man narrows his eyes. "And what do you know of them?"

"What I know is King Martin has given us all a second chance at a normal life, yet here you are doing nothing with yours." The man stands up and holds the throwing knife in between two fingers and shakes it at Sir Anthony. "Put those away. I'm not here to fight you". The man glares at Sir Anthony, then lowers the knife and tucks it away into his belt. "Are you loyal to the king?" Sir Anthony asks.

"I am not loyal to anyone anymore. I am only loyal to myself and what is good for me," the man replies.

"And King Martin?"

The man pauses before answering. "And King Martin," he finally says. "But even King Martin has us fight for him. What freedom is that?"

"There is not as much freedom as we would all like, but at least he does not send you out to kill an enemy that was never there in the first place."

THE ENEMY WITHIN

The men stare at each other. "What is it you want, old man?"

"There are men here who wish to cause harm to this kingdom and to King Martin. I would be grateful if you would find them for me." Sir Anthony leans on his staff.

The man chuckles then bites into the carrot. "You serve King Martin?"

"Like you, I serve for myself. We are both black knights, as it were. If King Martin helps to get me where I wish to be, then I will help him get there as well. In the end, we both win, don't we?"

The man narrows his eyes. "Alright, I will keep my eyes and ears open. What makes you think there are men here anyway?'

"In any siege, the best weapon is the one inside that starts scaring the people. We have to watch out for one another like we always have. This is just us watching out again, don't you think?" Anthony nods and walks away, leaving the man to eat his carrot. He reaches a soldier's den, and fashions himself a table with a handful of other soldiers drinking ale and eating chicken legs. Five other circular tables are squeezed next to each other, with even larger men squeezing around them. The backs of each chairs knock into the others.

"I heard that a scout has returned. Does anybody know what he saw?" a soldier from Sir Anthony's table shouts to the crowd.

The men lower their voices to a murmur. "I heard he was at the other castle," a soldier from the next table answers.

"And what did he see?"

"I don't know."

"He saw that the French were having a good time at the fair," another soldier adds.

"You think the King might show up?"

"Where? Here or at Quarry Castle?"

The soldier shrugs his shoulders. "No. The French are keeping him busy."

THE NEW QUEEN

"Would you let that army walk into the castle?" Sir Anthony asks pointing with his thumb towards the gate of the castle.

"Who is going to stop them?"

"I know if they were to enter the castle, I would stand before them, or are you a coward not fit to wear that uniform?" Sir Anthony challenges.

The soldier stands. "Old man, you would not have a chance against one man, never mind that army. Watch your tongue."

Sir Anthony stands, leaning on his staff. "I already bested the one man once before."

The soldier chuckles. "I doubt that."

"You dare to call me a liar, boy?" Sir Anthony glares at the soldier.

"Sit down, old man, or I will take you outside and make you beg for my forgiveness."

"I think it's time to teach you a lesson. Let's step outside and see what kind of soldier you really are." Sir Anthony shuffles out of the cabin, his staff thumping along the wooden floor. He stands outside, waiting for the soldier to join. The soldier, dressed in full armor and sword in hand, stands opposite of Sir Anthony as a crowd gathers around them. Some men clasp their chicken legs, others with goblets of ale. "I will give you a chance to apologize now, but if you don't, you may not live to get the chance again. As a matter of fact, I may kill you just to prove to your fellow soldiers that I am more than a simple man."

"Shut up, old man," the soldier responds and swings his sword at Sir Anthony.

Sir Anthony deflects it away with his staff. "My dead mother could swing a sword better than that!" The soldier circles Sir Anthony, hopping and jumping from side to side. "I see you have never fought a real man before."

"Old man, I have fought many more than you." The soldier lunges at Sir Anthony, using his entire weight to bring down his sword.

Sir Anthony sidesteps out of the way before the sword clangs the ground. "You will dull your blade that way," Sir Anthony remarks.

In a fit of rage, the soldier swings his sword sideways but Sir Anthony jumps out of the way and continues defending the blade against his staff. With one quick motion, Sir Anthony stumps the staff hard on the soldier's foot. The soldier shrieks in pain and the surrounding soldiers laugh.

"That's it! Teach the old man a lesson!" a soldier from the crowd shouts and they all laugh and holler. Sir Anthony steadies himself, ready for a violent attack at this outburst. The soldier snarls and charges straight at Anthony, swinging his sword from side to side. Sir Anthony stands firm and blocks each attack. When the soldier gets close enough, Anthony uses his free hand and slaps the man across the face. The soldier stands, eyes wide and mouth agape, staring at Sir Anthony. Sir Anthony stomps the staff down hard on the man's other foot, making sure to break a few toes. The man howls in pain and falls back to the ground, squeezing his foot. The crowd breaks out in laughter again, some re-enacting the attack holding their goblets. The soldier pulls out a knife from his boot and swings it towards Anthony.

"You could not hit me with your sword. What do you think you can do with a knife?" Anthony asks. The soldier struggles to stand, then lunges at Anthony but is blocked again. Anthony plows the base of the staff into the man's face, knocking him back onto the pebbled ground. Blood gushes from his nose. Anthony stands over the man and leans on his staff. "If this is the best you have, then I will not lead you into battle. That was pitiful." Sir Anthony leaves the injured man wincing on the ground and leaves the den.

THE NEW QUEEN

He listens to the men helping their friend to his feet and aiding him into the safety of the room.

The Black Army soldier leans against a stone wall off to the right, chuckling to himself as Sir Anthony approaches him. "They don't know you are a teacher?"

"They are ignorant of many things," Sir Anthony responds. "My only fear is that they will all plan an attack against me at some point."

"What honor would there be in that?"

"These young men are nothing more than boys. They do not know honor as we do," Sir Anthony answers, leaning on his staff and rubbing his lower back.

The Black Army soldier exhales. "I find no discipline to be found, either."

"No respect, no discipline, and no manors for the elderly."

"If they only knew..." The Black Army soldier pushes off the wall. "All of the Black Army will fight for Martin. Anyone who will not would have already left."

"So it is up to me to make these soldiers loyal to the king? How can I do that, I wonder..."

"You are the teacher! Make them learn, just like now," the man replies. "If you are looking for respect and discipline, you sure got it from those boys."

Martin awakes in his room, sandwiched between Elizabeth and Samantha on his bed. "The bed is not big enough for the three of us!" Martin shouts in annoyance. Both women jolt their heads up and yawn. Samantha tosses the wool blankets off of her and leaves in silence.

Elizabeth keeps her eyes closed and sighs. "No need to shout, your highness," she says sarcastically.

THE ENEMY WITHIN

"What are you doing here, Elizabeth? Why is your sister here, too?" Martin shuffles away from her to the opposite side of the bed. The fire crackles in the fireplace.

Elizabeth rolls over to face the wall. "We were wandering around, and then we became cold. It's fine."

"You can't just—" Martin starts when the bedchamber door swings open. Samantha enters with a tray of breakfast: hen's eggs, sliced ham, charred buns, and apples.

"Time to wake up! Elizabeth, get up. The king needs to eat." Elizabeth rolls out of bed and sits at the edge, yawning. Her red hair knots and spirals in all directions around her pale face.

Martin sits up and leans against the headboard. "Uh, thank you, Samantha," Martin says as Samantha places the tray on top of his lap. She heads towards the fireplace and pours Martin a chalice of hot water from the container of water resting on top of the fireplace ledge.

"Samantha, I'm heading back to our room. I'm still tired." Elizabeth yawns again and leaves the bedchamber. She closes the door behind her.

"Have you heard any news from King Louis?" Martin asks Samantha.

"No, sire, I am not privy to such things going on." She places the chalice of water on his tray next to the ale.

"Please fetch Mark for me," Martin asks Samantha with a mouthful of ham. Samantha remains silent.

With a mouthful of eggs, the king realizes what he had said. The king places the tray on the floor beside his bed and tosses off the blankets. "I am sorry, Samantha but I need to know if there is any news on the fight. I'm still in shock over Mark's death."

Samantha nods. "Yes, sire. No news that I know of."

The king searches for his suede clothing in his cabinets, and on the bed, but they remain missing. "Where the blasted is my clothing?" he hisses to himself. "That will be all, Samantha!" he says, dismissing Samantha as he searches for his clothing under the bed.

Samantha quickly returns and shuffles into the room with the king's clothing folded in her arms. "Here you go, your Majesty. All clean and ready to wear."

Martin stands up and faces Samantha. "Oh, thank you," he says, taking the clothing from her. She leaves again, and Martin scrambles into his wool sweater and leather pants. The king enters the courtyard as the kingdom commences their morning in a bustle of activity. He spots Garnet along the wall-walk, commanding the soldiers to keep building the castle wall. Some men yawn and lift boulders sluggishly, their heads drooping. As Martin makes his way out of the iron gate, another five feet of wall surrounds him, complete with a wall-walk. Just beyond the extension of the walls, four large holes line up in a perfect square for the towers to connect. All around Martin, the men cut stone while others mix mortar, lifting it to the men along the wall-walk. The king approaches Garnet, moving past a group of men carrying a boulder. "Garnet, I see the wall is moving quickly!" he yells to Garnet.

Garnet turns around. "Your majesty, you called?"

"I am amazed by how quickly the wall is coming along," Martin elaborates.

"Ah, yes. The wall. We have been working all through the night, and I reckon I should send some of these men to get some rest soon. I have some news. I believe we will run out of stone before we reach the end of this side of the castle wall. We won't have enough to extend it to the tree-line."

"I see." Martin nods. "What will you do then?"

"I have already sent a rather large convoy to Saxton's old castle, and they will gather as much stone as they can and bring it back here."

THE ENEMY WITHIN

Martin's eyes widen. "Is that wise?"

"Well, we have been doing this for an entire week now and no one has caught us yet."

Martin nods again. "How long until you finish this side of the wall?" He points to the wall around him.

"For it to be completely done? One hundred days including the towers in place."

Martin scans the wall again. "It looks to me that there are not as many men present than I'm used to seeing, Garnet."

"I have the men on four rotations. Most of the rotations are retrieving the stones and others to bring them here. Then they have half a day to go back as we keep expanding to find more stones. It's a long process, but all the men work hard to make it happen," Garnet says with a large smile.

Martin turns his attention towards the other side of the unmade courtyard where the next wall is to be made. "That is going to be one very long wall."

"It may seem to be a long, straight wall, your majesty, but I assure you there is not one straight part in it. It is all of my own design, you see. It winds in and out as the towers remain on the outside of the wall. Of course, the wall itself is two walls in one, with hay insulating between the two." Garnet folds his arms across his chest. "If one were to see the wall after it is finished, it would look to be six to eight feet thick in some spots, but only the towers are truly six feet thick. My secret is that the two walls remain stacked with stones and sand. If enemies try to dig underneath the walls, the weak ground will crumble, and the waste between the walls will empty onto them, filling their tunnel."

"How long until all the walls are done?" Martin asks again.

"Three to four years, sire," Garnet responds.

"But this wall you are working on now, will be done in one hundred days or so?"

THE NEW QUEEN

"Yes, but we have winter to contend with, your majesty. You cannot make mortar in the winter, and the men would freeze to death cutting the stone in the snow."

"Do you think the walls are high enough, Garnet?"

Garnet glances at the walls. "Do you not believe fifteen feet is high enough?"

"I am worried that it may not be," Martin responds.

"If we go too high, the wall can topple over on its own, especially with the weather."

Martin scratches his chin. "I think we can go higher. However, I just want it to be done as quickly as possible. Finish it at the height that has been set, and if we get time after that, we will raise the wall."

Sir Anthony rides his horse towards the gates of the castle as Douglass chases after him. "Where are you going?" Douglass asks, grabbing hold of the reins.

Sir Anthony slows his horse to a trot. "It has come to my attention that we do not have a large enough army to fight King Henry or this army. I must look for an army to protect this kingdom. While I'm away, I want you to go to the other castle and inform the king that I will be gone for some time. I plan to visit my friends where I was sent to train years ago. If I am successful, we will have a few great men by our side." Sir Anthony pulls his horse's reins, and it jolts forward, leaving Douglass out of breath as he watches Sir Anthony ride off.

"Won't they kill you?" Douglass shouts after Sir Anthony without an answer.

Douglass heads back to the courtyard, squeezing between narrow alleyways jammed with boxes, crates, waste, and hay. His leather boots clap against the cobblestone paths as he jogs, his sword bumping against his hip. As Douglass turns down a wider alleyway, he hears a group of small thumps behind him and notices a group of men jogging after him. Most look like poor farmers but two are dressed in leather pants and boots. He turns around and sees five men chasing him with their swords drawn. Douglass draws his sword and faces the group. "Five against one? You're brave," one man chimes.

The group of men stop running. "You attacked my man, sliced open his wrist, then ran away like the coward you are," a dirty looking man yells at Douglass. His leather jacket and boots contain rips and holes and stained with mud. His brown hair clumps in knots at the ends.

"Your man attacked me with his friend. I was outnumbered and did what I had to do."

The men snarl and step towards Douglass as another man, dressed in all leather with a matching leather hat and feather protruding from the side, places his sword to one of their necks from behind. "I do feel that five against one is a bit heavy on one side, so I decided to help even the odds." The group turns their attention to the mysterious invader. "So, my good man, I will take these four thugs, and you take the mouthy one in front of you," the man continues.

The unkempt man lunges at Douglass while another of his partners attacks Douglass from the side. Douglass spins out of the way and fences both men at the same time, increasing their lunges with force and speed. He picks up on their predictable patterns and recognizes that they are trying to flank him; when Douglass attempts to strike, the second man guards the way, forcing Douglass to re-position his attack. The swords and shouts from the group create onlookers watching from the main laneways. The adults hold their children back, pulling them away from the crowd.

THE NEW QUEEN

Douglass pushes one man onto some barrels, sending him smacking onto the ground as the crowd laughs. Douglass turns and attacks the remaining man, but he blocks each attempt until the second man jumps back onto his feet. A bystander, a middle-aged man, forces himself into the fight and pushes Douglass between the two men, cornering him. Both men point their swords at Douglass, their chests rising and falling with each breath and eyes narrowed. The man with the leather hat and thin feather interweaves and attack the second man. Douglass uses the diversion to strike the first man and they fight side by side.

"Like I said, I will take four and you take one, or are you greedy?" the man in leather asks Douglass with a smile.

"No, please, help yourself," Douglass responds as he fights hand to hand with his assailant. Douglass knees the man in his groin then spears him with his sword. The man falls to the ground with a thump. Douglass turns around and finds his new friend standing with one foot on the man's chest, while the other three lay around in pain.

"Now how about that! Wasn't that fun?" the man asks with a smile. "I take it that these are the last of the supporters of the army then?"

Douglass looks about. "All I know is that they attacked me, my good friend." Douglass reaches out his hand to shake the man that helped him. "My name is Douglass. What might yours be?"

"Names are not as important as loyalty to the king. Shall we string these up, lock 'em in the stocks, or just chop off their heads?" The man looks at Douglass for an answer.

"We should lock them up and have the king say their fate," Douglass concludes.

The man smiles so wide that his yellow teeth peek underneath his curled lips. "Lock them up then!" A few guards push through the expanded crowd and escort the band of bandits out of the alleyway. "And where are you off to now?" the man asks.

"I have to inform the king about Sir Anthony, and I guess I will tell him about this lot as well. You think you can keep the peace while I am gone? I don't suspect to be back until late tomorrow."

"I can do that, Douglass," the man says with a bow. The tip of his white and brown hawk feather waving in the gentle breeze.

"I am trusting you."

"I have always been trust worthy as I am part of the black army sir." Douglas knew he could trust the man.

The sun hangs low in the sky by the time Douglass leaves for the brief journey to Martin's smaller castle. At the halfway point, pausing between both castles, Douglass glances at the darkening sky. Thick, dark clouds eclipse the sun and cast darkness across the land. A thunderous roar echoes the sky, followed by a quick flash of lightning. The horse kicks its front legs, shrieking in fear before it bolts under a collection of trees. Douglass clings tight to the reins until the horse's shaking decreases. The rain falls hard, splattering onto the dry ground like bullets as the lightning continues. "Looks like we will have to wait it out," Douglass says to the horse, dismounting it. He pats the horse's face and it exhales and snorts, nuzzling into Douglass' neck. He lifts the small pack from the horse's body and empties its contents on the grass. He grabs his tinder box and furiously rubs two dry sticks together, sparking the flint. He adds fallen branches and leaves in a mound, forming a small fire for him and his horse. He sits in front of the fire as the horse strolls off to the side, chewing on some tall grass sheltered by a canopy of trees. Douglas eats a few handfuls of cured meat, washing it down with a few sips of ale from his leather canteen before curling up in front of the fire and falling asleep, clutching his sword as the storm rages on.

THE NEW QUEEN

The break of morning shines through the heavy clouds in the east as a light drizzle sprinkles the valleys and forests alike. The fire dies to a few glowing embers at the base of the fire pit. He tosses a handful of dirt on the remaining embers and packs up his small campsite, then grabs his horse standing off to the side when he notices a series of footprints nearly ten feet from the fire pit. Douglass stares at the different sized footprints one last time before mounting his horse, wondering what those people wanted and why they didn't attack him during his sleep. He directs the horse back onto the path towards Quarry Castle but the trail becomes difficult to travel from the mud, fallen branches, and other debris from the violent storm. Douglass guides the horse off the path towards the grass instead, listening to the horse's hooves squish into the soaked grass. They continue riding towards the castle when Douglass notices the same series of footprints from the campsite in some of the hardened mud, leading in the same direction he travels. Cautiously he keeps his hand by his sword, eyes narrowed, and continues his journey through the drizzle to Quarry Castle.

Martin looks out towards the channel and Hope Castle. "You should send them help," Elizabeth announces, startling the king. Martin turns towards her, holding the stone face of the wall-walk.

"And who should I send? The last of my men are playing soldier to keep this army at bay that we don't even know who they are!" He snaps raising his voice.

"You know, if Castle Hope falls, this one will be next." She walks to the other side of the king, looking out towards the way of Castle Hope. "Are we sure it's not the one and the same army?"

"Hmm, well it would make sense..." the king says. "It's why we cannot find them anymore, either..."

"March the army over there. You know Simon is there already."

"But he cannot get into Castle Hope, so what good is that?" he interrupts her.

"If Simon is anything, he is resourceful. I think he would find a way to keep the army from fighting or being able to fully siege the castle. The scout said that Simon got one man inside the castle and he wanted to go back and fight, too. Anyone who would go back to fight overwhelming odds must think there is some chance at least." Elizabeth pauses before she starts again. "I think we should march the men back and show the army a sign of force...if it's not too late."

"It's not too late, Elizabeth. I have scouts watching them carefully, and they would have told me if the castle had fallen."

"Then what are you waiting for?"

"I am just not sure. You would think with everything we have been through I would know what to do?"

"No. You are a good king and a good king never jumps to a decision." Elizabeth leave him on the wall walk to think it over.

Chapter 25
Looking for the Enemy

Only four guards remain in Simon's party from the nightly attacks from the Great Army. Simon knows the men are tired and hungry, he knows they want to stop fighting and leave, and he also knows they would not be able to survive much longer. Each time a group of men would come hunting for them in large numbers, they would kill enough to make Simon's party leave.

"I think my wrist is broken.," a soldier says quietly over the fire. The soldier sits around the campfire, holding his swollen wrist.

"Can you fight still?" Simon asks.

The man looks at his wrist and shrugs. "I guess I have no choice, do I?"

Simon lowers his head when one of his soldiers rushes over. "Look what I found," the soldier says, holding a handful of dried meat and a cask of ale. The other men smile as the food is divided out between them. Each man takes a considerable long drink of warm ale and a fist full of meat, gobbling it down as quick as they can.

"Where did you get this?" Simon asks.

"One of the dead guys had it on him. He was a fat one, too," the guard answers with a full mouth.

"Is there any more?" the soldier with the broken wrist asks.

"I don't know. I was so excited that I didn't check anyone else."

The group chuckles at the comment when a branch snaps by a nearby tree. Simon stands up slowly, looking around the campfire when an arrow flies by, grazing his shoulder as he dives down to the ground. The men scatter in every direction behind trees, leaving Simon alone by the fire.

Rollo and King Louis sit at a table in King Louis' tent at the end of another successful battle against the English with minor fatalities from the French and the Vikings.

"I will gladly send my men up the coast towards where we fight, but if there are more battles to be won, we will not be there to fight at your side," King Louis says. "There's no need for us to stick around."

"Yes, but this is my land! Not the English, not Martin's, and not yours!" Rollo raises his voice.

"My dear fellow, we have been fighting with the English since the beginning of time. My father's, father fought with them, and my children will fight with them. I see no end in sight!" Louis remarks.

"We once owned that land they now reside on, and we thought that if we let them live there, they would stop fighting with us. They want everything they can get. All the land, all the food, and

THE NEW QUEEN

all the people. Anyone who does not obey their orders is sent away or is executed."

"Ah yes, like King Martin?" King Louis asks, taking a swing of wine from his ruby-encrusted goblet.

"King Martin is a good king and a great warrior. He is quite excellent in combat, given his young age, and his people will surely follow him to their deaths if he ever commanded it. He has their undying support." Rollo taps his fingers on the wooden table, then stands and starts to pace. "It will be in both of our interests for his kingdom to succeed and grow. No one can get by him without him knowing and in turn, he could warn you of the passersby. He is also a good ally for us both because if his kingdom grows, so will his army. If we cleanse this land of all the English, then both of our kingdoms will survive another day."

"I suggest we form an alliance with all three of our kingdoms. This will give us great strength if one is attacked," Louis concludes, standing up. Rollo outstretches his arm and Louis accepts, agreeing on their new terms.

At the break of dawn, the armies leave their campsites in search for the rest of the English. They packed enough supplies for their search, expecting to be traveling for months on end. Rollo approaches the nearby village that the English destroyed; most of the small buildings either burned to the ground or contain severe burns, almost too brittle to stand on its foundation. Wisps of smoke and the choking scent of burning wood blends with the crisp morning air as a flock of blackbirds fly overhead.

"How many were lost?" he asks an elderly lady, slumped against a crumbled well.

"All the men, some boys, and many women were stabbed and killed. It will be difficult for this village to flourish after this attack." The elderly woman wheezes and lowers her head.

LOOKING FOR THE ENEMY

Rollo frowns. "Do not weep for them. The gods will grant them access, you can be sure of that."

"I have no more tears to weep with," the woman replies. "The time for crying is over. We must go on with what we have." She hangs her head.

"We will find the men who did this. I promise."

The old lady gives him a slight smile, then sighs. "We cannot go through life revenging after one another. The consequences are too grave." The lady sighs again and turns away. She bends down to gather long grass in her bruised arms.

Rollo leaves the lady, watching the French gather long grasses for huts and basket weaving. He places his hands on his hips and exhales. "Do not make camp here. We will move further," he shouts to the group of French men and Vikings closest to him.

A French soldier walks over to Rollo, scratching his head. "Ermm, is this not a perfect place to build camp?" The man points to the land around him. "No grass to move away, and no rocks to fight with... why should we move?"

Rollo looks back at the elderly woman, now further in the fields. The collection of tall grass piles in her weak, limp arms. "It's the only place left for these people. If we stay here, we are taking more from them, and they have already lost enough."

The French soldier glances at the old lady in the field, then turns around. "Pack up!" the man yells in French. The massive army slowly moves out of the decimated village, some on horseback and others on foot. They continue their slow trek for eight miles, exhausted and famished, until Rollo and King Louis instruct their men to scout out the land while the rest prepare camp.

One of Rollo's scout's returns, dismounting his horse. "Well?" Rollo asks him, approaching the man.

"I know this land," the scout responds, holding his horse's reins. "I was raised here and I know there are no neighboring

THE NEW QUEEN

villages nearby. There is a large oak tree that shows the entirety of the land for a mile around, and I could not see anything."

Rollo smiles at the scout and pats him on the back. "Well done. Now go help the others set up camp."

King Louis snores loudly inside his tent, already erect under a collection of pines. While the rest of the armies prepare their suede and linen tents, the remaining scouts from both armies return with confirmed news that the area is safe.

Dusk approaches as Rollo orders a small group of guards to be the night watch around the campsite. The fifteen men disperse to separate posts around the camp, some extending to the edges of the forests. In the distance, four unknown men approach on horseback. Rollo commands the armies to load their bows and keep them aimed at the impostors. As the men slow their horses, Rollo notices their armor from King Martin's kingdom and commands his men to not to fire. They lower their bows.

"You are getting too far away for us to keep a supply line going," a man says as he dismounts his horse. The other three dismount, untying three boars and a large bag of buns from the backs of the horses.

"Did Samantha bake the bread?" Rollo asks.

"I'm not sure, why?" He hands the bag to Rollo.

Rollo takes out two loaves of bread and claps them together. The loaves squish into each other, and some parts crumble to the ground. "No, she did not. If she did, we would be using them as weapons instead of food!" the Vikings and King Martin's men laugh as they turn their horses around and head back to the kingdom. Some men lift the boars and bag of bread, preparing a spit roast. Rollo rips a piece of bread from a loaf and heads to his tent.

Elizabeth and Samantha have the task of cleaning up after the French had left. Each tent had to be emptied and scrubbed cleaned. The buckets of waste were taken to the channel and dumped into the current, away from the castle.

"Hey, I found some gold.," Samantha yells out.

Elizabeth runs to Samantha. "Shhhh! Do you want everyone coming here and looking through our mess and finding the good stuff?" Elizabeth opens the flap of the tent. "Whoever used this tent left everything," she comments as she notices as all of the bedding and lamps remain in place.

"Elizabeth, this is my tent! You have yours over there!" Samantha points to the other side of the tented area. Samantha picks up a wool blanket. "Wow, this must be worth a lot...it looks new!"

Elizabeth takes the blanket and unfolds it, letting it hang as she inspects it for holes and moths. "Yes, it is a very nice blanket," she says, dropping it next to her sister. Samantha sighs at the unfolded blanket. Elizabeth leaves the tent and walks into the nearby tents in search for a similar find until she smells something pungent and rotten. "What is that?" she asks herself and continues into each tent until she finds the tent used for waste. The tent contains a chair with a hole in the centre where waste falls through, and into a large hole in the ground. Elizabeth covers her mouth and nose with her arm as she runs out of the tent. "Oh MY!" she exclaims, alerting Samantha.

Samantha runs out of her tent and looks for her sister. She walks towards her sister then catches the terrible scent. "Oh my, Elizabeth, what in the world is that smell?" Samantha covers her face with her arms. "It smells like someone relieved themselves all over the place."

THE NEW QUEEN

"Oh, they did! The whole tent is filled with it! I'm not cleaning that!" Elizabeth walks towards her sister, still covering her face. "I think I can taste it, too." She gags and spits on the ground.

"It's our job…we have to clean up after these pigs!"

Elizabeth looks at Samantha over her arm. "Then you clean it! That's the worst smell in the world!"

"It is bad, isn't it?" Samantha asks.

"Oh, Samantha I can't clean that. The smell is stronger inside, too." Elizabeth pleads with her sister. "Please, please, please, do this one for me?"

"Not a chance. It's your side so you do it." Samantha walks back towards her area of tents as Elizabeth takes a deep breath and walks towards the smell.

"Oh no!" Samantha exclaims. "I got a smelly tent, too."

Elizabeth runs over to Samantha's tent and pokes her head inside. "It's not as bad as mine."

Samantha crinkles her nose and closes the tent entrance. "I think it's time we eat. I don't want to look at another tent for awhile."

Elizabeth grabs Samantha's hand and they skip back to the castle together, pointing at the flock of ducks flying towards the channel.

The afternoon sun shines brightly making everyone feel a bot brighter than they should. Martin waves at Douglass as he enters the castle gate. "Douglass, how are things at Hope Castle?"

"We are under siege, sire. They have not attacked in full force as of yet, but they continue to march around the castle time and time again. A show of force, I think. We only have a few archers, and we come to ask for help."

"We have the English attacking the Vikings, and the French are helping to hold them back. If they get through the Vikings, we are next to battle the English. I am not sure we can spare anyone at this time, Douglass." Martin shifts uncomfortably.

Elizabeth and Samantha walk through the gates. Elizabeth notices Martin and runs up to him. "We are going to go eat. Would you like to join us, your majesty?" Elizabeth turns to Douglass. "What are we talking about?"

"I asked the king for help to stop the siege at Castle Hope," Douglass repeats with a panicked face.

Elizabeth narrows her eyes. "Martin, I thought we discussed this and you were going to send them help?"

Martin glares at her. "We did not discuss such things and we cannot send anyone since the English are lurking nearby!"

"If we can stop the siege, then there will be more men to help stop the English when they get here," Elizabeth responds.

"Elizabeth, you do not know what you are saying."

"Martin, you know if we march the men there and scare off this army, then they can march back here all before the day's out! How tough is it?" Elizabeth places her hands on her hips.

"What would happen if we end up fighting this army and lose all of our men? Remember I am the king and you are my subject." Martin turns and looks at Douglass all red in the face. "That will be all."

Douglass walks away holding the horse's reins as it follows him with a bowed head.

Elizabeth stands crossing her arms in front of Martin. She waits for Douglass to be far enough away before turning to Martin. "My king? And me, your subject? If anything, I am your adviser! And you said you were going to help Castle Hope if it falls. All we have is this castle and if it is under siege, where will we be? We need that castle to be free. It will show that you care about all men in

THE NEW QUEEN

your kingdom and you will protect each man, woman, and child. Think about it, you know I am right. Time is running out and you need to send some men as soon as possible. If you send them in the morning, they can be back near nightfall."

"You are a stubborn woman. No one would dare talk to me that way. I should have you..."

"Put me in the tower again? Once isn't enough for you?"

Martin takes a deep breath. "No, I would never do that to you or anyone. Elizabeth, just sometimes you make me so mad!" Martin storms off and approaches a nearby guard. "Take three men. Ride for half the night, then return and tell me if you see any signs of the English. I want to know when I wake up in the morning."

Simon falls as he tries to walk away from the fight to a safer part of the forest as his men continue to fight. Out of arrows and ready to drop, Simon watches as the last of his men finishes the fight by knocking the soldier down and driving his sword into the man's throat. Simon rests and pants against the large tree as three more of his men rest beside him. "Our numbers dwindle. We can't keep going," a soldier says out of breath.

"I know," Simon replies quietly with his eyes closed. Blood and sweat run down the side of his face. He opens his eyes and looks at a soldier holding his hand as blood drips between his fingers. Simon rips a piece of cloth from his vest and gives it to the man. He watches through thick woods as the army starts to move further away from the castle. "Oh, that's not good," he says as the other soldiers stand around him. "They are moving away from the castle. It can only mean that the castle has fallen or the enemy is planning to attack us from all sides with everything they have." Simon stands and faces his tired men. "Stay here. I want to see what the army is up to." He limps along, following them deep inside the forest at a far distance between the trees. He notices a dead soldier and leans over it, searching the body for weapons. He finds a bow and a full pack of arrows, attaching them across his back. He looks around, and in the distance, he sees the army still moving around the forest, dividing into small groups. "It's an attack from all sides!" Simon whispers. He backs away from the army and rushes back to his soldiers.

 Sir Anthony wanders through the courtyards, keeping an eye on the kingdom. Guards station themselves by the drawbridge and at the entrance of the courtyard, searching through the pockets of every visitor for weapons while the archers stay along the wall-walk, watching the army from a distance. Guards search through the goods of foreigners wanting to trade within the castle, and questioning any commoner entering and exiting the castle. Sir Anthony notices two foreigners dressed in dark brown cloaks and wooden sandals with leather ties, carrying a container of holy water and a leather bound Bible under their arms. The two men ponder through the courtyard, keeping silent and with their heads lowered. Sir Anthony follows the Black Army guard who also pursues the mysterious foreigners. The guard and Sir Anthony follow the foreigners into a side alley, where they pause and talk to a peasant woman selling fruit. The Black Army guard peeks around the corner, and Sir Anthony hides behind a barrel of hay.
 "Excuse me, miss. We heard there was a witch here," one man says in a low voice to the woman.
 "Yes," the peasant responds, looking up, "but she was set free some time ago. They say she had the king under her spell, unlike the Captain of the guards, and that's why she was locked in the tower."

THE NEW QUEEN

The foreigners glance at each other. "Where is she now?"

She steps closer and scratches her arm. "Oh, no one knows for sure. Most people think it was by magic, but I think she somehow escaped and went back to the other castle, away from here."

"Other castle?" Both foreigners glance at each other.

The woman nods and directs the foreigners towards Quarry Castle. "Why are you looking for a witch, anyway?"

"We are here doing God's work, under a holy mission. A witch is the devil's work, and we must end this dammed creature. Good day." The foreigners nod their heads to the woman and walk away in silence.

The Black Army guard turns around and jumps in front of the men, holding his sword forward. "Why do you seek the woman who was wrongly accused as a witch?"

The men stare at him and pull back their hoods, exposing their shaved heads. "Who are you to ask?" the man with deep blue eyes and a wrinkled face asks in a calm voice.

"Do you work for that army that keeps us at bay?" The men try and walk around him, but he twists his sword sideways and cuts them both off.

"It would be wise of you to stay out of our way. We are doing God's work," the other responds, narrowing his brown eyes.

"What do you intend to do with this woman?"

"That is none of your concern," the blue-eyed man snaps back.

"I think it is," the Black Army soldier persists, standing his ground. Sir Anthony grips his staff.

"Are you a God-fearing man, sir?"

"Why should one fear God who gave one life?"

"We are here to rid the evil in the world," the younger of the two responds. His brown eyes remain calm. The elderly blue-eyed man glares at his accomplice.

"And you believe this witch is evil?" The men pass around the guard in silence, but he turns around and shouts, "What about the falsely accused or the misunderstood?"

The older man turns around. "I'm warning you now, it would be best to stay out of our way while we complete our holy mission."

The soldier narrows his eyes at their decreasing figures among the crowd, and darts after them. Sir Anthony hurries in the opposite direction, thinking of a plan to save Elizabeth's life.

King Martin opens the front gate and steps outside, tripping on new stone steps and stumbling onto the dirt ground. He quickly scrambles to his feet and rubs his knee through his leather pants and dusts off his cotton shirt. Two nearby guards rush to his side. "When did this happen?" Martin asks the guards, pointing to the steps.

Garnet rushes to Martin's side. "Are you alright, sire?"

"What happened here?" Martin looks at the choppy steps. "You could have made a better entrance way to the castle. This is sloppy."

Garnet scratches his chin. "I have all the stone coming in from Saxton's castle as fast as possible. On the opposite wall of the castle, I have men cutting the stones as well." Garnet points to the far side of the castle wall. "I have three teams retrieving stone and two teams placing them. I am happy to say we are expanding the wall by ten stone bricks per day and night." Martin smiles and Garnet continues. "Without the towers, we will be done in four weeks if the amount of stone holds out. We will need another four weeks per tower afterward." Garnet smiles and places his hands on his hips, looking up at the men along the wall slowly moving a stone slab. His grey beard and hair hang in knots around his dirty face, and his white cotton shirt drapes loosely off his body, covered in

THE NEW QUEEN

more dirt and small rips. Calluses cover the insides of his rough hands and a thick layer of dirt wedges under his yellow nails.

"When did you last eat, Garnet?" Garnet pulls out a bun from his pocket. "I mean a decent meal?"

"I eat when I can, your majesty, just like the rest of us." He nods at the working men and takes a bite of bread.

Martin nods. "You are doing a great job Garnet, but I cannot have you looking more like a peasant than one of my most trusted leaders. I order you to have a proper meal and more importantly, clean yourself up and look like a trusted leader." Garnet bows and heads back into the castle. A scout returned from the night and approaches Martin from the wall-walk, climbing down the staircase and across the courtyard. Martin turns to him and they walk towards the unfinished wall. "How is the stronghold across the channel coming along?"

"Sire, I scouted for the English like you asked, but found none!" Douglass walks up to the king and waits for a word.

The king turns to Douglass. "What is it?"

"I want to inform you that Sir Anthony has left Castle Hope and has gone to get help to fight the army. I will be leaving to get back to the castle and try my best to hold it against this army, your majesty." His eyes are bloodshot, and large bags darken his under eyes.

"I have decided to send half of our army back with you. They may not be real soldiers, but they look the part. Some know how to fight, but most do not. That should scare off the army," Martin says.

"If we can get back into the castle, then we can have them keep the peace while we come up with some sort of plan," Douglass adds. He bows then leaves Martin to gather up the men he needs.

Martin turns to Garnet. "Tell the men to make twice as much mortar and to secure the rocks a little better. For now, we have the time, so use it for the mortar." Martin's attention diverts to the swaying of a large oak tree in the distance, crashing to the ground with a boom. He watches a group of men hack off the smaller branches and carry the larger branches back to the castle for timber. He walks towards the wall-walk, followed by Garnet, as they climb up the staircase and lean over the ledge. "We should build another tower on the other side of the landing."

"Yes, but the wall should be finished first. We don't have enough supplies and men to separate into smaller groups to work on multiple projects at once."

Martin sighs and nods in agreement, watching wagons filled with stone from Saxton's kingdom pull into the courtyard. Martin continues along the wall-walk with Garnet following closely behind. Martin stops at the joining of the new wall to the old, impressed with the excellent work. "This progress is all very well. I am impressed with the handiwork of the wall. The stronghold is what needs work, so make sure more mortar is being made for it. I want the stronghold to have the same handiwork as this fine wall." Martin pats the wall and runs his hand over the smooth ledge.

All of a sudden, a horn sounds, echoing off the castle walls. Martin and Garnet rush down from the wall-walk and towards the iron gate. They peer through the bars as one thousand men march towards them in military formation, just over the hills in the distance. Archers line the wall-walk, while soldiers in full armor pile in front of the gate, and spare men pour onto the field, ready to fight outside the unfinished castle. Martin's heart pounds at the thought of war finding its way into the kingdom all over again. They all wait in silence. From a distance, Martin notices a familiar man walking towards them. He squints at the approaching figure, and Martin clenches his jaw, unsheathing both of his swords in each hand.

THE NEW QUEEN

Sir Jade leads the army and drops to one knee in front of Martin. A guard draws his sword. "Your majesty," Sir Jade starts, "do not fear. I have not wavered in my service to you. I found these men who had lost their way. They would like to show you that they are still loyal to you, your majesty."

"Rise, Sir Jade," Martin responds.

Jade stands up to explain. "I found them not too far from here, laying traps to stop approaching intruders. They are scared and hungry and feel ashamed for leaving a long time ago."

"Your majesty," a man starts, stepping forward, "We did not think you would accept us back. After Henry was killed, most of us fled to save our lives and that of our children."

A long scar covers the man's cheek, and Martin recognizes him as a Black Army soldier. "How many are you?" Martin asks.

"I do not know the exact number, but I would say around one thousand or so," he responds.

Martin places his hand on the Black Army man's shoulder. "Tell them there is no shame found here, only loyalty."

Two short horns sound and the king moves quickly to the wall-walk by the front gate. He looks out and sees the French returning. Martin runs out of the castle walls towards the French. The soldiers stop and form two lines for King Martin to move through to see King Louis. "How is the fight?"

"Though barbarians are great at fighting, they fight without honor," King Louis comments.

"You mean the Vikings?" Martin asks.

"Yes," King Louis says with a large smile. He wraps his arm around King Martin's arm and they march back to the front gate. "We killed most of those English, so I have decided to go home. It has been many weeks longer than I had planned to stay away. I think we might finally be near the end of this blasted war once and for all."

"I'm very pleased to hear that, your majesty. What about Rollo?"

"He will be fine. Like I said, we chased the English out of my land and his land." King Louis notices all of Martin's men waiting in rows in front of the castle. "You were sending more men to help us? Ah, Martin, you truly are a man of honor."

"Well, now that you don't need them, they will go and fight the army that has Castle Hope under siege. I am greatly outnumbered with this other army, and I suspect the English."

King Louis scratches his chin. "Are you sure they are English?"

"All I know, your majesty, is that my castle is under siege by an unknown army. If this army takes my castle, then there is no one between you and the English again and maybe they will march towards you next."

King Louis' eyes widen. "No, that must not happen." He thinks for a moment. "My army will march alongside your army. I will not risk the lives of my kingdom to anyone, especially the English!"

King Martin turns to a Black Army guard. "Prepare the army for war, and then, we march." King Martin and King Louis stand side by side along the wall-walk as the war horn rings above them.

Chapter 26
Reinforcements Come and Go

Ten thousand men march side by side towards Castle Hope. Most French are dressed in their royal blue coats with a yellow comber bun and King Martin's army are dressed in their dark coats with their armor underneath. A light, misty rain made walking miserable, for each step is slippery in the mud. After marching straight to the halfway point, the men stop to break. Most look for some sort of shelter.

The soldiers who ride on the wooden wagons approach close to the castle and take cover from the rain in a treed area. Each soldier carefully stays with his partner in order to not fight alone. Sir Jade takes the lead into the forested area, his sword drawn. Jade looks carefully once inside of the forest. "I don't like this," he says to a few soldiers who walk behind him. "It would be too easy to ambush someone in here." Sir Jade stops, and the men stop as well.

REINFORCEMENTS COME AND GO

A bush moves and a bunch of arrows fly into it from all directions, then they watch with no one moving. Silence fills the air when a boar walks out of the bush and walks away. The men grow increasingly quiet as each step is cautiously placed in front of the next. "I feel something is about to happen," Sir Jade says to the man next to him, but the French man does not understand. All of the men suddenly stop as they see a body not far from them. They spread out, making sure they are not all one easily accessible target. Slowly they walk in a solid line towards the body with Sir Jade taking the lead. He rolls the body over to find a soldier who has been dead for a day or so. He looks at the body, checking it for any clue as to who he might be. Sir Jade checks through all of the pockets but finds nothing. The man's sword is within arm's length, and he has several wounds inflicted by a sword or a knife.

Jade rolls the body back the way he found it and looks through the heavy treed area to see many more bodies. He motions for the men to divide into two groups while he stays in the middle, gilding the men with each step. He stops when he realizes there are no birds singing or any rodents searching around for food, just a boar eating berries in the bush. More soldiers come from behind him, and he continues to walk slowly, making sure there are no surprises. Crossbows are loaded and aimed in front of the eye of the soldiers carrying them. They come to yet another body, and again, Jade carefully turns it over, checks for anything they could use. He looks around at the hundreds of bodies that are spread out all over the place. "An easy place for an ambush," he repeats aloud.

A guard comes up behind him. "There are a lot of bodies here. Are they ours?"

Jade looks at the guard. "No, I don't think so. This has to be a trap. Take your sword and test each body before turning it over."

"Yes, sir." The guard moves to his first body and sticks his sword into it. Flies buzz around but the body does not move.

THE NEW QUEEN

He turns it over, finding the man's face partly eaten by ants. He pushes the body back and motions the men who follow him with crossbows to the next body. One by one they search the entire area, finding only death.

After a long search of all the bodies in the area, the guards and Sir Jade meet together. "I found nothing," one guard says.

"Our castle has fought well," Jade says.

"But who are they? There are no flags and no armor that would show the kingdom they fight for."

A French soldier points to a body then to himself. "Are they French?" the guard asks Sir Jade in French.

Jade takes the French man's arm and leads him to King Louis. "Did this man do something wrong, Sir Jade?"

"We found a bunch of bodies but do not know who they are. This man seems to say something, but I do not speak French." The king asks the man and they have a small conversation. Jade grows irritated with the two talking in French. "Well?" he interrupts.

"My soldier believes they belong to the King of Castile. We have been allies for some time, but for them to get here they would most definitely have to cross through my kingdom, and our treaty would not let that happen unless they asked to."

"Why would they attack our castle?"

Louis shrugs his shoulders. "I have no idea. Also, they would not know King Richard was dead, either so that would mean they wanted to attack King Richard. That would make sense since we both were his enemy."

"How large is this army?"

"I do not know, but I thought it was fairly small compared to mine."

"Well, there is at least a hundred bodies spread out all over the forest floor, like fallen leaves."

REINFORCEMENTS COME AND GO

King Louis scratches his beard as he thinks what could have happened. Jade calls over a man who watches the horses. "Ride back and tell King Martin what we have found and tell him we are going through the forest to get to the castle." Jade turns and walks back into the forest. He walks to where the men continue to search, finding even more bodies. "There must have been a few battles in here, not just one. The winning army took their men's bodies already, but the losing army did not get theirs as of yet. Make sure you use your swords first! I don't want to be surprised and find ourselves in a fight!" he yells out.

King Martin shows just how nervous he is as he walks around the wall-walk with his arms folded in front of him. Elizabeth walks towards him, holding up her old gray gown from touching the damp stone floor. "I heard you sent the army to fight at Hope Castle."

"Yes I did, what about it?"

"I also heard you lied to King Louis so he would send his army as well."

"I didn't lie, Elizabeth," he pauses as a slight smile crosses his face. "I just pointed out that it would be in his best interest, that's all."

"You made him think that it was the English that has Castle Hope under siege!" Elizabeth crosses her arms.

"Yes, there was no way our army could win. They are all farmers and boys, nothing more than a show of strength. Now the only problem I have is that we have no army here to protect us in case of attack."

"Who is left to attack us anyway?"

"There is always someone who wants what you have. Try not to be so naive. You know as well as I that there could be an army around the next tree line."

THE NEW QUEEN

"Martin, what about Saxton's kingdom? Can you not claim it as your own?"

"I'm sure there will be others rushing to claim it. He had a few barons and a duke, I think. They will most likely fight among themselves until they figure who they want for a king. It happens all of the time."

"But if you claim the kingdom as a spoil of war, then they cannot say no to you." She leans up against the wall, placing her foot behind her. "I think you can do that. You did win the war, you know."

"But King Saxton fought against the Great Army and lost, so really England has the right to claim the kingdom as a victory."

"But was King Richard not the King of England?"

"Yes and no. He was the King, yes, but he was making Hope Castle a kingdom on its own, so no, he was not the King of England when we won the war. If King Henry knew we were the ones who won, he might send the Great Army to fight us now."

"I think that is all the more for you to claim the kingdom. If King Henry takes Saxton's kingdom, then they will surely come to get this one next and then the French will be forced to fight against you and England. If the French find out before you claim the kingdom that you could have stopped it all, they might want to fight you. It will be best for everyone if you claim the kingdom."

"That would make this kingdom a very large kingdom indeed. In turn, everyone would want to beat a large kingdom, making us a target, even for the French."

"But don't you think there are some good soldiers in that kingdom? We could start training men to fight and get a large army together and fight the English on their land."

"No, no, no. I would never go and wage war against the English. Remember, that's where most of us come from. It would be like waging war against the Vikings and they are good people!"

REINFORCEMENTS COME AND GO

Elizabeth walks towards the end of the wall-walk then turns back and looks at King Martin. "This is the perfect time to claim that kingdom. No baron or duke or earl would dare go against an entire kingdom. You have beaten Richard who controlled the entire area, and no one dared to try and fight him. This just goes to show that you are the rightful king. I think the barons and earls will be grateful when you take the kingdom under your flag! Martin, think about what I have said and remember that King Louis is not winning the war anytime soon. He told me they are evenly matched and no one moves. He cannot fight you and the English at the same time, so you do not have to worry about him. The English trot along our kingdom at will. You will have to put a stop to that soon, or else both the French and the Vikings will not be your allies." Elizabeth turns and walks down the stone steps, holding her gown up once again.

Sir Jade watches Elizabeth walk away. "She sure does test you," Jade says as he approaches Martin.

"I thought you went with the rest of the army," Martin says, glancing at Jade.

"No, I plan to talk with Mark and see if he wants to go hunting."

Martin shifts uncomfortably and clears his throat. "I guess you have not heard, but Mark died in his sleep."

"Are you sure? I mean, he is dead?" Jade stares at Martin, waiting for more information.

"It was a serious infection from when he fell off the horse. It ate him up from the inside. I met him at Castle Hope where he saved my life when my leg was hurt. He was a good man." Martin pauses, waiting for Jade to say something before he continues. "Sir Jade, it is my honor to ask if you would be my personal guard. I can't think of anyone better to serve me than you."

THE NEW QUEEN

Simon wakes up in a puddle of his own blood. His leather pants are shredded around his wound along with a few nasty cuts on his hand. Feeling dizzy, he tightens his bandage on his leg, hoping the bleeding will stop. His sight blurs from the loss of blood and the sweat runs into his eyes while he sleeps. He tries to pull himself up and leans against a large tree next to him, but does not have the strength to do so. Simon looks around through the sun shining through the trees and grabs the sword that lays beside him. He fights to lift it up but struggles under its weight before laying back down. "This must be the end, as God wills it," he says before passing out once again.

Garnet brushes off some dirt from his long robe, then kicks off some dried mud from his wooden sandals as he directs a few men where to lay the next stone. Garnet places both hands on his head and stops some men who enter the gate with more large stones. The king watches as Garnet runs over to the men and looks out seeing many more on their way, like a trail of ants. Garnet grabs three men and rushes them over to where the mortar is being made and tells them to make more mortar as fast as they can. "We need lots more mortar. The stones are coming too fast!" he yells at them. Three small children dressed in little more than rags sit and break up small stones to help.

King Martin approaches the children. "You are doing great. Keep up the good work." He then approaches Garnet by the front gate. "Garnet, things are moving very quickly."

"The men found a lot of stone that has already been cut and they are coming back faster than mortar can be made. I need the men who bring it back to put it in place, too but we do not have enough manpower to do both."

The king scratches his chin before answering. "Make three more groups to make mortar. Make one of the groups who are bringing the stone to also make the mortar. That way, the stone will not come as fast, and mortar will be ready when stones arrive." The King smiles then leaves.

Elizabeth rushes around the kitchen, packing food into her small satchel. "He needs our help."

"Elizabeth, Martin knows what he is doing," Samantha says as she follows her sister around the room.

"He is too scared to do what is right." Elizabeth stuffs some fresh bread into her satchel. "If I can make the barons and the earls see that he should be their king, then they will come to his aid and fight beside him instead of against him."

"Elizabeth, you're a woman and no man will listen to a woman." Samantha grabs Elizabeth and gives her a firm hug. "You are the most headstrong fourteen-year-old I have ever known, but the men would use you as they see fit and you could do nothing about it."

"I will say that I have be sent by the king. They would not dare touch me then."

"Yes, they would. The barons would not believe you, a woman, was sent by our king, especially if you are alone."

Elizabeth pushes away from her sister's grip. "I have to try," she says as she leaves the kitchen.

Samantha follows Elizabeth to the side gate as Elizabeth grabs a horse from the stable. "Elizabeth, no!" she screams. Samantha tries to block the path but Elizabeth turns the horse around Samantha and exits out the front gate. She runs up the stone stairs to the wall-walk and looks out towards Saxton's old kingdom and watches her sister ride over the top of the hill. Samantha lowers her head and begins to cry.

Sir Jade approaches Samantha from behind the corner of the wall-walk. "Samantha, what's wrong?"

THE NEW QUEEN

"Jade, you can help. Elizabeth has gone to talk to Saxton's heirs to convince them that King Martin is their rightful king. I just saw her go over the hill on a horse." Samantha cries.

"Hang on, I will go find her." Sir Jade hurries down the wall-walk and jumps onto a nearby horse, riding quickly out the front gate.

Captain Witter rides his horse while he moves the army around the forest. The land is uneven, The wagons rock and bounce along the uneven land. Captain Witter is dressed in full armor in the kingdom's colors, of red and purple. He is ready for another battle.

"We are down almost a thousand men, Captain.," a guard says riding his horse up to Witter. "And what about the catapults? Are we just leaving them there?"

"I left a small group to start the fight in the morning. They are to continue attacking the castle. As long as that castle is under attack, they will not think we would move away to our other duties."

"Other duties?" the guard asks.

"We are going to take Saxton's kingdom. Our queen is the rightful heir and will claim the kingdom for herself. It is only a two days march. We will march west, then turn south and claim the kingdom when we arrive. Once we take the castle, then we will call out to all of the noblemen and have them serve our queen by first getting rid of this new king who thinks he can hold King Richard's castle from us."

"But captain, a few catapults will not break the castle."

"They are not there to break the castle, they are there as a distraction. Once we have things in order, we will take the castle with all of our army and weaponry." Witter watches as the men perfectly march forward.

REINFORCEMENTS COME AND GO

A scout quickly rides up to the captain. "Sir, it looks like the French are the ones inside the forest. They must be the ones we have been fighting all along, that's why we lost all of those men. You think they are here to claim the castle?"

"If we are seen in a fight with the French, it could mean war with them." Witter stops his horse and looks around. "How many Frenchmen do you think are in that blasted forest?" The scout shakes his head. "Well, it has to be a lot if they killed over a thousand men." Witter turns to his guard. "Have all of our men move faster. We have to get away before the French know we are here. Go as far west as we can for the rest of the day, and maybe we can lose the French." Witter then turns his attention to the scout. "You must ride back home to tell the Queen what has happened and tell her we are heading to claim the throne under her name. And one more thing, tell her we did not know the French were the ones in the forest." Witter nods his head and dismisses the scout. "As long as the French don't find us, we will be fine." Witter says as he sighs showing his nervousness.

Simon opens up his eyes as he is rocked side to side on a makeshift stretcher while four men carry him through the forest. He is rocked to one side and instinctively grabs the side of the wooden frame in order not to fall off.

"Oh, he's awake," one of the men carrying him says out loud. Another looks down at him and says something in French then places his hand lightly on Simon's chest and gently pats it. Simon looks down at the man's hand, then rests his head back and falls asleep.

"Well there he is and still alive!" Simon recognizes his men's voices and struggles to see through the bright light. "Woah, woah, you have to stay lying down or we will drop you." One of the men

THE NEW QUEEN

grabs Simon's arm. The men place Simon into a large tent, sitting him down on a long table where two men wait with large knives. They place a piece of wood into his mouth that is covered with a rag soaked in wine.

"Bite down on this, son, this is going to hurt," a man says in broken English. Simon feels them tying his arms down to the stretcher while someone else ties his feet. He lifts his head and watches them cut his leather pants away from the wound and sees that it is infected. He watches the first man slowly push the knife into his thigh. Simon bites down hard on the wine-soaked wood as tears well up in his eyes. He yells quietly as the man cuts away parts of his leg.

Simon awakes in a yellow and red striped tent. He moves his head to the side and looks around. Simon sees a few more men sleeping on tables. Slowly he raises his legs bending it in more of a stretch. He tries to flex his other leg but pain throbs down his leg when he moves it. He lifts his head and looks down at his legs as he fights to get up onto his elbows. He sees that his legs have branches tied all around it, wrapped with a cloth over top.

"Hello?" he shouts. He looks towards the door and sees a man looking at him. "Where are we? What have they done to us?" The man blankly stares at Simon and says nothing. Simon fights but is unable to get up. Finally, he flops his head down onto the cloth filled with grass, and he holds his legs in pain. The man across the tent waves towards Simon, motioning for him to stay put. "Where are we?" Simon asks him. The man says nothing then places two fingers on his mouth. He tries to talk, but it is so mumbled that Simon thinks they cut out the man's tongue. "Good God!" Simon exclaims. The tent door flaps open, and one of Simon's guards walk in.

REINFORCEMENTS COME AND GO

"You're awake," the guard says, walking towards Simon. "You're in good hands. The French king had these guys fix your leg. It was badly infected, but they cut that out and sewed it all up."

"Are we safe now?" Simon asks.

"Yes, sir, we are. The entire French army is here, and they outnumber that other army three to one. They are still searching the forest, then they will attack the catapults." The guard leans against the table next to Simon. "We have some wounds, but nothing as bad as yours. One of us has a broken wrist, so we are told. I have a broken rib or three." The man stops and looks at the other man on the table across the room. "Does he speak?"

Simon lifts his head. "I think they cut out his tongue!"

The guard walks over towards him and looks at the man. "No, they didn't cut out his tongue, he's French. You French?" he asks the man.

"Oui," the man responds in a hoarse voice.

"That means yes." The guard holds up one finger, suggesting to wait. He leaves for a brief moment then returns with a Frenchman who walks over to the man on the other table. The two start talking immediately.

The guard walks back to Simon. "Did the king send everyone to help us?"

Simon rolls his head side to side in pain. "It is a large army. We had to stay inside the forest where we had a chance. We killed so many, but they just kept coming. I lost some great men." Simon lowers his head and grabs his legs.

"Well, it looks like they lost more. We found hundreds of men dead in that forest," the guard responds.

"Tell the king we did our best to save the castle," Simon says as the pain throbs down his leg until he passes out.

Chapter 27
HELP

The king walks out of the castle and back to the wall-walk that had come to be a common occurrence of his daily routine. He has been so concerned about the new curtain wall that he until now had not noticed how the kingdom has flourished. The farms expand still told what to grow that gave the kingdom a marking where their catapult could reach. Crops sowed are now starting to bloom, and cattle and chickens multiply, providing meat, eggs, milk, and transportation. Oxen plow more fields for crops, and more land for roads. Farm huts are rebuilt for the farmers to temporarily reside in during the night instead of in the castle's keep due to the sudden overpopulation. Guards in pairs scatter around each farm hut during the night for extra protection. Martin takes a long good look around, almost surprised by what he sees.

Garnet stands proudly, staring over the group of men labouring over the curtain wall. "The construction of the castle curtain wall on the south side is almost complete. The first wall surrounding the

HELP

forest area remains erect, while the second wall towards the forest shows promise as the trench is dug for the stones to be placed," Garnet says, yelling up to the king. Garnet has a group of men building flanking towers on the finished curtain wall, starting with the two towers that stand in the middle of the long wall. Each tower is over ten stories, rising over the hill that once faced King Saxton's kingdom. Each tower contains a deep foundation in the ground as a defense strategy, blocking the option for enemies to tunnel underneath. On the crown of the tower rests a catapult or trebuchet.

To help with the walls and security of the castle, Martin divides the extra men into scavengers for stone, or scouts on the lookout for any armies that might be about. Instead of bringing back only boulders from Saxton's, the scavengers also bring back furniture such as wooden tables and chairs, and even a few royal tapestries if they have room in their wagons. Some men return to the kingdom after bringing back extra boulders from Saxton's castle with help from the stronghold across the channel. Nightly shifts are divided among a few others, taking turns scouting different parts of the land at night for possible invaders.

"We may have to work into the winter, so be ready for that!" Garnet announces.

"How will we make mortar or cut stones in the snow? I mean it's not impossible," Martin starts. "Remember when our king asked to make a stronghold in midwinter? We did it. We built that huge wooden structure over us to keep us warm and protect the stronghold from the snow and ice. We should build one of these, but I worry about the surrounding armies. We may end up in battle, and I don't want to be unprepared."

Garnet thinks for a moment, remaining silent. "I think this could work. I will think up a plan and be prepared when the time comes." He leaves Martin and heads back to the wall as torches start flickering around the castle.

After hours of riding, Elizabeth enters a thick treed areain a place she had never been. Elizabeth fights with low limbs and the odd branch. Elizabeth lifts her head and sees a large body of water in front of her. "I don't remember anyone saying anything about a lake..." She dismounts, wraps the reins around a branch, and walks towards the water. The rough waves crash on to the shore with a loud crash one after the other. She takes a large breath and smells the salty water, tingling her nose. She stares into the horizon, not able to see the other side of the ocean. She walks along the cliff ledge, staring at the shoreline. "We must be in Saxton's old kingdom, maybe even past it..." Elizabeth rests along the cliff's ledge as mist sprinkles her face. "Ah, I hope I'm not lost..." Elizabeth sighs and stares at the ocean.

"You're not lost," a voice responds.

Elizabeth jumps up and turns around to see Sir Jade walking towards her.

"How did you find me?" Elizabeth stands up and walks towards him.

Sir Jade smiles before answering. "You didn't have too much of a head start from me. I followed the path I believed you to take, and I used your remaining campfires as evidence that I was on the right track. Each fire I came across was still warm, so I knew you weren't much ahead of me."

Elizabeth nods her head. "I see. Well, I'm not going back if that's why you're here. I have to help the king." Elizabeth crosses her arms.

"Why don't you tell me what your plan is, and maybe I can help," Sir Jade says as he wraps his reins around a large rock.

HELP

"King Saxton's kingdom is in shambles, and if King Martin lays claim to it, he can expand the kingdom and then have more men to fight King Henry. I think if I went to the barons and the dukes and whoever else is in charge, then I could convince them to join our kingdom." Elizabeth leans against a nearby tree and Sir Jade follows her.

"That is truly honorable of you, but do you think this king will listen to you? These men have had to fight for everything they have. Do you think they would listen to a girl?"

Elizabeth glares at Sir Jade. "I'm a woman at fourteen years old! I am not some child with a wild idea!"

"Yes, a woman, but a girl just the same." Jade pauses for a moment hoping she would continue explaining her plan. "What would you say then? I mean really, what could you say that noble men would just join a new kingdom?"

"It's not about just telling them to join a kingdom, it's much more than that! I would have to explain everything that has happened from King Richard to King Henry and how King Henry burned down Saxton's castle. I would have to tell them how smart Martin really is, and how he beat Richard at a war he had a little chance of winning at. And I will tell them how nice and kind he is, not just with me but to everyone; how he took in people who had no place to go and he fed them all for nothing. Did you know he never asked for anything in return?"

"Well, that's not exactly true. The king has them growing food and making weapons and working different jobs to strengthen the kingdom. Some make cabins, while others are helping to build the castle and expand it. Some men fight, too," Sir Jade explains.

"There must be someone in this kingdom who will listen," Elizabeth remarks.

"Elizabeth, there are hundreds of kingdoms all around us. This is not Saxton's kingdom...we are way past that. Over there, past

THE NEW QUEEN

that hill, is one kingdom while we stand here in another. If you look far enough, you can see another kingdom towards the smoke. The kingdoms around here are small, and they think everyone should join them, not the other way around. I once traveled through these kingdoms; some are friendly, but most do not welcome strangers in their kingdoms without paying homage."

"Then we will have to just make all of them understand that they have to join us because we are bigger than they are!" Elizabeth stomps her foot.

Jade smirks. "Well if you put it that way..." He stretches his arms. "They might take that as a threat, Elizabeth. Telling them we are bigger than they are, I mean. You have to appeal to their needs, that's what these noblemen understand."

"You mean we bribe them?"

"Yes and no. You make them see the benefits and how they will become profitable from joining the kingdom. The value needs to be greater than their current way of life."

They walk back to their horses and ride together along the cliffs. "I think we still have to try," Elizabeth says after riding in silence.

"Very well. I will do my best to help you on your quest, but you better know that not all men will listen or even talk to a gir-... woman. These leaders are different from Martin."

"I know. Some men are pig-headed, while others are rabbits that run without thinking," Elizabeth says with a smile. Jade laughs and shakes his head at her. They grip their reins and ride together into the forest, leaving the emerald ocean behind them.

Two men wearing dark brown robes with hoods hanging past their eyes enter through the main gate. The guards glance at the men and let them enter without a word. Martin watches the

HELP

mysterious men, trying to figure out who they are. He waves over a guard. "Find out who those two hooded men are. The guards seemed to think they were safe, but I don't recognize them," Martin orders.

The guard nods and heads towards the hooded men. Martin watches as the guard speaks with the men than returns moments later. The hooded men hang their heads low and speed through the keep. "They are two monks from France, your majesty. They wish to give service to the kingdom."

Martin watches the monks weave between groups of people. "Tell them they can give a service late tomorrow."

"But they will be gone by then, your majesty," the guard replies.

Martin thinks for a moment before giving an answer. "Tell them they may give a short service in the keep."

The guard bows and leaves to inform the monks. King Martin watches the guard search for the monks when Douglass approaches Martin from the side.

"Your majesty, I would like to inform you of the monks in the castle," Douglass starts. Martin nods. "You see, they are here to kill Elizabeth, not to give a service. They said they heard about a witch and are looking to cleanse the world of all witches."

Martin gasps. "Do they not know she is not a witch? I mean, Simon just wanted her out of the way. I think we should send them away."

"Your majesty, we cannot do that." The king looks back at Douglass with a curious facial expression. "They said they are here to do God's work, so how are we to stop the men appointed to do it?"

Martin looks away as fear sinks into his thoughts. "We know she is not a witch and losing her will not be right." Martin places his hands behind his back as he locks his fingers together. "Send them on their way. Tell them she is not here, and we do not want them causing problems."

"They have already started to tell the people that they will give service and most have not had service in a long time, your majesty."

"Very well, but they are to leave right after the service."

"Yes, your majesty." Douglas bows and leaves.

King Louis IX sits in his tent at the edge of the forest not far from King Martin's Quarry Castle. King Louis opens the tent flap at a commotion nearby.

"Your majesty," one soldier says to him. "The army is still using catapults to attack the castle, and the castle is not fighting back. I fear they have been pillaged by now."

"How many men are left of this army?" King Louis asks.

"I do not know, sire."

"How many people are left in the castle?"

"I do not know, sire. All I know is that the catapults are shooting at the castle as we speak."

"We cannot just run into battle without knowing what we are up against. Send a few scouts to see what awaits us before we march." the soldier bows and leaves the tent. The King looks around at his men who sit and rest. "When I was their age I did not need as much rest as they do today." he says to himself, then turns and goes back into the tent and looks at a map of the area that has been hastily drawn to give him some idea of what he is up against in the terrain. The candle on a small table flickers and the king watches it for a moment when it goes out all by itself. "I hope that's not a sign." he says looking back at the map.

HELP

Simon wakes up hearing a commotion outside of the tent he lays in. Gregory is still sleeping on the floor next to his bed. Simon tries to move but the wound in his leg shoots an intense pain and Simon yelps. Gregory wakes and jumps up quickly holding a knife. "Sorry I tried to get up." Gregory places his knife back into its sheath. "Go see what's going on and let me know," Simon tells Gregory.

Gregory opens the tent flap as a flash of light brightens the room. Gregory looks around, seeing the French and Martin's men moving quickly towards the forest with swords drawn. Sir Gregory calls over one of the men.

"What's going on?"

"We found the army, and we're going to go and fight them to save Hope Castle in our king's name!" The man runs off, and Gregory watches for a few moments before opening the tent flap again to tell Simon. "It looks like they found the army and we are going to attack them." Simon sits up, causing pain to shoot through his entire body. "Relax, you can't do anything anyway."

Simon nods with a frown on his face. "I know." Simon looks around the table he is on.

"What are you looking for?" Gregory asks him.

"Where are my things? My sword, my knives, my pants?" Simon realizes he has no pants on or a shirt and is wrapped in a sheet.

"Relax, Simon. Your things are around somewhere, so don't worry. I will find your things henceforth, but you have to relax. It will be a long time before you are able to get on your feet again, my friend."

THE NEW QUEEN

Simon rests his head down against a pillow made from hay and takes a deep breath, listening to the sound of his men running about the camp.

Sir Anthony waits for the rain to completely stop before exiting the cave. He mounts his horse and heads towards the village where Anthony grew up learning to fight. "We have a long way to go still," he says to the horse. The pair continue on their journey until Anthony spots a pack of wolves trailing behind them between bushes. Anthony kicks at the horse to make it run faster, but the wolves quickly catch up. Sir Anthony looks around at the growling beasts. "These old eyes don't see as well as they once did." He looks for a place to take shelter like the cave but sees nothing that might even come close to the good shelter they had before. Anthony directs the horse into a clearing and quickly dismounts, grabbing his staff.

Out of the corner of his eye, he spots a wolf in the distance, crouching as it approaches. In the other direction, Anthony sees the snow cap mountains he was aiming to reach by the end of the day. He moves the horse as close as possible to the entrance of the thicket, then cuts a few thorny branches and starts to make a wall in hopes to save the horse. He watches intently as the wolves move quietly towards them but still maintaining distance. As Anthony tries to straighten a long group of thorny branches he snaps it like a whip. "Oh, that might be better than a wall." He quickly puts together a small wall and ties them together as the wolves walk into the open area in a group of three. The horse sees them and moves side to side, thrashing its head about.

A wolf growls behind Anthony and he turns to see six more wolves behind him. He snaps the whip in their direction and one wolf raises its paw at it. The three wolves move closer and the horse

HELP

begins to kick wildly in the small walled area. Anthony snaps the whip in their direction catching one of the wolves as it yelps from the inflicted wound. One of the six wolves jumps onto the thicket bush, only to find there is no way in and only a pile of hurt to get out. Two of the three in front of the pack charges the wall where the horse continues to kick. These wolves too land on a soft wall of thickets and thorns and are thwarted by their attempts.

It wasn't long until the horse knocks down the wall from thrashing its legs and the wolves jump into action trying to get at the horse. A wolf manages to get through the thicket and Sir Anthony is face to face with the creature. His staff is no good in such a small space, although he keeps the wolf away from him and his horse. The animal shows its teeth, growling at Anthony. The wolf watches Anthony with its orange eyes, almost glowing as it stared at him. Its yellow teeth and sharp claws seem to glow in the darkness as it approaches closer.

All of a sudden, the rain starts to fall, growing heavier and heavier. Anthony locates where his weapons remain: his knife is in the satchel tied to the horse and his sword is also strapped to the side of the horse. The heavy rain makes it hard for Anthony to see the wolves in front of him as he grips his staff tighter.

Rollo walks through the tall green grass with his two-sided battle axe resting on his shoulder. "We have not seen one Englishman in days. I don't know if that's good or bad." Another Viking leader walks beside Rollo. He is shorter and has a red beard braided into two locks.

"I will say it is good because if the English are here, they are hiding and if they are not here, then they have left," the other Viking leader answers. "I am told we sent out three boats filled with women and children to safety."

THE NEW QUEEN

"Where to?" Rollo asks as he looks across the empty field.

"The new land. It will be safer there than here."

Rollo nods in agreement. "We have to make a stand. We have to get every leader together and fight these Englishmen once and for all."

"I understand your reasoning but the English are wildfire, once you kill one, another replaces its spot." The Viking pauses and observes Rollo. "You see something, don't you?"

"No, just a feeling that we are being watched." Rollo kneels down and quickly divides his men into two groups, sending them to surround the area. He observes other Vikings moving through the tall grass, then he catches a pungent scent; that awful smell of the English men heading his way. He raises his axe, ready for battle. He runs in the direction of the smell, his axe raised above his head, as the other Viking follow closely behind. The two Viking leaders run quickly, soon meeting up with one of the groups that approaches from the side. Rollo looks around, confused that there are no Englishmen. He stands tall on his tiptoes looking around as the second group arrives to join them.

"Maybe it is nothing?" the Viking says to Rollo.

"No, it's something, but I am just not sure what." He looks around, then spots something sticking out of the tall grass. He strains to see what it is when five Englishmen rise from the grass. "Ambush!" Rollo yells. The Vikings scramble in all directions, running as fast as they can to the English. Arrows start shooting across the field, and Rollo holds his two-sided battle axe to hopefully block any incoming arrows. Two Vikings get hit by arrows almost immediately and tumble to the ground, rolling in pain. Rollo lowers himself and moves around to come up behind the Englishmen. He moves as fast as he can, trying not to draw attention to himself.

HELP

"Attack!' The Vikings yell, and they rush towards where the arrows are coming from. They break through the tall grass to find no Englishmen but a few broken bolts and trampled grass. The Vikings look at one another as they start to assess where they went, finding footprints leading in one way. The Vikings run in that direction when arrows begin to fall around them once more. They push along the path but find that it is a dead end and there are no Englishmen about. The Vikings run in the direction of the arrows once ore, this time separating into three groups.

Rollo looks around the tree to see if he can spot the men who were shooting at them. He looks carefully and then sees a large group of men running close to a nearby bog. Rollo jumps up and runs to cut them off, trying to get in front of them. Rollo runs right into the lead groups as he swings his axe as fast as he can. Some of the men try to run around Rollo, rushing from both sides and landing in the bog as Rollo hoped. One Englishmen notices Rollo's plan and fires an arrow into Rollo's back. He screams in pain and drops to his knees as the rest of the Englishmen run past him and escape.

Chapter 28
SEND FOR OUR ALLIES

Elizabeth rides side-saddle with her gown dangling freely while Sir Jade rides slowly into the next village where the people watch them in complete silence. The ride was a good days ride from the last village. There are four small huts along the entrance to the village. Jade stops and looks at an elderly man who moves some wood from an old wagon to the side of a hut.

"Who is the king here?" Jade asks.

The man looks at him with wide eyes. His worn out stocking have holes in the knees, and his shirt barely covers his arms. The man looks around carefully before answering. "You need to get away before the king knows you are here," the man whispers.

"Elizabeth, we have to go, now!" Jade scrambles onto his horse and leads the way out of the village when four guards out of no where block their path. The guards dress in blue tights with leather boots and a bright yellow shirt, and a metal armor chest plate with a lion on it.

SEND FOR OUR ALLIES

"Halt!" One of the guards shouts. "You are trespassing this land!"

"We are from King Martin's kingdom, here to see the king!" Jade boldly responds.

The guards look at one another. "You will have to give a tribute to see the king."

"How much will this tribute cost King Martin?" Elizabeth asks before Jade can speak up.

"You let this girl speak for you?" the guard asks Jade while he glares at Elizabeth.

Elizabeth is about to speak when Jade quickly responds. "The king has sent her to speak on his behalf. She is soon to be the queen of King Martin."

The guards smirk. "What king would send a girl to do his bidding? She is nothing but a child."

"I would watch your tongue," Jade warns the guard.

The guard smiles. "And what could one man do with four guards?"

"Take us to see the king or leave us. It will be your death, not ours," Elizabeth blurts out.

The guards squint their eyes and purse their lips. "What do you mean by that?"

"There is a great army coming this way, and you will not be able to stop them by yourselves. In fact, only by joining King Martin's kingdom will you be able to survive. The king has many men and intends to hold this Great Army away from here, but we only have fifty thousand men. The Great Army has many more coming, so if you want to survive, you will take us to your king, now!" Elizabeth explains with a firm voice.

"...There is no such army," the guard says with a smile.

"King Martin had to fight King Richard and won in a full-scale war, and now the Great Army wants all of the land, including

THE NEW QUEEN

yours. Many kingdoms have joined us already to stop the Great Army, but if you don't want to fight with us, then I will tell King Martin to let the Great Army destroy your village." Elizabeth glances at the small crowd gathering around her. "You wouldn't let these people die, would you?"

The small crowd waits in silence for the guard to answer. Some wait with hands covering their mouths, while others softly murmur to their neighbors. The guards glance at each other, then nod to both Elizabeth and Sir Jade without saying another word. The guards lead them to a small stone house near the center of the village. They enter the house with the guards walking on the outside of Elizabeth and Sir Jade. A man, with long black curly hair, dressed in a fur coat and a metal crown, sits at a wooden table eating some duck. A guard walks up to him and whispers into his ear. The man laughs before waving them into the room.

"A great army, you say?" as he chuckles.

"Are you the king?" Jade asks.

The man chuckles again. "I am the ruler of this land, not a king. I was not born of royal blood." He takes another bite of his duck leg. "You do know you owe me a tribute," he says between chews.

"We don't have any money or gold," Jade says with his hand gripping a throwing knife.

The king shrugs. "Then I will keep the girl."

"She is the future queen to King Martin. It would not be wise to go against the king." Elizabeth steps closer to Sir Jade. "I take it you do not believe that a great army is headed this way?" Jade pries.

"I do not, nor do I believe this girl was sent by any king." Jade looks around the room as two more guards enter the room with their hands on the butt of their swords.

"Do you know who I am?" The man laughs. "I do not take nonsense from a stranger and his girl."

SEND FOR OUR ALLIES

"You will work in the fields until your hands bleed." the man tells Jade. Jade quickly turns and throws knife after knife into each guard's neck. "You will bow to the future queen or die. Now, which will it be?"

Captain Witter is happy to be far from the battlefield as the men happily march along. The sun shines through any sparse clouds keeping spirits high. No one knows that they had lost so many men, and even fewer knew that there was fighting at all.

A scout rides up quickly to Captain Witter. "Sir, there is a large army not far from here. I think it's the French."

"The French? What are they doing here?"

The scout shrugs his shoulders before answering. "I do not know, but they have other men marching with them who are not in uniform and it makes for a very big army."

"We will have to head further south. The last thing we want is to end up in a fight with the French. Turn the men." Witter looks out to where they will march ahead and sees a group of men heading towards them. "To arms!" he yells, and the men raise their swords while the pick men fall to one knee and hold their long spears. Witter rides his horse to the font of the line.

"Hello?" an approaching man shouts out. The man wears the same color as Witter's men but has the royal sash of green with gold trimacross his chest. "The queen has sent you gifts." A wagon follows the man and the coachman pulls out a sallet helmet, a large metal helmet that covers the entire face and flares out in the back, along with a large amount of quilted jack made from multilayered canvas, the best armor the queen could afford. "I did not think we would meet up with you this quickly. The queen sends her blessings and these thousand fighting men. Our queen wishes to know if you have taken the castle yet?"

THE NEW QUEEN

"Give these to the men right away," Witter orders the scout, pointing to the jacks. "Thank you. Tell our queen that the castle is under siege and we are moving to claim the throne in her name." Witter watches as the new recruits march up to join his army. "These soldiers look better equipped than we are. They have chains on their arms and covered elbows with gauntlet mittens."

"And they have the best-forged swords gold can buy. These are the best of the best our kingdom has to offer. The queen demands you to be successful or else suffer the consequences." Witter knows that means death. The royal wagon turns around, and ten men start back to tell the queen what they had learned.

One of the new men approaches Witter. "Captain, these are my men. They are the best of the best. We have been ordered by the queen to make sure this quest is successful and if necessary, to take command of the army."

"That will not be necessary, I know my duty." Witter pauses. "We will be successful in claiming the castle. I have a plan."

The French soldiers all raise their crossbows keeping them loaded. They moved around the catapults, surrounding the enemy soldiers that stretch almost halfway around the castle. The problem King Louis faces is that he does not want to lose any men from the catapults which could kill them all if they are not careful. A single burning arrow shoots through the sky from the forest, a sign to begin the attack. All of the French crossbows fire at once while King Martin's men run with the French, swords raised over their heads and yelling to instill fear in their enemies. As they reach the main camp, they find only injured or dead men, some crying while others begged for forgiveness, but no one will survive. The catapults are moved quickly into the castle and lifted into place on top of the wall-walks where previous ones fit, and new bases were swiftly made to help secure any new catapults to cover all sides of the castle. The castle is now able to defend it self once again.

King Louis parades into the castle wearing his newly polished armor. Peasants stare at him, surprised by his presence, while others even bow when he walks by. His guards surround him with their swords drawn and shields held high as they march in rhythm with his steps.

Douglass walks through the castle gate, a few men behind King Louis. He marches with the French guards when one of the peasants approaches Douglass.

"Sir, why are the French here? Are they not our enemy?" the peasant whispers.

Douglass beams. "We have the French to thank for stopping the siege."

"But we have been at war with the French for years. They even killed hundreds of our men! How can we be allied with them now?"

Douglass stops and hangs his head. "I knew this was going to be hard for the people here. The English have shown they are willing to go to war with King Martin and all of his allies. They have attacked the Vikings, the French, and they even crushed King Saxton to his very death."

"King Saxton is dead?" Douglass nods, affirming the peasants question. "And we have allied ourselves with the barbarians across the channel? I can't see this going well for us..."

"King Martin was thrown into a war against King Richard so we had no choice in this war. King Martin does not have faith in the King of England. He sees no recourse but to protect the kingdom and our allies. By having the French as an ally, we have a larger army and they will help in many other areas as well. That's all I am going to say." Douglas turns away from the man.

King Martin's Soldiers hurry by in the opposite direction with the French archers who take positions along the wall-walk next to

King Martin's guards that were already there. Each soldier looked out over the battle field hoping they would see tomorrow.

Sir Anthony wakes up in a twisted net of thorn branches and tall grass. He looks around and sees three dead wolves around him. He tries to move his right arm only to find it stuck in the mud as he lays on top of it. He raises his head ever so slowly and looks for a weapon. Sir Anthony sees his knife beside his hand that is buried in the dried mud. He tries to sit up but finds his arm and left foot are also encased in the dried mud. Sir Anthony pulls hard on his arm trying again and again to free himself. He lets out a long breath and tries to rock side to side to keep warm and hopefully loosen his binds. He looks through the thorn branches and between the tall grass when he hears movement beyond the shadows.

"How in God's name did you get in there?" A man stands over him as he looks at Sir Anthony and poking him with a staff. He dressed in a dark brown cloak similar to Sir Anthony's.

"I could use some help, this mud is like iron."

The man looks carefully over Sir Anthony. "This clay, once hardened, is like iron. I will have to use your sword to break it." Sir Anthony nods. The man moves below Anthony's legs and tries to pick up the sword. "It's stuck in the clay. I am Shu." He grabs the knife and begins to stab at the clay around Anthony's foot. "I think it's breaking, my friend." At that moment, Sir Anthony's foot kicks up and he slowly straightens his leg.

"Oh, that's better. I am Anthony," he says as he moves his leg up and down.

"Your arm is bent in a strange way, my friend," the man says as his breath brushes Sir Anthony's face. "I fear it may be broken." The man looks at Sir Anthony before he plunges the knife into the clay next to Anthony's head. Sir Anthony spits out small pieces of mud, then looks back at the man. Slight yelps come from each blow as Sir Anthony tries to keep quiet under Shu's digging. Finally, Sir Anthony is able to free his hand stuck in the mud. He wriggles his fingers.

"Lift your head," Shu says and cuts through Sir Anthony's hair to free him from the clay. "That clay will come loose in the water. It's not but a short walk from here." He helps Anthony stand, and they both look at his foot in a large mound of clay.

"It is very heavy," Sir Anthony says then raises his stiff arm. "I don't think I can get over the bushes." Shu puts his shoulder under Anthony's and the two fight through the thorns and bushes, freeing him from the thorny cage. Anthony looks around, spotting his horse grazing not far from the tree he remains tied to.

"If it was not for him, I believe you might be dead," Shu says, nodding his head towards a dead wolf. "Looks like he kicked that one, but I think he died from loss of blood. I looked at him before I knew you were there." As they carefully move towards the river, Anthony notices the similar robe that Shu wears.

"Are you from the Shaolin village?"

The man looks at Anthony, then looks at his clothing. "Are you a master?"

"Once, long ago, but the Shaolin village I come from is weeks away by horse."

"The village you speak was mostly destroyed by a great army many years ago. The people fled in all directions, and now my village is not far from here. We have but one master, Master Quan, while other villages have many more. We are taught the Shaolin ways daily, but with the new weapons we are slow to learn the new ways." The two reach the river, and Shu walks Sir Anthony straight into it. The clay quickly softens around his left foot and he brushes it off with his free hand. He soaks his right arm in the

THE NEW QUEEN

water, hoping it will free itself, but the clay stays firmly attached. The man gently wipes his hand over the clay as it slowly starts to wash away. "Master, what is your name?"

"I am Anthony, a student of Master Shin, but that was some time ago."

"Ah…I have also been taught by Master Shin. He was one of the last in the village. He fought many men until they used crossbows against him. They say he killed thousands of the men who attacked the village."

"And what is your name?" Anthony asks as he wiggles his toes. The man hesitates before answering.

"I am just a student, you see." He pauses. "I am Master Shin's son, Shu."

"You were not born before I left. Your mother still carried you. Do you know why you are named Shu?" Shu shakes his head. "Your father came to me one day when he found out about you. He asked me what would I call you if you were mine. I said, 'Shu'. He asked why and I told him it is because he has been so kind to me. 'Shu' means 'warmhearted'. Your father took me in when no one else would. Your father would be proud of the person you have become."

Shu bows his head. "I never got to meet my father." Anthony lets out a large gasp of pain as he frees his hand from the clay. "I fear your hand is broken." He continues to remove the clay. "It looks like it is your wrist, master." Shu carefully feels Anthony's hand and wrist. He helps his new friend to the shoreline and leaves briefly to gather one large branch, then carefully breaks it in half lengthwise. He places each piece on either side of Anthony's wrist and forearm. Shu pulls out a large amount of clay from a cloth and encases Anthony's arm around both sticks. Carefully he wraps a piece of his robe around the clay and sticks. "This will hold. You must not take this off for forty days until it heals properly."

SEND FOR OUR ALLIES

Anthony looks at his arm and feels the weight. "How do you know this, Shu?"

"Master Quan. Each student is taught the basics in mending the body, the mind, and the soul."

"Your father taught me to fight and defend oneself, we never got into healing or prayer."

Shu pulls out the sword from under his robe. "I managed to get this out of the clay, master. Do you fight with this sword?"

"Fighting comes in many forms. This sword is for nothing but show. As we know, it is not as great as our staff."

Shu bows and they head towards his village, pulling the horse behind them.

Garnet and King Martin stand in the keep, gazing at the curtain wall in complete awe. "Garnet, I would not have imagined that you would finish an entire wall in such a short time!"

"I also cannot believe that it is finished, even as I see it now, your majesty. The men brought more stone than I ever thought possible. And you were right, ordering more men to make mortar was the trick that was needed." Garnet walks towards the wall and Martin follows. They march up the steps and look over the finished wall-walk.

"Garnet, how much stone is there at the castle?"

Garnet looks out towards the hilltop. "I'm not sure. Maybe I should go and take a look?" Garnet's face changes as he watches a man riding his horse quickly towards the castle. The man rides up to the front gate where guards are posted. They wave over Garnet and the king at once. Both men rush down the stairs and over to the front gate.

"Your majesty," the guard says, bowing before continuing, "this man says there is a large army a day's ride from here, headed this

THE NEW QUEEN

way. I was gathering dandelion leaves to eat when this army came out of the forest. I counted over a hundred men, most marching but lots on horseback."

"Send a man to get our army back here right away. Have every archer we have up on the wall-walk. They can take up the entire wall until the army finds out it does not go all the way around the castle. The men can run the length of the wall-walk to the old part if they have to," Martin tells Garnet.

A man on horseback approaches the king as the guards leave a clear path to their king. Martin watches the man ride out of the keep headed for Castle Hope.

"Sir, do you think the French will come to help?" a guard asks.

"If it is the Great Army, then I sure hope so." Martin turns back towards the man who brought the news. "What did these men look like in the army?"

"Well, I was watching them but I did not notice what they were wearing, your majesty. I do remember some of them had these funny looking hats on, or maybe they were helmets. They did cover some of their faces, but not much."

"What were their colors?" Martin pries.

"Colors? Well, I cannot remember, your majesty, but I do remember that I did not see any flag, either. Their scouts rode horses and you could hear them coming from far away. That's why they did not see me; I just covered myself with leaves and mud and they rode right past me."

Garnet returns to Martin's side. "I sent the man on our fastest horse and have the archers at the ready, sire. Do you want me to send out scouts?"

"Yes, that's a good idea. Send out three scouts to cover what the man said. Make sure he is telling the truth and if so, we need to know where they are going. If it is here, we will need to be prepared and if not, we need to know where they are going." Garnet leaves

SEND FOR OUR ALLIES

and Martin turns to the guard. "Make sure he does not leave." The king points to the man as he tells the guard. The guard nods and grasps the man's arm. "Come with me."

Rollo and a fellow Viking wander around the village, taking note of what needs to be built, and other ways they can improve the remaining village when the fellow Viking points toward a small boy running towards them. The boy carries a short fishing rod over his shoulder. He falls to his knees in front of Rollo, breathing heavily.

"What is it, boy?" the man breaks the silence.

"Boats," the boy says between pants. "Lots of boats." The boy points in the direction that he came from.

Rollo and the Viking immediately rush to the edge of the water, their weapons in front of them.

"Do you think it's those Englishmen again?" the Viking asks Rollo.

"We chased the English out once before, and we will do it again if it is," Rollo responds. Both Vikings watch the large troop ships sail down the bay, men line the deck of the ship watching the shore, ignoring the Viking village as they pass by. "They are not stopping here."

"If not here, then where are they going?"

"They head for the channel. That's King Martin's realm." They continue watching the fleet growing smaller and smaller in the distance.

"The one who supplies us with food when we were fighting the English?" Rollo nods. "Shouldn't we help?"

Rollo looks at the man as he thinks of what to do. "It's too late to send a messenger, but we should help Martin anyways. Send word to the other villages that we have to save a friend."

Chapter 29
Assemblage

The kingdom of Castile marches closer to Martin's kingdom when a scout approaches Captain Witter. "The castle's not too much further up ahead. Do you want the men to spread out and surround the castle? It will make it look like we are taking it for our own."

"No, we are not taking the castle by force. We will simply march in and claim it in the name of our Queen." Witter continues to ride slowly with his scouts on either side of him. "On second thought, spread the men out in a long line so it looks like we are much larger than we are." The scout smiles and rides off. Witter holds up his hand as the entire army waits to hear their orders. "We are about to lay claim to a castle for our Queen as the last heir of Saxton's throne. We will march into the front gates. These gates are very large and may even look open, but do not be fooled, this castle is very fortified and with the right amount of soldiers on the

ASSEMBLAGE

wall, it cannot be taken. So if there are men on the wall, we will not walk through the gates. We will take the castle by force, if need be."

Sir Jade rides with Elizabeth at his side as the sun sets in the distance. Sweat runs down the side of his face, and he quickly wipes it away with his arm.

"How many more kingdoms are we going to go to?" Elizabeth asks. "We only get ten or so men from each kingdom that we visit. We will need to visit a lot before we have enough men to help King Martin." Elizabeth rolls up her sleeves in an attempt to help cool herself down.

Sir Jade looks over at her and shakes his head. "If you are to be the next Queen, you cannot go around showing your body off to anyone. Roll those sleeves down and be a lady, Elizabeth." She crinkles her nose towards Jade and does as he asks, rolling her sleeves over her arms. "Elizabeth, we must get at least a thousand fighting men before we are any good for the king. We need to visit another thirty kingdoms, and we have to tell them we need more than just ten or twelve men." Jade looks back at the hundred or so men who carry different flags from their kingdoms in a long line behind them.

Elizabeth looks back at the long line of men carrying kingdom flags with large lions on them. "I think I know how we can get more men from each kingdom...we have them sign a peace treaty that states while they are fighting with us, they cannot fight with anyone who is fighting with us." She pats her horse again. "And if they try to fight, then all of the armies with us will go against them."

Jade turns to Elizabeth. "Elizabeth, that is...brilliant." Jade pauses, staring at her. "Do you know how to write?"

"No, you don't?"

THE NEW QUEEN

"I left writing to the scribes. I just did what all men did: fight, farm and drink." Elizabeth chuckles at his honesty. "How are we going to get this treaty written and signed?"

"Hey, do you think most kings know how to read?" Elizabeth asks.

"I doubt it, that's why they have scribes. The scribes read and write for them." The wind blows Elizabeth's hair across her face, revealing a scar on the back of her neck. Sir Jade glances at the scar, then quickly looks away. Elizabeth pulls the hair from her mouth.

"I don't think any of the kings we have met thus far has a scribe, do you?"

Jade clears his throat and looks at her. "I doubt it. The kingdoms are tiny. Most are no larger than an average baron, so I guess they would not have any scribes. A scribe would have to be at the king's side at all times, and they do not have kings."

Elizabeth scruches her face. "I know how to write my name a bit, and I have seen a few written scrolls. We have to make a scroll up and tell the kings what it says and they will sign it. Then we will get more men."

Jade thinks before answering. "And what if they find out it does not say anything?"

"If we say it says 'no fighting' and everyone signs it, that would mean they all agreed to it, therefore, they have to do what they thought was written."

"You mean if they sign it no matter what it says, they have to do what they think it said?" Jade confirms.

"I think so," Elizabeth says with a blank face. "All we will need is a scroll, and I will write on it and sign it. We will make a bunch of lines on it for them to sign on, then we will get more men and get back to saving the kingdom." Jade raises his hand, signaling for the party to stop.

ASSEMBLAGE

"Let's break here for a bit," Jade yells out then looks at Elizabeth. "It's a good time to find out if any of the kingdoms know how to read and write." Jade jumps off his horse and helps Elizabeth off hers. She pats her horse on the neck and feeds him a carrot. The large party dismounts and walks their horses towards a grassy area. They tie up their horses to feed while the men make small campfires and cook some food. Some men drink ale while others drink wine from different casks.

Elizabeth notices a man carrying a small piece of cloth tucked under his breastplate. "You have someone back home?" Elizabeth asks innocently.

The man looks up at Elizabeth and pushes the cloth deeper into his breastplate. "I do, my lady. She was promised to me, then she gave me favor by giving me her handkerchief." The man lifts some flowers from the ground and places them together. "Here, a pretty lady should have some flowers," he says with a bow.

Elizabeth steps forward to accept them when Sir Jade knocks them to the ground. "She is the future queen, and you dare to court her? I should hang you here!" Jade glares at him.

"The night will be cold and I thought she would like some company, is all," the man explains.

"But you are spoken for, or are you just going to continue to lie to the queen?" Jade steps closer to the man.

The man takes one step back. "I saw her arms, she rolled up her sleeves," he explains. "Is that not a sign that she is a lady of the evening?"

"It is a sign that if anyone tries anything with her, then they will feel my blade. Do I make myself clear?" The man nods and walks away.

Elizabeth moves quickly beside Jade, her eyes wide open and her hands shaking. "I was hot. I wanted to cool myself down, that's all!"

THE NEW QUEEN

"Do not worry, no one will harm you, not while I'm around, anyway. But Elizabeth, you must keep your sleeves down." Jade pauses while Elizabeth hangs her head. "Make camp away from the men...best not to lure them into certain death." Jade walks away, leaving Elizabeth to stare at the smashed flowers in the grass.

King Louis calls his men back to the edge of the forest after conquering the siege. A scout walks up to King Louis and bows. "What have you?" he asks.

"Your majesty, like you had thought, the real army is circling around us to attack Quarry Castle." The scout takes a deep breath before continuing. "Sire, that army outnumbers us greatly, maybe four to one, sire!" The king looks away and takes a deep breath of his own. He calls for someone from Martin's kingdom and waits for them to arrive. "You two, I want you to go and keep an eye on the army. Keep at arm's length, understand?" The two scouts bow and leave right away. A slight wind blows past the king, giving him a shiver, when Gus arrives out of nowhere.

Gus holds his swords, one in each hand. "I am here in place of Simon. What can we do for you, your majesty?" King Louis looks over the old man: his ragged clothing, his flimsy pants, and patchy leather armor on his chest, shoulders, and thighs. Gus looks at the king and waits for him to say something, but the king continues to stare at his attire. "You called?" Gus asks in annoyance.

"Ah, yes. We have scouted the army and they are headed for Quarry Castle. I fear we have been lured here under false pretenses."

Gus looks at the King with anger on his face. "What do you mean?"

"I believe they planned to lure us here all along, then attack the other castle," King Louis explains.

"Who is this army? Where are they from?"

ASSEMBLAGE

"We think it's the King of Castile. But he has been a close ally to me for many years...I do not know why he would change his alliance now."

"No matter, we have to move to the other castle now," Gus urges.

"We just marched my men here half the day. If we march back now, my men will not be able to fight in the morning and will be no good to you or your king. We will camp and leave at first light."

"If we do not head back now, there may not be a castle or a king to help at first light!" Gus steps closer to the king and the guards step forward. "Your majesty, I would never raise a sword to you unless my king ordered it. And if he did so, those guards would not have a chance, anyway," Gus says, looking at the two guards. Gus steps back and places his hands on his hips. "We have to do something other than camp. How about we march until dark, then camp. Would you agree to this?" King Louis nods reluctantly, and the order is given to be ready to march.

Gus and King Louis lead the men at a quick pace until nightfall, reaching about halfway to the other castle, until the group prepares to set up camp. Two scouts approach King Louis with wide eyes. "Your majesty, the army is setting up to attack the castle. King Martin has his archers on the wall, but it is open on one side. If the army gets around the wall, I fear the castle will fall."

"We march before the first signs of dawn," King Louis responds.

Rollo and the young boy watch from a distance in a rocky area, as thousands of Englishmen disembarked their ships. "We cannot fight all of them?" the boy asks.

"I know there are ten of them to one of us. Even if we were to kill half of them, they would not be stopped." Rollo puts his hand

THE NEW QUEEN

on the boy's shoulder. "I do not believe they are all here yet." Rollo sits down behind a large tree in the far distance from where the English unload. A few Vikings crawl over to him.

"What's the plan?" A leader with long braided hair and a bread long enough to touch his waist, asks from another village.

Rollo thinks for a moment then looks at the boy. "I want you to go around the army and ride to the stronghold that sits on the channel. You have to get there before the English do and tell King Martin the English are on their way. Ride all night if you have to and do not stop until you get there." The young Viking crawls through the tall grass towards his village, then sprints to the horses.

Two more leaders arrive at Rollo's side. "What do you want to do? We cannot win this battle. Better to move back and live to fight another day, Rollo."

Rollo agrees with them after a moment of deep thought. "Let's move back, but we need one to stay and make sure they are not coming our way." Again they agree, with one leader assigning a young man to stay and keep watch. The rest of the Vikings quietly back away from the English.

A group of Vikings lead by a Viking leader fight with a group of Englishmen who were scouting the land. The Englishmen are just far enough that no English will come to help them. Rollo joins the fight with a roar, swinging his axe violently, but these soldiers are well trained and able to defend from Rollo's deadly attempts. The Englishman swings his sword towards Rollo but he steps out of the way, retaliating with his two-bladed axe. Rollo charges at the man, knocking the sword of his hand, and tackling the man to the ground. The man collapses with the weight of the Viking on top of him as Rollo quickly decapitates him, sending the severed head rolling towards a group of men fighting. Rollo turns to help the Viking beside him and the two are able to kill the soldier. After a

ASSEMBLAGE

long battle, Rollo takes a long look and sees he has lost more than half of his men in one small fight when a leader approaches him.

"These Englishmen fight well. I have never before seen such well-trained soldiers." Rollo nods in agreement. "We will be of little help to King Martin now. I say we go home and let him fend for himself."

Rollo sighs. "If King Martin was not such a good ally, then I would agree, but he has done much for us, so we must help."

"We are only good enough to tire the soldiers out. It took all of us to fight this one small group of soldiers and now we have lost too many."

Another leader approaches the Vikings with obvious signs of fighting with his shirt bloodied and his hair matted. "Well thanks to Oden, we fight another day." The man's face is cut and blood travels down his forehead to his cheek. "I have fought many Englishmen but never like this. They were good fighters.'"

"I am taking what is left of my men and going home." the first Viking announces.

"If we let the English win their fight now, when we have King Martin's army and the French to fight with us, we will win! And by Oden, the fight is now!" Rollo responds.

The Viking leader shakes his head. "I cannot take that chance for my people. We will move our village further north where the English will not bother us." Rollo and the other Viking watch the leader walk through the field of corpses with only his son by his side.

"We need to get to King Martin's castle before these Englishmen do. Any ideas?" The Vikings fall silent as they all kneel in the tall grass.

"Do you think the boy made it to warn King Martin?" a Viking asks.

THE NEW QUEEN

Rollo shrugs his shoulders, but the Vikings already understand Rollo's upset face.

Two young men carry Simon on a makeshift stretcher to the other caste under Simon's orders. Two other men accompany the group for protection as they begin their journey. Simon rolls side to side in the stretcher as the men jog along the bumpy terrain. They leave the campsite as the sun goes down. They walk for awhile until they reach the stronghold village between both castles. The village consists of three wooden houses and one stone home, all occupied by farmers. The stone house has a large tower on the side, and on top of the tower is where they light a signal to warn of impending danger.

The men stop at a mound house made of mud, grass, and wooden branches. They knock on the door asking for a drink. The man of the house gives them some ale and offers to keep Simon there while they continued on. Simon thanks the man but refuses to stop. The party continues their trip, back into the night.

"Stop!" the man in the front hisses. The men all stop and place Simon on the ground, one giving Simon his swords back. Simon and the two men carrying him wait while the other two walk ahead. Simon raises his sword when the two men came back running. "Get up, get up!"

"What is it?" Simon asks in a whisper, gripping his sword.

"There are a few guards headed this way. They look more like well-armed scouts."

Simon motions for two men to go in opposite directions to surround the scouts. The men dressed in their leathers easily camouflage in the dark as they quietly approach their foe. Two scouts emerge from the trees, swords already drawn. The scouts dress in metal armor breastplates and helmets.

ASSEMBLAGE

"Who are you?" they ask Simon.

"Who are you?" Simon responds, holding his sword by his side.

"We are the guard for Queen Castile, queen and rightful heir to King Saxton's realm."

"Really? I did not know that old Saxton had an heir." Simon tries to stand up straight, but pain shoots down his leg and he flinches. "I am Simon, Captain of the Guards for King Martin, who's kingdom you are in now."

"We are on the land forthright of Queen Castile."

"No, you are in the kingdom of King Martin, and you have no permission to be here. I will let you leave this time." Simon points westward, away from the castle. "That way, out of the kingdom."

"You three are here, but we are well-trained with the sword. You tell your king that he is on Queen Castile's land and he must leave now!"

Simon and his guards point their swords at the scouts. "No matter your training. You are in our land and you will leave. This will be your final chance."

The scouts laugh at the unconvincing threat while the other two guards approach from behind the scouts, placing their swords against their necks. The guards disarm the two scouts and has them sit in the center while the guards surround them.

"Tell me what your queen's intentions are with this land of ours," Simon asks.

"Our Queen is the rightful heir to King Saxton. She rules the land you wrongfully inhabit. You will not win against us, for we have an entire army here, thousands of soldiers, all trained to fight."

"That castle you speak of was built for the King, and it is only one of two he rules. If you did not know, King Richard's castle was taken by our king and it too is ours. King Saxton's castle is in disorder as the barons and earls fight over who should be the next

THE NEW QUEEN

ruler because they all know Saxton had no heir! Saxton's kingdom has asked to join King Martin's kingdom under our protection. You and your queen have made a grave mistake." Simon fights to stand up straighter and bites his lip from the pain. "My only concern now is: do we kill you here and now, or do I let you go so you can tell your queen to leave before the army inside the castle finds you here..."

"It does not matter what happens to us. We already have the other castle under siege, and it will fall soon."

"You think so? Well, I have some bad news for you and your queen. The men you left to keep the castle under siege are all dead." Simon pauses before continuing. "Yes, it was my men and me. And if that is the extent of your soldiers, I don't think we will need anyone else." He waits for their response, but the scouts remain silent. "Since you are enemies of the kingdom, I order you to be hung until your death."

The night is quiet and clear as the torches burn around Quarry Castle. King Martin waits until the dead of night before calling most of his archers back into the keep for safety. Scouts are sent out on a regular basis to report on the army that has camped out not far from the castle. Samantha approaches Martin along the wall-walk, dressed in a long white robe.

"Can you not sleep?" Martin asks her.

"How am I to sleep when we have an army about to attack the castle and my sister is gone somewhere and the French army is in a battle for Hope Castle?" She lets out a long sigh and rubs her forehead.

"Samantha, we don't even know if the army wants to attack us or just to move through. And I sent Sir Jade to retrieve Elizabeth, so she is safe with him."

ASSEMBLAGE

"Well, what about the English?"

"I think they will have their hands full with fighting the Vikings. It's one of the reasons I supplied the Vikings with food to help them fight."

"But what if the English defeat the Vikings?"

"I get daily reports from the Vikings. So far, everything is fine. It's the same with the scouts I have watching the army, I know where they are at all times and what they are doing. It's best to know what you are up against before having to start a battle." Martin looks up and notices a torch being waved at the end of the new wall. "What's that?" he asks himself out loud. The king runs up the steps to the top of the wall-walk towards the open end of the new wall. "What is going on?" he asks a nearby guard.

A guard points towards one of the lit torches as three men fight with a single scout from the army. The scout swings his sword with great accuracy, but the men are able to keep out of the way. They jab their swords back at the scout, keeping him from moving while another guard jumps on the scout from behind. Once he is on the ground, all three men jump on top of him, hoping the weight will suppress him. Everyone watches as they fight to bring the man into the front gates of the castle, still struggling to break free. The King runs the entire length of the wall-walk and down the stairs to see who this scout is.

"Kneel for the king," a guard orders the scout and kicks him behind the knees, making the man fall to the ground.

"I am King Martin, and who are you?" After a moment of silence, Martin backhands the man with his metal glove. The man's head rolls to the side as he moves his tongue around inside his mouth then spits. One of the guards punches the man in the face once again snapping, his head back and causing his nose to bleed.

"Answer the king, you fool."

THE NEW QUEEN

With a small smirk, the scout finally responds. "We will take this from you. We will kill your women and men, and take your children to be our slaves. This kingdom will burn to the ground with you in it. Captain Witter does not take prisoners and he does not take tributes, so you are done for!"

A guard holds a knife to the man's throat, and Martin nods at the guard. The man drops dead at his feet, blood soaking the grass.

"Send word to Hope Castle that we are being attacked and need assistance. Tell King Louis to bring his men and my men back here immediately." He leaves the wall-walk and walks out of the side gate, angrily throwing a lantern as far as he could. The lantern crashes down in a large burst of flames, making him jump back from the noise. Martin stares at the small embers when an idea crosses his mind. Martin returns to the keep where Samantha waits for him, holding Andrew's hand.

Chapter 30
ENGAGE

The night had fallen over the vast land as Sir Anthony looks up at all of the stars and lays quietly with his arms folded under his head. Shu lays beside Anthony, already asleep. Sir Anthony tosses the wool blanket off and sits up, looking around the village. He notices a well and makes his way over to grab a drink of the water. He sits on the side of the well and takes a long sniff of the fresh night air when a Shaolin warrior dressed in a long robe that separates into two pieces in order to move quickly if need be. The robe is brown in color and ties at the neck. The worrier emerges from behind a nearby hut.

"Are you here to stay with Shu? Where is he?" Sir Anthony points to the young man sleeping in the grass. The man glances over to Shu, then turns back to Sir Anthony. "You have to go back."

"Do you know who I am?" Sir Anthony asks.

"I know who you claim to be. I think you are a disgrace, claiming to be a master. Go back to where you came...a real master would

THE NEW QUEEN

not have hurt his arm, so easily." he says turning and planting his staff in to the ground as if he is disgusted by Sir Anthony.

"Oh? Are you a master?" Sir Anthony asks.

"I am one level below master," the warrior bitterly responds.

"Let's see how much one level below knows. Place your hand on the well." The man glances at Anthony with mistrust. "If I am not a master, then you have nothing to worry about, do you?" The man hesitantly places his hand on the well. "Now tell me, what do you see?"

The man peers into the well at the dark pit below. "I see nothing."

"Then you must be blind."

The man points into the well. "There is nothing to see in the well!"

"Keep your hand on the well and look again."

Once again the man looks into the well. "I see nothing but the rocky wall as it disappears into the darkness below."

"You slowly open your eyes, but still, you see nothing."

The man moves his hand off the wall and firmly holds his staff. "What do you see, then?"

"There is much to see all around us," Anthony opens his arms and waves towards the huts and the rest of the village, "yet you only see the well and inside of it."

"You asked me what I saw in the well."

"I simply asked what you saw. You assumed I asked about the well, but I never once mentioned the well. A master sees much and more than a simple well in a vast village."

The warrior shifts uncomfortably in front of Sir Anthony. "Go sleep!" he yells at Anthony. "I still do not believe you to be a master."

"Then how about we practice your fighting style?"

ENGAGE

The man takes his stance and grips his staff. "Get back or I will hurt you."

"Let's practice our skills, and you can show me what an almost-master can do!" Anthony taunts him. After a few minutes, the warrior bolts at Anthony but Anthony uses the staff to push him into the well wall. With a loud crack, another man emerges from behind one of the huts. He sees his fellow comrade get up slowly with blood running from his face. The man runs towards his friend and attacks Anthony. They both attack Anthony with their staffs while Anthony fights them one-handed, the clay still stiff around his other hand. The man attacks with both sides of the staff as Anthony stands his ground.

The sound of staffs hitting one another wakes the village up, and the people slowly come out of their huts to watch the fight. Anthony stands his ground as the man tries desperately to knock him down. Finally, Sir Anthony sees the man's weakness, his stance is incorrect and there fore not ready to move his feet at any given moment but continues to fight, waiting for the right moment to attack. He watches as the man slows his attack, becoming tired from the fight so far. Anthony uses the staff and stomps it down violently, breaking the man's foot in one attack. Anthony places the staff next to his side showing he will not attack. Now both men surround Anthony, ready to fight him.

"Stop!" Master Ying yells. The older master stands in a red robe much like all of the other men in the village, he too carries a staff with a yellow band around each end. "He has shown you mercy, and that tells me he is indeed a Master of Shaolin." Sir Anthony bows towards the village master and tosses the staff back towards the first man and walks back to where Shu sleeps. Both men stare at Anthony as he retreats into the distance. Sir Anthony sits down and Shu turns to him.

"Why did you let them fight you?" Shu asks.

THE NEW QUEEN

"There was no other way." Master Ying interjects, silently emerging from a hill. "They would not believe that he was a true Shaolin master. Even I had my doubts, but I am puzzled…why did you leave when the village needed help so long ago?"

"I left long before the village was attacked," Sir Anthony comments.

"The stories we have heard says that the village was being watched for some time and it was the reason they knew when to attack and how to defeat our masters," Shu responds.

"The village had many scouts so I thought they would have known about any incoming attack. I once went with a scout, and I did my duty the best any one of us could have. I do not believe it is possible to scout a village for a long period," Sir Anthony explains.

"But still, do you not find it strange that the village was attacked and defeated in a single day?" the village master presses.

"I do not believe it. There were many masters in our village, even master Shin would have seen the army coming." Anthony walks around to the other side of Shu. "How many survived from my village?"

"Not easy to say. Many retreated to other nearby villages," the village master responds.

"Were you not from my village?"

"No, I was placed here to teach and develop young souls."

"I am the only one from our village, Master Anthony," Shu says lowering his head.

"It is not wise to claim shame for something you had nothing to do with, Shu," the village master says. "Master Anthony, I have sent word to the other villages about your request."

"Thank you, Master, but do you not want to tell them that I am a master from the village? They might see the wisdom in this fight."

The village master smiles at Anthony. "You already did.

ENGAGE

The next day, Anthony woke with the sun peeking through the trees. He opens his eyes and rolls over to see that Shu had already left. The women of the village are busy cooking and Shu is training with one of the men who attacked Anthony last night. With each movement, Anthony hears his body creak and crack. He finds it difficult to move with the heavy clay glove that he is forced to wear each day. Master Anthony walks over to where the women are cooking. They giggle and laugh when they look at him, both old and young.

Master Ying appears quietly by Sir Anthony's side. "Master Anthony, did you sleep well?" he asks softly.

"I find it harder to wake than to sleep."

Master Ying laughs and nods. "I understand all too well." He hands Anthony a clay plate and the women fill it with rice and rabbit. "The villages have agreed to send our warriors with you. It is our understanding that it was these Englishmen who attacked our village so long ago. We fight to regain our honor."

"A wise man once said there is a fine line between honor and revenge."

The village master looks at Anthony. "Sometimes they are the same." He leaves with his plate, and Anthony follows.

"Master, when will they be here so we can leave?"

"There are many villages and the elders have sent word to each to send their warriors here by nightfall. You leave tomorrow."

Anthony bows again and watches the master walk away. He turns his attention to Shu and watches as he fights with the staff and gets pushed back outside a circle that is drawn in the dirt. Anthony walks over and watches. When Shu is pushed out again, Anthony grabs the young man's arm and whispers into his ear, "Plant your feet as if the very clay you fight upon are molded to your feet." Shu gets back into the circle as the man attacks him, but Shu holds his ground as the man almost runs him over. Once again

THE NEW QUEEN

Shu is pushed out of the area and Anthony approaches him again. "Plant your feet. You know he will come at you so change your tactics and fight hand to hand. There is no need for your staff." Shu steps back into the circle and once again the man charges but Shu plants his feet and manages to foil the assault. When the man is close, Shu grabs his arm and flips him out of the circle. Silence falls over the spectators.

Gus lays down with his eyes open, looking up at the trees. He looks for any sign of the sun rising. He knows that Quarry Castle needs them, and they are not far away. Gus smells freshly burning wood as someone starts a fire. Gus walks over to the boy sitting next to a small fire. "The sun is not up yet. Why are you starting the fire?" The boy turns away and adds more logs to the fire. Gus realizes that the boy only speaks French. As he turns away from the fire, he catches a glimpse of the sun peeking above the treetops. "How would one know when the sun comes up?" he asks himself quietly.

Soon both cooks and soldiers wake and there is movement all around the village. As the sun rises, Gus finds King Louis and asks him to start the march for Quarry Castle. It took little time for the men to start their march to Quarry Castle.

The scouts ahead stop the army and return to report to the king. "Your majesty," the Frenchman begins, "many men are surrounding the castle. It looks like they are attempting a siege. The army has spread out in a long line, but they cannot get around the whole castle." The scout draws a map in the dirt of the area and explains further. "The castle is there. The wall goes out here, and the channel is here so they cannot get around the entire castle." King Louis nods in understanding.

"What is the problem?" Gus asks.

ENGAGE

"It is a problem for the other army, not for us. Your king is a very smart man. He picked a great location for the castle and by making the wall so long, it puts the army in a hard spot. If they try to take the wall, they will have to attack it from both sides at the same time, but the main castle can protect them from their walls. And they cannot attack the castle directly because of the channel, and the stronghold across the channel protects that. It is tough to be able to take the castle."

Gus nods with a smile. "That's King Martin, always thinking ahead. I would not be surprised if he has more men ready to fight than we know of. Anyways, what are we going to do?" Gus paces back and forth, while King Louis dismounts his horse.

"We have arrived in time, my friend. The army is not yet ready to fight so we are going to take the fight to them. I have sent my man to inform your king that we are here."

"I thought your scout told you that they were surrounding the castle as we speak?"

"They are, but they are not yet ready to start their attack." Gus watches soldiers rush east towards the channel.

"You want to lead the group?" the king asks.

"Yes, thank you, your majesty." Gus races to the front of the line where three soldiers lead the group. Gus orders the men into three groups, forming them in a long line starting from the channel towards the forest outside Quarry Castle. They wait for word from the king before starting their plan.

Moments later, a scout approaches Gus. "How do you say? Start?" the scouts tell Gus in broken English.

Gus orders the first group closest to the channel to start shooting their arrows. The first attack rises into the morning air without warning. Men fall with arrows protruding out of them in all directions. The trumpet sounds and the army turns to attack the archers. Gus smiles and orders the second volley to join the

THE NEW QUEEN

first group, firing at the same time. Now arrows shoot from two directions, and the enemy does not know where to hold up their shields. By the time the army gets out of range, less than a quarter of the men remain alive.

The king raises his arm and motions for the rest of the archers to fire upon the remaining army, but they were ready this time and moved back into a group of trees. Arrows fired from out of the trees back towards the French, stopping them from chasing the army into the trees. A horn sounds from the castle, as thousands of Englishmen storm over the hill from Saxton's old realm. King Louis could see he is tremendously outnumbered as thousands of red coats charge from over the hill towards the castle.

King Martin orders all of the catapults to fire upon the English that crosses the beet farms farthest away, and all six shoot at once. Most men in the way die instantly, but much to Martin's surprise, the large boulders they used start to roll back down the hill towards the castle, killing more men from behind. Catapults at the top of the hill are able to reach the grounds close to the castle but not hitting the walls directly and are stopped by the high corn stocks. "Load the trebuchets and fire at the top of the hill. Make sure we take out those catapults." The men try to load both catapults and trebuchets as the English run quickly towards the castle wall.

King Louis orders his men to attack the treed area as they were killing many of his men. Large groups of blue coats rush into the treed area where the sounds of swords clashing and soldiers screaming are heard just beyond the cabbage patches.

Gus moves his group around the channel side of the castle towards the English army. Staying low, the group creeps along the shoreline when they come across the ships not far from the channel. They watch as more men on small rowboats eject from the ships and cross the water to the rocky shore. Hundreds of ships are anchored not far from the beach. Gus orders a small group to

ENGAGE

continue to shoot at the rowboats, making sure there will be no more men coming ashore.

Gus leads the less than five hundred men through the rocky forested area towards the other side. Gus and his group get as close as they can but are stopped from the English guards who watch the area. Patiently Gus waits and watches as the English guards walk one by one. He quickly sees their pattern and sends a few men from his group with crossbows down the treed area where the guards rest. Gus raises his sword into the air then points it towards the guards as all of the archers shoot at once, killing the guards quickly and quietly.

Simon sits on the wall-walk with his leg in a splint where King Martin stands not far from him. "Adjust the catapults to shoot higher in the air and make sure those trebuchets hit those catapults on the hill!" Martin barks out orders.

Simon watches the French in battle in the treed area. "We will need the French if we are to survive and they are fighting in the forest."

The fight never seems to stop. Men scream while others cry for mercy. Bodies litter the landscape as hundreds of men lay wounded or even dead. The clashing of swords echo off the castle walls, as women and children run for their lives. The fire rages in the small wooden huts that are gathered against the wall-walks and the curtain walls as billowing smoke blinds both sides of the battle.

"You are lucky that both the French and English have not figured out how the farms are markers to tell us just how far our weapons can shoot," Simon says to the king. "But you changed your farms around."

"Yes, the corn stocks would hide the army's approach so I made them closer to the castle and if we have to light them on fire, we can kill many by doing so. I made carrots to be the furthest and then

THE NEW QUEEN

cabbage, lettuce and then beans and leaks. By the time they get to the corn, we should have them."

"How far will the trebuchets shoot?"

"Just past the carrots. The catapults shoot just past the lettuce, and some to the cabbage patches. The arrows reach to the end of the beans, and the oil can fall upon the corn stocks will make great kindling." The king smiles and winks at Simon.

"Whatever made you think that up? I mean planting this way?" Simon asks, adjusting his legs to better face the king.

"It just made sense to me," Martin says, looking out towards the French. "I don't think we have enough men to be able to beat the English though."

Simon raises his head and watches the French over the wall. "The English are drawing the French into the trees. There could be traps inside there. They will be wiped out."

Martin lowers his head and takes a deep breath. A guard runs up to the king and points towards the stronghold across the channel where a flag waves side to side. The king squints his eyes to see as the men in the stronghold point towards the channel away from the castle where ships approach.

"I think I see something!" Simon says, squinting towards the channel. "Yes! Yes! It's the Vikings! It looks like a lot of them, too!"

The king moves closer to Simon and looks where Simon points to. "I hope he can help." Martin grabs the man by the shirt in a fist full of cloth. "Get word to the Vikings to meet up with the French and to help them in the forest over there." The guard nods and dashes away.

The king moves down the stairs and heads towards the other side of the keep to see how the battle goes. Martin takes a quick glance out and sees that the English are already past the carrots and are making their way to the beans. "Everyone, load your bows and crossbows! Every other man will shoot on my command and

ENGAGE

then I will say when the last of you will shoot two rounds. Pick the first target you see, fire, then get down. Archers, get ready!" Half of the archers turn crouched down with their bows, ready to fire. "FIRE!" the king yells, and the archers fire. A large number of English fall. The men duck down again, and the king yells out. "Ready! The next round! Archers, ready!" The remaining archers crouch and turn to face the wall with bows in hand, just like the archers before them. "FIRE!" Martin yells, and he looks out quickly to see how well the group of arrows hit their targets. Many Englishmen fall, but there are lots more to take their place.

"Your majesty!" Samantha yells from the bottom step of the wall-walk. "Here are all the lanterns you asked for!" she says, carrying a full basket.

"How far do you think one man can throw this lantern?" Martin asks Simon.

Simon thinks about the fields below. "No further than the cornfields, your majesty."

A large cheer breaks out as Martin watches the English retreat up the hill. "Fire the catapults and ready the trebuchets!" All six catapults fire at once, catching the Englishmen by surprise and killing more than expected. Everyone watches as the huge rocks slowly come to a stop close to the front of the castle wall. "Everyone get those boulders back in here so we can use them again!" Martin shouts to the shoulders in the keep. "If we leave them there, those Englishmen will use them for cover." The men run out the small side gate and roll the huge boulders in one by one while other men guard them.

"Have they moved back up the hill?" Simon asks.

"For now. We will let the English collect their dead and then we will fight on. Simon, you will lead this side of the fight. I have set up three units: two bowmen and one crossbowman. It is simple to shoot one, then the other bowmen will wait until the Englishmen

THE NEW QUEEN

are close enough to use the crossbowmen. That should keep them from approaching closer," Martin says in a stern voice to Simon before walking down the steps.

Martin runs across the keep and makes his way up to the wall-walk, then along the long wall that protrudes into a field. Martin approaches one of the archers. "How goes the battle over here?"

"We have lost a few good men, sire, but we are holding them in the forest." The archer holds a long piece of leather wrapped around his hand and thumb. "We are almost out of arrows too, sire."

Martin looks down at the nearly-empty baskets of arrows, then looks out on the battlefield scattered with fallen arrows. "Send out a few men to gather what arrows they can and bring them back. Make sure they use the front gate if the English see that the wall ends here."

"Sire!" the man yells out, stopping the king from leaving. "I do not think the soldiers in the forest are English." Martin stops and turns around. "The Englishmen that attacked us from that side look different from this side."

Martin opens his mouth to ask a question when suddenly a horn blows in the distance. The king sees that the French are retreating back away from the treed area in a panic.

"Why are they pulling away from the wall? They can't do that! It will leave us open! What is Louis doing?" the king asks in a panicked voice. Another horn blows two quick sounds, signaling that the dead are to be collected.

Chapter 31
TROUBLES ALONG THE WAY

Sir Jade and Elizabeth ride slowly heading back towards their kingdom through the late afternoon. The clouds helped the men from the heat of the day as they started to march before the sun was shining. Elizabeth looks tired and worn, her nice green gown dirty, and torn, and her hair knotted no longer filled with nice curls. The shine in her hair and her face had vanished days ago.

Sir Jade was tired as well, but he kept his smarts about him, never letting down his guard around the thousand plus men they have accumulated on their journey. Most of the soldiers were on horse back but some had to walk or rode two to a horse on the well worn path that laid between most of the small kingdoms. Each set of soldiers carried their flag of their kingdom. 'How will you explain to the king about the list of names on the parchment you have?'

THE NEW QUEEN

'Me? It was both our idea. You explain it to him.' Elizabeth says somewhat shocked by the question. 'He will know it was a good idea when we come back with all of these men to help fight the English.'

'Maybe so, but he will read the parchment and ask what it means. All that scribbled stuff and a few hundred ex's and then we will have to explain.'

'Do you think the king can read?' she asks not sure if he could.

'I don't know! I never thought about it.' Jades face turned as he put some hard thought to the question. 'I know Garnet must be able to read, but I do not know if King Martin can.' Jade looks around behind him. 'We better not talk to loudly.' Elizabeth look forward and kicks Nay to move faster. 'Whats the hurry?'

'What if the fighting already started? We have been gone for a long time you know?'

'We are not to far maybe a days ride now, so tomorrow we will arrive and know.'

'I have a bad feeling Jade. I think we should push to get there today.'

'I do not think we can. The horses would not be able to keep that pace and remember there are men walking as well.' Jade pauses before talking again. 'We can push the men to go longer today then I will make them into groups and tomorrow we will move as quick as we can and should be there in the morning sometime.' Elizabeth nods her approval and Jade turns his horse around to tell the army that they pieced together. Elizabeth continued to ride heading up the front as six more men ride up quickly to flank either side of what they believed to be a queen.

A group of men ride quickly towards the army. Stopping in a narrow part of the worn path. The six horsemen ride out front to meet them. Elizabeth slows Nay to a slow walk when the six men all of a sudden are now in a fight, swords are drawn and Elizabeth did not see what had happened. Nay stops and starts to move backwards as the group of men come up from behind. One of the horsemen fighting who was guarding her, falls off his horse with a bolt protruding out from his chest. The group charges ahead of her as they wave their swords over their head and their shield at the ready as they charge into battle. Nay stops and stands still as Elizabeth shakes with fear. She watches as the fight rages on swords clanking against one another, men yelling and the odd thud from the sound of a shield being struck. Elizabeth did not notice Sir Jade standing off his horse beside her. One of the men from the group ride back to her and Jade.

'Sir a small group of men who wanted to take the queen for ransom.' Elizabeth looks at Jade surprised by him being beside her and the news.

'And you told then no?'

'I told them they would have to take her over our dead body's. They must have thought it was just us, because there were not a lot of them. We made short work of them sir.'

'Were or are there any survivors?' Elizabeth asks in a slight stutter.

'Not now my lady.' the man says with a hint of arrogance in his voice. She looks at Jade.

'We need to move now!' Jade holds the reins and looks up at her.

'Now is not the time to run wild Elizabeth. You have to keep your head.' He pulls her off the horse and she wraps her arms around him and buries her head into his shoulder as she fights not to cry. The men look at the two knowing she is scared.

'My lady, your majesty we will not let anything happen to you.' Elizabeth lifts her head and looks at the man.

'Thank you.' she says quietly.

THE NEW QUEEN

'We will ride until night fall then camp. Tomorrow we will ride hard to make the castle and I think we will get there in the late morning.' Jade tells the men. The group now divides into two groups one in front of Elizabeth and one behind with three on either side armed with cross bows, no one will get to her again. They ride without further incident and as the darkness fall around them they make camp. Elizabeth sat in a tent one of the kings gave her to sleep in the night. She sat quiet as she brushed her gown with her hands trying to wipe away the mud. Jade opens the flap and steps inside. 'Are you alright?' She looks up at him and her eyes begin to well up with tears.

'I'm not the queen.' she begins. 'Why do they want me?' she bangs her fist on her lap then wipes her nose. They said they wanted to kidnap me, me a girl from Martins kingdom.' Jade steps closer in the small tent then kneels down in front of her.

'Elizabeth no one will kidnap you. We have a thousand men who will make sure that will never happen.' Jade stops and looks away briefly. Elizabeth sees it.

'What? What is it? I know you know something Jade tell me.' Jade looks back at her. The tears are gone and anger fills her eyes.

'I been thinking that's all.' Elizabeth gives him a look that would scare the hair off a mule. 'The men who said they were there to kidnap you called you the queen.'

'So?'

'So we told everyone that you were the future queen, not THE QUEEN!'

'So? I don't understand.' Elizabeth was getting scared something Jade did not want to do to her.

'That means, that the word got out that you and I were getting men to fight the English and someone some where found out and thought they could either make some gold on the deal or get some power making King martin to help them some how. Either way one of the kingdoms that we got men from are trying to take advantage of this war.'

'What do you mean? What are you saying?'

'I think one of the kingdoms are going to break their word and try to take over other kingdoms well the men are with us.'

'They can't they swore to us they wouldn't.'

'Men lie all the time.' Jade sits down having to move his sword to a side to do so. 'I will place two guards at you tent from two different kingdoms, and I will be in the next tent beside just in case.'

Gus was one of the last few original shadow army soldiers. He along with others were trained by the children who were sent out to learn to fight, he was also one of the first to learn all eight different styles of fighting making him a shadow soldier. Gus had it all planed out as he sat in the rocky forested area close to the catapults the English had made. The french men he had with him were working out perfectly. They were able to kill all of the sentries that guarded the catapults and the two trebuchet that were just made, when a horn sounded and the army started back up the hill moving towards him and his small band of men. Gus motioned for the men to move back and lead them back to the channel where he wanted to meet up with the archers who he left to keep the boats from making it to shore. Gus was shocked by what he found. All of his archers lied dead, some from arrows most from a sword wounds, he never thought they would not leave their duties and die still trying to keep the Englishmen from making shore. The French men in his group were chatting with one another and Gus thought they might blame him but it looked like they just wanted to get back to their king as they now were leading the way back, over the rocky terrain that littered the coast line.

THE NEW QUEEN

Gus followed the men as they duct in and out of the trees and back to the channel, over the rocks and dead logs scattered about. He was grateful to see Quarry castle again as the french marched past the castle without so much as a thank you or see you later. A few archers on the wall saw them but let them past without a word. There was no sense giving them away if they were on king Martin's side.

The sun began to set and Gus walked through the castle side gate looking like a tired, dirty, old man. He looked around and saw Simon on the wall walk but no King. He walked into the main castle where Samantha offered him some bread and ale which he took without even thanking her and ate it like he had not eaten in days, in fact it was an entire day he had not eaten. Samantha was as beautiful as ever, clean and in a long gown with a black sash around her waist. Her hair long and straight had a yellow bow that made her brighten your day with. 'Do you know where the king is?'

'He has gone to meet with the King of France.' Gus sat down on the floor and grabbed another piece of bread.

Against everyone's advice King Martin marched out towards the French army well four guards ran beside him holding up their shields for arrows that would never come. Martin was dressed in his leather that were less then a year old but were well worn and looking old from all of the usage he got out of them. In fact he wore nothing else but his leathers every day.

As the king past the carrot fields he saw that they were all trampled on and the French had moved so far back he could barely see them standing just beyond them. King Martin was furious. Mad that the french gave up so soon, mad that the English were now enemies and mad that war was happening all over again. The french had chopped down a lot of trees and laid then down on top of one another to make a type of wall that surrounded their camp. With archers standing on logs inside the camp looking out, there would be no way for any army to get close without the french knowing. Martin marched past the guards who were going to try and stop him but decided it would be best not to get in his way as he carried two swords one in each hand. 'Louis where are you?' Martin yelled at the top of his lungs. Two guards came out of a tent swords at the ready, followed by King Louis. He looked at Martin with a disappointment look of his own on his face.

'What?' he yells at Martin. 'What do you want?' Martin rushes up to the king.

'Why are you not fighting?' Martin yells into the kings face.

'I loose to many men in woods.' he says in broken English. "We cannot fight good in woods.'

'If they get around the wall they will know the castle is not yet finished and we will loose the castle to the English and they will have a hold on this land right next to your land.' Martin yells well pointing to get his point across.

'I do not have my army here only men for visit. We can not fight so many.' Louis raises his hands in the air. 'I loose half man.' he says upset at the war. 'These we fight are from king Castile, but they fight like English man.' Martin looks back at the field and see nothing but french dead men. 'We cannot fight in trees.' Louis says more calmly. 'I send for more men I hope we can stay alive until then.'

'Louis. King Louis it will take to long for your men to get here.' Martin brushes his hair back off of his forehead where the sweat held it in place. 'Where did you send Rollo?' King Louis thinks for a moment.

'Oh Rollo! I send him to other castle to protect it.'

'No, no, no, we need him here to help fight here. The vikings can fight in the trees I mean the forest. Quickly send a man to get

THE NEW QUEEN

them and have them come back.' King Louis sits down and shakes his head.

'No its to late King Martin we have lost this battle today.' he says shaking his head as he places his hands on his knees.

'No! 'The battle is still not lost. We have held them from getting to the castle. We can do this Louis.'

'No I have sent for more men to get me out of here not to fight for you. You have lost!' He stands and walks away. Martin turns to one of his guards.

'Go get a horse go and get the vikings back we need them to clear the forest.' the guard runs across the field to the castle to get a horse, and King Martin walks back to King Louis. You knew there would be English here that wanted to fight, if you didn't have your army then why stay and fight at all?' Martin places his fists on his hips still holding his swords in his hands as he tries to fight to control his temper.

'I thought a few Englishmen not to many. We can handle a few but the entire army?'

'Don't you see Louis if their entire army is here then where is your army and what are they doing? Did they win in the north? What happened to them?' Louis looks around his breathing becomes quicker.

'I do not know!' he yells at Martin and goes into the tent. Martin kicks a log out of the fire pits and sparks rise into the air. He marches back towards the castle stepping over body's as he goes. Then he stops in the middle of the field. He leans down and pulls an arrow out of a body of a fallen french soldier. He looks at the arrow as if he had never seen one before.

'Aw your majesty we cannot stop here sire.' a guard says looking towards the forested area. Martin stands up holding the arrow in front of him not taking his eyes off of it.

Have you ever see an arrow such as this?' he asks the guard. The guard glances at the arrow.

'It's an arrow your majesty, there are hundreds around here.'

'Not like this. The tips are iron, they went right threw the armor that's why the french were falling so quickly. Their armor could not stop this arrow. Its like getting shot by a cross bow but these tips make it so they don't have to shoot with so much power and the arrow will go threw the leather armor.' The guard takes a closer look. Knowing that they have to get off the battle field before they find arrows aimed at them.

'Sire we have to go.' he says looking around towards the forested area.

'Have the men collect as many arrows as they can.' the guard leads the king towards the castle with the shields held up high to once again protect the king. Once inside the castle the king make his way directly to Simon who still has not move from the top of the wall walk. 'Simon' Martin calls out as he takes two stone steps at a time up to the wall walk. Simon sits on the top step with his legs strapped together with tree limbs and cloth still in his leather armor. 'After three days of battle you still have not left this spot.'

'Well its very hard to move, why don't you get Mark to do this duty?'

'Mark is dead and we need to talk.'

'Dead? How? When?'

'He died sometime ago just after you left on your vacation. We need to talk about Elizabeth.'

'Is she dead too?'

'No but she might have been if I did not pardon her. You had her jailed whipped and tortured why?' Martin was once again angry and stood with one foot on the top step and his hands on his hips. His swords put away on strapped to his back once again.

'Why would you call her a witch when you knew differently? You almost killed her.'

'Your majesty.'

'Your majesty my foot! Don't try to smooth this over, tell me what I want to know.' Martin unknowingly placed his hand on the top of his long sword that sat on his side. Simon notice right away and watched at the kings hand.

'Your majesty she was accused of being a witch by one of my men, she was said to make a sword out of the ground.'

'Oh come on Simon, no witch would make a sword or they would be wanted alive by every kingdom in all of the land. Don't be so stupid.' Simon was nervous and was being careful what he was about to say.

'Your majesty, I did place her in the tower but I did not order her to be beaten or tortured. I made sure she was to stay there so you could concentrate on your royal duties. Henry would have done the same.'

'Like hell! He was my friend and the captain of the guard like you are now, He would have made me keep her by my side. He knew she had a way to keep me centered. He in fact said she complemented me in other ways.' Martin stands up straight and takes the final step up onto the wall walk. 'Simon you did the wrong thing in a big way, I trusted you, but never again.' Martin turns and walks away along the wall walk inside the keep. Simon was sweating and let out a long sigh, knowing that if the king ordered his death it would have been right there and then. Martin turned around and walked back to Simon after walking to the end of the wall walk within the keep. 'Mark died from some type of wound when he fell off his horse, it made him sleep a lot then one day he never woke up, I miss him he saved my life and I owed him more then I could repay him especially now.' Martin left Simon on the steps as he made his way down the stone steps and crossed the keep to the other side where the wall continued out. Simon could tell that the king was able to calm himself in such a short time. Samantha came up to Martin. She kept her distance knowing he was very upset but she did not know what about.

'Are you alright?' she asks in a faint voice. Martin almost did not hear her but heard something and turned his attention to her.

'There is another break in the fighting so they can gather their dead again.' Martin sat down falling the last foot under him on to the wall walk. Samantha ran up to him holding her gown up as she did.

'Oh are you alright?' she grabs his arm, and looks at him. His eyes are blood shot and blackened, his nose running like a fast stream and he is shaking as if he were in the dead of winter. 'Your exhausted, when was the last time you slept or ate a good meal?' she tried to pull him up to his feet but he was to weak to help. He had been running on adrenaline and being mad only kept him going.

'Just leave me Samantha. I will just lie here for a bit.' he says leaning backward against the wall.

'You will not! Now get up and get to bed or I will throw you over my shoulder and carry you with everyone watching.' She raised her voice surprising him as he had never heard her yell before. He struggled to get up even with Samantha's help. Once standing he looks out over the farms where the French were fighting and sees women pulling the arrows and bolts from the dead men. Samantha guilds him carefully down the stairs and they start walking together through the keep. 'Did you ask him about Elizabeth?'

'Yes I did. He claims he did not order her to be tortured, but I don't believe him anymore and I don't trust him either.' Samantha pushes him into the castle and gets a guard to help them to his room. She closes the door behind them and sits him on the bed. She fights hard to pull off his boots and by the time she gets them off he is asleep. She pulls up the covers and leaves. Ordering the

THE NEW QUEEN

guard not to let anyone in until he wakes, telling the guard it was by kings orders.

Night started to fall and the forth day of fighting was over ending early so everyone could gather their dead. Gus walked past the French to where the vikings sat around a camp fire and ate a deer they caught. The fresh air let the smoke drift carelessly over the camp filling every ones nose with the smell of good food. 'Rollo. The king wanted to thank you for coming back.' Rollo offers some deer meat to Gus. 'Thank you.' he gratefully accepts the meat. Gus looks back at all of the vikings. 'How did you do fighting the English on your land?' Rollo swallows hard before answering as he waves the knife around in the air. The viking sits in his fur coat and cotton leggings, and leather boots.

'They ran away before we could really fight and when they came back they came in large numbers, so we could only fight so many. These English are well trained and know how to fight, they killed many a good men before we were able to kill them. They cut us in half before we killed the small group we were fighting.' Gus opened his eyes wide knowing just how good the viking were. Rollo cuts a piece of meat with a long knife. 'I hope your king does not mind us helping ourselves with the food?' he says holding up the meat, then looking down at some cabbage that were rolled into tight rolls and tied and cooked.

'Is this all the men you have left?' Gus asks as he nods his head towards the rest of the vikings.

'No many wanted to go home, these are the true worriers the men who want to see the end of all the battles. I do not trust these English, I think they might attack in the middle of the night, so I put my men all around the camp.' Gus agrees with a nod himself, then shoves the rest of the meat given to him into his mouth and gets up to leave. 'Here take some more.' Rollo gives him a large portion of meat to go. 'Tomorrow we will clear the forest for the French and make our way around to attack the English on the other side.' Gus accepts the generous token.

'I had men up close to the English they have more ships docked up from the channel. I saw a lot of soldiers, hundreds maybe thousands. I don't know if we can fight against such odds.'

'Yes we saw many ships come this way too, if we do not stop them here they will take all of the land even the French will not stop them.' Gus looks behind him where the French are camped.

'I think the French want to leave anyway, they got hit pretty bad right from the get go. It made King Louis afraid of the numbers.'

'I have my men all around so we will not be surprised by anything through the night.'

'I don't know how far the English go, they might even be all around us and taken castle Hope by now.' Gus says looking towards the path that goes to castle hope.

'We make our move tomorrow, we will first clear the forest.' Rollo stands grabbing his axe as he does and moves into a area where the vikings are sleeping on the ground. Gus stands and leaves quietly back to the castle.

The flap on Elizabeth's tent flies open and she opens her eyes from the light sleep she was in. She turns her head to see two men in dark brown robes enter her tent. Before she can even ask what do they want one grabs her and pulls her to her feet. 'There's the witch we have been looking for.' The man holds her almost off the floor with his hand around her neck as she holds his arm. His hand grasp her jaw and continues to hold her up.

'I am not a witch. The king pardoned me. I am not a witch.'

'Shut up witch, we are here on orders from the Popes.'

THE NEW QUEEN

'Stop calling me a witch!' she yells hoping Sir Jade will come running.

'What are you going to do witch put a spell on me, wheres your wand now?' Elizabeth pulls her knife out from under her night gown and thrusts it into the man, finding it under his rib cage and deep into his heart. The mans eyes widen as he drops her from his grip. He lets out a large gargle sound.

'I told you not to call me a witch.' she says pulling the knife out then thrusting it back in violently. The monk grabs his stomach as blood rushes out of the wound aided by the mans beating heart. The other monk pulls out a short sword seeing his fellow monk in despair then abruptly falls dead to the ground as Jade stands behind holding his bloody sword.

'They told the guards they were from the pope and were to talk to you.' Jade moves over to Elizabeth. 'It's over.' he says in a whisper taking the bloody knife from her hand and wiping it on his leg before giving it back to her. She starts to shake.

'I never killed a man before.'

'Wait here.' Jade turns to the tent flap and leaves standing just outside her tent as he orders the men to get the monks bodies out, explaining to them they were impostors and they were going to kidnap the queen. He then yells at them for giving into the trap so easily. After the bodies are removed Jade returns and sits beside Elizabeth and waits for her to cry.

'First they want to kidnap me now they want me dead? I don't understand? Tears well up in her eyes. 'At fourteen every one wants me dead.' she starts to cry as Jade puts his arm around her.

'No one will get to do that well I am around, I told you that before remember?' he gives her a slight hug being careful not to get to close. She looks up at him with her eyes full of tears seeing a blur she nods at his comforting words.

'I killed a man.' she cries.

TROUBLES ALONG THE WAY

Sir Jade lies her down and he lies by the door with sword out, throwing knives in hand. 'Go to sleep I wont be leaving from now on.' Jade falls to sleep quick enough and wakes during the night to find Elizabeth siting up with her knees pulled close to her chest and a knife in her hand. 'Go to sleep they wont be trying anything tonight.' he pleads with her. She lies back down until he was a sleep again.

The queen trusted no one. The queen of Castile rode with her royal guardsmen and the rest of her army, all ten thousand men, fully armed and fully trained to fight. She rode in her coach and sat with two maidens on a down filled cushions and enough wine to go around. The maidens giggled making the queen smile for the first time in a long time. It may have been the wine or the sheer boredom but everyone was in a chatty mood even the queen. 'Yes I'm the second cousin of king Saxton, the last remaining heir, so I am going to claim my throne.'

'Is his castle big? Was he a nice man? How big was his kingdom?' the maidens chatted. 'I heard the bigger the castle the bigger the man.' they all burst out laughing.

'Bigger what?' the queen asks with a large smile on her face. The maiden smiles and lowers her head.

'You know.' the other maidens start laughing all over again and the queen pours wine in everyone's glass.

'I will need you all to behave well we are looking through the castle, there will be many men wanting to take my hand in marriage it will be your job to intercept them before they try and ask for my hand.' the queen brushes her gown off of imaginary crumbs.

'Why, they must know you can not marry every man that offers their hand to you?' the lady's start to chatter again. 'Ya marry them all then think how big your kingdom will be, because you know the

THE NEW QUEEN

bigger the kingdom the bigger the man...?' once again they all break out laughing and the one maiden who asked the question the first time now blushes, as everyone continued to laugh.

'I do not want to embarrass any of the barons, doing so might cause an up rise in the kingdom and mistrust within and we do not want that.' It was hard to tell the maidens apart as they were all dressed the same in a light blue smock with black stockings and wooden sandals. Their arms covered with a white cotton top with the collar that covered their necks completely. Their hair was always in a bun a top of their heads and that too is covered in a white doily and tied with a small piece of thread. The maidens in the coach all had the same colour hair and were about the same height, with only one being older and taller then the others. The coach was built for ultimate comfort with the wheels supported on bent wood that would spring for an easier ride for the queen. It was colored in a bright yellow and green paint. The inside was done in a oak finish with compartments for the wine and food that the queen requested on her rides.

The coach came to a stop and the queen opened the small sliding window and looked out. They had stopped in the middle of a wooden area. The driver knocked on the door. 'My Lady we are stopping for a brief break, would you and they maidens like to have a break?' The door swung open and a maiden steps out almost falling as she had to much wine. But laughing she walked around the coach and opened the other door where two more maidens came out laughing followed by the queen who was trying to be straight and proper and not laugh. She stepped out as the driver ran around to the other side of the coach with a step for the queen. The queen stepped out and missed the step altogether but fell on her legs still standing. The maidens started to laugh as the queen put her finger to her lips.

TROUBLES ALONG THE WAY

'Shhhhhh' she says fighting not to laugh brought on by the wine. The maidens and the queen walked around surrounded by the royal guard not even the regular soldier could get close to them. The queen saw it was time to leave. 'Come on time to go.' she says slurring her words. The maidens start to climb the step and crawl into the coach then they start to laugh as the queen pushes on their rear ends to get them in. when it come to the queen to get in she to has to climb in on her hands and knees. The maidens laugh and pull her arms well the driver stands holding the door.

'Go ahead push!' one of the maiden yells out at the man. The queen turns her head and looks back at the man, giving him a look of touch and die. He stood up straight and continued to hold the door for the queen. The queen climbs up onto the seat and the maidens were all laughing. Just as the driver is about to close the door the queen asks.

'How much longer?' the driver looks at the queen.

'I do not know my queen but I will find out for you.' he closes the door and locks it then walks around the coach and asks the head of the royal guards. Moments later he knocks on the coach door. A maiden opens the small window slat. 'Tell my queen we will be there very shortly.' the slat is closed and he hears laughter once again. The Queen and her maidens bounced around inside the plush coach giggling and laughing brought on by the large quantities of wine consumed. The coach came to a stop and the Queen sat up straight.

'Quiet.' the queen told all of the maidens and silence fell inside the coach. They all listened to men talking but were unable to hear what was being said. Then the coach started to move once more. 'What was that all about I wonder?' she asked the small group with a stern face. The gurls know not to joke about this by her facial expression.

'Would my queen like me to ask?' one maiden asks bravely.

THE NEW QUEEN

'No I am sure it was nothing.' no sooner did the queen finish her sentence the coach came to rest again. The queen held up her finger to tell everyone to be quiet again. Once again there was silence in the coach and once again the queen could only hear men talking but not make out what they were saying. She looked around at the maidens and let out a long sign when a knock came from the door. The queen nodded to a maiden to open the slat.

'Yes.' the maiden asks looking out of the small slat.

'"We have arrived.' the door opened and there was a wall of royal guards on horseback surrounding the coach. The queen followed the maidens out of the coach. The driver waited for the queen helping her down then having her follow him around the coach. The royal guardsmen left a small path for the queen to follow. Each step she took she became more nervous. When she reached where the castle once stood her eyes opened wide and she looked on both side of the guardmen seeing no castle.

'Well where is it?' she demanded. One of the royal guardsmen dismounted and came over to the queen.

'We have been told it was burned to the ground and all of the stone was taken to another castle.'

'So there is another castle?' she lets out a joking sign wiping her eye brow of sweat that was not there. 'You had me nervous there for a moment.' the guard did not understand her humor or her sarcasm.

'My queen the castle is totally gone!'

'Yes this one is but lets go to the other castle and I will make my claim there.'

'No. My queen. The castle did not belong to Saxton that claimed the stone it belongs to another kingdom.'

'The same kingdom that took King Richards castle?'

'Yes my queen.' the guard confirms. Then she sees another army not far from them.

TROUBLES ALONG THE WAY

'Are we under attack?' she asks looking past him. He stands up and looks where she is looking.

'They are English soldiers my queen, they have declared was upon the kingdom who took the stones. They were gracious enough to let us see the castle but insist we leave after we see it.' the queen looks around the men towards the English. 'My queen they out number us twenty to one we have to leave.' the queen looks at the guard and turns and starts to walk back to the coach.

'Are they fighting at Richards old castle or just here?' she asks the guard.

'Just here my queen I do not believe they have the other castle yet.'

'Good take me to the other castle maybe we can meet the rest of my army and claim it as mine before the end of the day.' the queen crawls back into the coach and they leave with out incident from the English. The queen opens the slat as the coach begins to move and watches as the English line up to let them pass. She could see no castle will have a chance against such odds, including hers.

Chapters 32
THE BATTLE BEGINS

King Martin awoke with a crash against his bedchamber outside wall from the keep. He sat up quickly and did not even know where he was at first. He jumped out of the bed and ran over to the slatted window. The window that faced the keep, beamed with light as a new day had already started. He threw open the slats to see large boulders cash down inside the keep, then turned towards the door but realized he had no boots on and quickly jumped into them before opening the bedchamber door, to find the guards standing with their swords at the ready and Samantha running towards his room. 'Whats happening? Have they got into the keep?' the king asked and Samantha began to answered before the guards could.

'No they have a trebuchet on the top of the hill, with that over sized catapult they can hit us but we can not hit them.' she screamed in fear. Martin ran past her with three guards in tow. He dashes down the stairs with the guards who are unable to keep up. Martin flies open the castle door and a boulder lands and rolls

THE BATTLE BEGINS

hard against the castle wall but does not damage it. Simon moves over to the king walking with great pain.

'Sire you must leave we will not be able to take this assault much longer.'

'What about our trebuchet's? Why are they not shooting back?'

'Only the one on the tower could possibly reach theirs, then it would be a game of who can target the other first, and they have five maybe six that will shoot at us we only have the one.'

'Get all the men you can.' The king starts to say as another boulder hits the wall knocking men off of it as it crashes down onto the rocky keep below. Both Simon and Martin look on. 'Have some men lift the other trebuchet up onto the tower closest to the castle set it up now!' the king yelled his order as he runs off towards the tower that holds the trebuchet that is already in place. Simon stands for a moment looks at the tower next to the castle then shakes his head.

'I cant believe I'm going to do this! The trebuchet has a longer arm than the catapults I hope it will fit.' he says to himself then waves a man over to him.

The king runs up the stairs onto the wall walk then along the wall to the newly constructed tower that has a trebuchet on top of it accessed by wooden stairs. On the inside of the tower it has a walker a type of crane, that moves heavy things up to the tower when one or more men walk in a wooden circular cage. Martin reaches the top of the tower the two men there are fighting to load their trebuchet. He moves over and helps load the boulder. 'Sire we will do our best but I don't think we can hit it.' the man yells as another boulder hits the outside wall shaking the tower.

'You see this?' the king points the notches on the wheel that turns the machine side to side. 'Each notch tell you where the trees are on the hill.' the men look at one another. 'This here,' He points to notches on the long poles that loads the boulders. 'you pull it back to the end notch, that shoots the furthest. Are we ready to shoot?' the men smile.

'Yes sir, what one do we shoot for first?' the king looks out, the bright sunny day giving him excellent clear view and he can see the men loading at the top of the hill. He watches carefully at the one that is about to shoot next.

'See the one that is at the far left of the hill?' the men nod and start moving their machine using the notches to aim. Martin moves away and turns to see another boulder was coming above the tower wall.

'Ready and loaded?'

'Fire!' Martin yells and the large machine flings the giant boulder towards the other trebuchet, as it lifts the end up off the tower then slams back down. The boulder rides high into the air and came crashing down on top of their target. The men yells in celebration that was short lived. They struggled to move the new boulder onto the wooden platform, then they slowly roll the wheel back to load the trebuchet. Martin thinks. 'We have to be able to load this faster.' he says. The men look at him shaking their head no. The three men turn the wheel and load the boulder but not until one boulder hits the wall beneath them shaking the tower again. 'That's a distance shot, they don't have us yet!' The three men fight to wine the large wheel that pulls back the giant arm that throws the boulders. Another boulder fly's over their head. The king looks out and see that the army is ready to run down the hill once the wall has been knocked down. Between the three of them they are able to load the trebuchet in record time. Martin looks out for the next trebuchet that is being loaded. 'Number three tree just right of it.' the men turn the wheel adjusting the machine. Martin checks first for its accuracy then pulls the rope releasing the giant arm. The boulder rises up into the air and passes the trebuchet landing past the target but killing a bunch of soldiers in the process. Martin

THE BATTLE BEGINS

turns and looks for another boulder but it was not all the way up the wall yet. He looks over the tower wall to see three men struggling to get the boulder up. 'Get more men to help.' the he orders.

Gus ran out to the French and gathered the group he had days before. They followed him believing they were ordered to do so. The morning sun shining their way. The small group of thirty Frenchmen all dressed in their blue uniforms ran quickly outside the castle wall close to channel along the rocky coast and into the rock infested forest where they were a few day before, inside King Saxton's old kingdom, but this time it was mid morning. With six archers, Gus wanted to stop the assault on the castle before it was too late. He knew they were out numbered but a quick hit and run tactic he thought should work. They moved closer to the trebuchet's and catapults. Gus ordered everyone down on their belly's as they crawled towards their targets slowly. He ordered the men to shoot the sentries just like a few days before. The sentries dropped with little problem then the small group ran towards the catapults lighting their arrows on fire and shooting them on the bottom of the machines to help them burn faster. The one catapult grew on fire quickly while the other trebuchet took its own time to catch all well the men tried to put the fire out the archers picked them off one by one, making sure the machine would not be used again. Gus order the men to move to the next trebuchet but the soldiers that operated it had left, and they were about to find out why. He turned around to find several thousand men approaching them from behind. A move he had hoped they would not try, but his last thought was he had destroy two machines and hopefully gave the king time to escape. He died killing another six men with his two swords before crossbows found his back then his eyes closed one final time.

THE NEW QUEEN

Garnet arrived at Castle hope in the early morning and was greeted by Douglas the new sheriff of castle hope appointed by King Martin in a last minute decisions. 'How goes the battle?' Douglas asked. Garnet pulled on his robe and displays a sad look. 'Not good?'

'If the castle was finished I would say King Martin might withstand this assault but it is far from being close to being done. Douglas walked around in his suit of armor.

'If we are attack all we can do is close the gates. We can hold out for a year maybe but we can only fight with the catapults the french captured and gave to us other than that the few French archers that stayed are all we have to fight with.' the two walk around the castle curtain wall.

"I think the English sent their entire army to fight.' Garnet said as he examined the wall.

'Why would they do that? I mean they were fighting the vikings, the french, and the Scots. They would be spread out very thin?'

'Well they have two large armies, the one that attack you, and the one attacking the castle now. When the one that attack you gets back to Quarry castle Martin has had it.' Douglas looked at Garnet with a weird look on his face. 'What?'

'The English did not attack this castle Garnet. It was some other kingdom past the french kingdom.'

'Does King Louis know this?' Garnet asked.

'Yes he was the one who told us. What was the name of the kingdom? I cant remember.' Douglas places his hand on his chin thinking. A Frenchman on the wall walk passes above them.

'Excuse me.' Garnet asks in French.

'Oui?' the guard answers.

'Do you know who attacked this castle?'

'Oui King Castile.'

THE BATTLE BEGINS

'Thank you.' Garnet says.

'Yes Castile that was the kingdom.' Douglas says.

'I know.' Garnet replies. 'But is this Castile Kingdom enemy's of king Martin, and if so why? We did nothing that far west? We never even went close to the french kingdom.'

'I cant answer that, but all I know is that the french and this Castile kingdom are allies until now. I think the french are in a hard spot.'

'Douglas send a messenger to Quarry castle I think King Martin needs to know about this.'

Captain Witter marched his army as far west as they could go and not have to fight the English or the French. They had marched all day and night and now the men made camp. Witter was exhausted and fell asleep sitting on watch. The sun was up and the entire camp was sleeping after marching for so long. Witter slowly opened his eyes then shakes his head to wake. He quickly stands to find that he is the only on up. He checks the suns position finding it directly above him. He walked around the camp making sure nothing is amiss. His first thought was to wake everyone but they were not only tired but battle tired that meant they earned their rest. Witter started a small fire to cook some food for himself. He waited for the fire to catch and walked around taking a mental count of men in his head. 'Less then half of the men are here.' he says to himself. A royal guardsmen rides into the camp and Witter stands pulling his sword from its sheath.

'Are you not from Castile?' the guard asks. Witter puzzled looks at the guard before recognizing the queens personal guard.

'What are you doing here?' Witter says with a smile and extends his hand towards the guard.

THE NEW QUEEN

'I am scouting ahead for the queen.' Witter smiled dropped from his face.

'The queen is here?'

'Yes she will be just east of here. She will be glad to see you. Have you acquired the castle she told you too?'

'We have it under siege but as far as I know it has not surrendered. We were not able to get Saxtons castle.'

'We know, how were we to know it was destroyed. That was not your fault.' Witter stood silent. For a while well the guard looked around. 'Do you always let the men sleep so late?'

'No we marched all day and night. First from one castle to the other then back, we had to fight to get here.'

'You fought the English? What are you not in your right mind?'

'They attack us we did not attack them along with the french as well attack us.'

'You took on both English and the French and are still alive? I don't believe you.' witted stop to think what to say.

'It is why we only have half the men left. They killed us with great ease.' the guard fought with his horse as it turned around on him.

'Where are you going now?'

'We will march back to the castle we have under siege and take it.'

'The queen will be happy to see you. We should all march together. Maybe the large number of men will change their minds to surrender before we have to loose any more men.' Witter thought it was a bad idea marching with the queen but the guard rode off before his could express his thought.

The bright day made traveling a bit nicer than normal and Elizabeth, now exhausted, rode half a sleep beside Jade who was

THE BATTLE BEGINS

rested but still tired. The small army came to an abrupt stop and calls from the front of the line cried for Jade to come quick. Sir Jade arrived in the front of the line to find a large group of horsemen in the distance headed for them. Jade looked at the soldier who lead the way. 'Do you think they are here to challenge for the queen?' the man asks. Jade shrugs his shoulders.

'Let find out. Have the men at the ready protect the queen at all cost.' Jade moved his horse towards the approaching army of thousands of men. He took a deep breath feeling intimidated by the large amount of men out numbering him ten to one. The large army came to a stop and waited for Jade to get to them. The three horsemen that lead the way moved away from the group to talk with him. 'Peace be with you.' Jade said raising his hand in a friendly jester.

'And with you.' they answer together. Jade notices a great many different flags.

'Where are you going?'

'Who are you to ask?' Jade was now feeling the strain of the quest overwhelm him.

'I am Sir Jade, knight to King Martin.' the men smile at him jade was not sure what to think.

'Well great knight, much has happened since you left our kingdoms and we have been sent to make sure your quest is successful.' Jade wipes his brow of the sudden sweat that ran down his face.

'What?' He says in disbelief.

'Each kingdom believes that your queen can unite all of our kingdoms together. We have been sent to show our unity and our commitment to your queen. Jades mouth fell open shocked by what he was hearing. 'Don't be so surprised my good man, she showed great commitment to your king and to the unity of survival itself.' the men smile at one another and laugh at Jades shock that

THE NEW QUEEN

was on his face. "May we ride with you?' Jade waved his hand as if opening a door.

'Have half of your men fall behind us the other half to take positions on either side of the group to make sure there will be no more surprises.' Jade turns his horse and ride up to his now small army compared to the new much larger army and tells them to make room. Jade rides back to Elizabeth and stops his horse. 'I need to talk to you now.' Elizabeth dismounts her horse.

'What is it?' she asks nervously. The two walk away from the main group to talk.

'You know all of those kingdoms we visited?' she nods. 'Well they have come together because of you and want you to be their queen.' Elizabeth has a sudden overwhelming feeling of fear.

'Oh my!' she says as she squats down. 'King Martin is going to be very mad at me isn't he?' Jade smiles and pulls her up by her arm.

'Oh on the contrary. I think he will be very proud of you.' She looks at jade with tears welling up in her eyes. 'You have shone real royal quality in your service to the king.' Jade waits until she is able to control her emotions before telling her that the army has grown ten times its original size. 'Let get moving we don't have much more to go.' the large army continues to move towards Quarry castle. A guard rides up beside jade and Elizabeth.

'What is the name of your castle?'

'It's Quarry castle. Its a small castle not like Hope Castle.' Elizabeth answers as she gains strength from the news she just received.

'So you already have two castles?'

'Yes.' Elizabeth says as yells come from the front once again. Jade looks at her but says nothing then ride up to the front. He arrives with the entire army stopped far away from a man who has blocked the pathway with some logs and stands behind it. Jade looks at the men in front.

THE BATTLE BEGINS

'You afraid of one man?' he asks.

'One man could not move those logs by himself. It is surely a trap.' Jade nods slowly in agreement. He looks at the man standing in a brown robe with a hood and a staff, as if waiting to play king of the castle.

'Stay here, and be on the look out for the trap.' the men are ordered to have their swords at the ready and every soldier unsheathes their swords, well looking around for the trap. Jade ride slowly towards the man having the horse walk. He gets closer to find a man in a long brown robe. 'Hello.'

'No more shall pass.' the man says. Jade looks at the man and somehow he looks vaguely familiar.

'I once knew a man who wore a robe like that, did you take it from him?' Jade pulls up his shirt and reaches behind him grasping one of his throwing knives.

'I steel from no one. I am Shu a Shaolin monk.'

'And what is a Shaolin monk doing this far from home?'

'That is not your concern.' Jade scratches the back of his neck.

'I think I knew a Shaolin monk before. His name was Sir Anthony do you know him?' the facial expression told Jade what he wanted to know. 'So you do know him!'

'Where is this master you speak of now?'

'I never said he was a master.' But he is a friend of mine, do you know where he is?' Shu looked around not sure what to do. He takes out a small wooden bamboo stick and blows into it. Making a wind sound. Shaolin warriors stand up all around the army. Men on horse are astonished that they were beside them all along and did not know. Shu yells out in another tongue that Jade did not know and Sir Anthony pats Jades leg before he knew he was even there.

'Hello my good friend.' Sir Anthony says surprising Jade completely from behind. Jade turns and see his friend.

THE NEW QUEEN

'Hello.' he says then noticing his hand. 'what happened?' he asks pointing at Anthony's hand.

'Its a long story.' Both Sir Anthony and Sir Jade walk back to Elizabeth well Jade explained all that had happened thus far during their journey. Elizabeth jumps off her horse after seeing Sir Anthony and hugs him. Jade looks shocked by her reaction.

'This is the man who saved me from the tower.' she tells him. And gives Anthony another hug with a big smile. 'Are you alright? What happen to your hand? It looks heavy.' Sir Anthony holds up his hand stopping Elizabeth from continuing to talk then looks at her with a small smile upon his face.

'I am told you are the queen now.' Anthony says loud enough with a wink and a nod. Elizabeth smiles.

'I guess so.' Anthony bows and takes a knee well holding Elizabeth's hand.

'Your majesty we will protect you and the kingdom.'

'Then lets get going.' Jade interjects.

'Not so fast my friend. There are thousands of English men. A frontal assault will not work we will need a plan.'

King Louis ordered his men to gather their things. He had changed into his battle armor that was made up mostly of medal with a chest plate with the kingdoms crest on it. He told them they will be going home. 'Going home?' Rollo asks the king.

'Yes we are out numbered, and I have lost enough men for this fight that is not ours to fight.' the king stood tall not afraid to stand up to anyone.

'King Martin need our help, you heard him he told you that the English will gain a strong hold here if they win and they will set their sights on you soon enough.' Rollo was getting mad, raising his voice.

THE BATTLE BEGINS

'My good man, one must know when to stay and fight and when to regroup to fight another day.' the king walked away not wanting to get into a fight. Rollo looked around in disbelief, he motioned for his men to gather around him and told them what the french were doing. Each man was frustrated with the French but they were not going to make an enemy of them. King Louis sent word to King Martin that they were leaving.

'What way will you travel back?' Rollo walked back over to talk with King Louis to make good he said to himself.

'I have to get the rest of my men from Castle Hope then we will be off. It will be weeks journey and hopefully my army will meet up with us along the way. I do not have many men left to protect me.' Rollo looks around at all of the men.

'Oh I think you have plenty of men sir.' King Louis looks around.

'Not for me.' he says and once again walks away from Rollo. Rollo noticed that the king would not talk to him for any length of time. Rollo waves one of the viking leaders over to him.

'We need a plan.' Rollo says watching Louis get ready to leave as he mounts his horse. 'Lets talk to King Martin.'

'If this is a lost cause we must leave King Martin to his faith too.' Rollo nodded reluctantly.

Martin targets another trebuchet, as Simon mounts his trebuchet on top of the tower that was closest to the castle. Men worked hard to load the trebuchet and as fast as they can. Martin was happy to see that they too could start shooting. As men slowly heaved the next large boulder up, the king watched Simon work standing with his hands on his hips next to the wall, when a boulder comes crashing down knocking a man off the tower and hitting Martin trebuchet damaging it and almost knocking

THE NEW QUEEN

Martin off the tower too. Martin holds on to the stone tower wall and fights his way back up onto the tower itself. His back injured with cuts from flying stones, wood and rocks. The king reached the top and looked at his trebuchet then seeing the one man who was back trying to fix the machine. He moves over to the man as they now tried to repair the broken wheel that moves the trebuchet from side to side. The large boulder sat on the hoist that sits next to the tower wall waiting to be loaded. Martin moves to the the side where the hoist is. 'I need two more men up here.' he yelled down. Martin noticed there was five men loading the boulder now it gave him a bit of hope that the fight was not lost.

There were three trebuchet's left and Martin had no idea if they could destroy them before it would be too late. Martin loaded the boulder onto the machine and hoped it was aimed already as the soldier he worked with thought it was. The king pulled the lever and fired the machine. The boulder raised far up into the air, Martin was thinking it would never hit anything and would just go up into the air and land short. Everyone was amazed when the boulder hit directly onto the enemies trebuchet and destroyed it in one solid blow. The English next trebuchet fired at them hitting the wall and bouncing off falling into the keep with a loud thud of rock hitting rock. The boulder splitting into two pieces. Two men came up the wooden stairs that were falling down in parts. Martin told them to load the trebuchet and aim for one of the two left. The king looked at Simon's efforts to load his machine but he was having great problems as there was not enough room to properly secure the trebuchet. Simon was having wood placed around to try and secure it the best he could. Another boulder hits the wall shaking everyone on the tower and Martin grabs for the wall to help hold on. The next boulder was already up on the hoist and the king pointed at it and the men moved quickly to load it. Martin start down the stairs as the men physically move the

THE BATTLE BEGINS

heavy machine to aim at their next target. Martin watched as they pulled the lever and fired the weapon. He could not see if it hit as he moved carefully down the wooden stairs that lead up to the top of the tower. Once he got to the wall walk the king looked out as the man cheered and scrambled off the tower down the wood stairs. 'What happened?' the king asked as the men came running down the stairs.

'We hit one of them sire but our machine fell apart.'

'Fell apart?'

'Yes.' another man answers. 'The main arm broke and the wheel broke and fell in to two pieces.' the man said running past the king. Martin heard the trebuchet shoot from Simon's tower and the whole machine falls to the ground from the sudden shift in weight. Three men going with it. Simon falling down on top of the tower. Martin turns to see the last shoot was successful and destroying the last trebuchet. The king along with the soldier on the wall walk all cheered together. But the cheer was short lived as thousands of Englishmen come running over the hill much more then in previous attempts to take the castle.

'Five the catapults! The king yelled and all were shot with larger boulder then before in hope to kill as many as possible. The archers all had their new bolts with the iron tips taking from the french battle just days before. The English shields split in half some even letting through the bolts and into there targets. Many of the English fell to their death by the bolts but the king could see they did not stop as many as he had wished it would. Martin ordered all archers on the wall walk and fire at will. But long bow and cross bow archer fired hundred of arrows and bolts alike but not stopping the on coming advance.

Rollo moved his men into the forested area thinking the English would try and flank King Martin. He had his men hide and wait quietly for the English to come through covered in fallen leaves and sticks and twigs found abundantly around. Not surprised they do. A few hundred men start to move through the forest but the vikings are ready and spring into action. A two side axe was the weapon of choice in a close quarter fight in a heavily treed battle. The English could not swing their two handed swords in the trees and they tried to move out using their shields but the Vikings had battle knowledge with the English and two vikings to every one Englishman and victory in this battle would be won today.

King Louis rode away hearing the battle behind him. He did not turn to look knowing in his mind that the battle would be lost. He did however hang his head for the lost of an ally. The long single file of blue uniforms marched away from the battle, each soldier feeling humiliated having to leave. Some of the soldiers looked back with tears in their eyes. 'we could have beaten them.' They say to one another. The king was close to the front of the retreating French upset no one understood why he was leaving and even the vikings stayed to help the king who invited them for games of fun not a war.

'No one wants war but one must be ready.' Louis says to himself, remembering what his father had told him. It did not take long to be away from the sounds of battle and it was not soon enough for the king. He normally never joined his men in battle and now was a starch reminder why, it fell heavily on his shoulders, a weight no one else could take away. King Louis always rode his horse he did not care for the coach as he felt it was hiding from the reason one would leave their castle to go out. Weather it be for a visit of war one can not hide from it.

THE BATTLE BEGINS

The English had most of their men on shore, with a large number of over two hundred men protecting the shore line. Most men stood around laughing and joking not expecting to be attacked as the battle was some ways away. The rocky shore and treed area would be hard not to be noticed by sound or sight, but they had not fought the Shaolin before. Their training unlike any other, they could walk unheard and hide unseen. All eight hundred Shaolin monks had one duty to take the shoreline and take it quickly. They moved quietly using their brown robe to help hide them in the rocky treed area, and their staffs helping them blend into their surrounding. The out skirt scouts were the first to go. They were easily spotted being dressed all in red coats and swords that dangled on their side. Taken out with sharp rocks thrown or throwing knives, none of English scouts saw it coming. The monks moves quickly into place and one by one with out being notice started to kill the unsuspecting Englishmen. The English were down to less than half of their men before they knew they were under attack. Each man drew his sword but that would not help when a Shaolin used his staff to disarm you before killing you, all in seconds. Once the shore was taken the archers shot arrows of fire to sink the ships, very few were far enough away to escape the onslaught. There would be no going back for the English. Sir jade waited for the Shaolin to give them the sign and continue to the next assault. Sir Anthony would have to wait for his friends to finish one task before moving to the next. They were fighting incredible odds. The entire army had to wait well the shore was to be secured. It was very hard as each man was excited and wanting to fight. They had over ten thousand men against what was over one hundred thousand men. Sir Anthony watched as the men got quickly into place for the second faze of the fight. The Englishmen were set up to attack in waves, the first wave had been launched and the three thousand men were being held off thus far, and any one

THE NEW QUEEN

getting close enough would land more and more arrows until he would be forced to drop his shield from the sheer weight then he would receive a few more into his body. The battle field was littered with body's, but this time the English were not stopping to collect their dead, the fight today would continue.

Sir jade waited with the army just beyond a grove that hid them from being spotted from any English scouts that might be about. Jade was nervous not knowing what to expect and only having new from Sir Anthony. Jade like to see for himself what odd he was up against. Not to be surprised Jade had a group of soldiers span out on either side in case one of those scouts got through the Shaolin monks even though he thought that to be unlikely. Jade had also assigned a group of soldier who were new to the group to protect the queen. They swore they would protect her with their very lives if necessary.

The Shaolin moved to the edge of the coastal rocky forested area that the English thought they controlled. With thousands of soldiers waiting their turn to attack the small castle the signal was given.\, and the Shaolin monks picked up as many sharp stones they could find as well with their throwing knives they were going to attack from the shadows, never to be seen or heard.

Sir Anthony waved his arms to signal the army to attack, they were to attack from the far side of the treed area, away from the coast and push the English backward towards the Shaolin monks so the English would be attack on two fronts, but not know it, until it was to late. Jade lead the army into position and charged towards the English. Jades eyes open wide when he saw the English take a stand, drop their shields into the ground and held them up with one hand while their other hand pointed a spear towards them. 'It's as if they knew we were coming.' Jade says to himself. Jade pulls back on the reins and holds up his arm stopping the charge. Men were confused and waited to hear what he was going to say. Two

THE BATTLE BEGINS

man that ride with Jade stop their horses and see the defense the English had put up. 'If we charge them they will kill the horses for sure the only way to get threw that line is charging on foot.' the English had started to march towards Jades army. 'Dismount!' he yells and everyone dismounts but a few in the rear. Jade put his long sword away and pulls out a short sword as the shaolin had ask them to carry. 'I never thought I would be fighting with a short sword in my life.' he says to the guy next to him. Everyone had their short swords out. 'Charge!' they cried and began to run towards the English ready to deflect their spears and jump into battle. Ten thousand men now run towards the English in a line over a mile long. Both sides screaming as they ran. Jade reached the line first and deflected the spear to one side and jumped up onto the soldiers shield as it collapse back down onto the soldier. Jade drives the short sword down making sure this soldier was not getting up to fight again.

Chapter 33
Retreat

King Louis was happy to see that Hope castle was not under siege and that the gates were open. The bright day only added to his relief. He marched his men right into the gates and ordered them to get some food and rest. Douglas asked how the fight was going. 'Not well, they are badly out numbered, I doubt they will stand for another few days.'

'A few days, that means King Martin is doing well thus far.' The French king just looked at Douglas and shook his head. Finding it funny that a man would wear his armor all of the time. A horn blew from the top of the gates and King Louis was puzzled by the announcement. Douglas looked at the king puzzled as well but ran up the steps up to the wall walk where he could see a large army surrounding the castle. 'Close the gate close the gate Douglas yelled in a panic. The gate were slow to close but they were as the army shoot a bunch of arrows to wards it. The archers fired back killing a few more of the army then they had anticipated. Louis reached the top step.

RETREAT

'Too many steps to get up here.' out of breath he looks out but the army stayed low and far back. 'Do you know who they are?'

'All I do know that its not the English they have red coats.' Douglas continued to look out. 'And you have no idea?' King Louis looked stone face at Douglas.

'I am thinking it maybe Castile. I will send a man out to find out if it is and why they have come here.'

'I would be grateful.' Douglas says knowing that his archers could not hit them where they pulled back to. The French king waves a man over with his finger. The french soldier hesitantly moves towards his king. Louis says something to him and the man bows and walks to the gate. 'You told him to go out and walk up to them? They will shoot him before he gets there.'

'He has a shield he will be fine.' the two watch as the soldier walks out holding a piece of cloth up high. A few arrows land around him but not close enough that he would need his shield. It was a sign to stop. He stands still waiting when a horse man rides towards him. The soldier in a half a bassinet and a medal chest plate and stockings.

'I am Captain Witter of the kingdom of Queen Castile, do you surrender?' The french soldier looks at Witter.

'I am but a french soldier to King Louis IX, King of all of France. I can not possibly tell you we surrender unless my king say for me too.' Witter looks at the man.

'Is this your castle?' Witter ask nervously.

'Non'

'Do you know where all of the men who were here have gone?'

'Non'

'Do you know where my catapults have gone?'

'Non' the soldier says. 'Why are you here?'

'This castle belongs to my Queen rightful heir to king Saxton's and all of his kingdom. This castle was once his we are here to lay claim to it and all of the land.' The French soldier just look at

THE NEW QUEEN

Witter as if he were not in his right mind. 'Who owns this castle and why do you protect it?'

'I do as my king says. This castle is...' the soldier stops himself thinking how to word what he was about to say very carefully. 'This castle is occupied by the kingdom of King Martin, friend and ally to King Louis the IX.' Witter had to admire the mans careful wording, but it did not matter.

'Your king will be upset to know you were going to fight the Queen of Castile and you died trying to save a castle that was not even yours to save. If your king were here right now he would tell you to leave the castle and hand it over to us.'

'My king is here and he is in the castle, if you attack the castle you attack France. Good bye!' the French soldier walked quickly back to the gates and told the king what the man had said.

'If they attack it will mean war with Castile I tell you now!' Louis was very mad.

'What if you asked the Queen to leave us alone?' Douglas said.

'If I go out there they will know I have no army to fight with, and once they know that we will be attacked for days maybe years I will be stuck here at her mercy, I will not have that!'

Witter rode back to the Queen. 'Your majesty it appears the king of France is in that castle right now.' Her eye opened with surprise and a large smile came across her face of great joy.

'King Louis is hiding in the castle? Poppy cock. He would be the one to come out and challenge me for every inch of land. He would tell my husband that we would go to war if he did not give him the land on their side of the river. We took it fairly but the king was to scared of war. If King Louis is in there have him come out and see me face to face.' Witter mounted his horse once again and rode out to the middle of the battle field waving a cloth in his hand.

RETREAT

'I think they want to talk.' Douglas says to the king.

  Jade had not anticipated that the English would push them back towards the heavily treed area. Each man and each kingdom fighting for their very survival. Jade kept fighting but would have to take a few steps backwards in order to swing his small sword. The English push the entire army back using their shields as well as their long swords. It was clear that the English were seasoned soldiers and more than capable to fighting off an attack. Jades army was fighting well and not backing down, it had looked to Jade that the fight was even, as when they lost a man so would the English. But they were truly out numbered. Jade could see every man he had, wore armor and it was saving them with each attack. The red coats pushed forward pushing Sir Jade back. He did not want to get pushed into the trees but it might help them with the short swords. Jade watched as the English sent another wave of men towards the castle. He could not believe they had enough men to fight with his army as well as send more to attack the castle. The army was starting to tire and they had been pushed to the edge of the forest when some of the men were being physically pulls back into the forest then they would continue backing up Jade had no choice but to follow his man. Once they were half way through the forest jade thought they were going to loose when men sprang up behind the line on Englishmen and starts slaughtering them from behind. The English Soldiers did not know what hit them. The Vikings were all over them before they could turn around and when they did they were dead by Jades army of a viking. Vastly out numbered the forest put the odds in Jades favor. The red coats could not swing their long swords in the forested area nor could they charge with their shield held up over their eyes. The two handed battle axes made short work and Jade was grateful for their help. As Jade stood

THE NEW QUEEN

and watched and to catch his breath there was a slight loll in the fighting and he thought about how Sir Anthony was doing with Elizabeth, and the Shaolin fight was going. Did they even start? Jade was patted on his back by a soldier.

'If we can lead them in to here we can beat them.' the man says holding his sword up to signal the next wave to attack.

'Have the men fight at the edge of the forest then back away in to it so they will follow.' The soldier smiles.

'I already told my men to do just that!' Jade smiled at the man and followed him in to battle again. The English were waiting as yet another wave came at them some with cross bows but the men were ready for that tactic and had their shields at the ready. The fight drew on for what seemed like days but was only hours. When a lull came a second time Jade wanted to see how many men were left and was pleasantly surprised to see not as many as he thought. In fact they had loss less then ten percent but the English had loss many more Jade did not think it was close to ten percent. Jade jumped up on a log to see into the English and how many more were there? He could still not see across the clearing where they gathered to attack the castle. He had a lot of men but the English had many more, it was the only thought he had in his mind, could they out last the English.

Jade got to the forest edge and saw yet another wave and red coats headed towards the castle. He saw Rollo and moved close to him. 'How is the castle doing? He yelled. Rollo looked at him after he was clear.

'Worry about this battle then we will fight the next one.' Jade nodded as he deflected a red coats sword again.

The Shaolin monks wait for the best time to attack. The English soldiers are lined up to charge the castle in waves again

RETREAT

and they face the castle placing the English sides to face the Shaolin monks. The monks wished the soldiers would have their backs to them but they wait and the fight does not go well by the looks for the army on the far side. The soldiers are not even paying attention to the army, a problem for the monks. Shu climbs a tree to get a better look but all he can see are soldiers all the way across to field to the trees far on the other side. He climbs down and a few monks look at him wanting to know what they are to do. 'I do not see the army, they may have not even attacked yet, we will have to wait and give them more time. Master Anthony must be told.' Shu looks at another monk who is still only two levels away from master, and with out saying a word the monk was off to inform master Anthony. The Shaolin monk once again hid them selves in plain sight where no one would see them. Shu waited wanting to attack but knowing it would only work if they fight together. A soldier walks in to the treed area where the monks wait and sees a monk sitting still behind a rock. The soldier pulls his sword and yells at the monk.

'Hey what are you doing here?' the monk remains motionless. 'I said what are you doing here, who are you?' he taps the monk on the shoulder with his sword when two throwing knives land in the back of his head just above his armor. The soldier falls to his knees grabbing the knives in one hand. The Shaolin monk slowly turns his head then knocks the man unconscious with a quick blow with his staff. Two monks retrieve their knives and go back in to hiding. One monk covers the soldier with leaves and dead branches and dirt lots and lots of dirt.

'The young Shaolin monk runs out of the forested area away from the battle and back towards Sir Anthony where he waits to direct the fight. 'Master Anthony, when will the army be in place to fight?' A puzzled expression falls upon Anthony's face.

THE NEW QUEEN

'They have been fighting for some time now. Have you not started?'

'No Master, Shu has said that he sees no fighting from the army.' Anthony stands up from the boulder that he was sitting on. He looks over towards the treed area where the army had went into and where a scouts squats low in the grass watching for instructions. With simple hand movements Anthony asks what is happening and is answered they fight in the treed area with the vikings. Anthony looks at the young monk.

'The word is given.' he says and the young monk bows and runs back to the Shaolin monks to tell them to fight.

The last one hundred soldiers guard 'Queen' Elizabeth, taking their job very serious. They set up a perimeter of twenty men and a inner wall of forty men who had logs and rock wall to stay behind and the last men guarded the queen in the tented area. Elizabeth was nervous wanting to know any bit of news she could get. She changed her clothing into her bright red dress, in case the men came back all bloody she could still tend to them with out looking dreadful. The last thing she heard was the army had attacked the English. No one knew how the battle was going or who was winning and that made Elizabeth more anxiety then knowing they were loosing. She would sit for a minute then stand, then walk, then pace then do the whole thing over again. When a soldier came up to her to help take her mind off the battle she was truly thankful.

'Your majesty.' he began. 'My king had told me that you were the one who gathered this army together.' Elizabeth looked at the soldier and smiled before she finally nodded towards him. 'Did you know that having every kingdom sign your declaration that you for the first time ever, that all of the kingdom will fight together? No

RETREAT

one has ever achieved such a great task. You are truly a gift to every kingdom.' the soldier bows.

'I thank you for your kind words sir, but it was only due to our plight that I was motivated to take on these challenges. Every great kingdom, yours and mine need to know that we can build a better future together then apart.'

'But is this King of yours the one who should lead all of our kingdoms?'

'King Martin is a kind and very smart man. He won the war against King Richard and we lost very few men but Richard army was completely and utterly wiped out. King Martin made friends with the vikings who we all know are savages yet they respect my king, and no nobleman thought of leaving as they too saw the greatness of the king. There are almost no taxes as they are paid for in labor and not gold most of the time. So a great King who can run a army with little or no money must be the smartest king, not taking more than what is needed.'

'And you must be from a great kingdom too my majesty as he would choose wisely a queen to help stop to fend off a war?'

'I come from King Richards kingdom one that is already fallen, King Martin fallows no traditions only his heart.' Elizabeth took a deep breath and stood up once again. 'And what about you? Where do you come from?' the soldier places his foot on the rock and his hands on his knee.

'My kingdom was once a great kingdom. It was made up of three bigger ones, then a baron said he was king and all war broke out soon our kingdom was divided into three smaller ones. It is how the entire area is. Many smaller kingdom as you would know majesty, you were there. What we need, what every kingdom needs is one leader who can and will unite us together, so if this English come again we can fight them off once and for all.' Elizabeth smiles.

THE NEW QUEEN

'That will only be a dream if we do not win this fight this day.' a small boy come over to the queen with a bucket of water.

'Water my lady?'

'The queen does not drink from filthy water boy!' The soldier about to back hand the boy. Elizabeth moves in front of the boy.

'He is trying to be of service. How can you not be grateful for such a small boy wanting to do honorable service?' She turns to the boy. 'Yes please.' she takes the ladle and takes a drink giving the boy the ladle back and placing it into the bucket. The soldier still looking mad watches as she turns towards him. 'I rather will drink the filthy water of men who will put their lives to save mine then to drink the fresh water on men who wish to take our freedom.' The boy is shown away by her hand and the soldier stands in awe at her brilliance.

The archers were running out of arrows rapidly, they stood on the wall walk firing arrow after arrow as the English would run towards them then turn and run back away up the hill. King Martin could see the archers were only able to stop a few at a time but most arrows would be used senselessly. 'I think I figured out what the English are doing.' Martin stands on the wall walk as Simon moves to sit beside him on the stairs. Simon's legs showed signs of bleeding through the cloth that held it in place. His leather armor did not cover his legs as it hurt to much to put on.

'What are they doing?' Martin asks suspiciously. Sweat ran down his forehead from the leather armor he wore in the heat of the day, and his legs shook from not eating.

'They intend to make us use all of our arrows so when the real charge comes we wont have enough to hold them off with.' The king looked out at all of the arrows sticking out of the ground.

RETREAT

'That makes sense.' Martin says looking at the almost emptied baskets that held arrows for each archer. 'We have to hold off shooting until they are almost at the corn fields then fire at them.'

'Now that makes sense.' Simon says with a smile. The king walks along the wall walk telling the archers to hold off shooting until the English reach the corn fields that were low and had not had much time to grow to full height.

'Your Majesty what about the cross bows? When are they to shoot?' a archer holding a cross bow asks. Martin thinks for a bit. Cross bows take the closest man bowmen shoot to hold off the man approaching behind them, but not to far behind we need to conserve our arrows.' The man yelled on the wall walk as the next wave started to come running down the hill yelling at full pace. This time no one shot at them. The men slowed as the bottom of the hill approached, still no arrows shot at them. They English stopped at the bottom of the hill holding their shields up and began to walk slowly towards the castle, looking around their shield every so often. They get closer then begin to run towards the castle once more. As they gain speed they reach the corn field and cross bows rise and begin to fire upon them. The iron tip arrows shoot right through the shields and the soldiers begin to fall quickly. Some of the soldier think it is a trap and turn around to run away but the bowmen are able to pick them off killing over a hundred men in a single charge. Some of the archers had lit their arrows on fire and were ready to light the corn field on fire but the word form the king never came and the charge was stopped for the first time. The king turned and looked back towards Simon. Simon raised his eye brows and gave him a slight smile, Martin smiled back, trust was building once again.

'Where are the vikings?' Simon asks.

'They went into the forest on the other side of the castle to fight the English there. If I know Rollo he will chase them all the way back to England it self.' Martin lets out a chuckle at the thought and Simon gave a big smile at the same thought. The smile soon left Martin's face when he thought about what was happening. 'How many times do you think they will charge at us before the real charge comes?'

'I don't know. The real question is how many more men do they have? You can tell if its always the same men charging, they all sound differently, I haven't heard the same yelling yet.' Martin jumped up onto the wall and looked as far as he could.

'Holy, there are a lots of them. I can see that they are from forest to forest wide but I can not see the end from here.' Martin jumps down off the wall and looks down at the catapults. 'How many boulders do we have left? He yells down off the wall walk.

'There is a lot sire, we were using what they sent us and gave it back to them.' A man yells up from the keep with a chuckle in his voice. The king looks over towards the wall that extends out past the inner wall. The men were just standing around and it looked like their baskets were full and he had twice as many men on that wall then the wall that faced the hill. The king waves over a small boy and he runs up the stairs with great enthusiasm. With a shirt and stockings that was the only thing covering his feet he was a typical peasant boy.

'Yes your majesty.' the boys say standing straight back his arms straight at his side.

'I have a important message for you to deliver.'

'yes sir you can count on me.'

'I want you to go over to the extended wall and tell the men in charge to send half of the archers to this wall by kings orders, got it?'

'Yes sir right away sir.' the boy ran down the stairs and jumped off the bottom step then took a few more steps and fell flat on his face. He quickly jumped up yelling. 'I'm alright!' and continued to

RETREAT

the other side where he told the men what the king had ordered. The archer began to move quickly down the long wall walk towards the keep and across to where the king waited. He ordered them to fill any open areas on the wall walk and filled them in on when to begin to shoot. Each man brought his own basket and the baskets were combined and set between every two archers. Simon could hear the charge coming.

'They are coming again!' Simon yelled as he slowly stood up to look out over the wall. A charge was coming, by the sheer number of men running down the hill Simon knew it was not the great charge they were expecting. Once again the soldiers stopped at the bottom of the hill but this time they went no further. Instead they planted their shield into the ground and hid behind them. 'Hold your fire!' Simon yelled out then walked as fast as he could down the line having every cross bow ready with the iron tips bolts. They took time to choose who they would target before shooting, then Simon yelled loudly. 'FIRE!' The archers stood up and shot their bolts that went threw the shields and the man fell wounded or dead as their shield fell on op of them. Then half of the bow men shot their arrows high into the air and the remaining archers shot directly at the shields as they raised their shield to take cover from the high arrows the direct arrow landed in their targets. Soon every Englishman that sat at the bottom of the hill was dead. Both the Martin and Simon could not believe their good fortune. 'Reload!' Simon yelled. The cross bows were reloaded quickly being the first line of defense. Simon heard another charge and looked over the wall with his legs soaked the cloth around it with blood, as he put pressure on it with his hand. The king looked over the wall as well to see a many more red coat soldiers coming over the hill then ever before.

'This is it! Martin yells. Ready the catapults, archers take aim.' The row of archer aim their bows up high into the air waiting for

THE NEW QUEEN

the order to shoot. Martin yells out.' Fire!' and the archers fire a umpteen arrows in to the air. The king waits for a few seconds to go by and drops his arm to signal the catapults to shoot. All six fire at once throwing large boulder up into the air, and right after he orders the archers to fire another round. With all of the arrows coming at the English they will keep their heads behind their shields but that wont help them against the large boulders that will follow. The men will be trying to protect themselves against the arrows they wont see the boulders rolling down the hill behind them. Everything Martin thought was going to happen did. The arrows killed very few men but the boulder killed a great many more then expected. 'Load quickly' the king yelled out towards the men loading the catapults. He knew it was a timely task and you could not hurry it up much more then what they were already doing.

'Here they come!' Simon yells out. As the English now stand up and head towards the castle. The archers try the same trick to shoot high then shoot low as the men would try and protect themselves from the arrows coming from above. It did not work so well this time. It looked like yet another wave was coming over the hill top. The king knew they did not have enough arrows for all of the soldiers. The cross bows were now firing stopping the soldiers from reaching the corn fields. But there were too many soldiers and a ladder hit the wall. A dozen arrows shot threw the opening loop of the wall to stop anyone trying to get at the ladder. Martin knew this would come and had his men ready each archer popped up and fired a flurry of arrows down at the soldier that held bows then a man would push the ladder away or pull it up if he could. The men of the far wall that extended out from the main castle began to shoot soldiers as they came around the wall in the much smaller curtain wall of the main castle. The catapults fired again killing more but not as many as the first volley, due to not having

RETREAT

all of the arrows to make the soldiers take cover. Martin walked to the end of the small wall walk and lit his lanterns then threw them with great force down at the soldiers below. Most of the red coats caught fire and it started the corn field on fire as well. One by one the king threw the lanterns over the wall to stop the attack. The Englishmen pulled back due to the flames then the cross bows finished any that they could see. As the smoke rides high in to the air Martin and Simon could see hundreds of red coats scattered bodies on the battle ground. There were more closer to the wall trying to get past the flames as the archers picked them off constantly. Some were trying to run back when other men would stop them and tell them to continue to fight. Martin told the men if they turn and run let them go.

The young monk came running back as fast as he could. A few monks saw him and looked for a sign. He stopped seeing Shu and gave him a thumbs up when a arrow killed the boy where he stood. He slowly fell to his knees when a second arrow plunged into his chest killing him instantly. All of the monks saw and took it personally the archer was dead before the boy hit the ground. The monks were lined up and started killing the soldiers as they tried to run pass to join the next wave against the castle. The monks had killed over a hundred soldiers before anyone could react fast enough to attack the monks in the rocky treed area. The English were now realizing they were surrounded taking damage from all sides. A flag made the men fall into a square box for defensive plan of action. The waves to attack the tiny castle were ordered to stop, and one side of the box was ordered to attack. The shoalin monks were ready for such an attack. They had not used their throwing knives yet and their staffs were lying beside them. The Englishmen held up their shield and started to march towards the monk but

THE NEW QUEEN

soon found out that the many pot holes made them trip and fall then a knife or two would fine them dead on the ground. Soon many red coats were dead on the ground against a small army of defenseless monks. A arrow shoots at Shu and he moves out of its way as the arrow fly away behind him. Out of throwing knives the monks now raised their staffs and headed into battle determined to make a difference in the war.

Like many men the English were no different and they assumed that the monks would be easily defeated once their throwing knives were used up, but they find out quickly that they were wrong, dead wrong.

The first red coat came running into battle and swings his sword, the shaolin monk deflects the sword away using his wooden staff, making lots of room to move, as he crashes the other end of his staff down hard on to the soldiers foot breaking a toe or two with a single violent blow. The soldier screams in pain and hobbles around now wanting to protect his toes. The soldiers now mad that the monk got the better of him charges flings his sword wildly at the monk well trying to control his sword and at the same time use it for quick defense. It did not help that the monk was taught to fight such a conflict and he moves the soldiers shield out of the way using his staff and when he tries to move it back he would receive several blows in the stomach then another blow into the mans face, all before the monk would forcefully jam the staff into the soldiers face crushing his skull, under his helmet, ready to move on to the next.

Shu tried to stand his ground having two soldiers attack him at the same time. Falling back into bad habits, Shu continued to step backwards as the two soldiers continue to attack. He was scared but started to remember what master Anthony told him and stopped moving backwards. The one soldier step forward and Shu moves quickly stopping his staff on the mans foot then swinging it around

RETREAT

to block an attack from the other soldier causing the soldier to drop his sword. Shu swung his staff as hard as he could upwards knocking the shield out of the hand of the first soldiers before turning around and swinging his staff with all his might across the soldiers head, all well the second soldiers retrieved his sword. Shu stood still assessing his surrounding before continuing to fight the second soldiers. Out of the corner of his eye he caught a cross bow aimed at him and ducks down as the bolt flies past him and into the second soldier as luck would have it. He stood up once again and again looked around finding another monk fighting two soldiers, Shu attacked from behind, using his staff to spread the mans legs apart before breaking the his leg with a blunt stab on the mans knee. The soldiers crumples in pain before Shu swings his staff well holding only one end and swings it around his body across the soldiers chest. It would only take one of these violent hit to make sure the soldier did not get up again. Shu smiles at the remaining soldier who swings his sword in one hands and holds up his shield in the other. Shu jabs at the soldier with his staff making the him use his sword to defend himself while the other shaolin monk stabs the mans shin with his staff, breaking the mans legs in one solid blow, Shu moves to look for another fight as his brother finished the job.

Three English red coat soldiers surround a shoalin master, Shu watches as the master taunts them. Each soldier moves around trying to surround the master but is foiled when he moves before they do and stops the soldiers from attaining their first goal in the fight. When one thrust his sword towards the master his sword is directed towards another soldier then the master swings his staff very low hitting the last soldiers ankle. The man backs away in pain. The last two look at one another when the master hits them both in their faces causing both of their noses to break and makes their eyes water. It is easy to finish the two off before they can see what was happening. The last of the three soldiers attacks from

THE NEW QUEEN

behind, but the master pulls his staff hard backwards, making the soldier to run into the staff knocking the wind out of himself. The master turns around quickly and smashes the staff across the soldiers head. Shu smiles at the master and the master nods back then moves towards the line.

'A soldiers attacks Shu but he is ready and stops the sword before any damage can be inflicted. Shu blocks the mans attack as the soldiers uses both sword and shield. Shu is pushed backwards once again when just behind the soldiers and cross bows is shot at a monk and makes contact killing one of the monks. Shu shocked with what he just saw, and the soldiers continues to attack. He relies on his automatic reflexes to block the attack as he breaks from the shock and returns to his mind set and begins to fight back. In little time the Shaolin monks find a fighting style that is able to beat the red coats.

The monks start to advance and soon realize that the red coats were retreating backwards and moving slowly towards Saxton, s castle. The monks fight more carefully knowing that they maybe lured into a trap. Each step they take they look for cross bows and archers waiting in the wings.

Sir Anthony sit not far from the battle field. He watches carefully as the war rages until he sees a few English soldiers approaching. The army behind him that are guarding the queen quickly run to Sir Anthony's defense. Each man holding his shield and sword ready to fight. The Englishmen stop and look at the thirty soldiers standing at guard waiting to see what they were going to do. The guards who watch Elizabeth move her away to a more safe area. 'Where are you taking me?' Elizabeth asks as they hold her by the arm and run with her.

RETREAT

'The war is coming your majesty.' the guard tells her as she look out towards the fight to see the army slowly moving towards them.

'Hurry, hurry their getting close!' she say hiking up her gown and running as fast as she can. The guards running almost completely backwards, well the outer ring of guards now stand ready to engage the onslaught. Hundreds of red coats attack the guards but they are determined to hold them off for Elizabeth. Soon the guards are completely surrounded by the on coming army but they refuse to stop fighting killing three four Englishmen until they themselves are killed. The guards run as quick as they can moving Elizabeth to a horse where they put her onto it and starts to move her away.

'Your majesty ride as fast as you can we will try and hold them off for as long as possible.' the guard says. 'If you ride to our kingdom maybe they can get you to safety.' Sir Anthony comes riding a horse out of a treed area.

'All of you follow me.' He says and all of the guards and Elizabeth ride and run into the treed area well the Englishmen run by them towards Saxton's destroyed castle. Sir Anthony stops everyone from running deep inside the treed area. 'They are retreating so nothing will stay in their way to escape a fight they can not win.' the guards and Elizabeth watch as this massive army runs and moves past them. Their archers continue to shoot arrows behind them not really looking where they are shoot. Elizabeth sees Rollo and the vikings running after them. Then she sees Sir Jade close behind Rollo and his archers are shooting arrows back towards the red coats but aiming much more carefully.

'There's Jade.' Elizabeth points out, the guards turning to see and are happy with what they see. Sir Anthony ride out onto the battle field and stops the men from pursuing. Rollo stops and is upset from the sudden stop in pursuit. 'What is he doing? Why wont he let them finish them off once and for all?' Elizabeth looks confused and looks around for anyone to give her an answer. She

THE NEW QUEEN

pushes her horse and rides away from her guards and out onto the battle field towards Sir Anthony.

Martin thought the castle was going to be over run. 'Fire' he yelled sending his catapults crashing as they shoot huge boulders over the wall and through the think smoke of the fire raging as the corn field burn. The boulders kill more red coats, the archers were now out of arrows and could only watch as the army was running down the hill when a horn blows. The king watches as the entire army stops half way down the hill and turn around, even the men who are already at the wall turn and run away back up the hill with out being shot at from the castle. Simon looks at the king puzzled.

'What happened?'

'I don't know! Did you hear the horn?'

'Yes, but that cannot be it. The horn means to attack.' Martin looks out at the men running away and his hand shake violently, so he grabs it with his other hand and tries to stop it. A archer moves over beside the king.

'Wish we could get some of those arrows back.' Martin turns and looks at the archer.

'That's a great idea.' the king says, and turns towards Simon. 'Simon send out ten men to get as many arrows as they can collect.' Simon turns to him with a look of fear on his face.

'What?' he whispers and the king motions to go. Simon points to a few men and opens the side gate as they run out the fetch the arrows as quickly as they can. Hoping not to get killed in the possess. Martin gets up onto the wall once again to get a better look and sees the army running away through the smoke and haze caused by the heat of the fire below. He strains to see why and sees an army running out of the treed area and giving chase to the red coats.

RETREAT

'Simon get the sword men ready and get the pike men too we leave at once. The army is on the run and we will give chase!' the swords men were all ready standing by the gate in case they broke through. Simon had the men line up outside of the wall and start to march towards the hill every other man held a shield in hope they could protect the archers and the swords men in case of an arrow attack. Martin mounted a horse and rode behind the his army of just over a hundred men, making sure the sides of the battle field were not filled with archers or a small group of red coats who were going to attack. The men marched up the hill to find Sir Jade, Sir Anthony and Elizabeth stopping the army from following the red coats. The king rides up seeing his friends.

'What the blazes is going on? Why are you not following them? Finish them!' Martin says mad from being stopped.

'Your majesty.' Sir Anthony starts holding his hand out as if to stop the king himself. 'Never corner a wild animal for it will turn and attack you. And this army has had the fight from the beginning. It's best to let them go. They will most likely go home and away from here and we will be able to fight another day. The king lowers his head then slowly shakes in agreement.

'Of course you are right.' the king looks around at the large number of soldiers. 'Who are all these men? Sir Jade smiles.

'Your Majesty you have Elizabeth to thank, sire. You would be proud of her. She had many, many kingdoms come together in order to save your kingdom and fight the English. All of these kingdoms came together for the very first time to help you all because she told them if they did not the English could and would most likely turn to them next. Every king she talked with agreed to help with out being threaten with us attacking them.' Martin looks at Elizabeth his jaw a gape. She look beautiful and the sun shined reflecting off of her red hair only added to her beauty.

'Is this true?' Elizabeth looks down before answering.

THE NEW QUEEN

'If I didn't help where would we be?' Martin moved his horse next to her and leaned over and kissed her on the cheek as he grasped her arm ever so lightly.

'God bless you Elizabeth.' he says then orders his men back to the castle. Elizabeth felt her heart beat a bit faster.

King Louis stood at the gate of Hope castle with Douglas beside him. 'You know once I go out there she will know we have no army to hold her off?'

'You have to lie your majesty or you and I will not live to see tomorrow.' Garnet announces. Douglas walks with the king out towards the middle of the field. Each step feeling like his last. Two guards one on either side of the king hold the french flag. King Louis stands and waits for the Queen to arrive. She rides out onto the battle field with ten guards all on horseback and in full armor.

'So you are here.' the queen states.

'Where is your king?' King Louis asks.

'He was murdered probably by you I guess.'

'Be careful what you say I am the king of France. I order you to leave this kingdom. It is under my protection, the protection of France.'

'We have no fight with you Louis, leave and I will pretend this conversation never happened.'

'My army is much bigger than yours, better trained, better equipped and experienced. All you have are farmers and a few soldiers.'

'And where is this army Louis? Hun? They could never fit in that castle nor would they hide in the castle. Your army is far away from here. Surrender the castle, you know it is mine anyway. The kingdom of Castile owned this land long before King Richard took it in a bad deal my husband made and I want it back.'

RETREAT

'That deal helped you to avoid a war. A war that would be fought in my kingdom. Your husband was very smart in giving it away very smart in deed.' King Louis stands up straight and sticks out his chest. 'Now leave or you will find a war on your land. This land belongs to the kingdom of Martin, not you, not the damn English will take it from him.'

'You avoid the question well Louis. Where is your army? Obviously they are not here so where are they?'

'They are around.' King Louis looks over where the path leads and sees the French flag coming up the path towards him. The queen notices them too. Thousands of soldiers riding to their kings rescue. The captain riding directly up to the French King.

'Your Majesty your army is here as summoned.' Louis looks at the queen. She turns her horse around.

'Another day Louis, another day.' she ride up to her captain and dismounts her horse. 'Ready to march now.' she yells as she gets into her coach. 'We do not stop until nightfall.' she continues to yell out orders as the men ready to march.

Chapter 34
THE NEXT CHAPTER

Douglas walked with King Louis towards the gate of Hope castle, still in full armor and the king in a leather robe that was a gift from Douglas and castle Hope. 'I could never be a king.' Douglas says making small talk. Both king and Douglas has to hold up their hands to block the sun.

'Oh why? To much pressure, you are brave, so it cant be that?' Louis continues to think why he would not want to be a king. 'Is it that you have to walk a fine line with everyone you meet and have to keep peace with people you don't like?'

'No.' Douglas starts to explain but is interrupted.

'I think it might be that you have to stand your ground. Like when I told the Queen she could not go through my kingdom on her way back. She will have to travel a great distance around and then take a ship across to get home. Hopefully that will teach her not to cross me again.' the two finally reach the gate. 'Well why would you not want to be king?'

THE NEXT CHAPTER

'Well its all of these guards that surround us, I feel caged in. I could not swing my sword without hitting my own men.' King Louis laughs with a large roar. He places his hand on Douglas' shoulder.

'My good fellow, they are the reason you do not have to draw your sword. And they are with me every bit of the day. Day and night.' he starts to laugh again as a tear rolls down his face from laughter. 'It took some time I must admit to get use to them, but after a year it was no problem.'

'No privacy I bet.' Douglas hands a bottle of wine. 'For your trip home your majesty, it may not be as good as you are use to but it will have the same effect on the journey.'

'You are a good man Douglas but that beard is a bit short, you need to grow a long beard and show the women you are a real man, hun, hun?'

'Are the guards with you when you are in bed too?' The king looks at him and smiles.

'It depends on who is with me.' He breaks out into a loud laugh and slaps Douglas on the shoulder. 'Good bye.' he says and walks over to a coach that waits for him surrounded by ten horse men that are fully armored. Douglas waves good bye.

The queen awoke in a bed that was kept for the owner of the house. The baron gladly gave up his home for the queen. Her maidens that were still recovering with headaches and sickness, helped dressed the queen in her long emerald green gown and polished her crown. They could not wait to be back in the coach again laughing with the queen on their ride back to home. The queen of Castile looked out at the large fresh garden and the sunny day that gave way to the odd cloud. Her guards surrounded the house and more men surrounded the entire estate that was now

THE NEW QUEEN

part of the kingdom of Castile. They wore green uniforms and were in their armor from head to toe.

Many of the barons had agreed to let her be rightful heir to what was once Saxton's kingdom. It would be known as The Castile of the north. North of France but still very much a part of her kingdom. Her kingdom would be separated on either side of France.

'A new castle will have to be built of course.' she said walking out of the small house. The baron nodded in agreement. 'I do not want it to close to King Martin's realm but not to far, so if we have to take that silly castle we can.' The baron wanted to say something and the queen could see he wanted to speak but would not let him. She held up her hand and continued to talk. 'We will expand this part of the kingdom to take all of the northern kingdoms. They are all small and wont put up much of a fight once they see our massive army, which you will help assemble of course. Once we acquire these we will then and only then squeeze the French so hard that they will pop like a pimple on a mans face.' she stopped and looked at the baron. 'Did you want to add anything?'

'Well it's just that King Martin had already claimed a large piece of land all the way up the coast to the other kingdoms. You see he gave everyone food when the harvest and the war was not doing so well. We had no choice in order to survive your majesty.' the queen looked at the man with a surprised look on her face.

'I will deal with that once every baron has agreed to kneel before me.'

'What if all of them don't?'

'They will simply loose everything they have.' she said candidly. The two continued to walk together. 'I do not like people who do not do their very best for me.' she says stopping looking at Captain Witter as he kneels over the chopping block and the soldier removes his head in one quick clean cut. His head falling into a basket. 'Do

THE NEXT CHAPTER

you know what I mean?' she asks in a serious tone well looking back at the baron who swallows hard as he watches the execution.

'I will always do my best my queen.'

'I hope so for your sake.'

Martin washed his face after waking. He sits in his bedchamber still feeling the effects of the long war. He thought about just how much food he ate last night. He ops for a cotton shirt and leather pants with his leather boots, glad that he would not need his armor today. The king opens the slats to the bright sunny summer day and looks out towards the keep finding it full of soldiers and vikings wall to wall. The door opens and Samantha enters the room with a tray of eggs, bacon and hot water. 'Your up?' she say surprised that he is standing already. 'I brought you something to eat and to thank you.'

'Thank me for what?'

'For bringing Elizabeth back safely.'

'That was all Sir Jade, Samantha. He took care of her.'

'But it was you who ordered him to do so, so it was really you. You are a king who looks after his people.' Martin smiled.

'Thank you.'

'Your welcome, now here eat.' Martin grabs some bacon and shoves it into his mouth then drinks the water completely in one chug.

'I need to be down there.', he says placing the cup on the tray and walks past Samantha giving her a peck on the cheek. 'Thanks again.' The king makes his way down the stairs that are lined with guards on every step all the way down. Martin looks into the small great room to see Simon getting new cloth put on his leg. For the first time he sees just how bad the wound was and griminess at the sight. The door is opened and the kings presents is announced. A

THE NEW QUEEN

large applause breaks out as many different flags line the walls on either side of the keep. The king looks at each of them and smiles.

'Your majesty.' a soldier says from an unfamiliar kingdom. The soldier is dressed in a bright red long cape with red armor. Martin turns his attention to the man. 'Sire you need to know how well your future queen represented you. She held herself in the upmost honorable way. If it were not for your Queen all of these kingdoms would surely be at war with one another.' the man yells over the applause. 'Not strong enough to fight off the English by themselves. Not only do we own you and your kingdom our thanks but we owe you our loyalty as well.' Another loud applause breaks out and loud cheers to the queen as well. Martin stood with his jaw open, not wanting to tell them that Elizabeth was not his queen.

'And I thank each and everyone of you and your kingdoms for your help against the English.' Martin gives a slight bow towards the man and moves away. Jade stands in the distance and the king makes his way towards him. Martin walks up to Jade and gives him a hug and whispers into his ear. 'My new queen? Whats that all about?' Jade smiles not wanting to let on to the crowd what he had to explain.

'I need to talk with you in private your majesty.' Jade says in his cotton shirt and stockings. Martin grabs Jades hand and lead him past the crowd and up to his bedchamber, the only place where he can have privacy. 'Your majesty.' Jade starts. 'We had to tell a few lies in order for us to be able to see and talk to some kings along the way.'

'Oh they would not talk with you even though I did not send you?' Martin say sarcastically.

'Elizabeth wanted to get more help for you. She felt she needed to do something and the truth is without the army she gathered you might not have won this war.' Jade walks over and splashes water on his face from the basin on the small desk by the door.

THE NEXT CHAPTER

'I did not ask her to do that.'

'I know but she gets things in her mind and that's, that. Every king we talked to was at war with another kingdom who they were next to. It was Elizabeth's idea to have them sign a document that they could not fight with each other well they helped us, that gave them a break in their war and they were able to send more soldiers to help us.' Jade stands straight up and faces the king making his face look serious. 'Sire every king thinks she is going to be your queen, if you tell them she is not going to be your queen they will think that we lied to them and in doing so they just might become our enemy and might even join the English.'

'If I tell them it was her that lied they will see the way.'

'No. They wont. They will think we told the lies for our own gain, they sacrificed hundreds of men for what? For our gain and nothing for them?'

'How will me taking Elizabeth's hand change that?'

'They will follow her if she marries you and in doing so they will join your kingdom and you will be their king.' Martin's eyes opened widely.

'But I did not want to be king Jade never.'

'Maybe that's what makes a good king, you are not out for yourself, you are out for everyone,' Jade stabs his finger into Martins chest. 'In your kingdom.' Jade moves back away from the king. 'And they see this and they want to be part of it. Think about it your majesty, they will have no more wars with one another, no starving people, no more boarder wars. We came across a kingdom that was no larger than this castle to the top of the hill, a few dozen knights and no one would dare attack them but they would not attack anyone else either. I am telling you sire we visited over fifty kingdoms all small but mighty in their own right.' Martin walks around his bed thinking.

THE NEW QUEEN

'Are you asking me to marry Elizabeth?' Jade looks straight face at his king not saying anything. 'Are you?' Martin asked not sure what was being asked of him.

'Yes.' Jade takes a deep breath. 'It will avoid a war with all of these kingdoms and strengthen your kingdom to unimaginable heights. It really is a win for you sire.' Jade walks over to the fire place. 'Plus sire she is in love with you.' Jade looks at Martin. 'I can tell you have feeling for her as well.'

'But not love that way, she is more of annoying sister than my queen.'

'I have seen how you look at her and I do not see that, what I see is pure love sire, I saw you looking at her as she walked away. Your stare was a gaze of love. You think she is pretty and I think you do love her, even more because she just save your kingdom and most likely your very life.'

'And if I don't marry her we will probably go to war?'

'Yes most definitely.'

'Then you have left me with no choice.'

'No your majesty I haven't.' Martin folded his arms in front of his chest and started to pace the room.

'I will have to think about this. And just so you know I am not happy being drawn into a lie.' The two walk out side when a large roar of applause starts again. 'Where is Elizabeth anyway?'

'I have not seen her since last night festivities sire.'

'Go find her we will talk.' Martin was shaking everyone's hands as he tried to make his way through the crowd. Then in the distance he sees Sir Anthony talking with a shaolin monk. Martin makes a his way towards him. When he reaches them Anthony bows his head towards the king. 'My goodness Anthony what happened to your hand?' Martin was surprised by the size of the wrap around his hand.

THE NEXT CHAPTER

'Oh your majesty I broke it but it will be fine soon. Your Majesty this is Shu my masters son who has become a shaolin master himself over these last few days.' Martin lowers his head towards the monk.

'I thank you for your service Shu, although I must admit I did not see your valiant effort in stopping the English.' the three men laugh.

'It was my people that own you, your majesty. With out this war we would not know how to train our worriers into masters. I had been trying to become a master for almost six years but there were no tests, no right of passage until you asked for our help.' Shu bows towards Martin.

'I believe we also owe master Anthony a thanks for him to step up and ask you for your help. We needed all of the help we could get.'

'I guess you owe your queen the most thanks then?' Anthony piped up. Martin took a quick breath at the notion.

'I need to speak with master Anthony would you excuse us?' Shu bowed and walks away. 'Ok I think there is a problem here.' Martin starts.

'A problem sire?'

'Yes Jade and Elizabeth lied to a bunch of kings that she was my queen.'

'Future queen sire.' Anthony holds up his finger as he interrupted the king.

'Yes, yes future Queen. But that does not make me want her to be my queen.' A loud roar began as Elizabeth stood in the doorway of the castle and the keep. Men started to chant hail to the Queen. 'I'm going to put a stop to this right now.' Anthony grabs Martin's arm as he starts to turn away.

THE NEW QUEEN

'A sign of a good king is when he is able to take solid advice and even though he does not like it, he still acts upon the advice.' Martin looks at Anthony. 'She will make an excellent queen for you.'

'She is to young for me.'

'Better for vitality sire.'

'She is pig headed stubborn and …' Martin stops as he catches her walking towards them. Her hair down in red curls and her face bright clean with a big smile, her gown a new cream colored with a lace trim. As she walks towards the king she holds up her gown with each step carefully placed.

'You were saying?'

'She's pig headed.' the king says almost in a whisper. Elizabeth arrives next to her king.

'Your Majesty.' she says while she curtsies. Martin just stood there unable to speak and just stared at her with his mouth opened. From her beuty and part anger. Anthony pulls Martin towards him.

'Did Henry not say she was good for you? I think he knew more then what he told you. Don't you?' Martin nods in agreement. Elizabeth face turns red and she seemed scared to talk any further as she turns away from Martin.

'Elizabeth.' Martin grabs her arm before she can walk away. You have put me in a very difficualt possition. Your lies have opened doors for the kingdom but at a great cost to me!'

'I can explain your majesty, honestly.' Martin pulled her towards him and manage to get both hand on her.

'Elizabeth pull yourself together.' he starts as she starts to cry slowly. 'Elizabeth you are not in trouble so stop crying.' She looks at him with confusion on her face but manages to stops crying.

'I'm not?'

'No how can I be mad at a woman who helped me save the kingdom.' the two look at each other face to face. 'You, that helps me keep it together. Henry was right we do need each other.'

THE NEXT CHAPTER

Elizabeth smiles and the two hug one another as the crowd erupts once again. A soldier comes up to the pair.

'Your majesty it gives me great honor to be able to tell you that my king will bow to you both once you are married.' Elizabeth looks at Martin with fear once again in her face. Martin smiles at the man and looks at Elizabeth for a momment as he compleplated he choices.

'Then lets not waste any more time lets get married well all of our friends and allies that are here today.' the crowd yells out a giant applause.

'But Sire my king would wish to be here, all of the kings would want to be here, it will take them three days a beg of you to wait.' a soldiers asks yelling over the crowd. Martin turns to Elizabeth.

'Well what do you think should we wait?' Elizabeth shocked by the news gives a large smile as tears stream down her face.

'Yes we will wait. In four days we will have the ceremony.' She turns around and raises her arms go and get your king and in four days we will marry.' the crowd starts to yells and congratulates the two.

Evening fell over the festivities but Rollo stood on the shore next to Quarry Castle. He had a large barge built and had all of the fallen vikings piled on it. King Martin and the future Queen Elizabeth stood by him. 'I am sorry for your loss Rollo.' Martin says, as Rollo pushes the barge out into the channel.

'They died fighting for what they believed in and we can not ask for anything more.' three archers from one of the many new kingdoms stand and light their arrows and wait for Rollo to tell them to light the barge on fire. It was soaked in lamp oil and flared up in little time. The body's burning quickly to honor the dead. The vikings standing with their axes in hand then they all raise them over their heads and yell. Martin was saddened by the whole

THE NEW QUEEN

ordeal. Elizabeth even cried a bit wiping tear away from men who she had never met.

Martin turned to see all the tents set up to help house all of the different kingdoms. 'We have to thank each and everyone.' the king tells his soon to be bride. As they walk up the hill that leads to the channel Elizabeth is welcomed by so many people along the way. She takes their hands thanks them and even kisses a few ladies along the way. Guards walk along side with her watching everyone around. It was the biggest party ever throne by anyone Martin ever knew. A knight in full armor walks up to Elizabeth.

'My lady I offer my service as a loyal and honorable knight.' the man kneels before her. Elizabeth almost starts to laugh finding the whole thing funny. Martin jumps in seeing her state.

'I thank you good knight, and I can only hope that we will never have to call you into service. Now rise and enjoy your time with us.' the knight rises and bows as he leaves. 'Elizabeth you can not laugh at men who are giving you their lives to do with as you wish. You know one day you may have to send him to his death to save your own.' Elizabeth looks up at her king and starts to laugh.

'But not tonight.' she stops laughing and smiles holding Martins arm as her arms wrap around it. The two continue to walk to the first tent to find no one in it. 'They must be out celebrating still.'

'yes I guess they are.' Martin stops and Elizabeth takes a step ahead then turns around.

'what? Is something wrong?' she ask worried her dream was about to change into a nightmare.

'I never told you how beautiful you look tonight.' Martins voice was serious. Elizabeth smiled.

'I bet you say that to all the ladies.' She laughs again and they continue on to the next tent.

THE NEXT CHAPTER

The wedding day arrived along with thousands of people who had come from all over the kingdom and the kingdoms that helped fight the English. 'My people said they saw the English boarding some ships about four days from here.' Simon says to King Martin. Martin looks at Simon's leg as he limps along walking in side the keep with a tree branch as a crutch.

'I saw your leg unwrapped a few days ago. It looks like it hurts a lot.' the two continue to walk together.

'I am at your service you know that. I never stopped.' Simon say sounding sincere.

'Simon I can see that you put yourself out to help save the kingdom, don't think it went unnoticed.'

'Are you sure you want to marry Elizabeth?' Martin looks at Simon then looks away taking a deep breath.

'Its complicated but it is best for the kingdom.'

'It will not be best if you are not happy.'

'I will have to control her better but she will help me be a better king too.' Martin stops walking as they fight through the crowd then he turns towards Simon. 'You have to take order from her when she is your queen you know that right?'

'I will do as your majesty asks of me.' Simon stands leaning on the branch heavily. 'I have a wedding gift for you two later too.'

'Thanks I better get ready for the wedding. Gwyneth made me something to wear for the wedding. Apparently I have to look very royal for the wedding, I don't even have a real crown. I will talk to you later.' Martin walks back to the castle, where Samantha come out of the castle door almost bumping into him.

'There you are.' she says all dress up in a royal green dress. I have been looking for you.'

'Oh something wrong?' he asks as tears well up in Samantha eyes.

THE NEW QUEEN

'I can't believe you are going to marry my little sister. She always wanted to marry you. Shes been in love with you from the first time we met you.' tears stream down her face as she smiles.'

'Why are you crying?'

'I'm just so happy.' she says and breaks out into a full crying session. She falls into the kings chest and they hug. 'I am so grateful your majesty for everything you do.' Martin gives her a hug. 'Once I thought you and I might marry. Did you ever think that?'

'Well I did not think of marriage to anyone before now.' they continue to hug.

Elizabeth insisted on me wearing the green dress and she is going to where a white dress that Gwyneth made for this wedding. Gwyneth will be in green too, she is one of the brides maids. She has never been asked to be in a wedding before.'

'I have to go Samantha.' the king says slowly breaking the hug.

'Don't go to the small bedchamber that's where Elizabeth is and if you see her before the wedding its bad luck.'

'I know.' Martin leaves and heads up to his bedchamber where two maidens wait for him. 'Who are you?'

'We are here to help you get ready for the wedding sire.' they dress the king and walk him down the stairs that are lined with soldiers on each step that are dressed in suits of armor that have been polished and shine like new. The door opens and Martin steps out into the keep where all the different kingdoms make a line right through the front gates. Simon stands waiting for the king.

'I have a gift for you. 'Simon announces. Simon hands Martin a new crown made with silver and gold with rubies and gems mounted in it. Martin places it on his head and is pleasantly surprised that it fits perfectly. 'There is another one for the queen your majesty I gave it to the monk doing the wedding.' Martin walked through the long line of kings and Queens and knights

THE NEXT CHAPTER

until he makes it just outside the front gates where a large platform was made and he walks up onto it and waits. Shu and Sir Anthony wait by Martins side on the stage.

A symphony of horns sounded announcing that the new queen was coming. Everyone knelt before her as Samantha walked her sister down the isle. When she came through the gates Martin saw the most beautiful women ever. Elizabeth was dressed in all white dress mostly a lace trim dress with a gold color stitching and white shoes that he had never seen before. With Gwyneth on one side and Samantha on the other Elizabeth was highlighted by green on either side. Martin was dressed in a brown leather robe with gold trim and a white cotton shirt also with gold trim and a high lace collar. Martin had placed his crown on his head. Beside him stood Simon and Rollo and Sir Anthony who was doing the service. Elizabeth was walked beside him and they stood side by side in from of Master Anthony. Martin could not take his eyes off of his bride to be and she could not take her eye off of him.

'I welcome everyone here today to witness their king to marry our new Queen.' Anthony started. 'Before we begin it is custom to ask anyone who may have an objection why these two should not be married to stand and announce your reason now.' Silence fell over the crowd. 'So I ask Elizabeth do you and will you do everything your husband asks faithfully, to honor and obey his every word?' Elizabeth looks deep into Martins eye.

'Anything her commands.'

'And your majesty will you be faithfully to your queen, to hold and comfort when need be, to protect and love until death do you part?' Martin's eyes well up.

'I will.'

'Then as the hold word allows me to join you two together I make you both husband and wife, King and Queen until death do you part. Kiss your Queen my majesty.' Martin and Elizabeth kiss

THE NEW QUEEN

for the first time making Elizabeth weak in her knees. A crown is placed on her head and a large cheer come to life.

'Hip Hip hooray!' the crowd yells as Martin takes Elizabeth's hand and they walk down the steps off of the stage and are greeted by more kings and queens that they will rule over from this times forward. The two walk towards the gate when a large coach arrives in front of them.

'This is a wedding gift from one of the kings' Simon tells them. The royal blue coach has gold trim and large wooden wheels painted black. The door opens and the two get in and are driven through the gates where everyone kneels as they past. Elizabeth waves to the people from the open window. The two are going into the castles main hall that has been emptied. They walk in and Elizabeth turns to Martin.

'I can't believe it I'm a queen!' she hugs Martin well tears stream down her cheeks.

'Now the hard part begins, uniting all of those small kingdoms in to one.' the two look at one another knowing their job has jest begun.

Thank you

To all my fans
To my brother Clint who always tells it like it is
To Lyndsay Sinko for giving your time to edit this book
And to my wife without you there is no me.

"The New Reign is likened to a new Game of Thrones"

CPSIA information can be obtained
at www.ICGtesting.com
Printed in the USA
LVHW092006171019
634576LV00001B/1/P